THE
TENDERFOOT

ROB LEININGER

Novels by Rob Leininger

Gumshoe
January Cold Kill
Killing Suki Flood
Maxwell's Demon
Olongapo Liberty   (R rated)*
Richter Ten
Sunspot (previously published as *Black Sun*)
The Tenderfoot

* The way it *really* was to go on liberty in the Navy during the
Vietnam War. (Not for the squeamish.)

Writing as Gwendolyn Gold

Nicholas Phree and the Emerald of Bool
(*a children's story* written *for adults*)**

** for the young at heart who like to laugh, who
remember all those good old stories that really
took you away. This one will take you away.

ROB LEININGER

THE TENDERFOOT

The characters and events in this book are fictitious. Any similarity to real persons, living or dead, is coincidental and not intended by the author.

Contact: robleiningernovels@gmail.com

Website: www.robleininger.com

1

I checked my watch. Nine forty-four and already the day was so hot flies had gathered in the shade. I closed my eyes, comfortable just the way I was on a chair tilted back in the shadow of the train station, when I heard the whistle of the engine about a mile south of town. I peered at my watch again. Nine forty-five; fifteen minutes behind schedule, but not all that uncommon for the run up north from Rock Springs. I was the stationmaster in town, not that there was anything in particular for me to do, so I just watched as the train steamed in.

My eyes widened some when Andy Stillman stepped off the coach and stood there on the dusty wooden platform, gazing first over the empty cattle pens then taking in the mid-morning languor of Willow Creek, at least what he could see of it from there, at the far end of Water Street. I sure hated to see him just then, showing up so unexpected-like. I counted myself a friend of Andy's, and back then, in 1885 in Willow Creek, that wasn't something I'd have cared to call out at the corner of Main and Water Streets. In those days, Wyoming Territory was still pretty rough. Andy was back, and that couldn't spell anything but trouble. Likely it meant trouble for Andy alone—but then, trouble has a way of spreading itself around, and it seemed possible it might just spread out far enough to include a few of Andy's friends, so I wasn't entirely happy to see him that hot morning in June, standing on that platform in a tired-looking, black broadcloth suit, wearing a short-brim eastern hat. I didn't want to see Andy get hurt, and, the sad truth was, I didn't want to see myself get hurt either.

He stretched his arms, then lifted his hat and ran his fingers through his hair, which was cropped to a medium length. His hair was deep black, like his eyes, reflecting the Indian blood he'd inherited from his mother who was the daughter of an Irish farmer and a full-blooded Algonquian squaw. I watched as he set his hat comfortably on his head, not wanting to say anything just then, not knowing what to say, in fact. It looked as if he'd grown some since I'd last seen him, 'bout two years ago. Going to college at that eastern school must've agreed with him. Andy was my age, twenty-three, and he was about an inch shy of six feet—a couple inches taller than me. He'd filled out some, gained a few pounds, and he carried himself like a man you wouldn't normally want to mess with—except now Dean Tripp was in town, along with Snake Haskins and Kid Reese. Reb Cotton and his men were working for the Circle-K too, and eighteen or twenty other regular cowhands. The deck was badly stacked against the Stillman Ranch—which was mostly called the Bar-O around Willow Creek, and I was sure glad I wasn't Andy Stillman just then.

Andy looked around and saw me sitting there in the shade so he wandered over. "Morning, Tom," he said. "What's new?"

That was a question me and probably every other telegraph operator answered at least fifty times a day, asked by just about everyone we came across, but I didn't want to be the one to tell Andy the bad news so I just sort of tiptoed around it by saying "Nothing much, Andy," which was a shameful lie that gave me a guilty shudder way down in my gut. I asked, "What brings you back just now, Andy? City life ain't agreein' with you?"

For an answer, he pulled out a crumpled letter and handed it to me. It was from his father, Henry, dated about three weeks ago, asking Andy to get his tail back to Willow Creek as soon as possible because of trouble that was brewing with William O'Meara's outfit, the Circle-K. It was a short letter; didn't say much more than that. "Trouble brewing," it said with Henry Stillman's typical western understatement. I handed the letter back to Andy. "Sorry, Andy," I said quietly. "Reckon you best be gettin' out to your pa's place."

"Trouble?" He tilted his head at me, echoing the words in his pa's letter.

"Yeah," I answered. "There's been a mite." I'd been raised out West of the Mississippi since I was four; guess I'd learned a thing or two about understatement myself.

He folded the letter and shoved it into a pocket of his suit. "Thanks, Tom," he said. He picked up a worn duffel bag and left.

* * *

I sat there outside the station office watching the iron horse belch steam, bleeding off pressure, feeling strange somehow, seeing Andy again after so long. Two years doesn't sound like much and I suppose it isn't, but Andy had changed a lot in those two years. I'd seen him for less than three minutes but already it was obvious. He'd grown in ways I didn't quite understand right then, but I sure enough felt it, like the cold nuzzle of a horse's nose against my neck, and for some reason I felt suddenly glum and inadequate, mired in my life, sitting there in the morning shade, feeling my life drift by in the same old fly-buzzing routine.

Not that I wanted any part of Andy's action with the Circle-K, you understand. I sure ain't no hero. But for as long as I can remember I'd always wanted to be a telegraph operator. When I was just a kid I drove my ma plumb crazy tapping out Morse Code on the back of an old shovel with a hunk of wood, translating that book of Herman Melville's, Moby Dick, into ephemeral dots and dashes by the light of an old oil lamp. I darn near did the whole thing, well, half anyway, I reckoned, before my ma took up my stick and shovel with a whoop and a holler and I never did find out the end to that story. But I learned Morse Code, and a sight more about whales than I cared or needed to know. Four years before Andy showed up that day in June I landed the job as telegraph operator and stationmaster for the railhead spur that was built north from Rock Springs to Willow Creek. My father, Lyle Booth, was hoping I'd help out at the mercantile, but I had other, more grand ideas. Or so I thought. Now, seeing Andy, I wondered.

After Andy strode off into town I watched the engineer pull the old 4-4-0 down a side track to where several men were waiting to unload the boxcar. A sudden, unexpected feeling of pure dissatisfaction with my life rolled over me like the sound of thunder, aware that at the age of nineteen I'd already realized my life's ambition and nothing much had happened in the four years since. Andy, on the other hand, was still learning, still growing, and it came to me that morning when I saw him step off the train that he was a man still going places, and I had already reached the end of the line.

Andy and me had been friends nearly fourteen years.

When we were a lot younger we spent time down at the Little Muddy, catching frogs and swimming—when the creek held enough water to call it swimming—and we both attended school under the kindly iron hand of Miss Kaufer over at the schoolhouse. I whipped him once, too. I don't recall what we were fighting about but it must have been all-mighty important 'cause we ended up swinging at each other like all glory and I landed a lucky punch that made his nose bleed. But we were ten years old then and I was bigger than him. Two years later he was taller than me and he never looked back.

You wouldn't catch me tangling with him now; I value my hide a sight more than that. The day he came back to Willow Creek he weighed about thirty pounds more than me, and none of it was extra. His shoulders were wide and he wasn't what you'd call lean, not filled out the way he was, but the way he moved you could tell there was rawhide under that tenderfoot suit of his. If you took the time, or the care, to look past the suit, that is. Some people don't.

Folks will tell a telegraph operator things they won't tell their own mothers. They have to, sometimes, if they want a message sent somewheres. The Blue Boar Saloon was the number one clearing-house for information in Willow Creek, the Lucky Lady Saloon was the second. I reckon I was the third. And I reckon I wouldn't be stretching the truth too far if I said I knew more about what happened that summer than just about anyone else in the territory. Except for Andy, of course, and possibly Bear. Andy was my friend and he told me a lot of it. Well, some of it anyway, as it was happening. And I count myself a friend of Bear Buchanan, the blacksmith, and Clevis Willis, the Circle-K foreman, and a host of others each of whom knew a part of the story. I kept my ears mostly open and my mouth mostly shut, paid for an extra beer or two (or three) over at the Boar, and as a result, I know pretty much the whole of what happened.

．　．　．

After Andy left the station he walked west down the short stub of Water Street, past Doc Simes' office, and turned left onto Main. He walked past the Miner's Cafe (In truth there never was much mining going on in the Wind River Range, but

Tincup Smith is still up there in the mountains somewhere), past the Sheriff's Office, the Lucky Lady Saloon, crossed the street toward Myra Nickolson's Confectionery & Bakery, and went past Beringer's General Store to the south end of Main Street where Bear Buchanan's Blacksmith Shop stood under half a dozen peachleaf willow trees.

When Andy walked up, Bear was under the lean-to, his back to the street, wielding a battered hammer and filling the early summer air with industrious, metallic sounds. Bear, like a lot of folks out in the territories, got his name from the way he looked. He had coal-black hair, a thick, black beard and a big moustache topped by a tiny nose and quick, alert eyes. His real name was Wallace, but Bear stood six foot five, weighed just over two hundred seventy pounds, and had darn near as much hair on his chest and shoulders as a range horse that hadn't shed its winter coat. Nobody ever called him Wallace. Some folks figured Bear could've shaped horseshoes with his bare hands and that heating them and beating them with a hammer was just an act, something he did so's people wouldn't think he was showing off. He was a few years past forty but he was still solid and there wasn't a more respected man in all of Willow Creek.

"Morning, Bear," Andy said.

Bear turned around. When he saw Andy a grin split his face like the cut in a tree just before it falls. "Andy," he said happily. "Gawd almighty, boy. How long you been back?"

"Just got in." Andy motioned toward the railhead.

Bear's grin faded and a gloomy look took hold of his face. "Sure sorry about your pa, Andy."

"My father?" Andy said, quicklike.

"You ain't heard?"

"Heard what?"

Bear set his hammer down and laid the shoe back on the hearth-brick. "They got him, Andy. Dirty sneakin' cowardly bastards got him."

Andy's face paled. "Got him? Pa? What are you talking about, Bear?"

"He—" Bear looked away unhappily. "He took a bullet, Andy. In the back." Bear paused again, at a loss for words, then added, "I sure am sorry, Andy. He's gone."

For a long moment Andy stood there in stunned silence as

Bear, who felt himself to be entirely the wrong person to have delivered the news to Andy, shifted his weight uncomfortably from one foot to the other.

"When?" Andy asked finally, a tremor riding his voice.

"Three . . . no, four days ago."

"Who did it?"

"No one seen it, an' no one's sayin'," Bear said unhappily. "Your pa was out mending fences a mile or two south of the house. But I'll bet a dollar for a dime that some of them new Circle-K hands had somethin' t' do with it."

Andy went quiet. His eyes narrowed. "What new hands?"

Bear let out a derisive snort. "Hands that seem a durn sight more familiar with guns and cards and whiskey than ropes or branding irons. O'Meara went and hired hisself some fast guns. Dean Tripp, Snake Haskins, Kid Reese."

Andy dropped his duffel bag in the dust with a muffled thump and looked down at his boots. "Tell me about them, Bear," he said softly.

"You et yet?"

Andy's shoulders sagged, as if he'd suddenly been reminded of some unpleasant chore he'd been putting off. "Sometime yesterday, I reckon."

Bear clapped a hamlike hand on Andy's shoulder and was about to say something when he stopped, fingers wrapped partway around Andy's shoulder. His eyes narrowed slightly. "What've you got in there, son? You been eatin' scrap iron?"

Andy gave him a wan grin. "Railroad spikes. U.P. serves up all you can eat."

For a moment Bear looked at him with one eye, then he shrugged and picked up Andy's bag. "C'mon inside. I reckon Abigail's cookin' oughta set well with you if you ain't had a decent meal in a few days."

"I should be getting out to the ranch, Bear."

Bear spoke quietly, but with some force. "Set a spell, Andy. Won't take all that long t' get you fed, an' I reckon the talk won't hurt you none either. This valley is gettin' t' be a dangerous place for Bar-O folk, an' I reckon the Bar-O's yours, now."

They moved on into the house which was set back from the dust of the street, deep in the shade of the willow trees. It was a comfortable house, fixed up with real upholstered furniture and pictures on the walls that had survived a covered wagon trip out from the East. There was even a rug on the floor in the living room, one of the few in all of Willow Creek.

The two men entered the kitchen and Bear said, "Look what the cat drug in, Abby."

Abigail Buchanan was one of the most beautiful women in Willow Creek. Half a dozen years younger than her husband and more than a full head shorter at five foot four, she managed to look more like twenty-six than thirty-six, which turned most of the town's womenfolk pickle-green with envy. She turned around and her blue eyes brightened. "Andy! What a surprise! My Lord, but it's good to see you again!" Then she bit her lip and glanced uneasily at her husband.

"He knows," Bear said simply.

"I'm terribly sorry, Andy," she said softly, her eyes filled with sadness and gentle concern.

An unhappy silence filled the room, until Bear finally said, "I promised Andy some of your cookin', Abby. He just got off'n the rails."

"Oh, you poor man," Abby said, wiping her hands on an apron, relieved that she had something to do. "Beefsteak, eggs, and fried potatoes?"

"Couldn't have said it better myself," Andy said, smiling.

Bear cast a longing glance toward the stove. "I could do with another bite my own self."

Abigail rested her hands on her hips and looked at Andy. "I swear all I do all day long is fill that man with food." She turned her back to them. In a casual voice she said, "Clair's out back, Andy. Hanging out the wash. I expect she'd be mighty pleased to say howdy. Besides, food won't be ready for a few minutes yet."

Andy glanced at Bear and caught the twinkle in the older man's eye. "Sure," Andy said. "I haven't seen little Clair in, well, two years, anyway." He started for the back door.

Without turning around, Abigail picked up a frying pan. In that same soft voice she said, "I reckon she's grown up some since then, Andy."

Bear grinned at Andy. "Reckon we'll talk later."

• • •

Abigail was right; Clair surely had grown up since Andy had last seen her—I know because I watched it happen. In those two years Clair changed from a funny, budding, sometimes awkward girl of fifteen, into a young woman of seventeen with a fine, slender, woman's figure, five feet three inches tall. Her hair fell four inches past her shoulders, a light chestnut color, soft-looking, loosely curled, and her eyes were filled with the deep, endless blue of the sky and a mischievousness the years hadn't changed much since she was ten. Her arms were slim and strong and brown; she had a pixie face with a button nose that time had transformed, somehow, and yet inevitably, into the face of a pretty, young woman.

In case you're wondering, I was in love with Clair Buchanan. I never said anything about it though, not to anyone and especially not to Clair, because after I paid fourteen dollars a month room and board over at Kinsey's Boarding House I had only eleven dollars left and that just wasn't enough to go calling on a girl. At least not a girl like Clair. So I kept my mouth shut and every time I saw Clair my heart just ached.

And that, of course, was my own damn fault.

· · ·

Andy went out the back door and found Clair pinning wet clothing to a line. She was hanging women's undergarments at the moment Andy walked up behind her.

"That yours?" Andy asked.

Clair jumped at the voice and spun around, a delicate shade of pink coloring her face. "It's mighty bad of you t' notice, Andrew Stillman," she said, embarrassed.

"I expect that means I'm right, then."

Her color deepened. She whirled, pulled the offending article of clothing from the line, and tossed it back into the basket at her feet. "Worse still for you t' mention it twice."

"It's good to see you, Clair."

She turned to face him, color still in her cheeks, hands on her hips. Her face softened and flushed again when she saw him, the way he was looking at her, and she straightened her dress self-consciously. "Please don't be lookin' at me, Andy. I'm a terrible mess right now."

Which, of course, was anything but true.

"You look fine, Clair," he answered with a grin. "Really."
They stood in the shade of a massive willow tree; to the left of
the house was a small stable and beyond that, a corral where a
pale buckskin horse rubbed its side lazily against a fence post
worn smooth as glass. Behind the corral, thick brush choked the
ground under a dozen aspen trees. Andy sat down on a nearby
stump. "You've changed, Clair," he observed. "Grown up a lot
since I was last here."

"A lot of things've changed since you were—" she broke
off and put her hand to her mouth in dismay. "Oh, Andy, I
didn't mean—"

"I know."

Her face was anguished. "Pa told you?"

"He did."

"Oh, Andy. I'm so sorry." She turned angrily toward the
clothesline. "Me and my big mouth."

"It's all right, Clair. You didn't mean anything by it."

She hung a pair of jeans in silence then said, in a soft,
subdued voice: "It's real nice t' see you again, Andy."

"Thanks."

Another long moment of silence went by, then Clair asked,
"You're not goin' t' get mixed up in it, are you?"

"You mean the trouble between the Bar-O and the Circle-
K?"

She nodded.

Andy looked down at his hands. "I don't know, Clair. I'm
not a rancher."

"But—" She stopped herself, biting her lip.

"Kit's the rancher in the family, not me," he went on. "I'm
an engineer now—a civil engineer, in fact, as of five weeks ago.
Nothing has changed that. I came back to help my father, but,
well, guess I got here too late." A deep sadness filled his eyes.
"I haven't had time to think about the future of the ranch."

"It's a fine ranch, Andy," Clair said lamely.

Andy nodded, not knowing what to say, and the lazy
morning quiet closed in around them again.

The screen door at the back of the house creaked and
Abigail's voice called out. "Food's on, Andy."

He stood.

"You going t' the Fourth of July picnic?" Clair asked. She

gave him a wistful look. "It's just a week off now."

"I don't know," he answered. "A lot can happen in a week." Her face fell and he added, more hopefully, "If I'm still in town on the fourth, I expect I'll be there."

Her smile brightened again. "I'm fixin' up a basket for the picnic auction, Andy," she said with the innocent devil of young womanhood gleaming in her eye. "Reckon it'll go for upwards of twelve dollars."

He smiled. "I bet it will at that."

• • •

"Before you go wanderin' around this here valley you'd better know where the chuckholes lie." Bear waved a fork at Andy emphatically, if not outright dangerously, as he spoke. "New ones, that is. Things've changed since you was last here, things you best pay attention to." Andy forked up a load of eggs and listened. Abigail said nothing, apparently paying no attention to them as she scrubbed out the skillet, but both Andy and Bear could feel her listening. "There's bad blood between the Circle-K and the Bar-O," Bear went on.

"Been that way for a long time, Bear."

Bear shook his head. "Not like this, no sir. Ever since your pa decided t' fence his spread and raise both cattle and grass, trouble's been building that just might split this valley into civil war. And the Bar-O ain't big enough t' fight a war with the Circle-K."

"William O'Meara might be Irish to the core, hot-headed even, but he isn't a stupid man," Andy said reasonably. "Cattle need grass. You'd think he'd see the sense of helping the range along, irrigating the land to make it more productive."

"Sense ain't got a durn thing t' do with it. It's tradition. More than tradition, Andy. Your pa closed off the range with his fences. The range has always been open."

Andy picked up a salt shaker and peered at it thoughtfully. "O'Meara's spread is ten miles from the Bar-O, Bear. He's just using that as an excuse."

Bear folded his arms across his chest and leaned back in his chair. He considered Andy's remark for a moment. "Yeah. I reckon he is at that," he said finally.

"O'Meara never was good at holding his cards close to his

chest," Andy said. "Too hot-headed. The Circle-K has been trouble ever since O'Meara decided he'd outgrown his share of the valley. He's a greedy man. It's no secret that he wants the Little Muddy. He wants a bigger spread. He wants more power, more money. Fences aren't the trouble in this valley, Bear, and neither is tradition. Water is. Water and greed. Some people never feel that they have enough."

"I reckon you're right, Andy, but that don't change one blessed thing, least not now. It's been a hot summer. Cricks are running low and tempers are wearin' thin. An' now, the bastards got yer pa. Big things are happenin', changes, an' like it or not you're a Stillman, which puts you right smack in the middle of it."

Andy pushed his plate aside. He kicked back a comfortable distance from the table and stretched his legs out.

"You said something about chuckholes. I'm listening."

"First off," Bear said, leaning closer, lowering his voice, "I'd keep me a good distance away from Dean Tripp."

"You mentioned Tripp earlier. I've never heard of him."

"Not likely you would, hobnobbin' around back East in all that la-de-da high society. But Tripp's a real bad customer, Andy. O'Meara hired him, as he says, to run cattle and protect Circle-K interests in the valley." He snorted. "Tripp wouldn't recognize a cow if one walked up and bit a good-sized chunk out of his ass—"

Across the room Abigail cleared her throat delicately and continued her scrubbing.

Bear grinned at Andy and said, "Anyways, I reckon you get the drift. More often than not you'll find Tripp over t' the Blue Boar rinsing out his mouth with whiskey, keeping his fingers loose shuffling cards. It'll be a warm day in January before you catch him with a branding iron in his hands. He's quick with a gun, too."

"Anyone seen that?"

"Not here, not yet anyway, but there're stories. Seems he killed a man over to Santa Fe and another in Tucson; fair fights both, if you believe the stories, but you can bet he had a hand in the provokin'. You want t' keep clear of him." Bear leaned around the edge of the table and peered at Andy's belt. He pursed his lips. "You ain't packin'."

"I've got a gun out at the ranch but I don't figure to use it. I'm no hand with a gun. Besides, guns aren't the only way to fight."

"Around here there *ain't* no way t' fight, Andy. Guns, swords, fists, words, it don't matter. O'Meara's got this town hog-tied, and that's a cold hard fact."

Andy folded his hands in front of him on the table. "What about the others you mentioned—Snake Haskins and Kid . . ."

"Reese. They came in with Tripp. I reckon they ain't quite as bad as Tripp himself, but they ain't good news, Andy. Snake is scum—dangerous, low-life scum. Don't worry 'bout gettin' shot in the chest by that one, but you watch your back."

"And Reese?"

"He's young and tough, pretty good size, carries a gun, but that's an hombre who likes t' use his fists. There've been fights in the Blue Boar lately and Reese usually ends up somewheres in the middle of 'em."

The kitchen door creaked, banged, and Clair backed inside carrying the empty basket. She put it aside, walked over to the table, and gathered up the plates and silverware. As she passed Andy she warmed him with a little smile.

"Turned into a right purdy little lady, didn't she?" Bear said with a grin.

"Pa!"

Bear got to his feet. "Reckon it's gettin' a mite close in here, Andy. Let's us high-tail it back out t' the shop."

Andy stood. Before he left he glanced at Clair and found her looking back at him. He asked, "What are you cooking for the fourth?"

"It's not right, your askin', Andrew Stillman," she said, her eyes glowing with ill-concealed pleasure. "If you're so all-fired curious, you can find out at the auction. If'n you bid high enough, that is."

"Twelve dollars?"

Clair glanced at her mother. "Well, ten at least," she said, a bit subdued. "Milly Shaw's basket brought twelve last year and Jill O'Meara's brought twenty."

Andy thanked Abigail for the food, said his good-byes to the women, and left the room.

In the shop Bear picked up the horseshoe with the tongs,

gave it a quick look, and set it back on the coals. He tended the fire and pumped gently on the bellows as he spoke. "There's more trouble in this valley than what I mentioned in the house, Andy."

Andy nodded. "O'Meara and his sons?"

"Worse. A few months ago O'Meara hired a man by the name of Reb Cotton. Reb brought five men with him—tough men. Oh, they're sure-enough cowhands, all right. But they're a bad crowd all the same. I reckon the real trouble started when they began workin' for the Circle-K. I don't recall all their names but I know one's called Dutch, another's called Gage, and one calls himself Reno. You might do yourself a favor and steer clear of that bunch, too."

Andy sighed. "That all?"

"Aaron O'Meara."

Andy's eyes narrowed. "Aaron?"

"He's gone bad, Andy. Changed. Near as I kin tell, anyway. Fancies hisself a fast hand with a gun. He fairly worships Tripp's boots. You best figger he's one of that crowd now."

"I'll keep it in mind, Bear." Andy wrinkled his brow. "How about Jason?"

"Jason? Can't say he's all that different. He's still O'Meara's son, still as ornery as ever, but I ain't seen him runnin' with Tripp or Reb Cotton's crowd, either."

Bear poked at the coals, spinning up a tiny whirlwind of hot sparks as Andy picked up his bag. "You an engineer now?" Bear asked.

"Civil engineer. As of five weeks ago."

"Well, that's a durn sight better'n bein' a rancher or a gol-durned blacksmith. Good luck t' you, Andy."

And that was all he said about Andy's education, right then.

2

Andy left Bear's shop and headed up Main Street toward the livery stable, fifty yards past the Blue Boar on the other side of the street, set off from the rest of the establishments a safe distance. The odors that carried out of Dugan's Livery weren't generally the most pleasant in town.

Andy walked into the cool shadows of the barn, looked around for a clean spot, then dropped his bag in the dust.

"Hello," he called. No answer. A half-dozen horses turned their heads and watched him from the corners of their eyes as Andy ambled into the darkness of the livery and looked around. The stable was large, two stories tall—a typical small-town livery with a haymow in the loft, a scythe or two hanging over the rafters, pitchforks and a shovel against one wall, and a sorry collection of saddles, bits, hackamores, and ropes that had mostly seen better days.

Other than the horses, the stable was empty. Andy walked through the livery, past the line of horse's rumps, and out the back door. An ancient buckboard stood tilted on three wheels, rotting quietly in the yard. "Hello," Andy called again.

An answering call came from the outhouse set back under the shade of an old water birch, and a minute later Len Peliter came out hitching up his overalls. Len was a gangly kid of fifteen with round, owl-like eyes, freckles, and comical, jutting ears. His father owned half-interest in Peliter & Owens Hardware Store at the opposite end of Main Street.

"Morning, Len," Andy said amiably. "I need a horse."

Len gawked at Andy momentarily in surprise. "Didn't know you was back in town, Mr. Stillman," he said. He stared beyond Andy at the livery. "Uh, Mr. Dugan don't let me rent no horses. I jest clean the stables and do the waterin' and feedin'." His face brightened. "Pays two bits a day, too."

Andy smiled. "You save some of that and you could end

up a rich man around these parts, Len."

"I aim to," Len said seriously.

"Is Max around?"

Len nodded. "Over t' the Blue Boar."

Andy smiled at Len. "Reckon a man needs to keep his whistle wet."

Len looked at Andy with a doubtful expression. "I reckon," he said.

• • •

Maximillian Dugan was an honest-to-god Remittance man, the only one in Willow Creek for which the townsfolk were mostly thankful. Some said he was once a Duke in England; others thought he might have been an Earl. Not one in twenty knew the difference between a Duke and an Earl, so it hardly mattered. Most folks had no particular interest in what Max once was and were satisfied just to call him the Whiskey Duke and let it go at that. Whatever he was, or once had been, every month or so a modest sum of money would arrive from somewhere and Max would spend the next week reeling around the streets of Willow Creek, bleary-eyed, reeking of cheap whiskey. Then he'd run out of money, drag himself back to the livery, pass out for a day or two, and finally he'd be his old mournful self again, full of stories of days gone by until the next bit of money came in. He was an institution in Willow Creek, a bit tiresome during his bad days, but the money that was sent to him was welcome in town. Folks mostly left him alone.

Andy walked back through the earthy, horse-scented dark of the livery and stepped into the street. He paused, looking toward the Blue Boar, then walked diagonally across the street toward the saloon.

The Blue Boar was a hell-pit, even as late as 1885. It was the first saloon to tap a keg in Willow Creek, and even when Truman Carlos put up the Lucky Lady three years later, the Blue Boar remained the "drinkin'-man's" saloon. For faro, poker, or craps, you couldn't beat the Lucky Lady (or so folks said, usually with a sly grin on their faces) but for serious drinking and maybe a good fist fight, the Blue Boar was the place to go.

Andy stepped up to the boardwalk and looked out at the

hitching post. Four horses were out front, standing three-legged in a ragged line with their eyes closed, tails flicking away flies. They didn't move an inch as Andy walked on by and pushed through the swinging doors into the saloon.

The room was as dim as a cave after the brightness of the street, and Andy paused for a moment to allow his eyes to adjust to the gloom. The windows were glazed with a thick layer of dirt and the floor was covered with drifts of coarse, dirty sawdust. A stale pall of smoke hung in the air.

After a while Andy was able to make out a man with a lean, hard face sitting at a table in back, dealing himself a hand of solitaire. A short, crooked cigarette hung from his lips. From Bear's description Andy knew it was Dean Tripp: six feet tall; longish, unkempt black hair; tough, wiry frame, about thirty-five years old. At another table to one side of the room, three men who had been talking in low voices fell silent and stared at Andy as if he were a strange bug that had crawled in off the street. Andy recognized Aaron O'Meara. The other two would be Snake Haskins and Kid Reese. Snake was thirty years old with a slight paunch, bad teeth, and shifty, dangerous eyes set in a dark, surly, unshaven face. Beside him, Kid Reese, with blond hair and pale blue eyes, stared at Andy with a sullen, yet somehow eager look in his eyes. Alone at a table by the front entrance sat Max Dugan with a bottle, red-eyed, unaware of the sudden tension in the room.

"Well, lookee here," Aaron's voice broke the quiet of the room. "If it ain't the new owner of the Bar-O." His voice was filled with contempt and Andy felt the sudden interest and quick appraisals of the other men. Max Dugan lifted his head and looked around with watery, unfocused eyes.

Tripp let out a short cluck of disapproval. "Tenderfoot," he said dismissively as he dealt another card to the table. Kid Reese let out a short bark of laughter at the comment.

"Morning, Carl," Andy said to the bartender.

Carl Springer nodded cautiously to Andy, picked up a glass and began wiping it slowly.

Aaron picked up a shot glass of whiskey and leaned back in his chair. "Heard your pappy bought the farm, Andrew."

The room had been fairly quiet before. Now it was silent.

"So I heard, Aaron," Andy said in a low voice. "I was told

he was shot in the back, so I reckon he wasn't killed by a man."
His eyes swept the faces in the room. Tripp appeared amused.
"Yep," Andy pressed. "My father was killed by a pure, plain
coward."

Snake's face turned chalky and his fingers gripped the
edge of the table in front of him. Kid Reese watched Andy
carefully as Tripp stood up and sauntered across the room.

"Those words could be unhealthy, spoke in the presence of
the man who killed your kin," Tripp said.

"I don't think so," Andy replied coolly, staring directly at
Snake. "Like I said, he wasn't killed by a man. It wouldn't be
dangerous as long as I was facing him since backshooters are
chicken-hearted, lily-livered bastards. Besides, I figure I'd
recognize him as soon as I saw him."

Tripp's eyes hardened. "How's that?"

"By the horse manure on his shirt."

"Horse manure—?"

"The kind of coward that shoots a man in the back
probably spends most of his time slinking around on his belly
like a snake. Around here, that's bound to leave manure on the
shirt."

Snake stood up suddenly. His chair upended and crashed to
the floor. The sound was loud in the room. He turned and
stomped out the rear door of the saloon.

"Well if that don't beat all," Andy drawled. "Wonder
what's eatin' him?"

Tripp smiled. "Belly ache. He's been complaining of that
just lately."

"That would do it," Andy said. He turned to Max Dugan
who was watching the proceedings with a vacant,
uncomprehending look on his face. "I need a horse for a few
days, Max."

Max forced his eyes to focus on Andy and he smiled a wet,
drunken smile. He raised a shot glass to eye level and drained it.
"T' yer 'ealth, Andy."

Tripp snickered.

"You got a horse I can rent, Max?" Andy asked again.

"Why sure he has," Tripp answered, his voice mocking
Andy. "Ol' Max has got a number of likely steeds, some of 'em
broke so's even a tenderfoot could likely mount up. Something

like ol' Spud ought t' serve you right well."

Max's milky eyes stared uncertainly at Tripp. "Spud?"

Aaron spoke up. "Another name for a potato," he explained to no one in particular. "That damn animal is half dead, half vegetable, but I reckon he's horse enough for a tenderfoot."

Kid Reese laughed and Tripp stood by the bar, grinning.

"Well," said Max, unable to separate Andy's request from Tripp's and Aaron's suggestions, "if'n y' want Spud it'll cost y' fifty cents a day, Andy. A buck if y' need a saddle and bridle."

"I will," Andy said.

Max jammed a cork into the bottle in front of him, stood up, and deposited it on the bar. "Hol' this fer me, Carl. I'll be back."

Springer set the bottle behind the bar and continued his nervous work with the glasses.

Outside, Max's balding head gleamed in the sunlight. He blinked and held a hand over his eyes as he and Andy walked to the livery, Max following an erratic course, tacking across the street in spurious arcs and curves. His cheeks were covered with what looked like a week's worth of stubble. Andy figured his poke had just about played out for the month.

"How are you getting by, Max?" Andy asked.

"Same's usual," Max answered without answering at all. He wheezed slightly as he walked.

"What's wrong with this horse . . . Spud?"

"Moody. Moody son of a bitch," Max mumbled. "Maybe you'd prefer a diff'rent horse."

"I'll look him over."

"Thought y' had a horse already, son."

"I just got back in town," Andy explained. "Been back East. I need a horse to get out to the ranch."

Max looked over at him. "Y' been gone?"

"Two years, Max."

But Max hadn't really heard him. Already his thoughts were on the bottle waiting for him back at the Blue Boar.

• • •

Having been raised on his father's ranch most of his life, Andy knew a thing or two about horses, but he didn't know anything about Spud. No one knew anything about Spud except perhaps the terse, grizzled stranger who rode into town two months earlier and sold Spud to Max Dugan for only six dollars. That was the only time anyone in town ever recalled Max getting taken.

I don't know if it's possible for a horse to be crazy or not. I know they can get deranged on locoweed but I don't know if a horse can be crazy, all on its own. If such a thing is possible then Spud was a crazy damn horse; if it's not, then Spud was even more a puzzle. Whatever went on in that brute's head, it sure wasn't natural. Anyway, everyone agreed that what happened next wasn't Andy's fault.

He and Max arrived at the livery and Max had Len put a bridle on Spud and bring him out front. Spud came out, docile as a sheep. Andy looked him over then counted out two dollars to Max to cover two days.

Andy laid the saddle across Spud's back like it was a silk handkerchief even though that saddle weighed nearly fifty pounds. Spud's ears flicked lazily at trespassing flies and he stood three-legged, dozing with the sun shining on his rump, reins wrapped around the hitching post to one side of the livery. Spud was a bandy-legged, barrel-chested, stocky little four-colored piebald. His eyelids drooped and his head hung low which was all part of the act. There's no telling what was going on inside that animal's head. The grizzled stranger had taken his six dollars and hightailed it out of town without another word.

Andy gazed down the street toward the Blue Boar. The front of the saloon shimmered in heat waves thrown off by the sun-scorched dust. He couldn't see any of the men who had been inside the saloon.

He tightened the cinch and Spud let out a little grunt but his eyes never so much as flickered.

Out front, Len leaned against the livery wall in the shade, watching. He said nothing. People out west generally do a pretty decent job of minding their own business.

"I'll bring him back tomorrow," Andy said to Max.

"Don't matter t' me, son," Max said. He belched. "Be a dollar a day fer as long as y' keep him."

Andy tied his duffel bag to the rear of the saddle, swung himself onto Spud's back, and Spud exploded, seesawing violently in the air as he whirled nearly a full circle. Andy was on that horse for maybe a quarter of a second, and then he was lying on his back in the dust and Spud was just standing there, eyes nearly shut, head hung low, ears already flicking sleepily at flies.

From down the street Andy heard whoops of laughter. Tripp, Aaron, and Kid Reese were standing in front of the Blue Boar, slapping each other on the back, pointing at Andy as they roared with delight. Further up the street, several townspeople turned to stare.

Tripp's disgusted voice carried up the street. "Tenderfoot."

Andy picked himself up and dusted off the seat of his pants. Len yawned and said, "That hoss sure don't much like t' be rode."

"Why in hell didn't you tell me?"

Len shrugged. "Reckon you didn't never ask."

3

Wyoming Territory was changing pretty quickly in those days. I went and learned Morse Code so I could be a telegraph operator, while back East some folks were using something called a telephone. A person could just talk into some kind of a box at one end of the line and their voice came out of a similar box at the other end—no need to bother with the dots and dashes I'd taken so long to learn. I reckoned it'd be a while before this telephone thing got all the way out to Willow Creek, but it was coming. Already I was starting to wonder what I was going to do when it got here.

But in 1866, the year Henry Stillman moved into the valley tucked into the folds of the Wind River Range, the country was still pretty wild. Henry was the first to settle in the valley. Two years later William O'Meara showed up and Henry was glad to have the company. There was still plenty of room, their herds were still small, and O'Meara's spread was some ten miles from the Stillman ranch. Around them was over one hundred thousand acres of prime grazing land and, occasionally, some angry Utes and Cheyenne. O'Meara's arrival gave them more hands to fight off the Indians.

In 1871 they combined their herds, drove them all the way to Denver, and the Wind River Valley was on the map. A year later, Willow Creek sprang up at the edge of the prairie in the shadow of the Tetons. The Blue Boar was the first building to see a roof. Out West, saloons tended to come first. Later came Beringer's General Store, the Wind River Hotel, Booth's Mercantile—my pa's store—and all the rest.

Henry Stillman had picked the location for his ranch with care. Little Muddy Creek ran right through the middle of his land. O'Meara took a place just the other side of Crooked Neck Ridge, a heavily wooded line of hills that pushed southwest into the valley. Badger Creek spilled out of the mountains around him and that was the main source of water for what finally became the Circle-K. It soon became apparent that the Little Muddy was more suitable for serious ranching than Badger Creek, which ran dry when the snow pack in the lower Tetons melted off. Most years the snow pack never did quite melt completely off and O'Meara did all right. But in 1873 the snow was nearly gone by mid-July and O'Meara had to sell part of his herd short then watch as thirty percent of the remainder died of thirst. The Little Muddy ran down to little more than a trickle, but it was enough for Henry's smaller herd to get by. Henry let O'Meara use what little water passed through his range to the south, which accounted for why O'Meara didn't lose more than he did.

O'Meara vowed never to let another drought get him. He went back East that winter to Chicago and ordered a hundred fifty feet of six-inch pipe and a valve that weighed upwards of three hundred pounds. The shipment arrived at Rock Springs in May on the Union Pacific, and O'Meara and Henry Stillman along with cowhands from both ranches went down to Rock Springs, picked it up, and hauled it back on a couple of freight wagons.

By then O'Meara had already begun construction on the Upper Badger reservoir. Badger Creek wound out of the Tetons and through a meadow six miles above the ranch house. A natural wall of rock cut off the lower end of that meadow. I heard someone say it was a moraine, left over from a glacier thousands of years ago when millions of tons of ice scraped out the hollow and pushed the rock into a low, circular ridge. Badger Creek had cut a path through that wall of ground-up rock but the channel wasn't wide at the lower end of the meadow and O'Meara's cowhands and a number of Stillman's as well spent the entire summer and part of the fall hauling rock and dirt on sledges across the grass to the lower end of the meadow. They set the valve into a framework of wood just below the dam face and ran a hundred twenty feet of pipe up into the meadow.

They didn't rightly get the dam completed that fall either. Half the next summer was spent adding height to it but even then it contained a sizeable body of water behind it. A hundred yards from the dam was a tiny island which some unknown person named the Rock of Gibraltar. When the reservoir was full that island wasn't more than three feet out of water but when the water was low you could walk right out to the knob on a low ridge that normally lay submerged out of sight. Most of the body of the reservoir lay to the north of the island.

Of course the whole thing froze over every winter. During that first year O'Meara was scared to death that the water would freeze back behind the valve and bust the pipes so they built a tiny shack around the valve as close as they could to the outer face of the dam and wrapped the rest of the pipe in straw and burlap. Inside the cabin a low fire was kept going all winter. The heat crept up the pipe under the burlap and kept the pipe thawed all the way into the dam. The next summer someone from back East showed O'Meara how to shut off the intake pipe inside the reservoir with a steel plate and a leather gasket. After that they simply shut off the pipe for the winter and drained it, leaving the valve open in case water seeped into the pipe over the winter months. O'Meara swore he'd kill any sonofabitch dumb enough to shut that valve in the winter.

In the late 70's, O'Meara's herd grew quickly. He sold only what he needed to keep going and he kept the rest for breeding. Then another drought gave him a scare in 1880. His herd had nearly outgrown the Upper Badger Reservoir (it was just called Badger Reservoir in those days) and when the snow pack melted off by early August O'Meara watched fearfully as the reservoir dropped steadily and the isthmus that connected the Tetons with the Rock of Gibralter rose out of the water, bold and prominent. O'Meara's face took on extra lines that summer. Then, in the middle of October, a pre-winter storm dumped six inches of snow in the mountains and the resulting run-off saved the herd. By that time O'Meara had already scouted the location for what became, the following summer, Lower Badger Reservoir.

Run-off from Upper Badger Reservoir filled the Lower Badger, two miles down the mountain. Lower Badger was only half the size of the upper reservoir but it gave O'Meara enough breathing room to keep expanding his herd.

By 1883 the Circle-K was five times the size of the Bar-O and had again just about outgrown the capacity of its reservoir system. O'Meara began to look across the valley at the Little Muddy and it was about that time that the far-seeing Henry Stillman realized that ranching on the open range was something that was entering the final stages of its existence. Irrigating the land to grow a finer, denser grade of grass was the next obvious step, and he took it. His cows took on more weight, used less land, and people who kept track of such things claimed they tasted better too. The efficiency of the ranch improved and profits were higher.

The Bar-O also strung fences on the range.

• • •

Andy gave Spud back to Max Dugan after suggesting several unlikely theories regarding the probable lineage of the beast and took instead a grey dun. By noon he was several miles out of Willow Creek, heading northwest for the Bar-O, loping easily through the prairie along a hardened buckboard trail. A few slow-moving puffy clouds rode the sky. A gentle breeze swept across the land from the direction of the Bar-O, cooling Andy's face. A hawk circled high overhead, scanning the prairie for field mice. In the distance, a dark line of willow trees marked the course of the Little Muddy. Beyond that, the Bar-O buildings were shadowed dots set in the foothills at the upper fringe of the prairie, five miles from Willow Creek and less than half a mile from the blanket of ponderosa pine and box elder that spilled out of the mountains into the western margin of the valley.

Before he reached the Little Muddy, Andy's way was blocked by a crooked barbed-wire fence. A makeshift gate crossed the trail and Andy dismounted, lifted the hoop of wire that held the gate shut, and walked the dun through. On the other side he rehooked the wire then mounted up and looked around. The range was no different on one side of the fence than the other, but in the distance, on the slope of the foothills beyond the ranch buildings, Andy saw large rectangular patches of irrigated grass that were greener than the rest of the prairie. To the north and south the stark line of fence disappeared into the gently folded contours of the valley.

Andy paused at the Little Muddy to let the dun drink. Ten minutes later he was in the yard leading to the front of the ranch house. A neat little cabin stood to his right; to his left were the corrals, next to the barn. The bunkhouse was set under several aspen trees nearby. In the yard a shallow pond reflected the blue of the sky, fed by the overflow pumped by a windmill thirty feet from the house. Andy hitched his horse at a post in front of the porch. The muted sounds of a hammer came from inside the barn along with the angry tones of a man cussing with great enthusiasm, but as yet Andy hadn't seen a soul. He untied his duffel bag from the saddle.

"Reckon the mail's gettin' a mite faster," a voice said. "Ain't been but two days since I sent you that letter."

Andy turned and saw his kid brother, Kit, standing by the side of the house. Kit was fourteen, taller by six inches than when Andy had last seen him. Andy figured Kit to be about five inches shy of six feet. He had the same dark hair and eyes as Andy and both had inherited Henry's lean, intense features. Andy was startled to see the colt hanging at the side of Kit's thigh in Henry's old holster.

"I never got it. It's probably no farther than Rock Springs by now," Andy replied. "How are you doing, Kit?"

"I'm jest fine. Pa's dead."

Andy paused. In a hollow voice he said, "I know, I heard."

"He was shot in the back like he was dirt. Like he wasn't nothin'." Kit's eyes were cold and bright, his lips pressed together in a tight, pale line.

"Where's Amy?" Andy asked quietly.

"Out back."

"Is she okay?"

"Still grievin'. Ain't eatin' much, but she's okay. They ain't shot her yet."

Andy picked up his bag and together they circled the house, a rambling, two-story structure built with heavy timbers and thick plank siding. It had been painted white some years back, a bigger house than was needed after Henry's wife, Leora, died in 1877 giving birth to Amy. Bigger still, now.

Andy pointed toward the cabin he had passed earlier. "That Miles' and Nell's place?"

"Yep."

The cabin was a new addition to the ranch. The foreman, Miles Harding, had tied the knot with Nell a year back. Andy had heard the news in a letter and was glad of it. Miles and Nell were both good people—they deserved each other—and Andy regretted having missed the wedding.

In the yard in back of the house Amy was sitting on a stump tossing feed in a desultory manner to a small flock of chickens that ignored her as they pecked energetically at the ground. With a pang of regret Andy noticed how much bigger Amy had gotten too. She was eight now, with dark, liquid eyes and long, black hair that fell halfway down her back. She still had a lot of growing to do yet, but Andy could see what the end result was going to be. In eight or nine years Amy was going to be breaking a lot of young men's hearts.

"Someone here t' see you," Kit announced.

Amy looked up and with a squeal of delight she slipped off the feed bag that hung at her side and ran across the yard to Andy. He squatted and she ran into his arms, gripped his neck, and pressed her cheek against his. Almost immediately her body began quivering and Andy realized she was crying. He turned his eyes up to Kit whose face had softened for the moment. A wave of helplessness washed over Andy. He held his little sister, patting her head gently, letting her cry.

"Oh, Andy," she sobbed in his ear, still clinging to him.

"P-Pa's been killed. Pa's dead."

"I know, button."

"T-Three days ago."

"I know." She wanted him to do something, wanted him to make it better somehow. When they were younger he had fixed her dolls when they had broken but this time there was nothing he could do. Wire pins and glue weren't going to bring pa back. He felt helpless, feeling Amy's tears on his cheek.

"Don't ever go away again," she said fiercely.

Andy said nothing. Amy needed comfort now, not cold, implacable logic.

•   •   •

The graveyard was almost half a mile from the house, high in the foothills just inside the line of trees that pressed out of the mountains. Amy walked with Andy. Kit stayed behind at the house.

They walked in silence in the bright June sun and when they were halfway there Amy reached up and took Andy's hand. Her hand was cold. He looked down at her; she was staring straight ahead, her face a tired mask of grief. He felt, for a moment, like a stranger next to this young girl who still trusted him so implicitly after he had unfailingly fixed her broken dolls and pulled slivers out of her tiny hands.

They stood at the foot of the two graves, one with a wooden marker already faded with exposure to the sun and wind and rain—the other freshly cut, set into ground that was still a shade darker than the earth around it. There was nothing to say. Andy stood quietly, staring at the unfamiliar grave, trying somehow to comprehend its meaning. It must be impossible for Amy, he thought. He glanced down at her and she looked up at him with a bleak face that had finally run out of tears.

After a while they turned and walked away.

"Are you goin' t' git them, Andy?" she asked, and Andy was surprised at the steel edge in her voice. Whatever hatred she'd felt up to now had been overshadowed by her grief, but it was there all the same, burning brightly inside her. He wondered what Kit had said to her.

"If I 'get' anyone, it won't bring pa back," he replied.

"I know. But—"

She left the thought unfinished; it hung heavily in the air between them as they walked back to the house.

When they got back, Kit had already put Max's dun in the barn. Andy took his bag up to his old room. Downstairs, Nell would be waiting to see him. The vision of the fresh grave was still with him, however, and he found he wanted to be alone. He went back outside and hiked down to the Little Muddy where it widened between polished banks of granite, shaded by gently swaying willows. The water moved in slow, placid eddies, reflecting sky and shadow, carrying bits of wood and leaves.

Andy sat on a fallen limb staring over the old swimming hole for nearly two hours, lost in thought.

When he returned the sun was low in the west and long shadows reached out from the Tetons. In the house Nell was waiting for him. Seven years ago, a year after Leora Stillman had died, Nell was hired on at the ranch as a cook. Over the years she had become much more. She was a friend to Andy and she was the nearest thing to a mother Amy had ever known. She was nearly fifty, plump, grey-haired, with clear, friendly eyes. One of the greatest joys in the valley was to be out at the Bar-O come suppertime.

She was standing in the doorway to the kitchen when Andy came into the house.

"Kit said you were back, Andy," Nell said quietly. "Reckon these are times a man needs a few moments alone."

Andy looked down at the floor sheepishly. "I was just coming by to see you."

"Thought you might." Her eyes brightened and she added, "Besides, a man's stomach will bring him by, sooner or later."

Andy smiled in spite of himself. "A man's still got to eat."

"How are you doing, Andy?"

"Adjusting It doesn't seem possible—pa gone and all."

She nodded, sadly.

He held out a hand then let it drop in a useless gesture. Finally he said, "Kit and Amy are taking it pretty hard."

"Reckon we all are, one way or another. But they're just kids, Andy. Amy'll be all right, in time. It's Kit I worry about."

"He's angry."

"He wears that six-gun all day long. He wore it to town the

other day when he mailed you that letter. Miles couldn't talk him out of it. He's got a temper, that boy does. He could get himself hurt."

"I'll talk to him."

Nell nodded again. "Soon, Andy."

An hour later, Bar-O cowhands started drifting in from the range. Andy went out to the bunkhouse to greet them. Paul Armstrong and Slim arrived first, then Stringer, Rolly, and Two-Bit. Everyone expressed their regrets over the death of Andy's father. They were polite to a man, but reserved. There was a silent, unspoken feeling that Andy wasn't quite one of them. Even Rolly held back a little. Andy was back from the East and according to current western folklore the East was a place populated by dudes, tenderfoots, tinhorns, effetes, and other inferior folk. He was Henry Stillman's boy, but he wasn't a cowboy. He wasn't a proper westerner any longer.

Andy went back to the house. Fifteen minutes later Miles sauntered in. He came in through the back door, to the kitchen where Andy was talking quietly with Nell. Amy was stirring a big pot of beans with a wooden spoon the size of a small oar.

"Andy!" Miles exclaimed, surprised and pleased. Then, in a subdued tone, he added his regrets to the others Andy had heard that day. "Didn't expect t' see you fer another two, three weeks," he said, peppered moustache bouncing on his cheeks as he spoke.

"Pa wrote three weeks ago, Miles. Said there was trouble."

Miles was a big man, over fifty years old, with a weather-worn face and a thick shock of white hair. He had taken on an extra ten or twenty pounds since Andy had last seen him. Nell was feeding him well.

"Never said nothin' about writing you," Miles replied.

"He wouldn't."

"No, I reckon not."

There was a pause in the conversation during which time everyone seemed to take an extra breath. Amy stirred the beans slowly with a troubled look on her face. Finally Miles said, with a wry grin, "Nell took on a heap o' trouble last year, Andy."

"So I heard. You married yourself a brave woman."

Amy smiled faintly.

Nell turned on them. "If'n you're going to stand around

jawin' you can take up spoons and help out. If not, you're takin' up space." Her voice was stern but the corners of her mouth wrinkled in her efforts to resist a smile.

"Reckon that's a hint even a mule could take to heart," Miles said, and he and Andy departed the kitchen in haste.

The ranch hands ate at the usual place at the usual time but Nell insisted the rest of the family sit at the dining table and have what she called, "a proper sit-down meal". This required that the participants wash up, and this in turn precipitated an exhibition of surly behavior on the part of Miles and Kit. They performed admirably and Andy noticed with mixed pleasure that Kit was able to hold his own with Miles, rounding out the obligatory grumbling with several phrases of his own invention.

The table was spread with a white lace cloth. Amy set the plates and silverware under Nell's direction. Amy moved proudly, smoothly, bristling with importance, and she even told Andy he was in the way once. Andy moved aside and Amy swept by him with her arms filled with dishes. Nell was wonderful for Amy, Andy thought, suddenly grateful. Amy was confident, graceful, already at home in the kitchen and around the house. Andy could see Nell's easy manner and quiet efficiency blooming in Amy as the seeds that had been sown inexorably bore their fruit. There was a lot of Miles in Kit too, Andy thought. Being around Nell and Miles had changed both Kit and Amy for the better. And now, there was little of Andy's past influence apparent in either of them.

At least, not any more.

4

They sat down to dinner. Miles said grace. He bowed his head and mumbled a few words of thanks in a low, embarrassed voice. Then food was passed around; to Andy it seemed there must have been a few dozen people invited he hadn't heard about who hadn't arrived yet, but were expected soon. Nell never skimped when it came to spreading a table.

Conversation started halfway through the meal, after everyone had worked off the first hard edge of hunger. It was Miles who first broke the silence.

"You done with college, Andy?"

Andy nodded. "Five weeks ago."

"That mean you're an engineer now?"

"A civil engineer," Andy agreed. "Of course I don't have any experience yet. Before I got pa's letter I was looking into several companies that sounded interesting."

Nell spoke up. "Exactly what does a civil engineer do, Andy?"

Andy had just taken a bite of steak so he turned to Amy and said something like, "Numpfh mmuummmph yuffph," causing her to giggle and squirm in her seat in delight. Nell smiled. Andy finished his bite and said, "A civil engineer changes the face of the land, Nell. Bridges, railroads, dams, roads, canals, and harbors, are all civil engineering projects. Even irrigation systems," he said, looking at Kit.

"Pa put in the irrigation system here, and he weren't no engineer," Kit said, defiantly.

"A lot of practical engineering is done using nothing more than common sense," Andy replied easily. "Any miner who ever dammed a creek learned something about engineering. A lot of bridges have been built by men who couldn't even write their own names. Engineering just provides a basis for being more certain of your work, of predicting how strong a bridge or dam will be, and often of doing the same job in less time with less money."

"You don't need t' know engineerin' t' throw a rope around a cow," Kit said. He was angry, not at Andy but at the loss of his father and at the unexpected and unwanted changes taking place in his life.

Andy received aid from an unexpected quarter. Miles looked across the table at Kit and said, "I reckon engineerin' ain't for ever'body, Kit. Some folks, like me, jest naturally got t' do what they do best, which is punchin' cows. An' some folks, like your brother here, was born with the brains t' do better'n that. Already engineerin' is changin' the country. Look at the Union Pacific. Look at O'Meara's reservoirs and our own irrigation system."

"They wasn't built by no engineers."

"Per'aps you ain't been listenin', Kit," Miles said. He turned to Andy. "That reservoir of O'Meara's, the Upper Badger; I reckon proper engineerin' could've built it a durn sight easier?"

Andy nodded. "They could have put in a temporary rail system and done it in half the time."

"There," Miles said, nodding to Kit. "You see?"

Andy noted Kit's pained expression. "Don't get me wrong, Kit," he said. "The Upper Badger isn't a bad dam. In fact it's one hell of a dam, probably twice the size it needs to be, and that's it's weakness as well as its strength. The point is, it doesn't hold any more water than a smaller, properly engineered dam would hold."

The conversation flagged temporarily and was again rescued by Miles. "I reckon you're the new owner of the Bar-O, Andy. You given any thought about what we're goin' t' do about the Circle-K? We're sittin' on a powder keg here, and that's a fact."

Kit's eyes took on an unusual brightness at mention of the Circle-K.

"I haven't been back long enough to make any decisions, Miles. I'm still not exactly sure what's happening here in the valley. I've got to know what we're up against before I make any decisions. Tomorrow I'll take a look at the changes around the Bar-O, especially the irrigation system. Perhaps if O'Meara were to come over and take a good look at—"

"Pa's dead, or doesn't that matter anymore?" Kit said bitterly.

"You tell me how to bring him back."

"I cain't do that, but I kin show you how to fix the coward that shot him in the back!"

"Who are you going to fix, Kit? Everyone out at the Circle-K?"

"If'n I have to, yes."

"They might take offense to that," Andy replied.

"Let'em. I ain't afraid."

For a second Andy's eyes blazed fiercely. "Maybe not. Maybe you're not afraid, in which case you're a damn fool, but you could catch a bullet all the same, Kit. There's no glory in death. Not a speck of it, and you'd better remember that."

"You tell 'im," Kit said, turning to Miles for support. Amy had been watching the heated exchange with big eyes, a mound of uneaten potatoes on her fork, and Andy felt a sudden pang of compassion for her. They were discussing her life and her ranch too, yet the only thing she could do was listen to the dangerous talk and worry, all alone. Andy reached down and took her hand. She looked up at him and gave him a sallow smile.

"Your potatoes are getting cold, button."

"I ain't awful hungry, Andy."

Miles looked down uncomfortably. "You're both right and wrong at the same time," he said, speaking to both Andy and Kit together. "Which is to say we got us a real mess on our hands here. Andy's right; if anyone else is hurt—" He left the thought unfinished. "But if'n we don't fight for what belongs to us," and now he looked straight at Andy, "then I reckon the ranch is done for." Andy started to protest but Miles held up his hand. "Those are the simple facts, Andy. O'Meara wants the Little Muddy and we'll either have t' fight him t' keep it, or we'll have t' move on."

"I ain't givin' up the ranch!" Kit said vehemently. "It's pa's ranch. My ranch, if'n he don't want it." Kit aimed an accusing finger at Andy. "I ain't handin' it over to O'Meara all wrapped up in blue ribbons."

"No one's giving up the ranch, Kit," Andy said firmly. "But if this thing turns into a full-blown range war you might as well pack your bags right now and get out with your hide.

O'Meara's got four times as many men as we do so you can forget about outgunning him. If you want to come out ahead on this one, you better start using your brains, not guns."

Kit retreated into a sullen silence that lasted for the rest of the meal. Amy's face was haggard. She picked at her food listlessly.

"You ought to eat something, button," Andy said.

"Ain't much hungry," she mumbled.

"You take a few more bites of that steak and I'll see if I can't find something in that bag of mine for you, something all the way from France, if I remember correctly."

Across the table, Nell smiled at Andy.

"What is it?" Amy cried. "What?"

"Oh, just a little something," Andy said. "Nothing much. Now, how about that steak?"

With her attention magically diverted from the leaden atmosphere by the promise of presents, Amy viewed her food with renewed interest. She was, after all, just a little girl. In a few minutes her plate had cleared remarkably and she pressed Andy again.

"What is it, Andy?"

Andy glanced around the table. "Is everybody through? Didn't I see a big apple pie somewhere around here?"

"I reckon there's time enough later for that," Nell said. "Right now you've got a little girl about to bust her buttons, Andy."

Amy cast Nell a grateful glance.

"Then we'd best be moving into the other room," Andy said. He turned to Amy. "How'd you like to get my bag from my room, button? No fair peeking though."

"I won't," she said. She hopped off her chair as if it had suddenly grown hot, and raced out of the room.

As the little company gathered in the living room Amy struggled down the stairs carrying Andy's travel bag. Andy took it from her and set it on the floor.

"Close your eyes and hold out your hands," he commanded. Obediently, she complied. Andy untied the bag, reached inside and pulled out a sturdy, oblong box. He opened it and from somewhere behind him Nell gasped. Amy trembled. Her eyes were shut so tight her nose was wrinkled. Andy pulled out what was inside and set it gently in her arms.

"Kin I open my eyes now?" she asked.

"Reckon you better before you bust them buttons," Andy drawled.

Amy opened her eyes and they seemed never to stop. They just opened wider and wider until Andy was certain she would hurt herself. Her mouth was formed into a perfect O of surprise and delight. In her arms was a doll, not an ordinary doll, but a beautiful, wondrously expensive doll with exquisite features, real hair, and a silk dress supported on layer after layer of petticoat material.

"Oh, it's . . . it's . . . so beautiful," Amy whispered in awe. "You mean . . . I can have it? It's mine?"

"All yours, button. Not sure what I'd do with it, myself."

With infinite care she set the doll down on the chair beside her then gave Andy his second big hug of the day. "It's beautiful, Andy," she whispered in his ear. "I'll keep it forever and ever."

He gave her a little squeeze then she turned back to the doll and began examining it in earnest, her face filled with rapture.

Beside Miles, Kit was squirming uncomfortably and trying to peer, unsuccessfully, into the depths of Andy's bag. "Reckon you could stand something from back East?" Andy asked him.

"How far east?" Kit asked, wary but thawing.

"Philadelphia."

Kit was clearly curious and his fidgeting was ruining his attempt at nonchalance. "I reckon," he said finally.

Andy reached into the bag and pulled out a box that had been tucked into one end. He handed it to Kit.

Kit opened it and in spite of himself his eyes widened as Amy's had just moments before. Inside was a dove-gray Stetson of the finest grade felt—decorated with a shiny silver concha attached to a fine leather belt that circled the crown.

He lifted the hat out of the box silently, with as much reverence as Amy had displayed with her doll.

"Now that's about as fine a hat as I've ever seen around these parts," Miles declared. Nell said nothing but she was smiling, enjoying the show.

Kit put the hat on his head and looked up, "How does it

look?" he asked, a youngster once again.

"Jest about as good as you think it does," Miles said with a grin.

Kit grinned back at him then turned to Andy. "Thanks," he said awkwardly. "It sure is a mighty fine hat." Then he bit his lip and stuck out his hand—almost like Henry would have done—and said, "I'm glad you're back, Andy. An' not just 'cause of the hat, either."

Andy took Kit's hand solemnly. "Things'll work out, Kit. You'll see."

Kit nodded then backed off and lost himself in a thorough examination of his hat. Andy reached into the bag again, pulled out a small, carefully-wrapped package, and handed it with elaborate ceremony to Nell.

"I sure missed your cooking while I was away," he said.

"Oh, my," Nell said, flustered. "You shouldn't have bothered, Andy."

"I suppose I can take it back."

"Not on your life," she answered. Inside the package she found a silk handkerchief, made in France, covered with such a rich, delicate design it took her breath away. "Oh, Andy. It's lovely," she said.

"Put it on," Amy cried, having looked up from her doll for the moment.

As Nell unfolded the handkerchief, Andy reached into that bottomless bag, pulled out yet another box, and handed it wordlessly to Miles. The grizzled old foreman took the box with an embarrassed look on his face and repeated after his wife, "You shouldn'ta bothered, Andy."

He opened it and pulled out a bottle of fine Kentucky bourbon. "On second thought, maybe you should have," he said with a chuckle.

Nell cast the bottle a reproving glance and Andy said, with a hidden wink to Miles, "For medicinal purposes only, Nell."

"That's right," Miles agreed heartily. "Reckon that twinge I'm feelin' is my rheumatism actin' up again. Join me in a little painkiller, Andy?"

"I wouldn't be averse."

Miles went into the kitchen to locate a couple of glasses. In a subdued voice Kit asked, "You bring back anythin' for pa,

Andy?"

Andy nodded, removed a book from the bag, and handed it to Kit. Kit read the title in labored tones: "Principles of Agriculture." He turned it over in his hands. "This a book about farmin', Andy?"

Andy nodded. "One of the best."

"Reckon pa woulda been tickled with it."

"You keep it, Kit. Pa would've wanted you to have it."

Kit nodded and tucked the book under his arm.

Miles returned with the glasses, poured two drinks, and together he and Andy ignored the feigned scowls that Nell occasionally cast at Miles as they drank the smooth whiskey in the midst of the happiness Andy had brought back with him from the East.

After the little party broke up, Amy and Nell went to the kitchen to clean up the devastation wrought by the evening meal while Kit went out to the bunkhouse to show off his new hat to the Bar-O cowhands. Andy and Miles were left alone in the living room.

"How bad is it?" Andy asked Miles after they seated themselves in comfortable leather chairs. It was the first real opportunity they had had to talk alone.

"Bad enough, and goin' t' get worse," Miles answered, his gentle blue eyes filled with concern. "They've left us alone since they killed Henry. Maybe they went a bit farther than they'd intended, but they'll be back at us again before too long all the same. O'Meara wants the Little Muddy, you know, and I reckon he won't stop comin' at us one way or another until he's got it. Mostly his men come at night and cut fences and shoot cows. We've lost upwards of a hundred head in the past three months and repairin' fences costs us wire and manpower we ain't got t' spare."

"How did pa die, Miles?"

Miles shook his head sadly. "I reckon I was the closest when it happened an' I don't rightly know myself. Nothin' I could swear to in court. Your pa an' me was out past the Little Muddy ridin' the fence line. Have t' do that a lot lately. We found a cut section an' Henry took it. I went on ahead, lookin' for more. 'Bout a mile south I found another bad section and I was fixin' it when I heard a shot. Pistol shot it was, an' I remember thinkin' Henry must've found hisself a rattler. It was a few minutes later that I remembered Henry wasn't wearin' his six-shooter that morning so I upped on my horse an' high-tailed it on back.

"He was lying face down in the dirt when I pulled up, Andy. Had a hole in his back, his horse not far off with the Winchester still in the scabbard. Whoever done it never gave Henry a chance.

"I looked around and I seen three men a couple miles off, riding north like the devil was after 'em, but I couldn't tell who they were." He gave Andy a long, sheepish look and said, "I didn't follow them, Andy. I don't ride so well these days an'—"

"I'm glad."

"How's that?"

"I'm glad you didn't go after them, Miles. One against three is just plain fool's odds.

Miles nodded then banged his fist down on his knee, hard. "But gol-*durn* it, Andy. We cain't just let'em wear us down. Soon enough they're goin' t' start with the night raids again, shootin' up our stock. We cain't afford it. If it goes on like this much longer the ranch is goin' t' just fold up and blow away."

"Then we'll have to figure out a way to stop them, Miles."

"Son," Miles said softly, "you figure out a way t' do that an' I'll be right there beside you." He paused then added, "I ain't normally a worryin' sort of person, but I've looked at this thing from ever' side I can think of an' I don't see any way out of it. We're outnumbered real bad here, and the law ain't no help at all." He stared at his rough, weathered hands with a glum expression on his face. "Way I see it, I reckon the Bar-O's a goner, Andy."

5

By midnight, the house had been silent for several hours. Andy was sitting alone in the semi-gloom downstairs, his eyes fixed on the fading glow in the fireplace, listening to the quiet settling sounds of the house, trying, somehow, to deal with the pain he felt at his father's sudden, senseless death. The house seemed gigantic now, strangely empty with the builder gone.

Andy's house, now. His ranch. His problems.

Years of college had taught him the value of temperance, of weighing alternatives with care, gathering facts before making decisions, and yet, in spite of all this training, he felt a blind, blundering rage inside trying to work its way to the surface; a rage, if loosened, that would strip his quiet, rational façade away and ruin whatever slim chance he had to save the ranch. And he couldn't let that happen. As he'd said to Kit that evening, it was a time to use brains, not guns.

He sat in the half-light, clenching and unclenching his fists, considering the merits of his own advice.

Behind him a padded footfall sounded, and like a shrunken ghost Amy appeared in her cotton flannel nightgown, a blanket wadded in her arms.

She made herself some room beside him on the couch, fixed the blanket around her knees, and snuggled against him. "I couldn't sleep," she said.

"Too much pie," he replied. She giggled.

They sat together in silence for several minutes. Finally Amy looked up at him with the orange glow of the coals on her face and said, "Are we gonna fight, Andy?"

"How good are you with a six-gun, button?"

"Not so good, I guess." There was a moment's pause and she added, "But I don't want t' leave neither."

"You might not be able to have it both ways."

"Maybe we don't have t' fight, Andy," she said hopefully. "Pa always said it takes two t' fight."

"I suppose that's true in principle," Andy agreed. "Even if someone corners you and starts hitting you, it's not a proper fight unless you defend yourself."

"We could go away, Andy. Somewhere where folks don't want t' fight."

"That we could, button, but you just said you don't want to leave here."

She looked up at him and bit her lip.

He rumpled her hair gently. "Let's try looking at this in a different way, what do you say?"

"Okay," she agreed.

"Let's suppose you were way out in the middle of the prairie and you looked down and saw a big sack of gold coins. What would you do?"

"Pick it up."

"Right after you do you look up and see four Indians riding straight for you, about two miles off. Your horse is faster than theirs so you know you can always outrun them."

"I'd take the gold and run."

"The gold is pretty heavy. If you take it your horse can't outrun the Indians."

"Then I'd drop the gold, skedaddle, and come back later."

Andy looked down at her and smiled. "The Indians know they can't outrun your horse. They won't chase you if you run off, but if you leave the gold behind they're going to steal it."

"No fair! You're making it too hard."

"Sometimes life is hard, button. So, what do you do now?"

"Fight'em!" she said tersely.

"Four Indians! You'd fight four Indians all by yourself?" he asked, his voice filled with mock alarm.

She hesitated. "Maybe I'd better leave the gold?" There was doubt in her voice.

"That's fifty thousand dollars you're giving up, button."

She sighed and thought a few minutes longer. "That's a tough problem, ain't it, Andy?"

"It isn't easy. And right now the Circle-K is riding down on us like that bunch of Indians."

She thought that over for a moment, then said, "And the

Bar-O is the gold?"

"You're a pretty sharp little waif, aren't you?"

She wiggled with pleasure then went still for several minutes. Finally she said, "It ain't so simple, is it, Andy?"

"No, button," he replied. "No, it isn't.'"

"What's a waif?"

"A little girl who keeps folks up all night asking lots and lots of questions. That's a waif."

She giggled and snuggled closer, smiling secretly into the rosy heat from the fireplace.

• • •

Early the next morning, after breakfast, Andy and Miles rode into the gently sloping prairie north of the ranch house to acquaint Andy with the Bar-O's new irrigation system. The morning air was crisp, laden with the dewy perfume of the hills; the sky a clear, unbroken blue. Andy left the dun in the corral back at the ranch and rode one of the ranch horses instead, a lanky bay someone had named Pete.

They rode in silence along a trail that wound through the prairie into the foothills. When they reached the timberline where the grass ended and the trees began, Andy looked back into the valley at the ranch house almost four miles away. A thin trail of smoke drifted from the chimney, the only sign of life at the main buildings. Out on the range, dark slow-moving shapes wandered between the meandering line of the Little Muddy and the western mountains. The grassland appeared sparsely populated with cattle, fewer than Andy would have thought. The range was deceptive that way, he knew. Distances were hard to judge in the clear air and there was more land and more cattle than it seemed at first.

Andy twisted in his saddle and gazed out over the valley. Miles away, Willow Creek lay in shadow at the base of the Wind River Range and beyond that, hidden by Crooked Neck Ridge, was the Circle-K. Bear was right, Andy observed. The Tetons had already given up most of their winter snowpack to the summer heat.

It was going to be another dry year.

They arrived at the diversion dam above the irrigated fields and traced the system from its source. As they rode, with Miles lecturing in a hearty baritone about the troubles they'd had putting the system in and the increase in quality of range grass that had resulted, Andy began to fully appreciate what his father had accomplished. It was a sound system. Henry had laid out the canals carefully, making thoughtful use of the natural slope of the land. A pumped system would have been prohibitive in cost so his father had designed it as a gravity-fed system with canals and simple locks. There was little Andy could see to improve upon except for a few places where the design might have yielded to the subtle pressures of mathematics. In time, the scope of the system might be enlarged and then it would pay to give it a more careful look. Damming one of the upper meadows like O'Meara had done would probably be necessary to supply the extra water such an enlarged system would require. But his father had done a remarkable job with less than five years' formal education, Andy thought. Like he had told Kit the night before, not all engineering was practiced by college-educated engineers.

"How many head of cattle do we own?" he asked Miles.

"Upwards of twenty-two hundred," Miles said. "Small potatoes compared to the Circle-K but it suited Henry just fine."

"Who do we sell to?"

"Anyone who'll buy. We sell some t' the Union Pacific, a little t' ranchers up north when they need fresh blood for their herds, an' the rest we ship out of the railhead in town t' one of them big conglomerates in Chicago."

"What's the current price?"

"That depends. It goes up and down month t' month, like a twister hoppin' across the prairie. But I reckon we could get about twenty-one dollars for every thousand pounds on the hoof." Miles laughed. "We regularly get one or two dollars more per thousand than Circle-K beeves an' don't you know that burns O'Meara's hide. Ain't no secret, Bar-O cows is quality beef."

· · ·

Later that morning Andy rode Pete into Willow Creek with Max's dun in tow, and Len Peliter put the dun up in a stall. Max Dugan was nowhere around. Andy didn't need to ask Len where he was.

Andy rode up Main, past the Blue Boar and Goldman's General Store, across Water Street, and climbed off his horse in front of the sheriff's office. Sheriff Heede was out front, as usual, leaning back on an ancient wooden chair with his feet propped against one of the posts that supported the porch overhang. He was a big man, soft around the middle, in his mid-forties, with a stubbly face and a bushy moustache that sometimes contained a little left-over cooking from the Miner's Cafe. Mornings, the jailhouse shaded the front of the sheriff's office. By early afternoon, when the sun beat fiercely on his own front porch, Sheriff Heede would be ensconced somewhere in a shady nook on the other side of Main Street.

"Heard you was back," Heede said, pulling cigarette makings out of a soiled vest pocket as Andy looped the reins around the hitching post.

"Thought you'd be out tracking down the men who killed my father, John."

Heede peered at Andy thoughtfully and said, "That's a mighty businesslike greetin' for a man what's been away two years. Right t' the point."

"Amy and Kit are taking it hard."

Heede clucked in vague agreement. "Durn shame, Andy, those two youngsters losin' their pa thataway."

"What I want to know is what you intend to do about it."

"Well, now that you ask, so businesslike an' all, mebe I ought t' mention that I rode on out there the very next day," said Heede dryly. He sprinkled a bit of tobacco on a paper, spilled some, and as he flicked the errant grains from his shirt he bumped his other hand and dumped the whole lot in his lap. He stared at the mess with a sour expression on his face and went on with his story. "Looked the place over where it happened, I did, and found a trail where three riders had taken their horses out of there at a gallop. Took up north, they did. So I followed, and what d'you s'pose I found?"

He continued without waiting for a reply. "Them tracks made a big loop up north, joined up with the Jackson Trail, an' ended up comin' right smack dab through the middle of town here, all mashed to nothin' by people's feet an' wagon tracks an' a hundred other horse's tracks. An' that's where it ends. They wasn't a hull lot more I coulda done."

"Convenient."

Heede's eyes narrowed and his mouth tightened. "Wasn't my idea t' have them riders lope their cayuses right through the middle of town. What would you've done different?"

Andy sighed, a low bitter sound. The worst of it was that Heede was right. Trying to match hoofprints would have been a hopeless task. O'Meara would have got wind of it, and he'd have put new shoes on a dozen of his horses including the three used by the men who shot his father. It wasn't Heede's logic that bothered Andy, it was his attitude. The man had done his job and was obviously relieved that the trail had ended as completely as it had.

As early as yesterday, only an hour after Andy had arrived in Willow Creek, he was pretty sure he knew who had killed his father. It was coward's work and it had Snake Haskins' name written all over it. Dean Tripp had probably been present too, along with either Kid Reese or Aaron. Talking to Miles the previous night and now, with Sheriff Heede this morning, was more a matter of form than anything else; a cleaning up of loose ends. Someone might have seen something. The trail might not have ended so ambiguously. It was unlikely, but justice might have been served. In time justice might yet be served, but for now Andy had another, more pressing, concern: the survival of the ranch.

"Miles tells me Bar-O cattle are being shot." Andy said.

Heede's face knotted with concentration as he balanced a line of tobacco on the cigarette paper and pulled the drawstring of the pouch shut with his teeth. "So I heard. Ain't none of my affair though. That there's range business."

Andy frowned. It was obvious that Heede had long since come to the conclusion that it would be safer to keep out of the trouble between the two ranches and that he wasn't going to give any partisan help, particularly to the smaller of the two sides involved. "Sorry to have taken up your valuable time, Sheriff," Andy said curtly. He turned to leave.

"That's a mighty dangerous chip you've got on your shoulder, son," Heede said with a shrug. "Don't bother me none. I do my job. But this town has toughened up considerable since you was last here an' I'd hate, as part of my job, t' have t' scrape you off'n the boardwalk after you was stomped into it by folks what taken offense t' your shortness."

"I'll try to keep that in mind, Sheriff."

"You do that."

Andy flipped the reins off the rail and led Pete down the street toward Bear's place while Heede, with legendary incompetence, continued his labors with his tobacco. Andy had just passed the Overland Hotel and was directly opposite Booth's Mercantile when he was brought to a halt by a woman's voice.

"Why, hello there, Andy Stillman. I heard you were back in town."

Andy turned and there was Jill O'Meara, standing on the boardwalk just outside the store.

•   •   •

The prairie wasn't a natural breeding ground for beautiful women. Abigail Buchanan was raised back East and she and Bear came out west in 1878. Clair picked up her good looks from her mother, but most of the women had a plain, weathered look to them—sort of cross between the backside of a shovel and my Aunt Elsie who some cruel but clear-sighted relatives on my mother's side once said had a face that resembled the southern end of a northbound buffalo. But not Jill. For the last two years, since she was sixteen years old, Jill had been the undisputed prettiest girl in the territory and it didn't hurt any that her father brought back thirty-five dollar dresses from Chicago that were made in New York, London, or Paris. They pulled her in at the waist and pushed her out in other places, until just looking at her was enough to make a man feel pain all through him. Her hair was the color of light honey, her eyes a luminous green, and her skin looked as soft as fresh cream. She was taller than most, five feet seven inches, and, well, like I said, she sure knew how to fill a dress.

Like everyone else, I felt my tongue go dry when Jill was near. There was no one special in Jill's life. She had her sights set on New York and no cowpoke or telegraph operator was ever going to take her there, which made us irrelevant and pretty much invisible.

I watched, from a distance, and kept my thoughts entirely to myself, same as with Clair.

• • •

Andy walked Pete to the hitching rail in front of Booth's Mercantile, draped the reins over the pole, and tipped his hat courteously. "Morning, Jill. Or what's left of it anyway."

"I'm so sorry about what happened, Andy," she said, glancing nervously up the street toward the Overland Hotel. "About your father, I mean."

Andy nodded and said, "So am I." He looked up at her. "Things have certainly changed around here."

Jill met Andy's gaze, cheeks coloring faintly. "I know things are awfully strained between the Circle-K and the Bar-O right now, Andy. I hope that doesn't affect our friendship."

"It doesn't have to."

Jill appeared relieved. "They say you graduated from college, Andy. Brown University, wasn't it?"

Andy nodded and Jill continued, wistfully, "It must be nice, back East. Father says finishing schools are nothing but a waste of money." Andy nodded, but said nothing, and Jill bit her lip, having blundered into a conversational dead end, then her eyes brightened and she asked, "Have you seen the Brooklyn Bridge, Andy? They say it's the eighth wonder of the world."

"I've walked across it. They charge a penny. It's a wonderful work of engineering."

"I'd love to see it," she said, her voice almost sultry in the mid-morning warmth.

"It's a sight."

"Are the women in New York as pretty as they say?"

"Depends on what they say."

Her gaze lowered demurely. "You know what I mean."

"I suppose there's a few that don't overly trouble the eyes."

It wasn't at all what she'd hoped to hear and her face knitted itself into a frown.

"I've got to be getting along, Jill," Andy said.

A quick look came into her eyes. "The Fourth of July picnic is next week, Andy."

"So I've heard."

"I'm going to auction a basket."

It was the second such invitation Andy had received in two

days and he was forming a careful, neutral reply to the question behind her statement when William O'Meara walked out of the Overland Hotel next to the Mercantile.

As O'Meara walked toward them, Andy, after a quick appraisal of the older man, decided the past two years hadn't been particularly kind to the Circle-K owner. His reddish hair had thinned some, and grayed, and he had taken on more weight. He was nearly sixty years old, barrel-chested, five feet seven inches tall and, with his stomach resting uneasily on his buckle, he now weighed at least two hundred twenty pounds. At one time, in Missouri, he had been known as a handy man with his fists, back when he weighed under one-eighty. In 1871 when his wife, Mary, died of cholera, O'Meara slowed down, gained weight, and began to show his age. And yet, in spite of a tendency to smoke foul cigars and drink excessively, he was still tough, still a man to be reckoned with, and he ran the Circle-K with an iron hand.

Beside him, in chaps and riding gear, was Clevis Willis, the Circle-K foreman.

At first O'Meara ignored Andy who was standing at the foot of the boardwalk beside his horse. "You find what you was looking for?" he asked Jill, his voice gravelly with age. Then, with a slow, studied air of discovery, he looked at Andy and grunted: "Heard you was back."

"They've nothing but cheap gingham and cotton, father," Jill replied. "And in the most awful colors, too."

O'Meara shrugged then turned from her to Andy. "Heard about your pa," he said. "Terrible thing, that."

"Murder usually is."

O'Meara's eyes narrowed almost imperceptibly.

"Morning, Clevis," Andy said to the Circle-K foreman.

Clevis nodded to Andy, a quick gesture containing neither warmth nor malice. He was a tall, rangy man several years older than O'Meara. His face was deeply lined and leathered with exposure to the seasonal extremes of weather. He had bushy white eyebrows and a thin, triangular beak of a nose that gave him a brooding, hawkish appearance. Unlike Tripp, Snake, Kid Reese, or Reb Cotton and his men, Clevis had but one duty and that was to run the Circle-K. Not even O'Meara could have forced him to pull a gun on an unarmed man.

"Lucky, my catching you in town like this," Andy said to O'Meara.

"Yeah? Why's that?"

"Saves me the trouble of riding all the way out to your ranch to talk, Will. Not only are there some murdering cowards somewhere in these parts, but there's vandals in the valley as well. Lately a lot of Bar-O cattle have been shot at night. Miles tells me we've lost nearly a hundred head in the past three months. I was wondering if you've had similar trouble."

O'Meara's face wrinkled in surprise. Then he grinned. "No. Can't say as I have."

"Guess it's just the Bar-O then."

"Guess so." O'Meara gestured around them. "Things are changin' all over the territory, Andy. Lot of riffraff driftin' through nowadays."

Andy shaded his eyes and glanced up the street in the direction of the Blue Boar. "I reckon there is at that, Will." He faced O'Meara again and in a soft voice he said, "I suppose there's nothing much to be done about it except to set up watch camps on the range at night."

"Takes a lot of manpower t' do that."

"It's a bother. Reckon I'll have to tell my men to shoot to kill, too," Andy said regretfully. "But these vandals have got to be stopped somehow. Just thought I'd warn you, Will, because if the Bar-O starts getting tough with them, they might just leave us alone and start in on your stock next."

O'Meara's face tightened and Jill gave Andy a frightened, anxious look.

"In fact," Andy continued, "if I have my men camp out on the range in concealed locations that change every night, one of these nights some vandals would likely pass within earshot of them and no doubt we'd stop one or two of them with a bullet. And, who knows, come daylight we might just recognize one of them. We might even figure out where they were holed up and who was behind them. What do you think?"

O'Meara's face had slowly turned an ominous shade of red. "Might work," he said tersely.

"If my men find out who's behind the shooting, maybe your men would like to join us in running the cowardly, sneaking bastards out of the territory, Will."

For a long moment O'Meara didn't answer. When he did his voice was thick with restrained fury. "We'll see." He turned to Jill. "We got t' be gettin' back t' the ranch. You finished here?"

"I guess so. Maybe next month they'll—"

"Then let's get a move on. I ain't got all day t' stand around jawin'." He grabbed Jill's arm and spirited her away toward a buckboard that stood in front of the Overland Hotel. Jill shot Andy an unhappy glance over her shoulder as they walked away.

Clevis nodded again to Andy. "You take care," he said and he left too.

At the Blacksmith Shop Andy told Bear what had happened. Bear hit a horseshoe one last time with his hammer, flipped it over, and inspected it critically. "You've ruffled his feathers, Andy," he said, his forehead wrinkled in concern. "Don't know what good it done you, neither. Now you watch out. Don't you turn your back on any dark alleys."

6

Word had it I was the best chess player in the territory. I didn't mind the reputation much, although it never turned Clair's head any.

By the time Andy showed up in Willow Creek Doc Simes had been coming over to Kinsey's Boarding House nearly every Thursday evening for the past four years. We'd set up the board and move the pieces around with Jack Peliter and Ira Goldman watching, groaning and carrying on. We must've played nearly two hundred games and Doc only beat me once. Most of the time I plowed through his pieces like Sherman marching through Georgia even though Doc was the second best chess player in Willow Creek. But then, chess was something of an oddity in town. Most everyone just played checkers. Still, more than once a man has arrived in town looking for a game of chess with me, usually some cowhand from somewhere who had beaten everyone at his ranch and fancied himself a pretty good player. Fact was, none of 'em could have beaten Doc. All this was akin to gunslingers looking to beat the fastest gun in the territory. We'd set up the pieces and I'd proceed to tear him apart; after the game was over I'd smile, shake his hand, and tell him he was pretty doggone good and that he really had me going there for awhile. Generally that was a bald-faced lie and we both knew it, but it preserved his dignity and that was mighty important to a man out west.

I had an unfair advantage, you might say, in that I could sit in my office at the station and study chess for an hour or two a day. I'd look over all the games I could find played by Paul Morphy and Pillsbury and Blackburne. I learned from the masters and in the dusty little town of Willow Creek the advantage I gained was overwhelming.

And, of course, I didn't mind winning all that much, either.

Now Andy was back from the East and he'd graduated from college. It seemed likely he'd played a little chess while going to school.

I wondered how good he was.

. . .

An uneasy peace prevailed in the wake of Andy's arrival back in Willow Creek, and from the time Henry Stillman was killed to the Fourth of July picnic there were no further hostilities between the two ranches. It was as if O'Meara had temporarily called off his assault on the Bar-O, waiting to see what, if anything, Andy would do.

In fact, it seemed almost everyone was waiting on Andy. In town, folks talked about the trouble between the ranches nearly every day, and yet, for Andy, the situation had quieted to the point that there wasn't very much for him to do except wait for the next outbreak of violence. He had more than just himself or the business affairs of the Bar-O to worry about. There was the safety of Kit and Amy to consider as well. And, although he had a fair idea of who had murdered his father, he kept away from the denizens of the Blue Boar and spent the intervening days at the Bar-O riding the range, checking fences, familiarizing himself once again with the land and the general orneriness of range cattle, impatient for the situation to be resolved one way or the other.

Later folks said that was just the lull before the storm, and that that week of relative peace only served to wind up tensions even tighter for what followed after the Fourth of July picnic. Be that as it may, everyone relaxed a little in those hot, quiet days and the mood in town became increasingly festive as the holiday drew near. It also gave Andy the opportunity to get to know the Bar-O ranch hands better.

The morning of his second day back, Andy traded in his eastern clothing for Levi's and a dark blue cotton shirt and became virtually indistinguishable, by appearance alone, from the rest of the Bar-O cowhands. They got some amusement in watching him as he tried to help out with the work. He had been away too long and his former skill at roping and riding had become little more than rusty memory. He'd throw the noose short or long and once, when the rope settled over a cow's horns, he wasn't quick enough in taking a turn around the saddle horn and that cow spent the next two hours dragging Andy's rope all over the prairie until Rolly roped the cow proper and retrieved it for him.

"Here you go, Andy," Rolly said with a slippery grin. "That cow took such a shine to your rope I almost thought t' give her mine in trade."

Andy accepted the rope humbly and thanked him.

But in the few days before the Fourth of July there was a slight but noticeable improvement in Andy's ranching skills and the day before the picnic even Two-Bit was easing off on the tenderfoot jokes. Andy spent some time in the bunkhouse and although the men were still a bit wary, watching him closely for some sign of relapse, they had more or less accepted him, with a few lingering reservations, as an almost legitimate member of the human race.

They were out on the bunkhouse porch on the third night of July—Paul and Rolly sitting on the steps; Two-Bit whittling a peg of wood down to nothing with steady intensity; Stringer and Kit playing a game of checkers as Andy watched over Kit's shoulder with amused interest—when Slim walked out of the bunkhouse, six-gun off, and stepped to the ground. Slim said nothing and no one paid any particular attention to him, even after he gazed determinedly toward the south for a long minute then took off running. Andy watched Slim's bowlegged shuffle as the man ran past the corrals and disappeared up the road.

"Now what's the matter with him?" Andy asked, attempting to conceal his astonishment, aware that this might be an elaborate ruse to expose him once again as a raw tenderfoot.

Rolly glanced up. "Slim's in trainin'."

"Training? What for?"

"The footrace at the picnic tomorrow. He figures t' give Aaron O'Meara his comeuppance this year." Rolly spat a brownish-yellow stream of tobacco juice into the dust and added, "Ain't got a snowball's chance, but he's got more hope than a barn full of wallflowers."

"Aaron's still winning then?" Andy asked.

"Four years straight. Reckon that boy is half deer."

At thirty, Rolly was the oldest of the Bar-O cowpunchers. Stringer was a year older than Andy and the rest had barely reached their twenties. Two-Bit was only nineteen. Like most cowboys, they all loved a good lie, a good story, and a good contest; probably in that order, too.

"Anyone else racing?" Andy asked.

Kit looked up. "I'm enterin' the horse race, Andy. There's a two-dollar entry fee, but I got the money saved up. I'm goin' t' ride Midnight."

Andy's eyebrows raised but he said nothing. None of them was through grieving over Henry Stillman's death, least of all Kit, but at least Kit was showing interest in normal pursuits again and had not worn the Colt since the evening Andy had passed around gifts.

Stringer looked up from the game he was playing with Kit. "You fightin' again this year?" he asked Paul Armstrong. The others laughed. Paul was a year younger than Andy. At six foot two and an even two hundred pounds he was the biggest of the Bar-O cowhands.

He grinned crookedly and shook his head. "Got more use for my face than to let Jason turn it into beefsteak again."

"Wouldn't have anything t' do with Grace Beringer, now would it?" Rolly asked him.

"Might, an' might not."

Rolly turned to Andy. "Paul's got his eye on Hank Beringer's daughter," he explained, sliding a crafty elbow into Paul's ribs. "You goin' t' bid on her basket, Paul?"

"Might, an' might not."

Rolly chuckled. "Might, hell! You'd spend six months wages if that's what it took. Still," he mused, "that'd leave Gracy with one hell of a fine dowry . . ."

"Aw, come on, Rolly."

Andy spoke up again. "What's this about a fight?"

Rolly grinned. "Somethin' the town council cooked up last year t' add a little spice t' the occasion. They set up a boxing match, open t' all comers. Paul here put up his money and got in the ring with Jason O'Meara. Whole thing lasted about six seconds—"

"Ain't there nothin' else t' talk about?" Paul said unhappily.

He was saved at that moment when Slim returned, blowing like a steam engine, sweating like a hard-rode horse.

Rolly looked around at the rest of the cowhands. "Well now, if that ain't one sorry damn sight," he said. "What d'ya say boys? Anybody here got a hankerin' t' put up for the night in the same bunkhouse with this bowlegged, lathered-up cowpoke?"

"Now don't you go startin' nothin', Rolly," Slim warned, breathing hard, bent over with his hands on his knees.

"Reckon not," Stringer said, answering Rolly's question. He got to his feet slowly. There was a general shift in Slim's direction and before Slim noticed what was afoot they had him and were carrying him toward the pond fifty feet away. Andy and Kit followed, grinning.

"You put me down you bobtailed, wall-eyed, no-account varmints," Slim shouted.

"You heard'im boys," Rolly said. "Put'im down."

With Slim yelling out insults and warnings they swung him three times in a low arc and chucked him out into the pond. He rose to the surface, sputtering, water streaming from his hair and a lily pad on his head, filling the air with imprecations and colorful imaginings of what he was going to do to each and every one of them.

But it was all for show and as soon as he pulled himself out of the pond he was his old self again, while back at the bunkhouse the men had already taken up their old positions.

"You think it's wise for the Bar-O to show up at the picnic?" Andy asked Miles. "The Circle-K could do a lot of damage while we're gone."

Miles shook his head. "Not with the whole town watchin'. Any Circle-K hands as didn't show up would be under suspicion right off. O'Meara ain't lookin' for that kind of trouble."

"What about Tripp and the others?"

"They ain't fence-cutters or stock-shooters. They're gunslingers. Cuttin' fence would be too much like work for that kind. We'll just watch for Reb Cotton and his bunch. If they're there we ain't got nothin' t' worry about."

"You know this valley better than I do now, Miles."

Miles chuckled. "Besides, what would you tell Amy? That young'n has been lookin' forward t' this for better'n a month now. You ain't tough enough a man t' tell her she cain't go."

"I reckon that's true enough."

"It'll be good for the boy's t' get out too," Miles said. "It ain't often they get the chance to go t' town. I know they've been lookin' forward t' this just about as much as Kit and Amy."

"We'll go, Miles. I guess I'll be counting on you to keep the men in line though. We can't afford any trouble."

"No trouble, " Miles said. "They ain't bad boys, Andy."

• • •

The next morning everyone gathered in the yard outside the house. Andy was amazed by the transformation the night had wrought in the Bar-O cowhands. Special chaps had been brushed off, conchas had been shined, their boots had received a fresh coat of polish, their guns gleamed, and they wore bright shirts, red neckerchiefs, and newly dusted hats. Even Rolly had been drawn into the spirit of the occasion and he gave Andy a discomfited grin.

Kit was proudly wearing his new Stetson and Amy was wearing a frilly white dress and shiny leather shoes.

"My, aren't you a pretty sight," Andy said when he saw

her. Her face lit up and she did a quick twirl for him.

Following some unspoken law they waited for Nell, and after she made her appearance and Miles had helped her into the buckboard alongside Amy, Miles climbed in beside them, snapped the reins, and the little procession moved off down the road in the direction of Willow Creek.

• • •

It was a fine day for a picnic, that summer day of 1885. The night chill burned off by seven in the morning and the sky was a deep blue over the Tetons. It was going to be in the low nineties by mid-afternoon.

I was up early, dressed in the best clothes I had. I wasn't any cowboy and never pretended to be. I just put on a pair of clean Levi's and a white shirt with a dark red bow tie, which seemed festive enough. Breakfast was earlier than usual at the boarding house. I can't remember seeing the other boarders looking so shined and polished and eager to get on with the day unless it was on the Fourth last year. I looked at them like they were strangers and got a few odd looks myself. I didn't usually wear a tie and I reckon it looked funny on me. Maybe they'd forgotten how funny it looked on me a year ago.

By eight-thirty I was at the telegraph office. I sent a hello down the line and Rock Springs answered, but there weren't any messages. I tapped out a 'no message' and signed off. The whole world was on vacation today, I reckoned, so I closed up the office and walked off to where the picnic was going to be held. In my pocket was a twenty-dollar gold piece. I wasn't going to enter any of the contests but I was going to do my best to be the highest bidder on Clair's basket.

Just being with Clair Buchanan would be worth the twenty, never mind the food.

The picnic was to be held a quarter mile southeast of town in the midst of a stand of old willows that grew by the banks of a small creek. The creek's name was Willow Creek but whether it was named after the town or whether the town was named after it, no one rightly knew. It flowed southwest out of the mountains then cut through the valley much the same as Badger Creek did, further to the south. Most years there was water year-round unless the snowpack was low. Circle-K cattle used the water in Willow Creek further to the south but it wasn't a reliable source of water in dry years.

The water was down to little more than a trickle that morning but the grass nearby was still green along the banks, water was still deep in the pools, and the trees provided ample shade from the sun. It was a near perfect place for a picnic. A wooden platform had been built facing an open grassy area from which Albert Fairbanks could make announcements to the crowd. The auction would take place on the platform too. Tables had been set up under the trees and yards of colored bunting had been wrapped just about everywhere imaginable.

William O'Meara had donated a cow for the event; it had been butchered the night before and prepared for the barbecue. By seven that morning it was already turning slowly over a pit of glowing coals. A crowd of about a hundred fifty was expected to turn out which included pretty near everyone in Willow Creek and the surrounding ranches. Tincup Smith was the only person within a radius of thirty miles not expected to show up.

By nine-thirty the bulk of the people began to arrive. First the townsfolk drifted in, Samual Shaw with his wife, Beatrice, his two boys, Doug and Danny, and his daughter, Milly. Milly was auctioning a basket this year, same as last. Then the Peliters, the Beringers, Doc Simes and his wife, Elizabeth, and Myra Nickolson with a wagonload of pies baked up special for the occasion. Max Dugan walked up, unsteadily, and sat under a tree with a flask of whiskey tucked into his coat pocket.

Shortly after that the Bar-O ensemble rode up. Andy rode Pete, Kit rode Midnight, and the cowhands rode their favorite ponies. Miles pulled the buckboard in a broad circle and everyone climbed out.

Sheriff Heede walked up. "You boys can leave them six-shooters with your horses or put'em right over there," he said, pointing to a table under one of the trees. "You ain't going t' need no guns today."

There was a round of grumbling as they unbuckled their guns and left them on the table. Like most cowboys they thought their guns made them irresistible to women, a fallacy they were loath to give up.

Ten minutes later the Circle-K arrived and were given the

same message. Reb Cotton and his riders weren't among them. Andy shot Miles a warning glance. He grew increasingly nervous until, five minutes later, Reb Cotton and his men finally appeared. They were rough-looking, unsmiling men who held themselves aloof from the rest of the Circle-K cowhands. Both Jackson and Gage were bigger than Reb Cotton. Reno was about the same size and build as Reb—six foot one, a hundred and ninety pounds. Dutch was an even six feet tall and Stark was an inch shorter. Most of the men were in their late twenties. Reno was the youngest and Reb, at thirty-six, was easily the oldest. There was an iron-boned hardness in Reb that clearly made him the leader. His lips were thin, almost cruel, and he had piercing steel-gray eyes that never smiled.

Jill O'Meara was lifted out of the buckboard by her brother, Jason. She was wearing a stunning pearl-white silk dress that must have cost upwards of fifty dollars. It had puffed shoulders, short sleeves, and was snugged in at the waist without leaving so much as a wrinkle. She lifted a basket out of the back of the wagon and, with a significant glance in Andy's direction, she was escorted by her father, Jason, and Aaron to the three tables staked out by the Circle-K. It was the first time Andy had seen Jason in two years. Jason was wearing a blue-checked shirt and black Levi's. At six-foot four, two hundred thirty-five pounds, he was the second biggest man in the territory after Bear Buchanan. He walked with an easy grace and folks just looked at him and shook their heads in wonder.

After the Circle-K had settled in, Dean Tripp, Snake Haskins and Kid Reese pulled up. The townsfolk gave them uneasy looks but the gunmen checked in their guns with the sheriff quietly enough. They walked through the crowd, Tripp looking at ease, Snake shifting his eyes from side to side, Kid Reese uncertain and wary, his hands balled into fists at his sides.

Truman Carlos drove up in a buckboard with Crystal Lee and Sue, the gals who worked in the Lucky Lady Saloon, beside him. Although the women wore dresses that were considerably more refined than those they wore during the evenings, most of the womenfolk at the picnic pursed their lips all the same, almost as if it were somehow required of them to register their disapproval.

Clair and Abigail arrived in a buckboard driven by Bear Buchanan. Abigail wore a quiet, blue cotton dress and Clair wore a lovely, ankle-length, pale-yellow dress with short sleeves and delicate white lace trim. She looked beautiful.

Andy walked over to them. "Morning Abigail, morning Clair," he said. He looked into the back of the wagon while Bear assisted the two women out of the rig. "Some mighty fine smells are coming out of this basket back here," Andy said, pretending to lift the cloth that covered the basket.

Clair slapped his hand away. "Shame on you, Andrew Stillman," she said in mock anger. "You keep your hands off'n that basket." She was unable to suppress a smile, however, that knocked all the stuffing out of her words.

Andy turned to Bear. "That's a mean woman, Bear," he complained.

Clair punched his arm.

"I know. I get the same thing at home," Bear said, his voice filled with great sadness.

"You two fools get along now," Abigail said. "We've got work to do."

"I'll see you later, Andy," Clair said, and she and her mother went off to find a place to settle.

"That's a mighty fine girl, Andy," Bear said when they were left alone.

"That's a fact."

"Reckon I won't have her around much longer though. Someone's goin' t' steal her away pretty soon. It's gettin' time."

Andy smiled and said nothing.

The steer was browning nicely over the coals and by ten-thirty that morning more than a hundred thirty people had arrived. Children ran through the crowd playing tag, laughing, burning off steam generated by the festive atmosphere.

Albert Fairbanks stood on the little stage, waved his arms, and called out to the crowd. He was a stocky man, fifty-some years old, with gray hair and blue eyes. He had an air of authority about him that was not entirely due to his status as Mayor of Willow Creek and the owner of both the best hotel in town and Willow Creek's only bank.

"Gather round. Gather round, people," he called. He waited a few minutes until a sizable crowd had collected around the platform. "Welcome to Willow Creek's sixth annual Fourth of July picnic," he announced in deep, oratorical tones. The crowd quieted. He delivercd a short speech filled with more rhetoric than meat, planning for the day, not far off, when Willow Creek's citizens would re-elect him mayor. When the speech and the enthusiastic applause concluded (the largest round of which came at the end, for good reason), he smiled and got down to the business at hand. "Entry sheets for today's events are ready for signing. If you can't write, an X will do, and if you can't manage an X, just tell Myra here, and she'll do it for you." A titter of laughter rippled through the crowd. "First event is the horserace. Same as last year—up the road, 'round the willow tree yonder, and back. Entry fee is two dollars and the winner gets all that's taken in. After that will be the footrace. This year the runners will start from here, run up the road to the other end of town, take a red ribbon from the fence just past the livery, return, and cross the finish line back here. Measures out at nearly a mile. You put those ribbons up, Max?"

Max Dugan looked up, his eyes bleary. "You say somethin', Al?" The crowd laughed.

"They're up," Len Peliter called out.

"Okay. Thank you, Len. Each runner will take just one ribbon, you hear? Any runner picking up more than one ribbon is disqualified right then and there. Entry fee for the footrace is one dollar and the winner gets all that's taken in." He paused, shuffled some papers, then continued. "The third event is the five-man tug-o-war. Elimination matches will be held out here on the grass and the final match will be held across the wide spot of the creek over there." He pointed toward the spot then added with a straight face, "Seems a tad muddy just now. Don't know how that coulda happened." That got another hearty laugh from the crowd. Men had been slinging buckets of water onto the muddy shallows all morning long. "Entry fee is five dollars for each team and the winning team gets all that's taken in."

Clevis Willis spoke up. "How about me signing up five of my mules, Al?"

"Just so long as they put an X on the entry sheet without any help from you, Clevis." The crowd laughed again and Clevis grinned foolishly.

"Last event is the boxing match," said Albert. "Same as

last year. Entry fee is ten dollars. There'll be elimination matches if need be and the winner of the final match gets all that's taken in."

"If you let Jason in, ain't nobody else goin' t' sign up," a voice shouted from the crowd.

"You going to be the one to tell him he can't sign up, Carl?" Albert asked, recognizing the voice. A nervous sound rustled through the crowd and Carl prudently remained silent.

"Anyone who boxes wears gloves," Albert continued. "We don't want anyone getting hurt." He pointed to the table below the podium where Fred Gorland, the bank teller, was seated. "Here's where the entry sheets lie, boys. Fred will be glad to take your money. Myra will help with the signing. Okay, let's get to it."

He stepped down from the platform. There were several whoops from the crowd and men surged toward the table with the sign-up sheets. Kit paid his two dollars and signed himself into the horse race while Slim set a dollar on the table and X'ed himself into the footrace. The crowd milled around the tables. Minutes later the Bar-O cowhands held a conference.

"What say we sign up for the tug-o-war?" Paul Armstrong suggested.

"Who's pullin'?" Two-Bit asked.

"Whoever wants. Shoot, we kin pull anyone into the mud, I reckon." It was the same unbridled enthusiasm that had caused him to sign up for the boxing match against Jason last year. Slim bowed out claiming he'd be no use after the footrace. That left Rolly, Two-Bit, Stringer, and Paul Armstrong.

"What do you say, Andy? You in?"

The cowhands turned toward Andy in a further loosening of their reserve toward him. He shrugged and said, "Sure, if you want, I'm game."

Paul collected a dollar from each of them and went off to sign them up. At the table Reb Cotton had just entered himself, and all of his men except Stark, in the tug-o-war. Two other groups had entered also, five men from town, and five other riders from the Circle-K.

Then Jason O'Meara walked slowly to the table and signed up for the boxing match. His was the only name on the list. He paid his ten dollars and walked away looking over the crowd with an amused, confident expression on his face. It was an unspoken challenge and not many men looked him in the eye just then.

In time, the activity around the sign-up table subsided. Half an hour later Albert Fairbanks called out again to the crowd. "Last call for the horse race. Race begins in five minutes. After that the footrace. The auction for the picnic baskets and the chance to eat with one of Willow Creek's pretty young ladies starts at noon sharp." He glanced down at the sign-up sheets and cleared his throat loudly. He looked out over the crowd. "Still got only one signed up for the boxing match," he said. "Can't have a match with only one contestant."

A voice grumbled from the crowd. "Ain't nobody goin' t' pay ten dollars t' get their skull split."

Albert Fairbanks shrugged and said, "Sheet's right here."

There was a last minute flurry of activity at the tables as a few more hopefuls entered one event or another. The riders who had signed up for the horse race were getting their horses ready near the starting line, churning up pale clouds of dust. Andy sat on a blanket next to Amy and Nell in the shade of a thick willow. He stood up, stretched, and said, "I'll be right back. Hold my place for me, button."

He walked over to the sign-up table and tossed down ten dollars.

"Reckon I'll sign myself up for the boxing match, Fred," he said.

7

The news swept through the crowd like an August prairie fire. People began talking excitedly, giving Andy looks filled with considerable curiosity. I must have gawked some myself. I remembered giving Andy something of a critical appraisal when he stepped off the train almost a week ago. Even now, he looked solid somehow—more confident and relaxed than he should have been for a man who had just paid ten dollars to have his head pounded sideways, but other than confidence and that curiously solid look there wasn't much to recommend him against Jason. Andy was five inches shorter and looked to be about a hundred seventy-five pounds, about sixty pounds lighter than Jason. And there wasn't anything to suggest weakness in Jason, either. He was light on his feet, broad at the shoulders, and wasn't carrying more'n two pounds of extra weight on him. If there was anyone in the territory who might have stood a chance against Jason it was Bear. But Bear was built more for wrestling than boxing so even that match-up looked unlikely. Of course, Abigail would never have allowed it anyway.

Andy had fought Jason twice in the past and had lost both times. Jason was two years older than Andy and had never weighed less than twenty pounds more than him. The first time they fought, Andy was just ten years old. It took place in the schoolyard right after school let out. Jason had been bullying Andy until Andy couldn't take it any more. Of course that was exactly what Jason had in mind. Jason was a natural bully. He loved to fight and he loved to win and he never seemed to care that his opponents were always smaller than he was.

So when Andy was ten they went at it and in no time at all Andy was sprawled in the dust with a black eye and a bloody nose. It wasn't a drawn-out fight. Jason got in two hits, Andy none, and it was over in ten seconds. I was right there watching and I remember thinking at the time how one-sided it was and how glad I was it wasn't me who'd tangled with Jason.

The next fight was five years later in the field behind the livery stable. I didn't see that fight but I heard about it firsthand from Jeff Hill who saw the whole thing. Jason was prodding Andy, pushing him around and bad-mouthing his father until Andy finally lit into him. But that had always been Jason's way. He'd provoke a fight then wade in with both fists. That fight lasted about three times as long as the first one. Andy got in one punch to Jason's midsection, a punch that had no effect on Jason at all, and except for some circling around that was it. Jason landed three punches. One knocked all the wind out of Andy, one opened a nasty cut over one eye, and the third knocked Andy colder than a fence post in January. Andy was out for upwards of ten minutes.

I reckoned Andy was about due to win one, but being due and doing are two entirely different things. Everyone was due against Jason but that didn't cut no ice.

· · ·

Andy walked back to where Amy, Nell, and Miles were still sitting in the shade beneath a tree. The news hadn't circulated back to them yet, but Miles was suspicious. "What'd you go an' do?" he asked.

"Just thought I'd give Jason a little competition," Andy said calmly.

Nell put a hand to her mouth and her eyes widened. Miles shook his head in dismay and said, "Boy, there's a few things they didn't teach you back at that there fancy school, an' one thing you should've learned was when t' leave well enough alone."

"What happened?" demanded Amy.

"Your brother here thinks he's goin' t' fight Jason O'Meara, that's what happened," Miles answered. "Reckon it's my job now t' talk him out of it." He looked up at Andy. "You ain't got t' fight him, Andy. You can forfeit the ten dollars an' you can bet no one'd hold it against you."

"I'll think on it," Andy said. "Say, it looks like the horse race is about to begin." He held out a hand to Amy. "C'mon, button. Let's go watch Kit win himself some money."

Miles sat next to Nell, shaking his head.

They walked over to where the riders were milling around the starting line and stood by the side of the road, surrounded by most of the people at the picnic. Clair stood nearby. She looked up at Andy with a strange, sad expression on her face and bit her lip. Bear edged his way alongside Andy and said, "That was a damn fool thing you done back there. What're you tryin' t' prove?"

"Nothing much, Bear. The boxing match was going to hell, that's all. No sport in that. Besides, I figure I can outrun Jason if the need arises." Andy's eyes twinkled.

Upon hearing this calm, outlandish reply, Bear squinted at Andy then shrugged. "Your funeral," he said.

The riders had taken up positions along a line drawn in the dirt across the road. Six hundred yards away stood the lone willow tree the riders had to circle. Nine riders had entered, mostly Circle-K cowhands. Andy was surprised to note that Two-Bit had also entered the contest. The young cowboy hadn't mentioned a thing about it. Len Peliter was in the line-up as well. On the back of the long-legged roan Len was riding he didn't appear nearly so gangly as he had the morning Andy had seen him in Dugan's Livery.

Albert Fairbanks stood to one side of the nervous, dancing line of horses. He looked over the riders and in a loud voice he called out, "Riders ready? On your marks. Y'all get set. Go!"

The mass of horses and riders bolted down the road. Andy noted with satisfaction that Kit had gotten off to a good start. So had Two-Bit, and the two of them led the pack toward the ancient willow. Andy hoisted Amy to his shoulder so she could see better. She clapped her hands and screamed in Andy's ear, "C'mon, Kit! C'mon, Kit!"

The pack thundered down the road kicking up clouds of gray-brown dust. By the time they reached the tree the group had spread out some. Kit was ahead by several feet when he made the turn but he swung wide and Two-Bit cut inside then kicked the cow pony he was riding and shot out ahead. Behind them, Len made the turn, nudged the roan, and the mare picked up speed like a boulder rolling down a mountainside.

"C'mon, Kit," Amy shrieked.

Kit pulled up next to Two-Bit and together they barreled down the road toward the finish line. Andy's eyes narrowed as he looked behind the leaders. What he saw was Len on that long-legged roan. Andy sized up the situation and nodded silently to himself. Len was catching up to the leaders like they were riding through sand. Two hundred yards from the finish line he passed them like they were riding wagon-train mules and never looked back. He was thirty yards ahead at the finish. Kit managed to edge out Two-Bit by inches.

Amy slumped in Andy's arms. "He lost, Andy. Len beat him."

"Can't win all the time, button."

"Don't have t' lose all the time, neither," she said, pouting.

The rest of the riders pulled in, dragging with them a thick cloud of dust. The crowd retired back to the picnic area and soon the riders came back, slapping dust off their clothing, trying to appear unconcerned over their defeat at the hands of the town stable boy.

Albert Fairbanks climbed the platform again and called out to Len, "Come on up here, Len. Reckon I've got something here that belongs to you now."

Len approached the stage, gangly once again, with a broad grin on his freckled face, ears tinged red, and amid scattered applause he accepted eighteen dollars from the older man.

Len stuffed the money in his overalls as he passed by Andy. "Looks like you're well on your way toward being a rich man, Len," Andy said to him.

Len grinned lopsidedly. "Sure am, Mr. Stillman. This here money's goin' straight t' the bank, too."

Andy felt Kit stir beside him. Kit watched as Len walked away. "Where'd he come from, anyway?" Kit said with wonder in his voice. "I thought it was just me an' Two-Bit and suddenly we were eatin' dust."

Andy laughed. "I reckon you've been hustled, Kit. Pretty good job of it, too."

Albert Fairbanks was still on the platform, leaning down talking with Fred Gorland. At last he straightened up and looked out over the crowd. "Footrace starts in ten minutes," he announced. "Last call for sign-ups."

William O'Meara wandered over to where Andy was

standing with Nell and Miles. Amy held Andy's hand. Jill accompanied her father, her arm looped through his; she gave Andy a quiet, demure smile.

"I see one of your cowhands is running in the footrace," O'Meara said to Andy.

"That would be Slim," Andy answered.

"Wouldn't care t' make a friendly wager on the outcome of that race, would you?"

Around them several ears perked up and heads turned. Betting was serious business out west. Ira Goldman edged in closer followed by Jack Peliter and Bear Buchanan. Clair was listening too, standing next to her father.

"Just Aaron and Slim?" Andy asked.

"Just them."

"Exactly how friendly a wager did you have in mind?"

Several of the men shook their heads. The crowd thickened. Doc Simes and Carl Springer nosed into the group. Reb Cotton looked on and Rolly stared at Andy, frowning.

"Twenty dollars sound fair?"

Andy looked doubtful. "I dunno," he drawled. "Aaron's lookin' mighty fit, Will."

"I'm giving odds."

"What odds?"

O'Meara glanced around the crowd that had gathered. He shrugged. "Three t' one."

"My twenty against your sixty?"

"That's right."

Andy appeared to consider this for several seconds. He hesitated, frowned, wrinkled his forehead, then shrugged. "Sounds okay to me, Will."

• • •

I was standing there the whole time. It was quite a performance. At least I learned one thing that Fourth of July. I never would play poker with Andy Stillman, and that's a fact.

• • •

O'Meara grinned like a hound dog with feathers caught in his teeth. "No need t' put up the money now, Andy," he said. "We'll just shake on it, if you don't mind."

"I don't mind, Will." Andy stuck out his hand and shook

hands with O'Meara.

Jason walked up and stood beside his father. Andy grinned at the two of them and said softly, "Maybe you'd like to make a wager on the boxing match too, Will. As long as we're layin' down wagers, that is."

O'Meara looked shrewdly at Andy. "That's right. I heard you'd signed up. Wouldn't have figured you for it somehow."

Andy shrugged. "I'd need odds though. Jason ain't goin' t' be easy."

O'Meara let out a loud, coarse laugh. "Ain't goin' t' be easy! Boy, back at that Eastern school you went to they sure taught you how to understate a situation."

The crowd that had gathered laughed too, but it was nervous, expectant laughter that held little humor. Bear watched Andy with bright, careful eyes.

O'Meara again faced Andy. His voice was suddenly cold and businesslike. "What sort of odds were you thinking of?"

Andy looked nervous. "I dunno. Six to one?"

O'Meara stared at Andy without blinking. "Three t' one."

Andy looked around at the gathered faces and licked his lips. "Five."

"Four."

Andy smiled shyly. "That it?"

"That's it."

"Reckon I'll take it then, Will."

A ripple of excitement passed through the crowd. Nell's face turned slightly pale and Mile's mouth tightened.

O'Meara smiled at Andy and said, "Your twenty dollars against my eighty?"

Andy looked around the crowd with a faint smile on his face, then he said in a quiet voice, "I was thinkin' more in terms of my two hundred fifty against your thousand, Will."

O'Meara's face drained of color and a gasp of utter incredulity swept through the gathered crowd. A sudden silence followed, broken only by the distant, musical laughter of children and the rustle of leaves in the trees overhead. Andy faced O'Meara. "Of course, if that's a little too steep for you—"

O'Meara found his voice and when he spoke the intensity of his anger made the crowd take an involuntary step backward. "Boy, they ain't no figure you could name would be too steep for me!"

"In that case, how about we make it my five hundred against your two thousand."

"Andy! No!" It was Nell. She held his arm, imploring him with her eyes. "No," she whispered. "This ain't right, Andy. Please don't do this."

Amy squirmed between Andy and O'Meara. In the tense silence that hung in the air she tugged on O'Meara's sleeve and said in a clear, defiant voice, "I got two dollars and I wanna bet it on Andy."

Nervous laughter spread through the crowd then died. O'Meara didn't look down at the little girl. He glared at Andy, a vein in his temple throbbing angrily. When he spoke it was in a surprisingly quiet voice. "Your five hundred against my two thousand. You game, boy?"

Andy stuck out his hand.

O'Meara looked at it for several seconds, then took it. A collective sigh rippled through the gathered crowd. The wager was sealed.

"What about her two dollars?" Andy asked.

O'Meara glared down at the little girl at his feet. "You still bettin', hotshot?"

"You betcha," Amy said firmly.

O'Meara looked up at Andy and an ugly grin spread across his face. "Five hundred and two dollars it is then." He pushed out of the crowd and stalked away.

8

Bear wandered over to Andy after the crowd had dispersed. "I reckon you know what you're doin', Andy," he said, but his voice turned it into a question.

Andy shrugged. "The Bar-O has lost nearly a hundred head of cattle in the last three months, Bear. That works out to something like three thousand dollars lost profit. Comparatively speaking, five hundred isn't so much."

"Still don't make no sense t' me," Bear said and he walked away with Clair and Abigail.

An air of uneasiness hung over the picnic grounds after the tense scene between Andy and Will. Everyone was grateful when Albert Fairbanks took the stage once again, this time to announce the impending start of the footrace.

"Runners get yourselves to the starting line," he called out. "Race begins in three minutes."

"Well, button, you ready to do some more cheering?" Andy asked Amy.

"I guess so," she said. "Are we gonna win this time?"

"I reckon not, but we'll cheer Slim on anyway."

"Why'd you bet on Slim if you think he ain't goin' t' win?"

"Just part of the game, button."

"What game?"

They walked out from under the trees and joined the crowd that was gathering around the starting line. Slim was walking around, loosening his legs which were hopelessly bowlegged for the task at hand. Aaron stood to one side, talking with his father with an easy smile on his face. There was no hope for Slim, of course. Aaron hadn't ruined his legs on the back of a horse as Slim had. Fourteen runners had entered the race, but at that moment all eyes were on Aaron and Slim.

Albert Fairbanks repeated the instructions to the runners then had them line up with their toes behind the same line used to start the horse race.

"Runners to your mark. Jake, you got a foot over the line; you want to get back a bit? Everyone set? Go!"

Immediately the pack was a seething ball of churning legs and flying elbows. Amy had once again taken up her position at Andy's shoulder and she dutifully shouted in his ear, "C'mon, Slim!"

But already it was hopeless. By the time Aaron had reached Main Street and had disappeared around the corner of the blacksmith shop, Slim was over a hundred yards behind. Slim pounded out the distance grimly and rounded the corner in eighth place.

"He ain't doin' so good, is he, Andy?" Amy said in his ear.

Andy looked at her. "He's doing just fine, button. Better than I can explain to you right now."

"But he's *losing*, Andy."

"Looked to me like he was beating a few of 'em when he went around Bear's house."

Amy cast him a doubtful look then turned her attention back toward town. The last of the runners had disappeared from sight and there was nothing to be seen for a while. Andy glanced at O'Meara and the stocky Irishman was staring back at him with a triumphant expression on his face.

Minutes later a rush of sound passed through the crowd and Andy looked back up the road. Aaron had rounded the corner and was racing for the finish line. Soon he was a hundred and fifty yards beyond the Blacksmith Shop and still no one else was in sight. It wasn't even a race. The crowd watched in near silence as Aaron approached, all alone, with a red ribbon in his hand. When he was two hundred yards from the finish another of the Circle-K cowhands appeared around the edge of the building followed closely by Ed Nickolson, Myra Nickolson's boy. This, at least, was a race—cowhand against town dweller—and the crowd warmed, yelling out encouragement to both runners. Slim appeared from around the building just as Aaron crossed the finish line, four hundred fifty yards ahead of the Bar-O cowpuncher.

In the final thirty yards Ed pulled ahead of the Circle-K

runner and came in second, much to the delight of the townsfolk, then the rest of the runners straggled in. Slim came in tenth, blowing hard, all heart and no legs. Andy set Amy down and walked over to him.

"Nice run, Slim."

"Nice run, hell," Slim wheezed.

"I mean it. You gave it all you had and that's what counts."

Slim looked up at him in surprise. He took several deep breaths before managing a smile. "Thanks."

Andy clapped him on the shoulder and went back to the picnic grounds. Albert Fairbanks stood up and announced that the picnic baskets would be auctioned off in fifteen minutes, causing a thrill of anticipation to ripple through the crowd. Both Clair and Jill glanced over at Andy, then, slowly, looked at each other. It was a moment of surprise for each of them, as if they had really seen each other for the first time that day. Jill lifted her head a fraction of an inch, turned her back on Clair, and took her father's arm again.

"Playin' for keeps this time, Andrew."

Andy turned toward the voice. Jason O'Meara was standing a few feet away. Andy smiled. "Morning, Jason."

"Just the two of us signed up."

"Reckon so."

"More fun that way," Jason said. He stuck out his hand. "Welcome home."

Andy took Jason's hand and felt the pressure immediately. Jason had big, powerful hands and Andy's hand was imprisoned in a paralyzing viselike grip. Jason smiled pleasantly, his face showing nothing of the force he was exerting and Andy felt the bones in his hand grind softly. Suddenly the pressure was gone. Jason looked down at Andy and his eyes were hard and bright. "Yep," he said again. "This time, Andrew, it's gonna be for real." Then he walked away.

When Andy turned around Miles was watching him. "How's the hand, son?" Miles asked.

"It's felt better."

Miles shook his head. "This fight ain't no good, Andy. Why don't you call it off?"

"Too late for that now."

"Ain't too late for anything yet, son. After the fight starts, that's when it'll be too late."

Andy managed to muster up a wan smile. "Handshaking isn't fistfighting, Miles."

"His hands ain't goin' t' feel any better against your face than they did around your hand, Andy. You better think on that awhile."

•   •   •

There was more going on at that picnic than you could shake a stick at and I was mostly just keeping my eyes and ears open, sometimes having a word with Doc Simes or Ira Goldman, looking over at Clair as often as I dared. The time was rapidly approaching when I was going to bid on her basket and everyone, Clair included, was going to know I had a good-sized interest in her, a twenty-dollar interest. Doc Simes already knew, but he was a man you could trust with anything and I had no fears on that account. I reckon he knew what I was feeling because several times he looked over at me and gave me a friendly wink. I smiled back, my insides all knotted up.

The platform that faced the picnic area had been fixed up with a small table and a chair when Albert Fairbanks climbed up to start the basket auction.

"Gather 'round. Gather 'round, people," he said in a loud voice full of good humor. "We're going to have ourselves an auction here."

The crowd gathered around the podium for the favorite event of the day. Milly Shaw was standing first on one foot and then the other, her eyes darting expectantly through the crowd. Grace Beringer looked down at her feet with a glow on her cheeks; when she looked up her eyes were fixed on Paul Armstrong. Clair stood between Bear and Abigail looking nervously around the crowd and at Andy. Jill was there too, looking too beautiful to be real, and four other girls with faces and figures that varied from kinda plain all the way to one, Hazel Yaw, from a ranch up north about fifty miles, who bore a fair to middling resemblance to my Aunt Elsie, God rest her.

Albert Fairbanks cleared his throat and said, "As you all know, each basket was made up special by the little lady who's auctioning it. The highest bidder on a basket gets the food and the pleasure of the girl's company for an hour. Longer if she's of a mind."

Soft laughter swept through the crowd and several of the girl's faces took on a bit of extra color.

"Bidding will start at five dollars. And I'll ask that you not embarrass yourselves by upping the bid by less than a dollar. Cash on the barrelhead, gents. If it's not in your pocket, don't bid it." He paused, and with a flourish he pulled a set of hand-lettered cards from his pocket and waved them in the air. "We're going to do this fair," he said. "Same as last year. Each card has a gal's name written on it. I'll have someone pick a card from the hat and whoever's name is on the card will sit up here on this chair beside me while her basket is being auctioned." He placed his hat on the table in front of him, made a show of stirring the cards into the hat, then presented the hat to the nearest bystander who happened to be Rolly. "Pick a card, son."

Rolly reached into the hat and withdrew a card.

"What's the name?" Albert asked.

Rolly handed the card to Albert with a red face. "You tell me," he said. The crowd laughed good-naturedly then quieted.

Albert read the card and said, "Grace Beringer. C'mon up here, Gracy, and bring your basket with you." Amid whistles and applause and several well-intentioned catcalls, Grace took a seat in the chair beside Albert, blushing furiously. A nearby group of girls eight or ten years old giggled into their hands.

"Some mighty inviting aromas're coming from this here basket," Albert announced after leaning down and inhaling deeply. He pulled a gavel from a back pocket, rapped the table three times for silence, then got down to business. "Who'll bid five dollars for this basket?" he called out.

"Five," said a cowhand from the Circle-K. Grace glanced toward the voice nervously.

"Six," another voice called out.

"Seven."

I was standing about ten feet from Andy and beside him was Kit, Nell, Miles, and several of the Bar-O cowhands, including Paul Armstrong. Once again Amy had been hoisted to Andy's shoulder so she could see.

Paul hadn't bid yet and Andy nudged him. "There she is, Paul. Go get her."

"Reckon I'll wait awhile," Paul said.

The bidding was up to twelve dollars.

"Twelve it is," Albert said. "Twelve. Going once . . ."

"Thirteen."

Heads turned and looked at the bidder, Sonny, from the Circle-K.

"Thirteen it is. Going once. Go—"

"Fifteen."

Paul had made his play; folks looked at him and smiled.

"Sixteen." Sonny was still in.

"Twenty," Paul said. A sigh ran through the crowd and Grace beamed at Paul in pure delight. Near the stage Rolly was grinning like a cat.

"Twenty," Albert said. "Going once. Going twice." He hesitated a second then brought the gavel down on the table with a final bang. "Sold. To Paul Armstrong from the Bar-O for twenty dollars. Now *there's* a hungry man, folks!"

The crowd relieved its tension with a burst of applause and excited conversation as Paul worked his way through the crowd to the podium where Fred Gorland sat at a table set discreetly to one side. Paul dug in his pocket and handed the money to Fred who put it in an envelope with Grace's name on it then put the envelope in a small metal cashbox. Paul held out his hand and helped Grace down from the platform. She handed him the basket and together they moved off toward the rear of the crowd to watch. When I looked back they were standing side by side, holding hands, and Grace's face was fairly glowing.

I was nervous though. Twenty dollars, and on the first basket too! That was all I had with me and it was as much as Jill's basket brought last year. It was shaping up to be a tough year, all right.

Other names were picked out of the hat. One basket went for ten and another for twelve. I started feeling better. Milly Shaw's basket brought fifteen and Hazel Yaw's brought but seven. She seemed happy enough just as soon as someone opened the bid at five.

Two names remained. Clair's and Jill's. Albert presented the hat to a Circle-K cowhand and my heart must have stopped for better'n four seconds.

"Clair Buchanan," Albert called. "Take the chair, little

lady, and bring your basket with you."

My heart started again, thudding hollowly in my chest. I looked over at Doc and he winked at me which did nothing to help the trembling in my knees or the numb feeling in my fingers. Clair climbed the steps to the stage and sat down beside Albert. She looked so pretty in that pale-yellow dress I thought I would die. Suddenly I knew with a dreadful certainty that my twenty dollars wasn't going to be nearly enough.

"Who'll bid five dollars for this basket?" Albert asked.

"Five."

"Eight."

"Ten."

It was going up too fast.

"Twelve."

"Thirteen."

"Fourteen."

A pause. "Fifteen."

It slowed. For a moment I thought there might be a chance, but only if I shocked the other bidders out of their slow, relentless escalation.

"Twenty," I called out.

A sound of surprise passed through the crowd and folks turned to look at me. I risked a look up at Clair and she was staring at me with surprise on her face. Surprise and pleasure, I thought, and my heart surged. Then her glance shifted to Andy, questioningly.

The crowd quieted. Albert paused and said, "That's twenty. Going once . . . go—"

"Twenty-five." It was Andy.

I reckon I'll never forget the way I felt just then. I just looked down at my feet and tried not to think. When I looked up, Clair was looking at Andy in a way I only dreamed a girl might ever look at me. Standing next to her father, Jill's face was clouded with undisguised anger.

The crowd buzzed and Albert smiled. "Twenty-five it is. Going once. Going twice—"

"Thirty."

The crowd gasped; heads swiveled, Clair's too, and there was Tripp, leaning against a tree with the stub of a cigarette stuck between his lips. Beside him was Snake Haskins and Kid

Reese, both with broad grins on their faces. Tripp had bid the
thirty dollars. Andy's face hardened and Clair looked at him in
horror, her eyes pleading.

"Forty," Andy called out. Clair cast him a grateful look,
but her eyes were still fearful. The crowd whispered, looking
from Andy to Tripp and back to Andy again.

"Forty," Albert said with a catch in his voice. "Forty
dollars is the bid." He spoke quickly trying to end it. "Going
once going—"

"Fifty."

A shocked sound blew through the crowd. Tripp had bid
fifty dollars. I watched as Andy dug in his pockets and came up
with three twenty dollar gold pieces. Clair's face was ashen.

"Bid's fifty dollars," Albert said unhappily, looking at
Andy.

"Sixty." It was all Andy had.

Tripp smiled. "Seventy."

Clair looked sick and I felt terrible for her. Tripp wasn't
interested in Clair or the basket. He was after Andy, using Clair
and the auction and the collective decency of the townspeople
as a kind of terrible whip. Albert Fairbanks spoke slowly.
"Bid's at seventy dollars." He looked at Andy and hesitated.
Finally he said, "Going once." He paused again and for the first
time that day he looked old.

I nudged Andy and handed him my twenty dollars. "For
Clair," I said. Andy took it instantly, a look of thanks in his
eyes.

"I'll pay it back," he said, unnecessarily.

"Going twice," Albert intoned.

"Eighty," Andy said. The tension in the crowd was awful
and there was a palpable sadness mixed with the tension. The
festive atmosphere had been torn apart. Tripp's smile mocked
not just Andy, but everyone there.

"One hundred dollars," Tripp said.

Silence squashed in around us. Somewhere a baby cried.
Then someone moved at the side of the podium and Bear
Buchanan climbed the steps. He picked up the basket, took
Clair's hand, and turned toward the crowd. "My daughter is
withdrawin' her basket from the auction," he said in a leaden
voice. Clair stood, her face white, numb with pain, and Bear

half-carried her down the steps, away from the stage to where Abigail was waiting to console her.

Andy turned to me and gave me back my twenty dollars. "Thanks, Tom," he said. At his shoulder, Amy stared at me with wide, dark eyes.

People turned to each other and talked quietly. Everyone felt just awful for Clair and some folks glared hatefully at Tripp. He leaned against the tree, ignoring everyone, and rolled another smoke.

Albert stood on the platform looking uncomfortable. The crisis had been partially averted but the fun had gone out of the auction. Still, another basket remained and not even Tripp would bid on Jill O'Meara's basket.

"One last basket," Albert said to the crowd. "Jill, you want to come up here?"

Jill nodded, her face a lovely, neutral mask, and she climbed the stairs with her basket. Sixty yards away Clair sobbed, her face buried in Abigail's shoulder.

"Who'll bid five dollars for this basket?" Albert asked, trying, without success, to force a measure of buoyancy into his voice. No one spoke and Jill's face paled; the seconds passed in terrible silence.

Albert stared at the basket before him on the table, nonplussed, unsure of what to say as another quarter-minute passed. Several young men in the crowd looked down at their boots in embarrassment and suddenly Andy realized that the auction was going to be as bad for Jill as it had been for Clair. He saved her.

"Five dollars," he said quietly.

A sigh of relief swept through the crowd and faded.

"Five dollars is the bid," Albert said. "Five. Going once." He paused. "Going twice." He paused again, his eyes searching the crowd for another bidder. There was none. "Sold. To Andy Stillman, for . . . five dollars."

There was a round of weak, scattered applause that broke up almost immediately. Andy hadn't expected to do any more than get the bidding going. Suddenly he was stuck with the responsibility of seeing it through to the end. He walked up to the table beside the stage, paid the money, and helped Jill to the ground. Clair watched, stunned, and burst into fresh tears.

Andy watched as Bear helped Abigail and Clair into the buckboard and drove the two women up the road toward town.

It was a year everyone would remember for a very long time.

9

The day warmed into the nineties as expected and the sun drove the crowd into the shade under the trees. The steer was taken off the coals and folks lined up to get a piece of beef. Pots of beans, bread, and salads appeared. The winners of the auction sat with their girls, apart from the crowd, on blankets by the trickle of water that flowed down the creek. To everyone's relief, Tripp, Snake, and Kid Reese departed. In time the festive atmosphere began to build again.

Andy carried Jill's basket to a patch of shade on a bit of grass overlooking the creek where he helped Jill spread a blanket on the ground.

"Five dollars," she said, her voice breaking. "Last year it was twenty. What'll folks think?"

"I imagine they're going to be too worried about Clair to worry about how much your basket went for," Andy replied evenly. They sat on the blanket.

"Even Hazel Yaw's basket brought seven dollars."

"That's so."

Jill bit her lip. Her eyes narrowed slightly. She wasn't quite so pretty when her eyes did that. "You bid eighty dollars on Clair's basket, Andy. Eighty dollars!" Although she kept her voice low, she cracked it like a whip.

"So I did," Andy said. "I don't suppose you noticed what was happening back there, Jill?"

"You're so terribly gallant," she said caustically.

Andy looked her in the eye. "I did the same for you, Jill," which wasn't the most diplomatic thing he might have said, but

Andy wasn't feeling particularly diplomatic just then.

"You *what*?" Her voice rose half an octave.

"No one was bidding on your basket."

Jill's eyes flashed. "Well thank you so much, Andrew Stillman, but I don't need your . . . *charity*. I can take care of myself."

Andy sighed and stood up. "Reckon that'll serve you right well now, Jill."

Jill paled for the second time that day. "What are you doing?"

"Guess I'll go on back to the Bar-O camp. Amy'll be missing me, I reckon."

Jill looked around in panic. "Andy," she hissed. "For God's sake sit down! People are watching."

Andy shook his head. "I reckon not, Jill." He turned to go.

"Why, Andy?" Her voice trembled with anger.

"I don't really think you want to hear the answer to that, Jill. Let's just leave it at that."

"Oh. Oh, you . . . you . . . I *hate* you, Andrew Stillman!"

Andy walked away and Jill's shrill voice followed him, "I hope Jason knocks your block off!"

"I reckon you're not the only one," Andy said, and then he was gone. The folks at the picnic were surprised to see him walking toward them and many looked back across the field just in time to see Jill pick up her picnic basket and fling it out into the creek.

· · ·

"Andy!" Amy said happily when she saw him coming. She was sitting on the blanket between Nell and Miles. Kit was sitting cross-legged on the other side of Nell. Amy looked around doubtfully. "I thought you were s'posed t' be eatin' with Jill," she said.

"Reckon it didn't take me all that long to get my fill," he said with a twinkle in his eye. "I'm starved. Where do I get a plate?"

Amy didn't comprehend the curious relationship Andy's last three sentences had to each other, but Miles grinned and handed Andy a plate without saying a word.

The festive atmosphere was unaffected by Jill's anger.

Most folks thought it was rather funny, although they kept their talk courteously low and tried not to stare at her. At least not too often or too obviously.

The afternoon wore on and there was a time of quiet when folks were full of food and feeling sleepy. Some of the men from the boarding house got to pitching horseshoes and there were two games of checkers going at one time, but most everyone was content just to stretch out on blankets, visit quietly, and watch the sun move slowly across the cloudless sky through the leaves of the willows. The water in the creek gurgled pleasantly.

At two-thirty several men wandered over to where the boxing match was going to be held. Four posts had been set into holes that had been dug in the ground and filled with thick mud. That had been nearly a week before. The mud had dried and the posts were as solid as hickory stumps now. Two men began stringing rope between the posts to form the boxing ring. This perked the interest of some folks and the picnic grounds began stirring once again. Some Circle-K cowhands got up and began throwing a rope around a stump, arguing loudly over the finer points of their technique.

Sometime before three in the afternoon Bear Buchanan walked back to the picnic grounds and he and Andy walked off by themselves for a spell.

"How's Clair?" Andy asked.

"Takin' it hard. Auctioning that basket was all she ever thought of since you got back."

"Reckon she wouldn't be so pleased to see me now, Bear."

"I believe she said she'd rather see a Gila monster in her shoe, or somethin' t' that effect. But I reckon I understand why you bid on Jill's basket, Andy. It was the proper thing t' do and Clair will see it when she quits hurtin'."

"I'm not so sure, Bear."

"She'll come around."

"I mean it might not have been such a good idea." He told Bear about his confrontation with Jill.

Bear laughed quietly. "Reckon I missed the best part. That little lady has had somethin' like that comin' for a long time."

From the podium under the trees Albert Fairbanks again called out to the crowd. Andy and Bear wandered over to listen.

"Tug-o-war starts up in ten minutes," Albert announced. "Four teams have signed up, one from town, one from the Bar-O, and two from the Circle-K. Ten minutes, gents. You'll find the ropes yonder under the trees."

Rolly approached from the crowd and said, "Maybe you ought t' sit this one out, Andy. You still got Jason t' worry about."

Andy smiled and shook his head. "Reckon I can use the stretching."

Rolly blinked, surprised. "It's your neck," he said finally.

The crowd gathered around the site where the elimination matches were to be held. The Bar-O was paired with a Circle-K team led by Clevis Willis. Andy looked over at Amy standing next to Nell and Amy waved to him. He waved back. Then Rolly shook hands with Clevis and the two teams began to position themselves.

A line had been drawn across the ground in the dust. Albert Fairbanks pointed to the line and said, "First man to cross this line and that team loses. When I give the signal, y'all start pulling." He looked up and down the rope at both teams. "Are you ready?"

Rolly and Clevis nodded affirmatively as a hundred people watched from the sidelines.

"All right then, ready, set . . . pull!"

The Bar-O dug in as did the Circle-K. The rope drifted back and forth and wandered from side to side as the air filled with the sounds of men grunting and straining and people yelling out encouragement. Andy heard Amy screaming out his name. Dust roiled under their feet and beads of perspiration stood out on the men's faces but slowly the Circle-K team was drawn toward the line. With a final burst of energy the Bar-O finished them off as Clevis was pulled across the line. The crowd gave the Bar-O a round of applause, then the other two teams took hold of the rope, the townsmen against the Circle-K team led by Reb Cotton.

"You won, Andy!" Amy said excitedly.

"It isn't over yet, button," he said. He rubbed her hair and lifted her into the crook of his arm again.

Albert Fairbanks got the teams started and there was only a moment's hesitation before Reb Cotton and his boys summarily dragged the townsmen across the line. It wasn't much of a contest. Bear grinned at Andy. "Reckon you fellers got yourselves a pull comin'."

"Looks that way."

For the final match-up, as promised, the rope was stretched across the muddy shallows of the creek. Folks gathered along both banks leaving a gap twenty feet wide for the men doing the pulling. The two teams took up the rope and Albert Fairbanks said, "I reckon there's no need for me to explain what constitutes a loss here." The crowd laughed and when the commotion faded into an expectant murmur Albert asked the teams if they were ready.

They were. Reb Cotton grinned wickedly.

"All right, then. Ready, set . . . pull!"

As before, the Bar-O dug in, clawing at the dust and the grass near the bank of the creek with the heels of their boots. The mud in the shallows had been recently watered and it glistened darkly in the sun. Two-Bit slipped and went down and the Bar-O was dragged five feet closer to the mud before he was up and pulling again. The line held and they gained a foot back before it stalled again. It remained motionless for nearly half a minute. Amy screamed for Andy to pull harder. Then Bar-O boots began to slide, slowly, relentlessly, moving toward the black, shining mud. They lost a foot, then another. Then five. Finally Rolly was standing in mud. His boots slipped, he fell on his back, and suddenly the Bar-O was being dragged through the slick mud on their backs and on their bellies. They were good sports and no man turned loose of the rope until he was deep into the mud. The throng cheered and in unison the Bar-O men stood up and took a good-natured, muddy bow. This brought more applause and more laughter, then the crowd drifted away and left the Bar-O cowhands to rinse off the mud in the water of the creek.

Andy came back, dripping, and Amy looked down at the puddle of water forming in the dust at his feet, accusation glinting darkly in her eyes. "Ain't we never gonna win *nothin'?*" she asked.

Andy walked down the road toward the big willow tree that had marked the halfway point of the horse race, letting the breeze and the sun dry his clothing. Kit walked beside him in silence and by the time they reached the willow Andy's clothes were only damp.

Andy stretched; Kit looked back toward the picnic area under the trees where the ropes now lay taut between the four posts, awaiting the boxing match. He looked up at Andy. "You really gonna fight Jason?" he asked, shading his eyes, looking concerned.

"Reckon so."

Kit paused, then asked, "We got five hundred dollars, Andy?"

"We could scrape it together if need be."

Kit plucked a weed and stuck the stem in his mouth, squinting thoughtfully at the horizon. He said nothing for a full minute, then said, "You gonna win?"

"Do you have any more money?"

"Six dollars."

"Might want to see if you can put it down on me, four to one if O'Meara's still in the mood."

Kit looked at Andy for a moment, then nodded. "Okay."

A few minutes later they walked back. The sun was still hot, blazing in the western sky. Andy was dry by the time they reached the picnic area. Kit bet his six dollars on Andy, then went to sit with Nell and Miles.

Albert Fairbanks walked up. "You ready, Andy?"

"Give me five minutes, Al."

Albert nodded and walked away. Bear wandered over. "Anythin' I kin do t' help?"

"No thanks, Bear. Unless you want to make sure the fight's fair, that is."

"It'll be fair." Bear's face was hard.

Andy went to the Bar-O buckboard. From a bag in the back he withdrew a pair of soft buckskin moccasins. Bear looked at them curiously. "Moccasins?" he asked.

"Only a damn fool would fight Jason in boots."

"Only a damn fool would fight Jason, period."

Andy grinned at him, pulled on the moccasins, and together the two men strode over to the boxing ring.

The crowd had gathered close around the ring. They'd spread blankets and were mostly sitting, except those who stood at the outer fringes. Amy sat with her back against Nell; Kit sat cross-legged beside Miles, looking over the crowd anxiously. People spoke in low voices, pointing here and there as they spoke. Albert Fairbanks stood beside the ring, talking quietly with Doc Simes.

Andy approached and stepped through the ropes into the ring. A quiet murmur rose on the afternoon breeze. Bear stood nearby, arms folded across his chest, eyeing Andy carefully.

Soon Jason left his father and his brother, Aaron, and stepped through the ropes. The murmur became an excited buzz that traveled through the audience as folks looked from one man to the other making quick comparisons. Jason was a mountain, formidable—dwarfing Andy. He smiled confidently, looked down at Andy's moccasins, and grinned. Before the gloves were placed on his hands Jason took off his shirt. His chest and shoulders were heavy with muscle and his arms were huge.

Andy took off his own shirt then and a sort of startled gasp went through the crowd like the first rattle of wind before a storm. Jill put a hand to her mouth and Bear's eyes opened some in surprise, then narrowed. He started to smile, a quiet smile that spread slowly across his entire face until his cheeks were puffed with joy and his head was nodding silently in comprehension. A shadow passed over William O'Meara's features and his eyes went cold.

Never before had the people of Willow Creek seen so much carefully-honed muscle on a man in all their lives. Jason was simply huge, as strong as a horse, but where his muscles clung to him like thick pads, Andy had muscle that appeared to be chiseled out of perfect, unflawed marble. When he moved, his muscles rippled. His stomach looked like the flat of an anvil; his arms corded in steel. No one had seen this Andrew Stillman before. The face was the same and the voice was the same but the rest of him had somehow turned into pure, sun-dried, winter-hardened rawhide.

"Good God almighty, ma," Miles whooped. "Looks like we got us a fight comin' up here!" Nell hushed Miles but not before his enthusiasm had drawn the crowd out of its stunned silence. The talk built quickly to an excited roar. At the side of the ring, Len Peliter tied the gloves on Andy's hands with the same quiet ease with which he had ridden the roan earlier that day.

"You watch Jason's right, hear?" was all he said.

"I will. Thanks."

Jason was still smiling but the smoothness had left his face. It was a hard, humorless smile now. His pale blue eyes glinted like chips of rare, translucent obsidian. Len finished with Andy's gloves and Andy leaned against the ropes, staring at Jason with a hard, purposeful look from across the ring.

Albert Fairbanks called for silence. The talk of the crowd faded to an excited, expectant hush. "There aren't going to be any rounds or fancy frills in this fight," he said. "When I hit this here cowbell the fighters will come out swinging and the one left standing at the end will be the winner. There'll be no kicking, no hitting below the belt, and no hitting a man while he's down or on the ropes." He turned to Andy and Jason. "That understood?" he asked.

The two men nodded.

"All right, then. I reckon we're ready to begin." From his pocket Albert Fairbanks pulled the gavel, looked around a moment, then at the two fighters, and gave the cowbell a single, sharp rap.

The sound was loud under the trees.

• • •

I reckon that's a fight that will be retold around open fires for the next hundred years in Wyoming Territory. And not because it was one of those knuckle-busters that last inordinately long, either . . .

Andy and Jason pushed off the ropes and Jason came after Andy without the slightest hesitation. He crouched and swung a left that missed Andy by less than an inch as Andy stepped sideways, pulling his head back in an easy movement. Jason unloaded a right that would have knocked a steer to its knees, but it didn't land. Andy danced effortlessly to Jason's right. Jason whirled and threw another left, and again it missed Andy by less than an inch. Andy backed off, Jason followed, and again Andy began circling to Jason's right with perfectly-timed, perfectly-placed steps that were a pleasure to watch.

"Get 'im, Andy," Amy's voice carried out of the crowd.

Jason threw his left again, missing by next to nothing, then punched with his right. As he did, Andy stepped to his left and sent a fist straight over Jason's right arm that connected solidly with the side of Jason's face. Jason staggered sideways and I reckon only he knew the force Andy put behind that blow. Amy screamed in delight, her voice almost lost in the roar of the crowd.

Jason shook his head, whirled, and another fist cannon-balled squarely into his face. Jason fell back against the ropes and slipped sideways to the ground. The muscles in Andy's back and shoulders appeared to have been poured from molten lava, liquid, rippling, deadly. He turned and walked back to his corner as Jason kneeled on the ground shaking his head, blinking, trying to focus his eyes.

"Get up, goddamn it!" William O'Meara's voice thundered out of the noise of the crowd.

Andy leaned against the ropes and smiled a smile that no one who was watching will ever forget, a smile that could have only come from someone so utterly in control of a situation that there was no longer any need to think. He stretched his arms out along the rope, waiting for Jason to collect himself, and I remember thinking it almost looked as if he was going to yawn.

He didn't. But thirty seconds passed before Jason pulled himself to his feet, cleared his head, and pushed himself out into the center of the ring again. A thin line of blood ran from his nose.

This time, having found some respect for his opponent, Jason covered up. Andy circled slowly to his left and Jason followed. Andy took another quick step, Jason twisted, threw a left, and Andy reversed like lightning—stepping to the right— and caught Jason on the side of the face with a right that sent Jason reeling back against the ropes. Andy moved in and Jason moved sideways, trying to keep out of Andy's reach, trying to clear his head. The crowd was roaring, but suddenly Andy broke off the attack, walked to one side of the ring, and leaned back against the ropes. Jason slung an arm around a post and hung his head, shaking it gently, breathing deeply. His left eye was beginning to puff up.

Andy waited for him.

Jason looked up and Andy smiled at him. An angry look passed over Jason's face and he started across the ring. Andy waited for him, hands hanging easily at his sides.

"Get away from the ropes, Andy," Bear yelled from the crowd.

Andy just stood there, an inch off the ropes, and Jason's eyes took on a gleam. He came in low, on the balls of his feet, and threw a haymaker straight into Andy's face. Except that Andy was no longer there. With a swift, catlike movement Andy twisted to his right, crouched, and threw a right that exploded against Jason's ribs under his left arm. Jason let out a sharp, involuntary cry and sank to his knees, his face a death-white mask of pain. Again Andy walked to one side of the ring and watched. He was breathing as easily as a person listening to a church sermon; a light sheen of perspiration coated his upper body. The muscles in his back stood out like strips of molded rawhide.

William O'Meara pushed through the crowd to the ropes and squatted down, facing his son. "You get up and *fight*, boy," he bellowed. "You get up an' start usin' your brains, goddamnit. Wear him down. Cover yourself up. But by God, don't you *dare* lose this fight!"

Jason nodded, slowly. He hugged his side where Andy had hit him as he pushed himself to his feet. Then he leaned against the ropes and looked warily out at Andy before taking a single step into the ring. This time Andy came to him. Andy danced up lightly and threw a soft right into Jason's face and a gentle left to his body. The punches weren't meant to hurt. Jason backed off, confused. Andy circled. Jason turned in place, keeping his guard up. Andy smiled and lowered his hands to his chest. Jason threw out a tentative right and Andy responded with a flurry of punches to Jason's face. Later folks said they never saw hands move so fast before in all their lives. Yet Andy kept the force out of those punches too, and Jason backed away listlessly, blinking in confusion.

And then, six seconds later, it was over. Andy turned his back on Jason and started to walk to one side of the ring. Jason watched Andy in surprise. In that brief moment a look of triumph returned to Jason's face. He pulled himself together and charged. Andy stepped to one side almost as if he had been pushed by an unseen hand and Jason sailed on by. When Jason turned, his head was low, hands tucked against his chest, and Andy hit him square in the face with a blow that had all of his iron strength behind it. Jason's feet flew out from under him; the first thing to hit the ground was his back. He lay like a stone, unmoving, in the dust.

Never before in the history of the town could anyone remember anyone being beaten so thoroughly. Jason hadn't landed a punch. Not one. And there he lay, like a sack of feed grain in the dirt with his face puffed and bloody. The crowd fell almost silent, looking at Jason on the ground, then up at Andy who had turned his back to Jason with a quiet, indecipherable expression on his face. William O'Meara stared at his son, his face white, trying to comprehend the disaster that had befallen him.

Andy stepped through the ropes and held out his hands to Len Peliter. "Reckon you could untie these now, Len?" he asked.

Len grinned. "Sure thing, Mr. Stillman." He unlaced the gloves as several men entered the ring and kneeled over Jason. Andy looked up and saw Jill staring at him with an expression of awe and fright on her face.

The gloves were removed; Andy thanked Len and turned to leave. "I reckon this is yours, Andy," Albert Fairbanks said, holding out twenty dollars. Andy's entrance fee, and Jason's.

Andy took it. "Thanks, Al," he said. Then he walked over to where O'Meara was standing near a group of men from town. He gave O'Meara the twenty dollars. "Here's the twenty I owe you for the footrace. You owe me two thousand dollars, Will. You can deposit it in the Bar-O's account at the bank. And you owe eight dollars to Amy and twenty-four to Kit, which I expect you can pay now."

O'Meara stared at Andy, emotion twisting the muscles of his face. "You'll get yours," he said finally, his voice choked with anger. He gave Amy eight dollars and shoved twenty-four into Kit's hands, then turned and stormed away.

· · ·

The little procession from the Bar-O left town as the sun was gliding behind the mountains to the west. All the way home Miles carried on about the fight.

"That was the gol-durndest, almighty finest doggoned fight I've ever seen in my life, Andy," he exclaimed, and he kept it up steadily for the next twenty minutes. "Dropped him like a rock! Like a rock, I swear I ain't never seen the like! Where in blazes did you learn t' fight like that?"

Andy said nothing, but a strange look came over his face, a look Miles noticed in a hurry. He peered at Andy closely. "There's sure somethin' fishy goin' on here," he said finally. "You've been awful quiet since we left town. You got somethin' you want t' tell us?"

Andy looked at Miles sheepishly then at Amy and Nell. Kit was listening intently as he rode alongside Andy. "You ever hear of Benjamin Montgomery?" Andy asked.

"Ain't ever'body?" Miles said. "Folks say he's the best fighter ever t' go t' college back there in the East. Never lost a fight his entire last two years." Miles gave Andy a sudden speculative look. "Come to think of it, that was that Brown College, same school you was at, ain't that so?"

"Same school."

"Well I'll be doggone. That where you learned to fight like that . . . from Benjamin Montgomery himself?"

"Sort of."

"What's that mean—'sort of?'"

Andy paused. "I'm Benjamin Montgomery, Miles," he said quietly. "I just took the name so pa wouldn't know I was fighting. I didn't think he'd approve."

Kit's eyes widened and Mile's mouth simply dropped open. "*You?*" Miles exclaimed after a moment of stunned silence. "*You're* Benjamin Montgomery?"

"Afraid so."

Miles recovered, then let out a whoop that folks must've heard all the way back in Willow Creek. "Great Jumpin' Jesus!" he cried.

"*Miles!*" exclaimed Nell.

"Don't put a bridle on me now, woman!" Miles howled. "Hot damn, Andy! Benjamin Montgomery! I'll be a lop-eared mule! I'll be hogtied an' hickory-switched! An' you went an' got Will O'Meara t' bet two thousand dollars against five hundred that Jason was goin' t' beat Benjamin Montgomery in a boxing match! If that don't beat all. By God, Nell, I want me a drink t' celebrate."

Then the Bar-O cowhands crowded around, staring at

Andy as if he had suddenly grown two horns and a tail. Finally Slim let out a call like a coyote, yipping into the shadows that were darkening around them, and the little company continued on to the ranch, laughing and shouting.

· · ·

"You beat him Andy, you really did," Amy said as Andy tucked her into bed.

"Guess I did at that, button."

"Well, I knew you would."

From a pocket of her jeans she pulled out the eight dollars O'Meara had given her and stuffed it into a jar.

Hesitantly, she said. "Kin I tell you something, Andy?" she asked.

"Sure you can."

"Promise you won't tell nobody."

"I promise."

"An' you won't git mad."

"No."

She grinned and said, "I didn't have no two dollars t' bet, Andy, but I went an' bet it anyway."

10

Benjamin Montgomery! The day after the picnic Miles Harding rumbled into Willow Creek in the old buckboard with several branding irons and an iron gate from the Bar-O irrigation system that needed repairing. At Peliter & Owens Hardware Store he bought a fifty-pound roll of baling wire, picked up three thousand feet of barbed wire, and told Jack Peliter about Andy being Benjamin Montgomery.

The news was all over Willow Creek within an hour.

Benjamin Montgomery had fought at Brown University on the school team as a middle heavyweight. In his last two years he'd never lost a fight, never split a decision, and had nineteen first- or second-round knockouts in twenty fights. Benjamin Montgomery was some kind of a folk hero, even as far west as Wyoming Territory.

As soon as I heard of it I remembered Andy stepping off the train just a week before and how it seemed he'd filled out some. Just shows how accurate first impressions can be, sometimes. It sure explained why Andy had appeared so much at ease just before the fight and how he had beaten Jason so easily. And the bet Andy had placed with Will O'Meara, well, it was simply a first-rate con job.

• • •

Sometime in the dark hours of the morning of July seventh the uneasy truce was broken that had existed between the Circle-K and the Bar-O since Andy's arrival back in Willow Creek. From far down the valley to the south, shots were heard, faint rolling noises like the distant sound of thunder. Andy woke in the pre-dawn darkness. His window was open to the night chill and he sat up in bed, listening.

There was no mistaking what the sounds were. The trouble had started again.

He saddled up with the others in the first pale light of dawn, before breakfast, and rode south through the rolling waves of prairie grass. Two miles from the house the riders fanned out, three hundred yards apart each, and covered a path a mile wide between the banks of the Little Muddy and the mountains to the west. It was Two-Bit who found what they were looking for.

He let out a call which was repeated up and down the line. Everyone came riding and gathered around the bodies of seven steers lying stiff-legged on their sides, thick blood matted around bullet holes in their sides and necks.

"Bastards," said Miles.

Rolly spat on the ground. "Reckon it's startin' again," he said. "Jest a matter of time was all it was."

"Any hope of trailing whoever did this?" Andy asked.

"None," said Miles. "We've tried it before but the trail

always ends in a creek or in town." He shook his head. "No, we ain't goin' t' catch them that way, Andy."

"Have we got any hard evidence that these raids are being done by O'Meara's men?"

"Hard evidence, no. Nothin' as would stand up in a court of law, that is. Besides, with twenty-five riders, O'Meara pretty much is the law in these parts, Andy. That's the hard truth of it; the law belongs t' the man that can enforce it. O'Meara's got nearly half the men in the valley riding for him. Men who are familiar with guns, that is."

Andy stared at the dead cattle. There was probably ten thousand pounds of beef lying there. Over two hundred dollars at the railhead. Already O'Meara had effectively recouped ten percent of his losses. Andy turned in his saddle and looked toward the southeast, toward O'Meara's ranch.

"Guess it's time for me to pay William O'Meara a personal visit," he said.

"Maybe that's not such a good idea, Andy."

"Something's got to be done."

Miles looked at him. "We'll camp out here, post guards, and drop 'em next time they come in."

"We can do that," Andy agreed. "But only as a last resort. First I'll have that talk with O'Meara."

The sun spilled over the edge of the Tetons and Andy felt the mellow warmth of sunlight against his face. Several flies crawled sluggishly on the blood of the cattle on the ground. "How much can we salvage here?" he asked.

"Hides," Miles answered. "We can jerk some of the beef for later and use some of it now. Most is goin' t' rot right where it lays."

Andy looked at the cows and nodded. "I'll take a hindquarter over to Bear's place on my way out to the Circle-K. Let's waste as little as possible."

•   •   •

"Kin I go too, Andy?" Amy asked.

"I'm not going to be in town long, button," Andy said.

It was Nell who saved her. "I've got a few things to buy in town, Andy. I could use the help." Her eyes twinkled.

"I'm outnumbered, then."

"It appears so."

"Goody," Amy said.

By mid-morning the buckboard was ready. In the back was a hundred and fifty pounds of beef wrapped in cowhide. At the last minute Kit decided to go along and he was on Midnight when Andy and the womenfolk came out of the ranch house and climbed into the buckboard.

An hour and a half later the little group pulled up in front of Goldman's General Store. Andy helped Nell and Amy out of the buckboard as Kit wrapped Midnight's reins around the hitching post out front.

"You'll find the buckboard over at Bear's place, if you need it," Andy said.

"Figured we'd wait for you," Kit answered.

"Suit yourself. I expect to be three or four hours though." Andy snapped the reins and clattered south on Main Street toward the blacksmith shop.

Bear was under the lean-to working the bellows. Andy pointed to the cowhide in the back of the buckboard and said, "Where do you want this?"

Bear looked up. "Hello, Andy," he said. "What've you got there?" He walked over to the rig.

"Fresh beef."

Bear's eyes narrowed. "Don't reckon the Bar-O slaughtered it."

"We had some help."

"Sorry t' hear it, Andy. How many did you lose?"

"Seven head."

Bear nodded. "Now what?"

"Now I go out to the Circle-K and talk to O'Meara."

Bear lifted a flap of the hide in the buckboard. "We kin use the meat, Andy, and thanks. But you be careful out at O'Meara's place. He ain't likely t' be pleased t' see you ... Benjamin."

Andy grinned. "You heard, then."

"Everybody in the whole valley's heard. O'Meara's not likely t' think it was funny, though."

They unloaded the meat from the buckboard. "Clair inside?" Andy asked.

"She's in. Reckon you'll get a more civil welcome out at

O'Meara's place than in there."

"I'll risk it."

"Keep your guard up, Andy. And watch her left."

Andy laughed. "Back in a minute," he said, and he went inside. The house was pleasantly cool from the night airing. He walked in the front door just as Clair was walking into the room from the kitchen. She took one surprised look at him, turned around, and went back into the kitchen.

Andy followed. In the kitchen Abigail was mending a pair of Bear's Levi's. "Good morning to you, Abby," Andy said. "Morning, Clair."

"Morning, Andy," Abigail answered.

Clair turned to her mother and said frostily, "I need a few things from Goldmans, ma." She swept out of the room without a second look at Andy and moments later the front door banged.

"Looks like an early winter this year, Abby."

"Give her time, she'll thaw. Then watch out 'cause she might throw off a fair amount of heat."

Andy smiled.

He spoke with Abigail a while longer, left the house, said his good-byes to Bear, and walked up the street toward Dugan's Livery. Kit had offered the use of his horse for the trip out to O'Meara's but Andy declined, preferring instead to rent the gray dun once again. With him he carried a small leather bag.

He had passed Beringer's General Store and Myra Nickolson's Bakery when Jill appeared on the boardwalk in front of him. She was wearing a light blue summer dress trimmed with white lace and her hair spilled down her back like a shimmering golden waterfall. Clevis Willis glanced out the door of the hardware store, nodded briefly to Andy, and disappeared back inside.

"I'm terribly sorry about my behavior at the picnic, Andy," Jill said, her head held low. "Can you ever forgive me?"

"I already have, Jill."

A look of relief passed over her face followed quickly by a slight blush. "I never saw anyone so strong before, Andy. At the picnic, I mean. I never would have thought anyone could beat Jason like that, but you made it look so . . . easy."

"Jason had it coming."

"I suppose so," she said. "But Jason isn't bad, Andy. Not,

well . . . not like—" She broke off abruptly, her face strained.

"Aaron."

She looked up and there was something like fear in her eyes. "Yes," she whispered. "Watch out for Aaron. He's mean, and," her face took on fresh color, "I—I wouldn't want you to get hurt, Andy," she stammered.

"I'll try to keep out of his way."

Jill nodded; she chose that moment to look up the street. Clair was two stores down, in front of the bank, walking slowly in their direction. Jill took a quick step closer to Andy, tilted her face up, and kissed him quickly on the lips. He backed away in surprise and looked up the street. Clair was standing on the boardwalk watching them with pain etched on her face.

Andy turned to Jill. "That was a thoroughly rotten thing to do," he said.

"A kiss, Andy?" she said with sugar in her voice.

Andy glanced up the street again. Clair was gone. He faced Jill again. "It takes a hell of a lot more than pretty dresses and smooth skin to make a lady," he said, then walked away.

On the dun again, he followed the course of Willow Creek as it wound south through the valley beside the trail out to the Circle-K. To his left, Crooked Neck Ridge ran southwest into the valley, growing smaller until it ended rather abruptly in a small, steep bluff.

Willow Creek carried water past the end of Crooked Neck Ridge on wet years, joining up with Badger Creek several miles below the Circle-K ranch buildings. This year it never made it past the end of the ridge. The water was little more than a trickle through town and over the next few miles the water seeped into the dry earth and evaporated until finally it just quit flowing altogether. It ended in a dark depression in the prairie where drying mud cracked and curled in the sun.

It was shaping up to be a dry year, all right. O'Meara's reservoirs would be receiving the last of the water from Badger Creek. At the picnic Andy had heard that O'Meara had added another foot to the dam of Upper Badger Reservoir and that the water was rising slowly beyond its previous high. The Circle-K would need every bit of it to get through the summer. It was no surprise that William O'Meara had set his eye on the Little Muddy.

As he rode, Andy looked up at the Tetons. A tiny patch of snow still lay in a ravine on the side of Wind River Peak, over thirteen thousand feet above sea level. That patch of snow was probably the sole source of the water in Willow Creek just then. There would be more snow on the northern slopes but most of that would either shed to the east, or into the Green River, and be lost.

Andy's thoughts turned to Clair. He shook his head. "Winter, hell," he said to the dun. "Next time I'm over at Bear's place Clair'll have an arctic blizzard in full swing." The horse twitched its ears, listening intently. For years horses had been the best damn listeners in the West.

Andy rode around the tip of Crooked Neck Ridge and turned almost due east. O'Meara's ranch lay two miles beyond in a protected basin formed by Crooked Neck Ridge to the northwest and the Tetons to the north and east. Badger Creek circled past the ranch house and ran out into the flat of the prairie to the south. The Circle-K wasn't a big ranch compared with many in Texas, Colorado, or even eastern Wyoming, but it was big for the Wind River Valley. Too big. O'Meara had nearly fifteen thousand head of cattle in the summer of 1885 and he was pushing the limits of what the range could support. The grass was rich, even for prairie grass, but it still took upwards of two acres to support each cow and the Circle-K's water supply consisted solely of Beaver Creek now that Willow Creek had dried up for the summer.

Andy noted all this as he neared the ranch buildings, the rambling two-story main house, the low, outlying bunkhouse, and several barns, equipment sheds, and corrals. He kept the dun at an easy lope until he reached the yard of the ranch house; then he reined the horse to a walk and crossed the yard to the hitching rail at the front of the house. As Andy looped the reins, Aaron stepped out of the house and leaned against a porch post. He was a smaller, leaner version of his brother, six foot one, a hundred sixty-five pounds, with dark brown hair and ice-blue eyes. Hard, pinched eyes now, Andy observed. Not like when he was a teenager.

"You got a spittoon's own brass, showin' up here after what you done," Aaron said. "Stealin' from my pa."

"I reckon you see a great many spittoons nowadays,

Aaron," Andy replied drily.

Aaron's eyes narrowed to slits. "This ain't exactly the best place fer you t' be shootin' off yer mouth," he warned.

"I'll have to write that down, see if I can remember it."

As Andy climbed the steps Aaron blocked the way with an outstretched arm. "Jest where d'you think you're goin'?"

Andy stared at Aaron's arm. "Pull it back or lose it," he said quietly. Aaron studied Andy momentarily then withdrew his arm. "Is your father in?" Andy asked.

"Pa? Sure, he's in. Don't think he'd care t' talk none with you, though."

"I reckon that'll be his decision, not yours," Andy said. "You want to call him for me?"

"Not hardly."

At that moment Jason appeared in the doorway. His left eye was partially closed and his lower lip was split. "You come t' see pa?" he asked.

Andy nodded.

"C'mon in."

Andy walked into the house. Inside, Jason offered his hand to Andy. Andy hesitated and Jason said, "Reckon it's safe enough this time." There was a faint, sad smile on his face. Andy shook his hand and Jason said, "I never thought anyone could go through me like you did at the picnic, but then I didn't figure t' be fightin' Benjamin Montgomery either."

Andy smiled. "Sorry about that, Jason."

"Nothin' t' be sorry about. It was a fair fight an' I lost. But, Gawd," he said touching his left eye gingerly, "I'd like t' know how such a little guy could hit so damn hard."

It wasn't the first time Andy had seen a man change almost overnight. Sometimes that happened, particularly in a man who had had some sense beat into him just at the moment he had the daylight beat out of him. Jill was right, Andy thought. Jason wasn't really bad; he'd just been king of the mountain for so long he'd never known what it was like to be anything else.

"Practice," Andy said.

"I'll bet."

"I wonder if I might have that talk with your father, Jason?"

"Yeah, sure. He's in the study." Jason led the way through

a door to the left of the living room and they entered a smaller but still spacious room with books lining one wall and a heavy oak desk at the far end. William O'Meara was seated behind the desk, crouching over a sheaf of papers. He stared at Andy as the two men entered the room.

"What the hell d'you want?" he asked tonelessly.

"We need to talk, Will."

"Ain't nothin' t' talk about, Andrew. Or should I call you Benjamin?"

"Take your pick."

A sour look crossed O'Meara's face. He leaned back in his chair, eyes fixed on Andy. "I ain't got all day. Hurry up an' say your piece, if you got to."

"More Bar-O cows were shot last night."

"That's too bad."

"That attitude isn't going to help solve this problem, Will."

"What problem? I ain't got no problem."

"You will if I find it's Circle-K riders that have been shooting our stock. I'm putting out guards, Will. We'll catch someone in the act one of these nights, and when we do I'll drive them and their outfit right out of the territory."

"Those are mighty powerful words for a jerkwater farm boy," O'Meara said. He glanced at Jason. "Leave us alone for a minute, son. And close the door."

Jason left and O'Meara withdrew a cigar from a box on his desk, rolled one end around in his mouth absently for several seconds, then lit the other end. He leaned back, drew deeply on the cigar, and sent a cloud of blue smoke toward the ceiling. "What you say is mighty interestin', boy. Mighty interestin'. I just don't see where it concerns me or the Circle-K."

"You deny that the Circle-K is shooting our stock and cutting our fences, then?"

O'Meara smiled, a grim and ugly smile. "I'm denyin' it. Until you come up with that proof you just mentioned, I'm denyin' it. And even if you manage t' come up with proof, I'll still deny any personal knowledge of it."

"That's just about as good as an admission of guilt right there, Will."

"It's an admission of nothin', boy," O'Meara's voice was hard. "Nothin' said in this room today will have any legal standin' anywhere. It'd just be your word against mine and I'd deny it along with any knowledge of the shooting of Bar-O cows."

"Who murdered my father?"

"Don't know nothin' about that."

"I'd hoped you would be interested in listening to a way to save both our ranches, Will."

O'Meara's eyes gleamed. "That ain't a ranch you've got over there. That's a farm. When you grow grass, you've got a farm. And when you put up fences, you ruin the goddamned range."

"Fences aren't the issue here."

O'Meara leaned back and scrutinized Andy shrewdly. "Yeah? Then what is?" he said finally.

"The Little Muddy. Water."

O'Meara sat motionless behind the desk for a long moment. Finally the sound of a wagon pulling into the yard outside came into the room. O'Meara glanced out a window. Jill was back from town with Clevis Willis. Tension hung heavy in O'Meara's study. He leaned forward suddenly and put his arms on the desk. "Suppose it is. So what?"

"The Little Muddy belongs to the Bar-O."

"It belongs t' whoever can hold onto it, boy."

"That's the criminal in you talking. Keep your men away from my ranch, Will."

"That's your worry, not mine."

Andy stared straight into O'Meara's eyes. "That's where you're wrong, Will," he said. "If I catch your men shooting Bar-O cows or cutting Bar-O fences, I'll dynamite Upper Badger Reservoir—so help me God I will—and if I do there won't be enough water left in the whole valley to keep three thousand head alive through the summer."

O'Meara's face turned white then went red with rage. "Boy, words like that could get you killed!"

"Like my father?"

"Just like any goddamn thing that's dead and picked clean by buzzards, goddamn it! You keep *away* from my reservoirs. I'm posting guards starting right now with orders t' shoot on sight—you or anyone else from the Bar-O found anywhere near those dams."

"Leave the Bar-O alone and you won't have to post those guards, Will."

"Get out."

"It doesn't have to be like this, Will."

"Get out. Now."

Andy turned on his heel and left. William O'Meara went to the door and called for Aaron. Aaron gave Andy a malicious grin as he walked into the study. Thirty seconds later he came out and went out the back of the house.

Jill was in the living room. "You said I wasn't a lady." Anger crackled hotly in her voice.

"I've been back East, Jill," Andy replied. "I've been around women. I couldn't be wrong about a thing like that."

O'Meara reappeared in the doorway to his study. "You ain't left yet?" he growled. "I'm havin' Clevis escort you off my land right now."

"That won't be necessary."

"It's my right."

Andy shrugged. "Okay by me. I haven't had a chance to visit with Clevis since I got back anyway."

Jill's eyes blazed at him as he left. O'Meara called for Clevis. When the weather-toughened foreman arrived, O'Meara gave him instructions. Clevis nodded and left.

Andy climbed into the saddle and spun the dun around. O'Meara's eyes never left Andy as the two men rode out of the yard, but when the men were a quarter mile away O'Meara's eyes shifted to the northwest, searching the prairie and the low-lying hills of Crooked Neck Ridge.

11

A hawk circled lazily in the invisible currents of air that swept up the sides of Crooked Neck Ridge. The afternoon sun cast a pall of heat over the land. The two men rode in near silence until they rounded the tip of the ridge.

"Reckon this is as far as I go," Clevis said. He pulled the brim of his hat down to shade his eyes as he looked into the trees of the nearby hills. "You watch your back trail for the next hour or so, Andy."

"I was thinking the same thing myself," Andy replied. He stared curiously at the older man. "Why do you stay?" he asked.

Clevis returned Andy's gaze impassively. Clevis was perhaps the best poker player in the territory. He could hold four kings with exactly the same bland expression in his slate-gray eyes that registered when he held a single pair of deuces. Leather creaked as he hooked a leg comfortably around the saddle horn. "Will O'Meara and I go back a long way," he said.

"What's happening here isn't right, Clevis."

Clevis spat into the dust. "I ain't got no part of that. I punch cows. Period."

"You could work somewhere else."

"Like I said, Will O'Meara an' me, we go back a long dang way—twenty-eight years to be exact—ever since Will had himself a little spread in eastern Missouri. Reckon I ride for the brand now. Maybe I don't approve of what's been goin' on lately but I ain't makin' it none of my affair, either. Will knows I'll punch his cows an' do a hell of a job of it in the bargain, but I won't be part of nothin' else." He gave Andy a long, cool look. "Now Reb Cotton an' his boys, they're another matter."

"So I gathered."

Clevis nodded. "Those men are mighty fine cowpunchers, some of the best I've ever seen, but they're mavericks, too.

They don't much care what job they're asked t' do an' they don't mind workin' late."

"How late?"

"Late. Although they're not the only ones."

Andy nodded his head toward the Circle-K. "Why's he doing it, Clevis? Why is he pushing so hard?"

The craggy old foreman scanned the hills again before he answered. "Will's a hard man, Andy. Hard an' proud. Sometimes those are good qualities in a man an' sometimes they ain't. Depends on how a man uses 'em, I reckon. Will looks around an' knows this is all he'll ever have. He's too old t' start over, an' besides, they ain't hardly no place left t' start over at. Country's gettin' plumb filled up everywhere. They ain't no place left for a big ranch an' that's all Will ever wanted. He always thought big, Will did. Never was any place quite big enough t' hold him."

"A man's got to stop growing sometime."

Clevis shrugged, uncurled his leg from the saddle horn, and stuck his foot back in the stirrup. "So long, Andy," he said. "You take care this afternoon, you hear." He wheeled his horse and rode back toward the ranch.

Andy kicked the dun into an easy lope and continued on toward town. He had ridden several miles when they came out of the hills, riding like the devil in his direction, two riders, hunched low in the saddle, and Andy figured they weren't interested in polite conversation. They weren't much over a quarter mile behind him when he spotted them. The town was still five miles to the north and a quick estimate told him he wouldn't be able to make more than two of those miles before they caught him. The dun was a fair horse for easy travel in open country but it wouldn't be much for running. Andy had no gun and he was out in the open. The cover of trees and brush on Crooked Neck Ridge was his only hope and he kicked the dun into a wild gallop toward the hills.

He looked back. The riders were gaining on him and had cut back toward the hills on a line that shortened the distance even further. It was going to be a close race to the trees.

The dun raced through the prairie grass, angling away from the approaching riders, and started up the slope. Its breathing became ragged as the trail steepened and its speed dropped as it labored up the side of the hill past outcroppings of rock and broken patches of shale.

The riders were less than a hundred fifty yards behind when Andy reached back and pulled the leather bag from the back of the saddle. He leaned forward over the dun's neck and encouraged the horse to go faster. Then they were in the trees. Andy ducked under a limb, guiding the horse toward a thick stand of pine and brush. Behind him, he heard the crash of pursuit.

When Andy reached the brush he jumped off the back of the dun and slapped it on the rear. "Go home, boy," he shouted and he ran up the side of the hill into the trees.

A shot rang out and a twig snapped wickedly off a tree to Andy's left, arm's distance away. "He's afoot," a voice shouted below him, not fifty yards off. It was Aaron. "He ain't got no gun and he's afoot. We got him now, by God!"

Andy ran up the slope, opening the bag as he went. He looked behind him and saw Aaron and Tripp leap off their horses. Another shot rang out. Andy heard the bullet rip through the brush beside him. He ran uphill a hundred yards then kicked off his boots. From the bag he pulled a pair of shoes—the buckskin moccasins he had worn during the fight with Jason.

They had no laces and Andy slipped them on quickly. A vision of Aaron racing for the finish line at the picnic two hundred yards ahead of the nearest runner crossed Andy's mind. He smiled. The stakes in today's race would be a lot higher. He crossed a little clearing and ran into the trees. There was less brush here but there was more room to run. He risked a quick look behind him and saw Aaron run across the clearing on foot, well ahead of Tripp. Tripp was already winded, but Aaron was only forty yards behind now and in that quick look Andy saw a triumphant expression in Aaron's face. Aaron's gun was out and he snapped off a quick shot. It went wide by several feet. Andy lowered his head, increased his speed, and dodged upward through the trees.

Then the race began in earnest, at least for Aaron. Andy ran up the side of the ridge until he reached its crest. He glanced behind often to insure Aaron did not fall too far behind. He kept Aaron about eighty yards back, close enough to keep him hopeful but far enough to prevent him from getting off a good shot. They worked their way up the backbone of the ridge for over a mile; Aaron had quit firing and Andy began to enjoy the run. The breeze was cool on his face; bright patches of sunlight pierced the cover of the trees. Andy ran easily, tirelessly, with the fluid grace of an athlete who had spent countless hours running, training more for endurance than for speed.

Aaron stopped and stood with his hands on his hips, breathing heavily. Andy gave Aaron a few seconds to catch his breath. Then he shouted, "Come on, Aaron. I thought you could run. I never would have figured you for a quitter. A yellow-bellied coward, yes, but a quitter—"

Aaron's eyes blazed. He fired again and the slug buried itself in the trunk of a pine tree next to Andy. Once more the chase continued as Andy led the way up the back of the ridge, heading northeast toward the Tetons. He slowed the pace so Aaron could keep up and soon they were well over two miles from where they'd left the horses.

Again Aaron faltered and Andy decided they'd gone far enough. He cut suddenly to the left and ran down the western side of the ridge. The slope was steep but Andy went down in a series of controlled leaps that brought him within minutes to the lower edge of the timberline. He stopped and listened. Birds sang and a mild breeze stirred the leaves of the bushes, otherwise it was quiet. Aaron had been left hopelessly far behind.

Andy stayed just inside the timberline, above the open expanse of the prairie. He ran along the side of the ridge in the direction from which they'd come, more swiftly now, dodging through the trees and rocks in near silence, warming to the run, feeling the earth through the soft leather of his moccasins. Over his right shoulder lay the town of Willow Creek, now only a little over three miles away, sweltering in the heat of the afternoon sun.

When he neared the place where the horses had pulled into the hills, Andy slowed, running carefully where he would make no sound, searching the trees for a sign of Tripp. Aaron would still be far behind up the ridge, but Tripp could be anywhere. Crossing the tracks made by the horses earlier, Andy slowed to a careful walk, following the tracks into the trees. He stopped, listening. For almost a minute there was no sound but the quiet of the hills—then a horse blew and stamped the ground somewhere up the slope.

Keeping to the trees, Andy crept up the hillside. Finally he saw the horses, picketed to a fallen tree in a clearing, probably by Tripp after he'd given up the run. Tripp was nowhere in sight. Andy eased his way past the clearing through a thick stand of greasewood, scanned the slope carefully, and located Tripp who was leaning against a granite boulder in the shade of several pines, rolling a cigarette with careless ease as he watched the ridge where Andy and Aaron had disappeared. A Winchester leaned against the rock beside him, its barrel pointed toward the sky.

Andy smiled. He crept back down through the greasewood to the edge of the clearing. The two horses eyed him nervously as he broke from under the trees and crossed toward them. "Easy there," Andy said in a low voice. "Easy boys. We don't need any noise just now." He spoke softly to them as he untied their reins. Holding the reins of Aaron's horse, he stepped into the saddle of Tripp's strawberry roan. Then, leading Aaron's horse, he walked the horses down the slope through the trees.

"Hey," Tripp's voice sounded from above.

Andy nudged the side of the roan and they went down the hillside in an easy lope. The trees thinned and they broke through the timberline into the open.

"Stop, goddamn it!" Tripp's voice sounded from far away. A rifle cracked in the hills and a slug whined far over Andy's head. He kept the horses at a steady lope as he rode into the shallow slope of the prairie. More shots rang out in quick succession but the sound of the bullets was lost. Tripp was shooting wildly, unloading his gun blindly in the direction Andy had taken.

Andy grinned and rode on toward town. When he reached the willow tree that had marked the turning point of the horse race at the picnic, he dismounted and stripped the saddles and bridles from the horses and set them under the tree. Then he slapped the horses on their flanks and shouted, "Get on home, boys!" The horses bolted in the direction of the Circle-K. Andy watched as they galloped away down the trail.

• • •

At about the same time that Andy and Clevis were having their talk at the tip of Crooked Neck Ridge, Nell was in Booth's Mercantile buying sewing supplies and several yards of material. Kit and Amy were crossing Water Street on their way to the field in back of Wilton Butterfield's Wind River Gazette and Printing Company to watch the unloading of the boxcars in the train yard. They walked past the front of the Wind River Hotel, an old, decrepit structure with tired, peeling clapboard siding, and started past the Blue Boar Saloon.

Kid Reese was leaning against a porch post out front. As Kit and Amy approached he stepped languidly into their path. Kit glared at Kid Reese and started to step around him but Kid Reese blocked the way again in an easy movement.

"Hey!" Amy cried. "You're in the way, mister."

Kid Reese grinned at her, then at Kit. "Don't see it that way, myself," he said, yawning. "Looks t' me like you're tryin' t' walk where I'm tryin' t' stand."

Kit grabbed Amy's hand. "C'mon," he said and he started to step off the boardwalk into the street. Again Kid Reese blocked the way. Snake Haskins appeared in the doorway to the saloon, grinning.

"Sure are in a hurry, ain't you two?" Kid Reese said.

"You're in the way," Amy said again.

"That's what she says," Kid Reese drawled, staring at Kit. "What do you say, boy?"

"Reckon she's got good eyes."

Kid Reese grinned at Kit. He looked at Kit's new Stetson. "Nice hat," he said, winking at Snake. Snake laughed, a short ugly sound. He watched from over the top of the batwing doors, the stub of a cigarette hanging from his lips.

"You leave us alone or my brother'll beat the daylights out of you," Kit said.

Kid Reese looked up at Snake in mock despair. "It's his brother, Snake. By God, we're in for trouble now." He looked around and lifted his eyebrows in feigned surprise. He glanced behind him then checked his pockets. "Well I'll be doggone, boy. I don't see him nowhere around."

"You better watch out," Amy said. "My brother is Benj'min Montgom'ry an' he's real tough."

Kid Reese's eyes went hard. "I know who your brother is,

kid." He turned suddenly and knocked Kit's hat into the street.

"Hey," Amy yelled.

Kit balled up his fists and held them up in front of him.

"Well, lookee here, Snake. Seems like ever'one in the family knows how t' use their fists." At five foot seven Kit was tall for his age but Kid Reese was a good six inches taller and at a hundred and eighty-five pounds he outweighed Kit by more than sixty pounds. He grinned, cold blue eyes narrowing into slits.

"You leave my brother alone," Amy screamed.

Kid Reese stepped from the boardwalk and held a boot over Kit's hat. "No," Kit yelled, charging forward. Kid Reese swung a left, landing a glancing blow just under Kit's right eye. Kit staggered and Kid Reese threw a right straight into Kit's face. Kit landed on his back in the dust, dazed. Blood ran from his nose which was bent at an odd angle.

Amy ran to his side. "Kit!" she cried. "Kit." She looked up at Kid Reese with tears in her eyes. "Go away," she sobbed. "Go away. Go away." She turned toward her brother again. Kit struggled awkwardly to a sitting position. Dust clung to the back of his head and to his shirt. Blood dripped from his nose.

"You're bleeding!" Amy screamed.

"I'm all right," Kit said, gasping. He took hold of her shoulders, quieting her, forcing her to look into his eyes. "It's just a little blood, Amy. I'm all right."

Kid Reese looked down at them. "Reckon I was wrong, Snake," he said. "Not ever'one in that family knows how t' use their fists." He turned, looked cautiously over his shoulder, and disappeared into the saloon.

•　•　•

Nell had been looking for Andy. When she saw him driving the buckboard from Bear's place at the south end of town she waved him over. He crossed the street to the front of the sheriff's office and stopped.

"Oh Andy," she said. "When we saw your horse come back without you we were so worried!"

Sheriff Heede appeared in the doorway to his office. Andy nodded to Heede, then said to Nell, "I ran into a little trouble coming back from the Circle-K."

"What kind of trouble?" the Sheriff asked.

Andy explained, omitting the part about how he had outrun Aaron, mentioning only that he had managed to circle around and take their horses.

The Sheriff grunted. "That'll be your word against theirs."

"You can check my story, John. I left their saddles under the old willow tree just south of town."

The sheriff squinted at Andy. "Suppose I went out there and found them saddles, son? Wouldn't prove a thing. Still be jest your word against theirs. They might even claim you stole them horses, an' by your own admission maybe that's just what you did."

Andy stared at Heede in disbelief. Finally Nell touched Andy's arm. "Kit's been hurt, Andy."

Instantly, Andy turned away from Heede. "Kit? How bad? What happened?"

"He's going to be all right, I reckon. He's over at Doc Simes' office. The doc says it's just a broken nose—nothing to worry about."

"A broken nose? For god's sake, Nell, how'd that happen?"

"I'm not quite sure, Andy." Her voice was low. "It had something to do with that gunman, Kid Reese. Let Kit tell it."

Andy turned to the sheriff. "What about it, John?"

Heede shrugged. "I checked it out. Nobody seen it happen. Reese denies it; says he ain't left the Blue Boar all day."

Andy's eyes flashed. His hands trembled. "Let's go," he said to Nell. He helped her into the buckboard and they left the sheriff standing in the doorway to his office.

Doc Simes' office was just around the corner next to the Miner's Cafe on Water Street, not far from the train station. Doc Simes was a short, gray-haired man, balding on top. He had quick, alert eyes set into wrinkled sockets under bushy gray eyebrows. He was in the front room when Nell and Andy entered the office. "How is he, Doc?" Andy asked.

Doc Simes smiled. "Pleased as punch, Andy," he replied. "His nose is broken. I reckon it hurts some but I doubt if he'd have it any other way. He's going to be mighty proud of the shiner he's got, too. He's in back with Liz." Andy started toward the back room but Doc Simes stopped him with a gentle hand. Doc Simes lowered his voice and his mood became more somber. "Kit'll be fine, Andy. There's no sign of concussion. But that Kid Reese—" He broke off. Then in a quiet, almost apologetic voice he said, "Willow Creek is filling up with trash, Andy."

Andy nodded, his eyes hard and thoughtful.

They filed into the back room where Elizabeth Simes was applying the finishing touches to Kit's bandages. Amy was sitting on a chair watching the proceedings with big eyes. "Andy," she said in delight when she saw him. She ran over to him. "Kit got beat up."

"So I heard. Hello, Mrs. Simes."

"Afternoon, Andy," she replied. Elizabeth Simes was a neat, trim woman in her early fifties with graying hair and sharp, clear eyes. "I'll be done here in a few minutes."

"My nose is broke," Kit proclaimed proudly.

Andy's voice was calm. "So I heard. You want to tell me how that happened, Kit?"

Kit told the story, with help from Amy, and as the story unfolded, Andy's eyes turned cold and distant, at least that's what Doc Simes said later. Right then I wouldn't have been standing in Kid Reese's boots for any doggone thing.

12

Long shadows reached across the valley as the little group from town pulled into the yard in front of the Bar-O ranch house. Miles watched from the porch as they arrived. Kit led the horses to the corral as everyone else filed up the steps and went into the house.

Miles stared at the bandage on Kit's nose curiously then followed Andy into the living room. "Kit get throwed?" he asked.

Andy explained what had happened in town. Miles shook his head. "So they're fightin' kids now. What's next?"

"I doubt if attacking Kit was O'Meara's idea."

"Mebe not, but Reese is still O'Meara's man. Things is gettin' out of hand, Andy. How'd your talk with O'Meara go?"

"He says he wants the Little Muddy."

"He said that? Come right on out with it?"

"Not in precisely those words but that was the substance of it." Andy recounted his conversation with O'Meara then told Miles about the later trouble he had with Aaron and Tripp.

"They're playin' for keeps now, Andy."

"We knew that when they killed pa," Andy replied.

"Reckon so." Miles sighed. "So, what do we do now?"

"I guess it's time we posted those guards you mentioned this morning. I've been thinking about that. We could set up two camps about a mile apart with three or four men in a camp. We can take turns standing watch. We could cover a reasonable piece of ground that way and one of these nights we'd be sure to surprise some Circle-K riders coming in to shoot our stock."

Miles considered this for a long moment. "Ought t' work," he said finally.

"I just want to catch them in the act, Miles. I want absolute proof that the Circle-K is behind the shooting of our cattle. I only wish there was some way to do it without risking anyone getting hurt."

"Those boys out there have been itchin' for a good fight, Andy. They ain't felt right about jest sittin' around while the Bar-O loses stock. They'll fight for you."

"The one thing we don't need is a fight, Miles. With luck we might be able to capture one of O'Meara's night riders. I'm hoping if we do O'Meara will call off his raids. If he doesn't, it's a fight we can't win."

"We cain't give up without tryin'."

"I reckon not." Andy stared out the window at the darkness settling over the southern range. "This was pa's home," he said in a tired, remote voice, slumping into a worn leather chair. "It's all Kit and Amy have left now. Seeing this through to the end is my responsibility, and because of them, I'll try." He sighed and stared into space for several seconds before continuing. "I'm out of my element here, Miles. Fact is, I'm an engineer, not a rancher. As soon as this trouble is resolved I've got to be getting on with it. I've given that a lot of thought lately. If things work out I'd like you to run the Bar-O, not just as the foreman, but as a partner; one-third for you, two-thirds for Kit and Amy."

Miles peered at him closely. "And what about you, Andy? What do you want?"

"I reckon I've already got it, Miles. I received an education. That's enough. Truth is, I want to build bridges. Later, Kit and Amy can decide for themselves what they want."

Miles was silent for a minute. "One-third partnership," he mused. "That's mighty generous, Andy. Mebe a mite over-generous."

Andy shook his head. "No. It's not. You and Nell are wonderful for the children. Besides, Kit won't be able to run this place on his own for several years yet. He's still got a lot to learn about the business end of ranching. Anyway, Miles, you and Nell are family—have been for years now."

"All right, Andy." Miles grinned awkwardly. "I'd be pleased t' accept your offer, if things work out like you hope, that is."

"It would have made my father happy too," Andy replied and the two men shook hands.

That night they set up camp in two groups, three miles south of the ranch house, on the west side of the Little Muddy two hundred yards from the creek. Andy, Slim, and Two-Bit took the position nearest the ranch buildings, while Miles, Rolly, Stringer, and Paul set up camp a mile further to the south. Ever since the fight with Jason at the picnic, Andy had been accepted not only as one of them, but as someone who had earned more than the usual measure of respect. Without question or reservation, the men followed Andy's orders.

Kit wanted to join the watch camps but Andy wouldn't allow it, explaining to Kit that someone was needed back at the house to protect the women. Kit was only partially mollified but he accepted the decision without further comment.

They set up their camps after dark and lit no fires. In Andy's camp the talk was low until everyone but Andy turned in. He had drawn the first watch. The horses were picketed nearby, saddled with loosened cinches. For several minutes the horses stamped the dust and blew fitfully but eventually they quieted down and Andy listened to the distant sounds of the high prairie. Far away a coyote howled. A gentle breeze stirred the grass with a somnolent rushing sound and occasionally the faint whispering rush of a bat sounded overhead.

Andy peered into the gloom that lay across the prairie. The dark mass of the Tetons to the east was marked by the absence of stars. There was no moon. Darkness and quiet settled over the land. Only the bright canopy of stars looked down over the valley and Andy stared up in wonder at the wide, misty band of the Milky Way.

He heard nothing. At midnight he woke Slim for the next watch.

They broke camp during the faintest light of dawn when the prairie was still shrouded in darkness. The Tetons were framed by the blue-black sky of earliest sunrise and the Milky Way had faded from the sky when they tightened the cinches of their saddles and rode back to the ranch buildings.

Two more nights passed before the night riders came.

The Bar-O cowhands were tired, but no one complained. The men were rotated in the groups since the night watch was easier on the camp with four men; they got more sleep than the men in the smaller camp. Andy was on watch at three-thirty in the morning in the camp with Miles, Slim, and Two-Bit. Rolly, Stringer, and Paul were in the smaller camp.

The night was cool and Andy sat cross-legged on a knob of earth that projected ten feet above the prairie floor, wrapped in a blanket, listening to the quiet sounds of the night. Something splashed in the Little Muddy. Far away, a cricket chirruped. A click sounded in the distance. Andy pricked up his ears. Several seconds later it was repeated, a distant metallic snap in the night.

Andy stood and stared in the direction from which the sound had come. Soon he heard the quiet rustling of horses moving. In the stillness of the prairie sound carried for miles; Andy estimated it to be nearly a mile to the north. That would place it near the smaller camp. Was it caused by the men at the other camp? If so, perhaps they had heard something even further to the north and were moving to investigate.

Andy decided to wake the others. They woke quickly, pulling on their boots and strapping on their six-guns. They were at their horses tightening the cinches when the first shots came. The electrifying sounds galvanized the Bar-O cowhands into action. In darkness they leaped into their saddles and rode quickly toward the north.

The pop of handguns intermingled with the deeper roll of rifle fire; the firing was sporadic, angry sounding. Suddenly it was gone, replaced by the urgent sounds of their own horse's hoofs and the dry rush of grass against their legs.

"Bar-O comin' in!" Miles shouted as they neared the smaller camp.

"Over here," a voice shouted back. It was Stringer. They circled him on their horses.

"Where are they?" Miles asked. "You get any of 'em?"

"Don't know," Stringer said. "Must've been half a dozen of 'em, but it was jest too blessed dark t' see much."

"Where are the others, Rolly and Paul?"

"Around here somewheres. We heard riders comin', split off, and shot into 'em from different angles."

They mounted a quick search and found Paul walking back to camp cussing. "Dad-burned horse throwed me," he said angrily. Wolf-bait cayuse didn't care much for all that flyin' lead, I reckon."

"Where's Rolly?"

"Out there somewhere," Paul said. "Shootin' up a storm last time I heard him."

Before daylight they found Rolly's horse but it wasn't until the yellow glow on the horizon had driven the last stars from the sky that they found Rolly himself. He was lying on his face in a thick clump of prairie grass when Miles discovered him. Miles fired three shots into the air then climbed off his horse and turned Rolly over. He had taken a rifle slug in his chest and had died just about instantly from the look of it.

"Oh Lord, no," Miles said in a low, anguished voice. "Oh Jesus, Rolly. Why'd you have t' go an' do that?"

Rolly was the only casualty in the fight that dark morning; at least the search for Rolly turned up no sign of the Circle-K, no bodies, no blood. They put Rolly across his horse and the little company rode slowly back to the ranch house. They were met at the door by Nell and Kit.

Kit stared at Rolly's body, stunned. "Heard all the

shootin'," he said remotely.

Nell's face was white, her fingers knotted around the end of her shawl. Behind her, Amy appeared in the doorway, her face waxen. "What happened?" Amy asked.

"Go on back in the house, button," Andy said.

She appeared not to hear. Barefoot, she walked out on the porch and stared at Rolly. Tears formed suddenly in her eyes and rolled down her cheeks. She looked up at Andy. "I-Is Rolly . . . d-dead?" she asked.

Andy climbed off his horse and held her. "I reckon so, button," he said gently.

She clung to him, trembling. "I-I liked Rolly, Andy," she said, her voice breaking. "I-I don't want him t' be dead."

Her tears seared his cheek. "Reckon none of us wants it, button."

They put Rolly in the bunkhouse and covered him with a blanket. Miles sent Two-Bit to town to notify the Sheriff. "Did Rolly have any family?" Andy asked Miles.

"None that I ever heard of."

"You know what part of Texas he came from?"

"Galveston. Or mebe Corpus Christi. Talked about the sea once in a while when he'd had a drink or two."

"Reckon we'll bury him here, Miles."

"Guess that's best," Miles answered.

Andy ate no breakfast that day. Shortly after his talk with Miles Andy slipped on his moccasins and ran into the hills to the west.

"Where's he goin'?" Kit asked.

"Reckon he needs a little time alone," Miles answered as he watched Andy disappear into the hills. "Reckon I know jest how he feels."

Andy ran up to the timberline and went north, parallel to the line of the Little Muddy. When he was in the trees he ran all out for several miles until he couldn't run any farther. Then he walked, circling the northern end of his father's ranch with its channels and gates and hundreds of acres of green grass, tiny patches of odd color in the endless sea of dusty-yellow prairie. A mile from the diversion dam he cut into the trees and ran up the side of the mountain for half a mile. The Looking Rock was still there: a massive granite boulder twenty feet high, still holding the tiny steps he'd cut into it years ago. The Looking Rock was where he had come to, dozens of times in the past, when he wanted to be alone. He scaled the side of the rock and stood on the smooth, rounded pale dome that overlooked the entire Wind River Valley. Crooked Neck Ridge lay fourteen miles to the southeast and the town of Willow Creek still hugged the morning shadow of the Tetons.

Andy lowered himself to a sitting position on the rock, sitting cross-legged facing the valley. Below him the Bar-O was spread out, three miles wide, twelve miles long, twenty-three thousand acres. It was all going to be lost. The years of work, all the thought and care his father had put into the irrigation system, the cattle they had nursed through hard winters, the hard times they had endured in the beginning and the quiet contentment that had come later. Already it was disappearing, Andy thought—fading away like distant mountains on a hazy day. Over a hundred head of cattle and two men had been lost in less than six weeks. Shadows were forming over the Bar-O; a bitter pall cast by Will O'Meara and the Circle-K.

Andy had known Rolly when Rolly was Two-Bit's age; Rolly started working for the Bar-O when Andy was younger than Kit was now. Time inched slowly by until, suddenly, ten years had passed and Rolly was almost as much a part of the Bar-O as were Miles and Henry. Now both his father and Rolly were gone. Who would go next if they continued to fight? Slim? Two-Bit? Maybe Miles. Possibly even Kit.

Unable to take your own advice, he said silently to himself, clenching his fists. The words he spoke his first night back echoed back to him —if you want to come out ahead on this one you'd better start using your brains, not your guns.

Andy shook his head. The ranch had been Henry's dream—but was it worth more than his father's life? What about Rolly's life? Was the ranch more important than the lives of those who would surely die if he continued to fight O'Meara? There were those who would fight and die no matter how little the gain, no matter how great the price, on the hallowed dictates of principle alone. But Andy wasn't one of them. He could fight and maybe even die himself, but what about his responsibility to Kit and Amy? What about Miles and Nell?

The Indians are after the gold, Andy thought. What are you

going to do about it? You can't fight them; you can't ignore them; you can't take the gold with you. And if you simply leave the gold the Indians will take it. Is that it, then? Is the gold worth fighting for? Maybe it was time to move on.

A hawk circled overhead, wings dark against the sky, and a pair of squirrels chattered noisily in the trees behind him. A butterfly flittered by in its erratic, aimless flight. The sun rose in the sky; the day grew hot. Yet Andy stayed on the rock, looking over the valley, thinking, pondering his situation.

He sat on the Looking Rock for the entire day. Slowly a plan evolved in his mind and he turned the elements of the plan over, searching for weaknesses. There were many and he considered these carefully. Apparent weaknesses were balanced by hidden strengths. Moves. Countermoves.

In time he had it. Not all of it, of course; it was impossible to anticipate every move O'Meara might make. What he had was an overall strategy; a general plan of attack laid out in broad outline. It was risky. He could fail. The Bar-O might still be lost. But as things stood now the Bar-O was doomed anyway and only a bold stroke could save it. An unexpected stroke—and his plan depended on the very unexpectedness of his next move. That and all the resourcefulness he could muster after the first move was completed.

The first move would be to bury the gold. Quickly.

·   ·   ·

He walked out of the mountains when the valley was again in shadow and the last golden rays of the sun lit the crowns of the Tetons to the east. He looked over the rich fields of grass, made possible by the ingenuity and foresight of his father, and he walked with a firm, purposeful stride, burned by the sun, dried, hardened—his mind spinning with the thoughts of his desperate plan.

13

Andy stood to one side of the living room staring out the window at the darkness in front of the ranch house. Kit straddled a wooden chair with his arms folded across the back and Miles sat in an easy chair near Henry's old desk. Nell and Amy sat quietly on the leather couch against one wall.

It wasn't going to be easy to tell them what he had in mind, he thought. Harder still because he couldn't tell them all of it. If they knew exactly what he intended to do they would put up even more resistance and he didn't need that right now. Things were going to be tough enough as they were. But there was nothing he could do now except come right out with the rest of it. He turned and faced the little group.

"I've decided to sell off all the Bar-O stock," he said, rather abruptly.

Kit was off his chair in an instant. "Andy! You can't do that!"

"We've got to, Kit."

Miles shook his head. "This ain't no time t' sell, Andy. We'd take a hell of a beatin' at the scales."

"There," Kit exclaimed. "You see!"

"I know it looks bad," Andy said, "but we've got no choice."

"We can fight 'em," Kit said.

"And who would die next if we did? Stringer? Two-Bit? Who would we bury next?"

"But we can't just give up," Kit cried angrily. "This is pa's ranch. He died for it. We can't just turn it over t' the Circle-K."

"Nobody's turning anything over to anyone," Andy said sharply. "We're not selling the ranch, we're just going to sell off the stock."

Kit sat down again. "Same thing."

"No it's not. We'll retain control of the Little Muddy and

we'll keep fifty or a hundred head on the range to show everyone we mean to keep the ranch."

Miles looked at Andy cautiously. "If you don't mind my sayin' so, Andy, what you're suggestin' don't make a whole lot of sense. What d'you have in mind?"

Andy smiled tiredly. "I reckon I'd rather not say just yet, Miles. I've got a plan and the first thing I've got to do to carry it out is sell off as much of the stock as I can."

"They'll skin us alive at the railhead," Miles said slowly. "We might get eighty-five cents on the dollar, if that."

"We'll take what we can get."

"It'd mean the same thing as losin' three hundred head, selling off that cheap."

"How many would we lose by staying?"

Miles stared down at his hands. "Mebe more, mebe less."

"And maybe the whole ranch."

Miles nodded miserably. "I reckon that's right too."

Andy stared out the window again. "Who can we sell to?"

Miles thought for a moment. "This ain't a good time t' be selling, but I reckon Weston & Schofield out in Chicago would buy. I know Nat Weston. He'll buy your beef, but he'll skin your hide."

"How are we goin' t' ranch if we ain't got no cows?" Kit demanded.

"We aren't, at least not for a while."

"What are we goin' t' do, then?"

For a long moment Andy didn't answer. The discussion had twisted and turned until, inevitably, it had reached this final point—the point Andy wished he could have somehow avoided. Yet they had to know what was coming; they'd know soon enough as it was. "I'm turning the Bar-O cowhands loose," Andy said. "And I'm sending all of you to Cheyenne for a spell."

"What!" Kit howled. He rose off his chair again as if jerked by hidden wires. "You can't do that, Andy! You *can't*! You're givin' O'Meara the Bar-O for sure!"

Nell spoke. Her voice was quiet but filled with concern. "Are you sure of this, Andy? It doesn't look right."

"I reckon I know how it looks, Nell. In fact, that's part of what I have in mind. Until the stock has been sold and is on its way to whoever buys it I want it to look exactly like the Bar-O is pulling up stakes and clearing out."

"Ain't it?" Kit asked sullenly.

"No, Kit," Andy's voice was firm. "It's not. But it's got to look that way to O'Meara."

"Wish it didn't look that way t' me, too."

Amy's eyes were round; she held Nell's arm tightly. "I don't want t' go away," she said in a tiny voice.

"Just for a little while, button? You'll have a good time in Cheyenne."

"You goin'?"

"Reckon I'll be staying behind a spell," Andy said gently.

"Then I don't want t' go."

"I know," Andy said. "I know how strange this must seem to all of you, but there's just no other way." He turned to Miles. "You'll still be on the Bar-O payroll, Miles."

"No sir. I don't take pay for work I don't do," Miles declared firmly.

"You'll be doing plenty. The work may be a little different for a while is all, but you'll be working."

Miles stared at him for a long moment. "Son," he said finally. "I wish I knew what you've got up those sleeves of your'n. If I knew that I might be able t' talk you out of it 'cause I got me a bad feeling about this."

Andy gave Miles a wry grin. "Reckon we'll go to town tomorrow and sell us some cows, Miles."

• • •

When Andy and Miles walked in the station I was looking over a chess game Paulsen and Morphy had played over twenty-five years earlier. It was a typical Paulsen game, tight, controlled, closed. Paulsen always seemed to play that kind of game. Reckon that's why Morphy didn't much care to play him. Morphy liked to dazzle everyone with his brilliance but Paulsen played so slowly he just about bored Morphy to tears. Still, I learned a lot by looking over their shoulders, so to speak.

When Andy and Miles walked into the station I set down the book I was studying and looked up.

"Morning, Tom," Andy said. "The line up?"

"All the way to Paris," I told him.

"I don't reckon we'll need to send a message quite that far," Andy replied. "How about to Chicago?"

"Sure. Just write it down here." I handed him the form. As he filled it out I sent a quick hello down the line to Rock Springs and when they answered I told them to check the line to Chicago, which meant they would relay the message through Davenport, Iowa.

Andy handed me the paper. I read it over and whistled. "You selling out?" I asked. I hated to see it but I'd heard about Rolly and I knew the Bar-O was in bad trouble.

"I'm selling off the stock," Andy agreed. "Can we get this man on the line in Chicago and negotiate a deal this morning?"

It wasn't a request I got every day but I'd done it before. I would send the message to Rock Springs who would pass it on to Davenport who would contact Chicago. The answer would come back the same way only in reverse. "It's slow," I told Andy. "But it's a durn sight better than shouting." When he didn't smile, I figured things were plenty serious.

In fact, it took nearly an hour to make contact with Nathan Weston. Andy had sent an open-ended offer requesting a bid on between eighteen hundred and twenty-two hundred head of cattle. I sure would have liked to have played Andy a game of chess in that hour but he was worried about more important matters, I reckoned.

The key began clattering and I sat down and copied out the reply. It was short and to the point:

Nathan Weston, Weston & Schofield
Meat Co., Chicago, Ill. Offer $16 per
thousand pounds at Willow Creek railhead.
Regards to Nell.

Miles groaned. "I told you he's a damn pirate, Andy. Counter offer twenty dollars. Mebe we kin get eighteen."

I sent the message. The system was running smoothly now and Weston's offer came back in under twenty minutes.

Final offer $16.80.

"We cain't take it, Andy," Miles said, fuming. "It's like

losing four hundred head; almost a year's worth of profit."

"Can we get him any higher?"

Miles shook his head. "I know Nat Weston. When he says 'final offer,' he means just that."

"Will anyone else take them, all two thousand head?"

Miles shook his head once again. "Not in June, Andy. If we can wait until September—"

"We don't have the time," Andy said grimly. He turned to me. "Accept his offer," he said.

Miles grabbed Andy's arm. "We kin fight 'em, Andy. We don't have t' go like this. If we hang on three more months we kin get ten, mebe twelve thousand dollars more for the herd, if you're still of a mind t' sell them then."

"It's hard for me too, Miles," Andy said gently. "But no one else is going to die nurse-maiding those damn cows."

I hadn't sent the reply back yet and now Andy turned to me.

"Sell 'em," he said.

•   •   •

Nathan Weston had several of his agents holding down rooms in Denver and before the day was over they had been notified of the sale. They would operate the scales and keep a tally book as the cattle cars were being loaded in Willow Creek; Miles would watch over their shoulders, keeping his own tally book at the same time. The Weston & Shofield Meat Co. would handle business arrangements with the Union Pacific; the first cows were scheduled to leave Willow Creek in just five days.

"Can we be ready that soon?" Andy asked Miles.

"It'll be tight, but we kin do it," Miles answered, "if'n we don't run into any trouble with the Circle-K."

"It looks as if we're clearing out. O'Meara doesn't want our cattle, he wants the Little Muddy. Once he gets wind of what's going on, he'll leave us alone."

"I jest hope you're right, son."

The impending sale of the Bar-O stock was the talk of Willow Creek for the next five days. It became a common sight for folks to stand at the north end of town and watch as the dust rose in dry, gritty clouds across the Little Muddy. Not many were eager to see the Bar-O pull up stakes and clear out. The

Bar-O cowhands and the Stillman family were well liked in the valley.

On the third day, O'Meara stood at the entrance to the Blue Boar watching the activity to the northwest. He said nothing to Clevis who stood in silence beside him. O'Meara smiled as his hungry eyes traveled the length of the Little Muddy.

On the morning of the fourth day, Weston's agents arrived in town on the train; the locomotive left twenty cattle cars on the spur over by the cattle pens, ready for the next morning's shipment.

During those days there was no trouble from the Circle-K. It appeared Andy had read O'Meara right—all Will O'Meara wanted was the Little Muddy. He was happy enough just to watch the Bar-O round up its cattle and leave in peace. But it was a sad time for everyone out at the Stillman ranch. The cowhands took out their frustration by cussing the cows through their bandannas as they rounded up the herd and corralled them in the southeastern quarter of the ranch. Every day they were at it from before sunrise to past sundown. The spring roundup had taken care of most of the branding already and they branded less than forty steers in those five days. Andy rode with them and helped out all he could.

On the afternoon of the fourth day the bulk of the herd had been gathered in a large milling mass that spanned both banks of the Little Muddy. Andy reined his horse at the camp where Miles was checking figures in a tally book. "How many head do you think are still out there?" Andy asked, waving his hand toward the hills to the west and south.

Miles thought about it for several seconds. "Thirty. Mebe forty. We cain't get them all." A few hundred yards away the herd swirled, bawling, churning up pale clouds of dust.

"Okay," Andy said. "Have the boys cut out fifty head from those we've got here and turn 'em loose. Just young ones; ones that aren't worth selling."

Slim cast Andy a curious look when Miles gave him the order but he and Two-Bit spent the next two hours weeding out fifty of the younger steers, turning them loose on the range. Miles struck off fifty cows from his tally book. The next time Andy rode up, Miles showed him the figures. "Two thousand an' thirty-eight head," he said.

The next morning Miles, Andy, Two-Bit, and Paul cut out four hundred head from the main herd and drove them to the railhead where Weston's agents were waiting to weigh them and load them onto cattle cars. The locomotive had made the trip to Rock Springs the previous day and had returned with twenty more cattle cars which were on the spur behind the Blue Boar Saloon awaiting the following day's shipment.

In five days five herds were driven across the valley to the railhead. On the morning of the fifth day the last bawling herd was weighed and loaded into the cattle cars. Andy watched, exhausted, as Miles and Weston's tallyman, Douglas Levy, compared figures. When they were through, Levy signed the paper, as did Miles, and handed it to Andy.

"Comes to just under two million eight hundred and ninety thousand pounds," Levy said in a high, reedy voice. "At sixteen-eighty a thousand that's forty-eight thousand five hundred and fifty dollars. Sign here." He pointed to a line at the bottom of the paper.

"Shoulda been nearer sixty thousand," Miles grumbled.

Levy grinned at him. "You shoulda waited three months," he said cheerfully.

Andy signed the invoice and Levy took it from him. "Where do you want the money sent, Mr. Stillman?" he asked.

"Wait a few days, then deposit it in the Bar-O account at the Wells Fargo Bank in Cheyenne."

Levy's eyebrows lifted slightly. He shrugged and said, "It'll be there." He turned and walked away.

"That's it then," Andy said, relief in his voice.

"It's jest as well Henry didn't have t' see it," Miles replied.

They stopped at the Willow Creek bank and Andy withdrew a thousand dollars from the Bar-O account. Then, in silence, the men rode back to the ranch. The prairie around the ranch buildings looked strangely barren after the excitement of the past five days; the dust had settled and the moving brown mass of cattle was gone. Andy looked to the south and saw one lone brown shape standing under the willows. Just one.

It had been decided earlier that they would vacate the ranch the following morning. Amy was standing on the porch looking forlorn and uncertain as the Bar-O riders rode in. Nell was in the house preparing the final evening meal. Conversation was muted as the men put up their horses; the wind seemed loud, now, in the trees.

At the cheerless meal Andy stood up and called for everyone's attention. The men fell silent as Andy stood at the head of the table. "None of us like what's happened," Andy said, looking around the table at the cowhands. "And I'm not going to make things worse by telling you things are going to get better here at the Bar-O. But I'm not giving up, either, in spite of how it looks—"

"You ain't got no cows, Andy," Slim said, pragmatically. "Cain't ranch without no cows."

"The Bar-O is still here," Andy answered. "Only the cattle are gone. I intend to fight O'Meara, but in my own way, on my own terms." He put his hands on the table before him and looked at each man in turn. "I'm going to give each of you one hundred dollars severance pay and I'm going to ask that wherever you go you keep Miles here informed of where you are. If the Bar-O gets back on its feet again I'll let you know. You may not want to come back and that's your choice, but you're damn fine men, and if things work out I'll be glad to have you back."

"That's nearly three months' pay," Paul said.

"You earned it," Andy answered.

No one else said anything at all.

The meal ended and the men retired to the bunkhouse to gather up their belongings. After Nell and Amy cleaned up the dishes, Nell put the finishing touches on the packing that had been going on for nearly a week.

Later, Paul Armstrong approached Andy. "I can't go," he said simply.

"Because of Grace?"

Paul nodded. "She an' I—" His voice trailed off "Well, you know how it is, I reckon."

"I can't keep anyone on, Paul."

"I ain't askin' t' be kept on, Andy. Jest thought you might like t' know I'll still be around."

"Just so long as folks understand you aren't working for the Bar-O, Paul. I figure there's going to be trouble. Lots of it. I don't want you mixed up in it."

Paul looked at Andy uncomfortably. "Wisht I could help."

"I appreciate that. But what I need right now is for everyone to stay out of it—and that includes you. I don't want to sound harsh but that's the way it's got to be."

"Then that's the way I'll play it," Paul replied. "Good luck to you, Andy. Hope things work out."

Andy sighed as he watched Paul walk away. He sat on the porch staring out at the blue-black sky of early evening. A quarter moon hung over the mountains to the west. He closed his eyes wearily and a tremor shook his body. So many people's lives were being affected by his decisions. It wasn't easy to play God, he thought. Nell had said nothing about the move ever since he had told them what he intended to do. She bustled about the house, packing clothes for Kit and Amy, sometimes asking him if a certain item should stay or go. The Bar-O was her home too, hers and Miles', and he was sending them away. It was home, too, for Slim and Stringer and Two-Bit and Paul. It was the only home Kit and Amy had ever known.

What if he was wrong?

Almost overnight he had turned the Bar-O into a piece of paper that would become forty-eight thousand dollars worth of gold in the bank at Cheyenne. He had buried the gold.

Now he would have to fight the Indians.

Amy came outside and sat down beside him. She sat close and leaned against him, hugging his arm, staring into the darkness with frightened eyes. "I don't know anyone in Cheyenne," she said, her voice small in the night.

What if he was wrong?

"Kit will be there," he said. "And Nell and Miles."

"I don't want t' go," she whispered in a trembly voice.

"I know, button. I sure do know."

• • •

They gathered at the station the next morning and I watched as Andy saw them off. Two-Bit left straight from the ranch and headed north toward Montana; Slim rode south to Rock Springs. Stringer was at the station, carrying his saddle, and I sold him a ticket to Salt Lake City. Everyone else bought tickets to Cheyenne.

The engine turned around on the side track in the freight yard behind the Blue Boar. Steam belched from its valves, swirling around its driving wheels.

Andy shook hands with Kit. "You take care of Amy, Kit. She's going to need you."

"We ain't comin' back, are we, Andy?"

"You are if I can work things out."

Kit's eyes glistened and he turned away.

Then Amy was in Andy's arms, her doll tucked carefully in the crook of an arm as she hugged him. "I still don't want t' go," she said in his ear, her voice bubbly with tears.

"Just for a while, button."

"Then make us come back soon, Andy." She hugged his neck fiercely then let him go.

Kit helped her onto the train. Nell said her good-byes and followed them. Miles held out his hand and Andy shook it.

"You ain't said what you're plannin' t' do," Miles said. "Been pretty closed-mouthed the past few days. But I reckon I kin guess at what you've got in mind an' I don't like none of it. What you're thinkin' is dangerous as hell an' only a complete damn fool would try it."

"Take care of them, Miles."

Miles stared stiffly at the western hills, closing and unclosing his big, work-hardened hands.

"When you get to Cheyenne open an account for the Bar-O, Miles. Hold the money for Kit and Amy. If anything happens to me, promise me you'll raise them proper."

Miles stared at Andy and blinked hard. When he answered his voice was husky. "We'll do 'er, Nell and me, if that's what you want."

Andy nodded. "Check the telegraph office in Cheyenne at least once a day, Miles. I'll be in touch."

"You ain't got t' do this, Andy. You kin come with us."

"No," Andy said. "No, I can't." He stared at the empty cattle pens, his eyes distant, unfocused, and sad. "Look after them, Miles."

"All aboard," I called, hating to interrupt them.

Miles stepped up into the coach and seconds later the train started forward. Amy pressed her nose against the glass as the train pulled away from the station. She waved without enthusiasm and I could see tears pouring down the sides of her face. Andy waved back until they couldn't see him any longer, then he stood on the platform watching the train for nearly five more minutes until it was completely out of sight.

14

Andy walked over to where I was sitting behind the ticket counter. He set five dollars on the counter top and I looked up at him, wondering what it was for.

"Keep it, Tom," he said. "If anything happens to me I want you to send a message to Miles Harding in Cheyenne."

I stared at the coin, feeling uncomfortable. I reckoned Miles had been right; Andy should've gone with them. "What would you want it to say?" I asked uneasily.

"If anything happens to me I want to be sure Miles hears of it. Just a short message telling him what happened."

"I'll do it, Andy," I said. He turned to go. "You be careful," I added, not knowing what else to say.

"Thanks, Tom."

• • •

Andy left the station and walked up Water Street to Wilton Butterfield's Gazette and Printing Co. He pushed open the door and found Wilton patiently setting type for the next edition which would come out in two days. Wilton was a tall, lean man of thirty with a dry sense of humor, already thinning on top, who wore a pair of fragile spectacles set into round, wire frames. He turned when Andy walked in the room. "Well, good morning, Andy," he said. "I was just setting type for the story about the Bar-O pulling out." He looked at Andy over the top of his spectacles. "You got something to add?"

"For the sake of accuracy you might want to mention that the Bar-O isn't selling out, isn't moving, and isn't giving up any of its holdings or any of its water rights to the Little Muddy."

Wilton stared at Andy for several seconds then he shook his head in anguish. "You mean all the work I've done this morning has been wasted effort?"

"Depends on what you've written, Wilt."

"The Bar-O isn't leaving?"

Andy pulled a piece of paper from his pocket, something he had written the night before. "This tells the story as well as anything else," he said. "I'd like twenty poster-sized copies made up as soon as possible."

Wilton took the paper from Andy and read it. "So you're staying," he said—a bit rhetorically after reading what Andy had written.

Andy nodded. "How long will it take?"

Wilton scanned the paper with a practiced eye. "Two, maybe three hours. Printed, and the ink dry."

"I'll be back for them this afternoon, Wilt."

"You sure this is wise, Andy?" Wilton asked. "I'm glad you're staying, but this is sure to cause trouble."

"I've already got trouble," Andy replied. "I'll be back later for the posters." He left the shop. At the corner he glanced to his left and saw William O'Meara standing in front of the Overland Hotel. Andy crossed Main Street, feeling O'Meara's eyes on him, and went into Peliter & Owens Hardware Store.

"Morning, Jack," Andy said. "Have you got axe handles in stock?"

Jack Peliter looked up at Andy, surprised. "Thought you were gone, Andy." Outside, boots scraped on the boardwalk.

"Nope. Still here. Pretty hard to figure where rumors get started sometimes."

O'Meara stood at the door, scowling. "What d'you mean, rumors?" he asked angrily.

"Why, hello, Will," Andy said pleasantly. "You know how rumors are—once they get started there's no stopping them."

"You sold out, dammit!"

"Don't know what gave you that idea, Will. I just sold off some of my stock, that's all." He turned to Jack Peliter. "You have that axe handle, Jack?"

Jack started. "Oh. Yeah, Andy. Sure." Reluctantly, he headed toward the back of the store.

"What is this?" O'Meara thundered. "Some kind of trick?"

"Not at all. I need a new axe handle."

"That's not what I mean an' you know it, goddamn it! The Bar-O's pulled up stakes—sold out. You're finished!"

Andy turned to O'Meara with eyes as cold and hard as winter glass. "As you know, Will, I was having a lot of trouble with a bunch of cowardly vandals. So I sold my stock to reduce my losses and sent everyone away so no one else would get hurt. But the Bar-O isn't going anywhere, Will. I mean to fight those vandals. Like I told you out at your place, I intend to drive them right out of the territory."

"You're crazy!"

"Maybe," Andy said. "Maybe not."

Jack Peliter came back with an axe handle and set it on the counter. "That'll be forty-five cents, Andy," he said nervously.

O'Meara turned on Jack furiously. "You'll sell nothin' t' the Bar-O."

"B-But—"

"But nothin'," O'Meara thundered. "Not an axe handle, not a roll of wire, not so much as a goddamned nail or a scrap of tin, or the Circle-K takes its business to Rock Springs!"

Jack Peliter paled. He stared at Andy, his face drawn.

"No problem, Jack," Andy said. "Reckon I can do without for a while."

"You've got no stock!" O'Meara bellowed, fury shaking his voice.

"I've got nearly a hundred head left," Andy said. "The Little Muddy belongs to the Bar-O. Keep the hell off my land, Will. Fight me and it'll be something you'll regret for the rest of your sorry life." He pushed past O'Meara and left the store.

Andy crossed the street in front of the Sheriff's Office and headed in the direction of the Blue Boar. With long, purposeful strides he walked past the decrepit front of the Wind River Hotel. Kid Reese was leaning against a post just outside the Blue Boar, staring out at the street. He looked up nervously as Andy approached.

When he was just three feet from Kid Reese, Andy stopped. "Heard you beat up my kid brother," he said.

Kid Reese paled; before he could react Andy's hand shot out and slapped him, hard, spinning him halfway around. Kid Reese drew his gun, turned, and Andy's fist exploded in his face. The gun flew from Kid Reese's hand and he sprawled on his back into the street.

"You're a big man with your fists," Andy said coldly. "You proved it once by beating up a fourteen-year-old kid. Now you're going to get the chance to prove it again."

Kid Reese stood up and looked around furtively. His gun was lying ten feet away in the dust. Several people had paused in the street and were watching, Ira Goldman and Myra Nickolson in front of Goldman's General Store, and Len Peliter over by the livery. Kid Reese licked his lips and glanced toward the Blue Boar. Snake stood in the doorway; he nodded imperceptibly in the direction of the people across the street and shrugged at Kid Reese. Snake wasn't about to pull his gun on an unarmed man with witnesses around.

Kid Reese took a sideways step toward his gun. He licked his lips again. "Must be some mistake," he said.

"No mistake," Andy replied. "And if you reach for that gun I'll break your back."

"That was *your* brother? Hell, I didn't mean no harm. I was jest funnin' and things sorta got outta hand." Kid Reese took another half-step toward his gun.

Andy stepped off the boardwalk, closing the distance between them. "Too bad," he said. "Too bad things got out of hand."

Kid Reese leaped for his gun and Andy sprang forward. Suddenly Kid Reese twisted—his hand slipped to his boot and he whipped out a knife, raking the blade across Andy's ribs in a short, vicious arc, then he held the knife in front of him. "All right, tenderfoot," he said savagely. "You want a fight, I'll give you a fight!"

He lashed out with the knife and Andy jumped back. Blood flowed from a cut on his ribs, visible through a ragged hole in his shirt. He circled warily, watching Kid Reese's eyes, vaguely aware that Mrya Nickolson was calling for the sheriff in a high, almost hysterical voice. Kid Reese moved in, ripping upward with the long blade in a quick, sinuous movement. Andy dodged and circled, his eyes flicking down toward the ground. He backed toward the boardwalk, reached down suddenly, and picked up a stick. It was a slender twig, twenty inches long, as thick as a man's little finger. Kid Reese looked at the stick and the corners of his mouth lifted in an evil smile as he moved in again.

Andy held the branch in front of him, pointed directly at Kid Reese's eyes. Kid Reese's grin faded. He circled but the stick followed him, too close to his eyes for him to close with the knife like he wanted. He slashed at Andy's hand instead. Andy jerked his hand back and the blade of the knife skinned a piece of bark from the stick. Andy circled. Kid Reese crouched, sweeping the air in front of him wickedly with the razorlike blade as Andy held the stick firmly, still pointed directly at Kid Reese's eyes. Suddenly Kid Reese closed again, slashing at Andy's hand. Andy pulled his hand back, twisted sideways, and swung a quick left to the side of Kid Reese's face. Kid Reese staggered then caught his footing. He touched the side of his face where Andy had hit him.

Andy laughed, goading him. "I was hoping I'd get to see you use your fists, Reese," he said. "I should have known a yellow-belly who fights children wouldn't fight a man with his fists."

Kid Reese's face clouded with fury. He charged Andy, swinging the blade in front of him. Andy lunged to the side and dropped to the ground, kicking the side of Kid Reese's left knee just below the kneecap with all his strength. Something in the gunman's leg snapped with a crack that was heard all the way across the street. Kid Reese screamed, dropped the knife, and toppled to the ground, writhing in agony.

Andy looked up at the saloon; Snake was nowhere in sight. In the street Kid Reese groaned, a low, anguished sound. Andy stared at the man for a long moment, his face impassive, his fists still clenched, then he turned and walked away.

At the corner he was met by the sheriff who was followed closely by Myra Nickolson. Heede glanced past Andy at Kid Reese. "What's the trouble here?" he demanded, out of breath already, eighty yards from his office.

"No trouble, John. Reese pulled a knife on me but then he thought better of it. Reckon I won't press charges."

Heede's brow knotted. He hurried up the street toward the stricken man.

"Thanks, Myra," Andy said.

Myra Nickolson stared at Andy with a frightened look on

her face. "You aren't hurt bad, are you, Andy?"

"No. Not bad." He thanked her again and left. A sharp, burning pain seared his ribs as he walked down the street. He lifted his shirt and glanced at the cut the knife had made along his ribs. Luckily, Andy had leapt pretty much out of Reese's reach as the blade went by; the cut was shallow, more annoying than dangerous. Already it had quit bleeding. Andy continued up Main Street to the blacksmith shop.

Bear was out front, as usual. He looked up as Andy approached. His eyes narrowed when he saw the blood on Andy's shirt. "That as bad as it looks?"

"Just a scratch."

"It appears someone ought t' lock you up for your own good, Andy. What happened?"

Andy explained. Bear shook his head. "Figgered you for more sense than that, son."

Andy gave him a half-hearted smile. "I didn't know he had a knife."

Bear set a heavy gate hinge on the anvil—one end of the hinge still glowing dully. "C'mon in the house," he said. "Let's let Abby have a look at that cut."

"How's Clair?"

"Still mad. But worried."

"Worried?"

"She's been watchin' the Bar-O sell off its stock. She ain't said much, but there's been a bad light in her eyes for days now, especially when anyone says anythin' about the Bar-O leavin'."

"Now why do you reckon she'd care?"

Bear grinned. "She's a mighty fine girl, Andy."

They went through the house into the kitchen. Abigail gasped when she saw the blood on Andy's side. "I'm not even going to ask how you got that," she said, lips pursed. "Just take off that shirt and let me see how bad it is."

The cut burned as Andy unbuttoned the shirt and pulled it off, muscles rippling with the movement. Abigail stared at him, nonplussed. She and Clair had left the picnic before Andy's fight with Jason so Abigail hadn't seen Andy with his shirt off before. She shot Bear a startled glance.

"Told you," Bear said, smiling. "Andy's been exercisin' some."

The kitchen door creaked open and Clair backed in, carrying a basket. She turned and saw Andy, her eyes widening as she saw the lean muscle that covered his chest and shoulders. Then she saw the red slash across his ribs. "Oh, Andy," she cried, dropping the basket. "You're—" She stared at him, perplexed and uncertain, vacillating between sudden concern and old anger. Finally, in a low voice, she said, "Reckon you got that by bein' foolish," and she whisked out of the room.

Andy looked up at Bear. "Pretty soon I'm going to get fed up with all this nonsense, Bear."

Bear grinned. "Ain't none of my affair."

The cut on Andy's ribs proved to be superficial. As Andy put on his shirt he thanked Abigail for looking after him and the two men went back outside. Andy turned to Bear. "I've heard Reb Cotton and his men sometimes hang out at the Lucky Lady, that right"? The Lucky Lady Saloon was on the other side of Main Street from the blacksmith shop, three doors down.

"Several days a week," Bear replied. "Hope you ain't got no big ideas about messin' around with that bunch, Andy. They ain't nobody t' be foolin' with."

Andy shrugged. "I need an axe handle," he said. He pulled some money from his pocket and handed it to Bear. "Maybe you could buy me one at the hardware store." He pointed to an unused corner of the shop. "I'll pick it up over there sometime later, maybe tonight."

"Sure, Andy. But if'n you don't mind my askin'—"

"O'Meara threatened Jack Peliter this morning," Andy said, anticipating Bear's question. He told Bear what had happened earlier in the hardware store.

"O'Meara," Bear said slowly. "The man can be a bastard when he wants to. But I know how it is. If the Circle-K quit comin' t' me, I'd be hard pressed too."

Andy stayed at the blacksmith shop for the next three hours, talking quietly with Bear, watching the big man form horseshoes, mend branding irons, and perform other miscellaneous tasks. He quizzed Bear about the capabilities of the little shop and looked through a rusting collection of scrap iron with unusual interest. Once he looked toward the house and caught a glimpse of Clair peering at him through a window. He smiled at her and she pulled back with a jerk, obviously annoyed that she'd been caught looking at him.

Early that afternoon Andy went back to Wilton Butterfield's Gazette. Wilton was setting type when Andy walked in, continuing his work on the next edition. "Are my posters ready?" Andy asked.

"Right there on the counter, Andy. If you like 'em, leave a dollar."

Andy examined them briefly then set a dollar on the counter. "They look fine, Wilton. Mind if I put one in your window?"

"Go right ahead, Andy. I never print anything I'm ashamed of."

Andy set one in the window of the Wind River Gazette then went across the street and put one in the window of the Miner's Cafe. He nailed several to the trees that lined Main Street, put one in the train station, one in the Overland Hotel, at Booth's Mercantile, at the Bank, at Ralph Kinsey's Boarding House, at the livery stable, and gave one to Sheriff Heede. He was making sure everyone knew what position the Bar-O was taking, and as he walked around town putting up his posters people watched him, talking quietly, sometimes pointing in his direction.

Near the Miner's Cafe he ran into Doc Simes. "That boy's never going to be quite right again, Andy," Doc said.

"Who's that?"

"Kid Reese. He'll never walk right again. Probably have to use a cane the rest of his life. That was an ugly break. Worst I've ever seen. It just about shattered the socket."

"Too bad he pulled a knife."

Doc Simes nodded in agreement. "Yes. Too bad."

It was late afternoon when Andy went to the livery and hitched up the buckboard that had been used to bring the family into town that morning. He watched the prairie warily as he drove back to the Bar-O with Pete trailing behind, reins tied to the back of the buckboard. At the fence he put up another poster then continued on to the ranch house. He circled the wagon in the emptiness of the yard in front of the house, stepped to the porch, and put up the final poster, nailing it right to the front door of the house. He took a step back to admire his work.

"What do you think, Pete?" he asked the horse. Pete

flicked his ears indifferently. The poster looked out of place on the door. The words were printed in heavy inch-high black letters:

PUBLIC NOTICE

Be it hereby known that the Bar-O
Ranch has relinquished none of its
holdings, its land, or its control and
ownership of Little Muddy Creek.
Fence cutting, stock shooting, and
any other acts of vandalism will be
dealt with severely.
by owner: Andrew Stillman

•   •   •

The sun slid behind the mountains and the ranch lay quiet in the cool shadows of early evening. The air was still. The windmill sat unmoving, a dark, spindly shadow against the sky. No cattle lowed in the distance, no men swore down at the corrals, no sounds came from the house. The stillness was deathlike. The very heart of the ranch had moved to Cheyenne.

Andy took stock of his situation. Everyone was gone except for himself; there were almost no cattle left; O'Meara was livid with anger and he wanted the Little Muddy. Shooting the remaining stock would be pointless now; even cutting fences would serve no purpose if the main objective was to get Andy off his land. Now O'Meara would be forced to shift his attack to all that remained of the ranch; to the ranch house and to Andy himself.

Andy sat on a chair on the front porch looking out over the valley. The house had been built on the mild slope of the prairie, in the lee of the western mountains, some two hundred feet above the floor of the valley. From the porch Andy could see the buildings of Willow Creek across the valley, and beyond that to the wooded slopes of Crooked Neck Ridge. When trouble came it would be from that direction, beyond the southern edge of the ridge where the Circle-K lay hidden. Andy didn't know when the trouble would come, but he figured it would be soon; O'Meara had always been a bull-headed, impatient man. He might even come tonight.

Overhead the quarter-moon brightened as the sky grew dark. Stars appeared and the prairie was bathed in pale moonlight. Andy listened to the quiet for nearly an hour, then he went into the house, collected a bedroll, his moccasins, and a rifle. He went outside and set out the bedroll under some brush near the aspens that framed Miles' and Nell's cabin. He cleared the leaves from the ground before he set out the blankets so there would be no noise if he had to get up during the night. Then he grabbed an edge of the blanket and rolled, keeping the Winchester with him. From where he lay, he had an unobstructed view of the yard, the pond, the bunkhouse, the corrals, and the front of the main house.

The night air turned cool. He looked up and saw a shooting star through the leaves of a tree. From far away a coyote called. Then he was asleep.

• • •

They came when the sliver of moon had just slid behind the western peaks. They made little noise but the night was quiet and Andy awoke, aware of a subtle change in the sounds of the prairie. He listened; a faint clink of metal on metal sounded in the distance.

Andy unrolled slowly from the blankets. He pulled on his moccasins, crept behind the trunk of a tree, and stood in the darkness, watching. Three men appeared in the yard, shadowy figures walking cautiously toward the ranch house, guns glinting in the darkness. One of them was carrying something heavy. From the direction in which they had come Andy heard the sound of a horse blowing softly.

The men went by, not forty feet away, and Andy stood in utter stillness like a part of the night. The men spoke in low whispers as they moved past the pond, an inky pool in the yard. Andy moved stealthily through the cover of the trees and crossed the yard to the side of the pond. Crouching down, he set the Winchester on the grass beside him, scooped up some mud and began smearing it over his face. As he did, he watched the dim figures in the yard in front of the house. They stood in a small knot, talking.

Andy crept back into the shadows and circled the far side of the pond. He went behind the bunkhouse, walked quickly to the far end, and peered around the edge of the building. One of the men walked around the ranch house toward the back yard as another knelt by the hitching rail working with something on the ground. The third walked back toward Miles' and Nell's cabin.

The yard was engulfed in charcoal shadows. The man in the yard stood up and carried whatever he had been working on up to the porch. Andy crept around the end of the bunkhouse and crossed the yard, moving quickly toward the figure on the porch. The man was barely visible in the darkness but Andy could hear the sound of liquid sloshing, then the man backed down the stairs, pouring something from a can. Andy was about fifteen feet from him when the man looked up. Andy made no attempt to conceal himself, but he held his gun ready. The gloom prevented either man from recognizing the other. Andy was walking from the direction of Miles' house. In the darkness the man mistook him for a friend.

"You finished already?" It was Aaron O'Meara.

Andy grunted, disguising his voice. "Uh-huh."

"See anyone?"

"Uh-uh."

The smell of kerosene hung in the air. Aaron turned, searching his pockets. He found what he was looking for and seconds later a match flared brilliantly in the darkness. Aaron's back was turned toward Andy; the flickering light silhouetting his body. Aaron tossed the match into the dark line of kerosene in the dust and flames erupted from the ground, licking toward the porch. Andy took a step closer and swung the stock of the Winchester against the back of Aaron's head; it landed with an ugly crack and Aaron pitched forward heavily on his face.

The flames had almost reached the porch when Andy kicked the kerosene-soaked dust away from the foot of the stairs. He kicked more dirt on the flames burning in the yard. The fire went out quickly and again the night was engulfed in shadows. Andy went back to where Aaron was lying in the dirt. A sticky matt of blood covered the back of Aaron's head where Andy had hit him.

Soft sounds came from the side of the house and Andy pulled back into the shadows. A dark figure walked into view. "I'm ready back there," Tripp hissed. "Aaron? Goddamn it! What're you doin'?" He bent over the body then looked up suddenly.

Andy levered a round into the Winchester. "Move and you're dead," he said.

Tripp froze.

"I know what you're thinking, Tripp," Andy said, his voice low. "I hope you try it."

Tripp crouched over Aaron. "Man don't shoot so good at night, boy. You'd never get two chances with that rifle."

"Maybe you'd like to see how well I do with one shot?"

There was a moment of silence then Andy heard Tripp's low chuckle. "Guess not. Even a tenderfoot can get lucky. Reckon I'll just get this feller back on his horse." Tripp crouched, levering Aaron onto his shoulders, then he turned and faced Andy in the darkness. "This ain't over yet," he said in a strangely quiet voice. "Ain't over by a long way." Then he left.

Soon Andy heard voices over by Miles' house, then the sound of footsteps fading into the distance. Several minutes later horses galloped away into the night. In time, the quiet of the prairie settled once again over the Stillman ranch.

15

From the narrow alley between Myra Nickolson's Bakery and the hardware store Andy listened to the muted strains of piano music riding the cool night air. The moon had set some minutes earlier, leaving the town in darkness; the only light now came from a fading glow on the western horizon and the pale yellow squares of light that reached the street from the Lucky Lady Saloon. A number of horses shuffled quietly at the hitching post in front of the tavern. Crickets chirred in the night's stillness. Except for the activity at the Lucky Lady, the town appeared asleep.

The previous night, Tripp and the others had tried to burn

down the Bar-O ranch house. After waking that morning, Andy had spent the day at the Looking Rock, gazing over the valley. Later that morning he saw two men leaving Willow Creek riding south toward the Circle-K, black specks in the distance. Later, one man returned: Doc Simes, who remained close-mouthed about what he had done, although in the days that followed it became generally known that he had treated Aaron's head and that it had taken fourteen stitches to close his scalp. When the sun set, Andy climbed down from the Looking Rock and rode to town, keeping off the main trails. He left Pete picketed to a branch under cover of the aspens behind Bear Buchanan's corral. In the blacksmith shop he found the axe handle just where he'd asked Bear to leave it.

Now, under cover of darkness, Andy held the axe handle in one hand, tapping it absently against a moccasined heel as he peered intently at the front of the saloon. Except for the horses, the street was empty; the music continued, punctuated by the sound of rough laughter. Andy stepped out of the alley and crossed the street to the opposite boardwalk. Through the windows of the saloon he saw Reb Cotton sitting at a table against one wall, accompanied by Stark and Dutch. Reno and Gage stood at the bar and Jackson was at a table near the front door, talking in low, earnest tones with Sue. As Andy watched the men a rush of anger went through him. Stock shooting and fence cutting was too much like work. It wasn't Tripp's style, or Aaron's, Kid Reese's, or Snake's. Especially Snake. Andy had little doubt that Reb Cotton and his gang were responsible for the night raids on the Bar-O. And Rolly's death. O'Meara had ordered it; Reb Cotton and his men had carried out those orders.

It was time to get rid of Reb Cotton.

There was a chance, however slight, that after Reb Cotton and his men were out of action O'Meara would change his mind about fighting the Bar-O—a slim chance, but a chance all the same, and it was this slender hope that prevented Andy from proceeding immediately with his original plan of dynamiting the Upper Badger Reservoir. The loss of the reservoir would ruin the Circle-K; certainly it would break O'Meara's power in the valley. However it would also be a hardship on the town of Willow Creek. In one way or another, the money brought into the community by the Circle-K ranch helped just about everyone in town. Andy didn't want to destroy the reservoir without giving O'Meara every possible chance to make peace in the valley.

Fighting Reb Cotton, Andy told himself, was just another way of fighting O'Meara, a lesser step than dynamiting the reservoir, yet part of him reluctantly admitted the truth: Reb Cotton and his men had killed Rolly. Now, just as Kid Reese had paid for what he'd done to Kit, Reb Cotton and his men would pay for what they'd done to Rolly.

Cautiously, Andy eased down the boardwalk, down the alley to the area behind the saloon where he scouted the terrain, noting the location of boxes, barrels, and packing crates which were stacked in disarray, getting the feel of the path that wound among them. On a large wooden box near the rear door of the saloon he left the axe handle where he could locate it swiftly in the darkness.

Pausing at the front of the saloon, Andy took a deep breath then pushed open the bat-wing doors and went in. A chair banged against the floor as one of Reb Cotton's men saw Andy and leaned forward suddenly. A number of townspeople and several men from one of the northern ranches were in the room along with a sharp-eyed faro dealer and a man running the roulette wheel. The ever-vigilant owner, Truman Carlos, turned and looked at Andy. Reb Cotton was at the same table as before, talking with Dutch, but Stark had moved and was now sitting at a table by the back entrance with the dark-haired, dark-eyed Crystal Lee. Against the far wall a man in a brightly-colored shirt played a piano, not well, but engrossed in his work, hunched over the keys. When Andy entered the room the conversation tailed off but the piano player played on, not yet aware of the change in the atmosphere that had come over the place.

After a quick glance around the room Andy strolled over to the long, wooden bar, as close to the rear of the saloon as he could get, and stood next to Gage. Reb Cotton's eyes narrowed. Andy slapped five dollars on the bar and said, "Gimme a beer, Red."

Red Dufresne shot Andy a warning glance. "You sure?" he asked in a careful, neutral tone.

"I'm sure, Red," Andy answered, loud enough that

everyone could hear. "Protecting my property against cowardly, night-riding scum is hard work. I've found it dries a man out somethin' awful."

The piano player quit abruptly and turned around. The room was silent except for a series of high-pitched giggles from Sue and Jackson's low voice telling her to shut the hell up. Andy stood with his back to the bar looking in Reb Cotton's direction, aware of Gage, not three feet away, who was peering at him with an ugly expression on his face. On the other side of Gage, Reno set his mug carefully on the bar, the beginnings of a smile playing across his face.

Reb Cotton pulled out papers and a pouch of tobacco from his vest pocket and began to roll a cigarette. He shot a quick look at Jackson who quickly dispatched Sue and took up a position by the front door. Reb Cotton smiled. "You're Andrew Stillman," he said languorously. "Bar-O. Ain't that right?"

"Yep," Andy replied. "Heard about you and your men. I sure could have used your help recently."

"That right?"

"Uh-huh. Maybe you've heard about the trouble I've been having, cowardly bastards shootin' my stock, cutting fences. Why, I'll bet if I'd hired you to protect my ranch, none of that ever would have happened."

Reb Cotton sucked in his breath. The room was suddenly electric with tension. Several feet from Andy, Gage trembled.

"Yep," Andy pressed. "I reckon if I'd hired you and your men, the fear it would've put into those hydrophobic sons of bitches would've kept them away, even if I'd sent you and your men all the way to Tucson. As proof of that, the Circle-K hasn't had any trouble with those worm-ridden, yellow-bellied—"

Gage filled to the breaking point and exploded. "Goddamn it!" he roared, swinging a bottle at the side of Andy's head. "Enough!"

Andy, who'd been watching Gage more closely than the others, spun, ducked, and landed a powerful right to Gage's face. The burly man flew backwards into Reno, knocking both men to the floor. Andy whirled and leaped toward the back entrance. Stark was just getting up from his chair, just starting to pull his gun, when Andy kicked him in the chest as he went by. Stark pinwheeled across the table and sprawled in a heap against the piano.

Then Andy was through the door and out of the building. Although the dark of the alley was almost impenetrable after the brightness inside the Lucky Lady, Andy found the axe handle and managed to traverse the broken path through the litter quickly. Moments later a man burst out the back door. Andy picked up an empty crate and threw it in the direction of the rear entrance.

A man yelped in pain, then yelled, "Goddamnit!"

Scraping noises were followed by a crash and muttered curses as a stack of boxes fell over. Andy heard someone struggling through the debris toward him, and he swung the axe handle blindly, chest high, with all the force he could put into it. The handle struck something soft, a man screamed in pain, and a gun went off, pointed at the ground. Something crashed heavily into the litter at the side of the building.

The darkness filled with men's curses.

Another shot rang out. Andy crouched and ran toward the back of the Overland Hotel. As he crossed the alley between the saloon and the hotel, another man turned the corner at the front of the saloon and walked rapidly down the alley in his direction, carrying a gun, backlighted by the pale light in the street cast through the windows of the Lucky Lady. Andy pressed himself into the shadows at the corner of the hotel, watching the approaching form, listening to the confused sounds of the men in back of the saloon. His eyes hadn't yet adjusted to the darkness, which meant Reb and the others were also still night blind. The man reached the end of the alley. "That you, Reb?" he called out. It was Jackson. "Where are you?"

"Over here," Reb Cotton's voice came out of the darkness. "Got Dutch with me. Reno's hurt pretty bad. You seen 'em?"

"No, I—"

The axe handle landed with sickening force between Jackson's shoulder blades. He pitched forward on his face without making a sound. Andy sprinted up the alley toward the street. Behind him he heard Dutch call out in a strangled voice, "Sonofabitch, Reb!" Then a shot rang out and a bullet whined past Andy's ear. He dodged sideways, crouched, and ran around the edge of the saloon. He checked the street, saw no one, and sprinted diagonally across to the narrow alley between the bakery and the hardware store.

From the corner of Myra Nickolson's Bakery Andy watched as Dutch ran out of the alley, Reb right behind him. Both men looked uncertainly down the length of Main Street. Just then, Gage pushed through the doors at the front of the saloon and stood unsteadily on the boardwalk, holding his jaw. "Where is he?" he asked Reb and Dutch.

"Didn't see him after he ran out the alley here," Reb said. "He got Reno and Jackson out back. How's Stark?"

Gage glanced back into the saloon. "He's comin'. Jest had the wind knocked out of him is all."

Soon Stark came out of the saloon and the four men held a brief conference in the middle of the street, staring into the blackness around them. "Looks like the sonofabitch has got hisself a club of some sort," Reb said. "Bastard knows how t' use it too."

"Want us t' spread out an' look for him, Reb?" Gage asked.

"We do that an' he'll pick us off one by one. Let's stay in twos—me an' Dutch an' you an' Stark. But find him, goddamnit! I want his hide nailed t' the bunkhouse wall!"

Andy watched Reb and Dutch jog south toward Booth's Mercantile; Stark and Gage went north. Andy went through the alley and into the cluttered yard behind the hardware store. His night vision had almost fully returned by now. In the gloom he found a ladder by the back wall of the store. Near the ladder he located an old nail keg that weighed about six pounds, partly full of rusty nails. With a tight, grim smile he placed the ladder against the wall of the hardware store and went up, holding both the keg and the axe handle. He scrambled onto the roof. Once he cleared the low parapet he pulled the ladder up silently behind him.

The night was still. Andy kneeled on the roof, watching the ground below, listening. Across a broad, tree-shaded yard to the northwest, lights shone from several windows in Kinsey's Boarding House. Beside him lay the keg and the axe handle.

A board scraped then fell with a clatter in the alley between the hardware store and the bank. Something rang with a dull, metallic sound. A man cursed in a tired, angry voice. Andy positioned himself by the parapet, crouching low to avoid silhouetting himself against the starry sky. Whispered voices came from somewhere below. In the yard, two slow-moving figures appeared. They stopped, glanced about uncertainly, then began threading their way through a narrow path between the rear wall and a jumbled stack of packing crates behind the hardware store. Andy recognized Gage and Stark. Dim light reflected off their guns.

Stark was in the lead. He passed beneath Andy. When Gage was directly below, Andy released the keg over his head. His aim was true, the keg landed with a horrid thud on Gage's head, the old wood shattering. Gage crumpled backwards to the ground.

"Sonofabitch!" Stark yelled, his voice pitched high with fright.

Andy grabbed the axe handle and hurried to the north side of the hardware store, hung from the roof and dropped into the alley beside the bank. He pressed himself against the side of the building and listened.

"Over here! On the roof of the Hardware!" Stark shouted. Scrabbling footsteps sounded behind the store and Stark came into the alley, walking quickly, staring up at the roof of the hardware store with his gun aimed at the sky. "Goddamn," he muttered. "Goddamn, goddamn."

Andy swung the axe handle into the pit of Stark's heavy belly. Stark's gun went off, echoing through the town. He dropped the gun, doubled over, staggered backward, eyes wide, and Andy caught him full in the face with a roundhouse that sprawled him in the dust, unconscious.

Behind the hardware store, Andy checked Gage. He was out cold and blood was oozing from a huge welt on the top of his head where the keg had hit him. Andy grabbed him by the collar and dragged him around the building to the alley where Stark lay breathing raggedly, a trickle of blood draining darkly from his nose. Andy collected their guns, looked around quickly, and tossed them to the roof of the bank. He stretched Stark and Gage out, side by side, and covered them both with a piece of moldering canvas.

At the entrance to the alley, Andy searched the length of Main Street, checking for movement in the shadows on the opposite side until he was sure it was safe, then he darted across the street and passed through the alley between the Sheriff's Office and the Miner's Cafe. He crept behind the buildings until he was again at the back entrance of the Lucky Lady. A man was standing in the shadows, one arm pressing against the side of the building, the other dangling limply at his side. From his silhouette Andy recognized Reno. Reno was staring at the limp form of Jackson still lying in the alley between the saloon and the hotel.

Andy stole up silently behind the man. "You boys oughta quit while you're still standing," he said.

Reno whirled. His good hand dropped like lightning for the gun at his side, and Andy swung the axe handle once again, cracking Reno on the side of the head. Reno fell heavily to the ground and was still. "Told you," Andy said woodenly, remembering how Rolly had looked that dismal morning when Miles had found him in the field. He took both Reno's and Jackson's guns and tossed them to the roof of Booth's Mercantile.

Many of Willow Creek's citizens awoke when the first shots were fired behind the Lucky Lady that night, listening uneasily to the sharp sounds. Some displayed brief curiosity then withdrew, pulling their shades against the night. As the minutes dragged by, the town settled into an uneasy, listening quiet. Sheriff Heede kept out of it. As time passed most of the townspeople assumed the trouble, whatever it had been, was over. They didn't know what had happened and, like Heede, were content to leave well enough alone and ask questions in the morning.

But for three people the trouble wasn't over yet. For the next thirty minutes Andy hunted for Reb Cotton and Dutch, finally locating them behind Doc Simes' place where they were searching the yard. At one point they passed within twenty feet of Andy, crouched in the soft, black earth of Elizabeth Simes' garden, hidden by pole beans.

"Let's go on back, Reb," Dutch said.

"Go if you want," Reb replied angrily.

"Aw, Reb. It's jest . . . this ain't no good, out here. But I ain't goin' t' leave you out here by yourself."

"Then shut up, Dutch."

"Hell, Reb. Mebe he's gone. I ain't heard nothin' in

better'n half an hour."

Reb looked up. "That's true," he said thoughtfully. "Reckon we ought t' go find the others."

The two men walked through the alley between Doc Simes' office and the Miners Cafe, turned, and went up Water Street to the corner where they stood staring up and down the length of Main Street. Andy crept out of the garden and went up the same alley. The men were still standing on the corner with their backs to Andy; faint, black figures against the darkness that had grown ever deeper as the moon retreated farther behind the hills. Andy peered across Water Street; twenty yards away a dim alley opened between the Wind River Hotel and Wilton Butterfield's Gazette.

He took one last look at the men on the corner then sprinted across the street, intentionally luring the two men toward the alley and into the broken fields that lay behind the Union Pacific loading docks.

"There he goes!" Dutch cried. A shot rang out just as Andy reached the alley, the bullet shattering a window of the printing shop.

Another shot boomed in the darkness. The slug thudded into the wall beside Andy, tearing out splinters of wood and leaving no doubt at all about the murderous intentions of the two men. Andy raced out the back of the alley and into the blackness behind the hotel and the Blue Boar, passing a water birch with a thick, gnarled trunk, leaves silhouetted darkly against the sky, then he picked his way through a field of short, dry grass littered with packing crates, broken barrels, stacks of lumber, and weathered storage sheds near the loading docks by a side track. In the distance a boxcar sat opposite a wooden loading ramp.

Reb and Dutch sprinted into the clearing behind the hotel and the saloon and stopped, guns drawn.

"You seen him?" Dutch asked hoarsely.

"No," Reb Cotton hissed. "An' keep your mouth shut an' your ears open, goddammit!"

They searched the yard slowly, peering cautiously into the shadows behind the printing shop and the hotel. Several minutes went by before they passed the Blue Boar and began to search the field behind the loading dock. Dry, brittle grass crackled under their boots.

Hiding behind a small storage shed, Andy listened to the sounds. He tightened his grip on the axe handle.

Somewhere, far away, a dog barked.

The men approached on the west side of the shed. Andy waited, the axe handle held motionless over his head at the top of its swing. The men were twenty feet away.

Fifteen.

"I don't much like this."

"Shut up, Dutch."

A gun appeared around the corner of the shed, then a hand. Just as Reb Cotton's arm appeared, Andy brought the axe handle down on his wrist as hard as he could. Bones snapped. Reb screamed and Andy flicked the axe handle upwards, catching Reb in the forehead. Reb collapsed in a heap and Andy turned and ran the length of the shed.

"Goddamnit!" Dutch cried hoarsely. A single shot echoed in the night as Andy rounded the far side of the shed. He sprinted across a small clearing, reaching a second shed just as Dutch came into sight. He picked up a pebble and watched as Dutch walked into the clearing, gun swinging in short, nervous arcs.

Andy waited until Dutch was near then he tossed the pebble a short distance to Dutch's right. Dutch whirled and fired into the shadows. Andy jumped forward, axe handle raised, and said sharply, "Drop it, Dutch!"

Something in his voice must have gotten through, because Dutch hesitated only a moment before dropping the gun at his feet. He turned slowly, fearfully. As he did the fight suddenly went out of Andy. He found he didn't want to hurt Dutch; he simply wanted never to see the man again. In the darkness Dutch stared at the axe handle in Andy's hands with wide, frightened eyes, licking his lips.

"It's time for you to clear out, Dutch," Andy said, his voice cold and diamond-hard. "You and all of Reb's rotten little gang. Fast and far. Tell Cotton and all the rest of them that what I did tonight is nothing compared to what I'll do if I see any of you within a hundred miles of Willow Creek again. Do you understand?"

Dutch let out a tiny sigh of relief. In a faintly sullen voice he said, "They ain't goin' t' like it none."

"I'm not interested in what they'll like, Dutch. I'm just telling you what'll happen if you or any of the others stay in Willow Creek. The next time I see you there won't be any warnings. You'll die without knowing what killed you."

"Don't know if I kin git the others t' go along."

"Try to convince them. Try real hard. And if you can't, then get out yourself. If you don't, you won't live to see next week."

Dutch moistened his lips again. "How long you givin' us?"

"Sunset tomorrow ought to be enough time to pack your things and clear out. When it's dark, I'll come looking for you. Anyone still in town won't live till morning."

Andy picked up Dutch's gun. "Reckon you won't be needing this. If you want to stay alive, what you'll need is a ticket out of Willow Creek."

He kept the gun and walked away.

16

When Andy returned to the Blacksmith Shop he found Bear pacing the shadows under the lean-to with a shotgun cradled in his arms.

"Heard the shots," Bear said. "Sounds like there's been trouble afoot most of the evening." He glanced at the axe handle in Andy's hand. "Course, you wouldn't know nothin' 'bout that, would you?"

"I had a bit of a run-in with Reb Cotton and his men," Andy replied.

"Found your horse out back. Figured I'd wait for you." He stared more pointedly at the axe handle. The wood was darkly stained at one end. "Looks like you already got some use out of that."

Andy held up the handle. "Came in handy. It's got a good swing to it. Nice balance."

"Want t' tell me about it?"

"There's nothing much to tell, Bear. I went to the Lucky Lady for a drink and one of Reb Cotton's men took offense to something I said."

"Since when did you start drinking?"

"Took it up earlier this evening," Andy said, grinning. "But I've quit since then." Then, quietly, he told Bear about his encounter with Reb Cotton and his men.

Bear shook his head in exasperation. "You could've been killed, Andy. You ought t' quit while you're ahead."

"Not until O'Meara decides to live in peace with the Bar-O or pulls up stakes himself."

"He ain't likely t' do either, Andy."

"Then I'll keep trimming him back until he does."

"Or until you're dead?"

"Maybe," Andy said sharply, then his voice softened. "But I don't think it'll come to that, Bear. It's just something I've got to do, that's all. My father fought pretty hard for that land. Reckon I can do the same. It's all Kit and Amy have left."

"They've still got you. So far." Andy was silent and Bear added, "Thought you was an engineer now."

"I am," Andy said, staring into the blackness.

"Then quit while you've still got your hide. You can't keep this up." Bear nodded in the direction of the Blue Boar. "You already took a knife across the ribs. Tonight it might've been a bullet. If you want t' be an engineer, then you ought t' clear out an' get on with it."

"I can't do that, Bear."

Bear nodded toward the house. "What about her?"

"Clair?"

"Yes, Clair. She's a woman now, Andy, and she's had her eyes on you ever since you got back."

"She doesn't much care to have me around these days, Bear."

"Hogwash! What're you usin' for brains? That girl's so much in love with you she's on fire, Andrew Stillman. Course, if *she* ain't what you're lookin' for, then that's another thing."

Andy said nothing for several seconds and the stillness of

the night closed in on them. "She's a mighty fine girl," he said finally.

"And?"

"And after this trouble with O'Meara is over I reckon I'll be coming over with chocolates and flowers and all the rest of it."

"Doggone it, Andy! You are the most stubbornedess cuss I ever did see! You an' Clair was just meant for each other but you're just itchin' t' get yourself killed instead, I reckon."

"I'm going to save the ranch," Andy said tiredly. "What I need to do next is to set up a meeting with O'Meara."

"That's right," Bear growled. "Just like a college feller t' change the subject." He peered at Andy. "What d'you have in mind?"

"Just talk. Here in town. Tomorrow. I split Aaron's skull the other night out at the Bar-O, and tonight I busted up Reb Cotton and his men. Hurt some of them pretty bad, I imagine. They'll probably be leaving soon. I figure now's a good time to see if Will O'Meara will listen to reason."

"You want me t' set it up?"

"I'd appreciate it if you would. I reckon it's best if I'm not seen much in town these days." Andy handed Bear a dollar. "Give this to Len Peliter and have him ride out to the Circle-K tomorrow. Have him tell O'Meara I want to talk with him at the Overland Hotel at, let's say, two o'clock tomorrow afternoon. No guns, no trouble, just talk. I'd like you to be there as well, if you don't mind—and Albert Fairbanks and the sheriff."

"I'll be there, if'n you want."

"Thanks Bear. Guess I'll be getting back out to the ranch now." He turned to leave.

"Maybe you ought t' stay in town tonight."

"Where?"

"Right here, of course. We kin stretch you out on the couch. It'd be a durn sight safer than you staying out at the Bar-O by yourself, an' it'd give you a fresh start tomorrow."

"Abigail wouldn't mind?"

"Course not. It's late an' it's dark. We'll jest put your horse out of sight in the stable an' you can hole up in the house until the meeting tomorrow."

Andy was tired. He accepted Bear's offer gratefully and

together they went into the house. Bear explained the situation to Abigail. She was delighted to have Andy stay the night and she told him so. While the men got Pete settled she laid out blankets for Andy on the couch. When Andy and Bear returned, the bed was waiting and Abigail was gone.

"Looks mighty inviting," Andy said.

"Get all the sleep you can," Bear responded. "The way you been stirrin' things up around here lately, I reckon you can use it."

Andy was more tired than he thought. It wasn't until after breakfast that he awoke to the sounds of Bear beating on a piece of hot iron outside in the shop. He awoke facing the back of the couch. For a moment he stared at the unfamiliar arabesque designs of the material, blinking, unable to remember where he was. Suddenly he sat up and faced the room.

"It's about time you were gettin' up," Clair said, her voice huffy and filled with resolute anger. She was wearing a lovely white cotton dress that Andy had never seen before. It fit her well, snugged in firmly at the waist, and it made it clear indeed that Clair was now a woman. It was also clear that she had put on that particular dress after waking and discovering that Andy had stayed the night.

"Good morning, Clair," Andy said amiably.

"You missed breakfast," she said in a cool voice.

Andy swung his feet to the floor and smiled at her. "Maybe you could fix me a bite."

"Maybe Jill could fix you something better."

Andy was reaching for his moccasins as she said this. He paused and stared up at her. "This is going to have to stop pretty soon, you know," he said softly.

"What's going t' have t' stop?"

"This pig-headed foolishness of yours."

"Pig-headed foolishness!"

"That's what I said."

"I'm not the one who . . . who—"

"Who what?"

Clair sputtered. "Y-You know perfectly well what, Andrew Stillman. You an' Jill—kissing right out there in the middle of the street."

Andy stood and stretched, loosening the muscles in his

arms and shoulders. "I didn't kiss Jill, Clair. She kissed me. There's a difference. And she only did it to upset you. Looks like it worked pretty well, too."

"You bid on her basket at the picnic," Clair said, her eyes flashing.

"After what Tripp did to you, no one would open the bid. I was only trying to get it started, help things along."

"Well, that's a likely enough story."

"It's the truth. I didn't want to win the bidding."

"But you did."

Andy ran his fingers through his hair and grinned at Clair. "I'm hungry."

"You know where the kitchen is. Fix it yourself."

Suddenly Andy stepped toward Clair and swept her off her feet, into his arms. "What are you doing?" she shrieked. "Put me down this *instant*, Andrew Stillman!"

Andy carried her through the kitchen, past Abigail's startled glance, and out the back door of the house. "What're you doing?" Clair cried. "Where're you taking me? Put me down!"

"You've got a hot temper, little lady. I aim to cool you down a mite." Andy carried her across the yard to the corral. He held her in one arm as he unlatched the gate, then carried her into the small enclosure where a large horse trough sat on the ground by the fence. Bear's pale buckskin horse stared at Clair and Andy curiously, munching hay. When Clair saw the horse trough her eyes widened.

"No. Oh, no, Andy. You wouldn't *dare*." She started kicking, futilely, in his arms. She twisted and bucked. "Pa," she called. "*Pa!*"

Bear's head appeared from behind the lean-to. Clair saw him and shrieked, "Pa, help! *Make him stop!*"

Bear grinned. "Wouldn't think of it," he said, disappearing.

"Pa," Clair wailed. She looked down, poised in Andy's arms right over the water. Just that morning Bear had pumped in fresh water. It was crystal clear, over two feet deep. The sides of the trough were coated with bright green moss. Clair stared, wide-eyed, into Andy's eyes. "No," she whispered. "You wouldn't dare!"

He set her gently into the water then pushed her head

under. She surfaced, sputtering and blowing water, hair hanging in clumped strands across her face. She gripped the sides of the trough and tried to stand but Andy pulled her feet forward and she slid down into the water again. She swept her hair out of her eyes with one hand. "Oh, you . . . you—"

He crouched and kissed her gently on the lips, then pulled back a foot or so and watched her.

Her face clouded with confusion. "You—," she said weakly. "I—"

He put his hands on her shoulders and kissed her again. She didn't pull away. Her hands touched his face, and when Andy ended the kiss she gasped and stared at him, blue eyes wide. "Jill's a spoiled brat," he said quietly. "One of those in Willow Creek is plenty."

"I—uh—"

He kissed her again, a long, tender kiss. Her hands found the back of his neck and held him timidly. When at last the kiss ended she gasped again. "Oh, Andy. What're you doin'?" she whispered.

"Putting out your fire."

She stared up at him with bright eyes. "I don't think so," she said, her voice trembling.

He looked down at her and a tiny smile played across his face. She followed his gaze, inhaled sharply, and quickly folded her arms across the front of her dress. The water had turned the material partially transparent and it was clinging to her, molded to the curves of her body. "Oh, Andy," she cried in dismay. "Don't you dare look!"

He lifted her out of the water toward him, until they were both sitting on the edge of the trough. He kissed her again and she responded with quiet eagerness as water dripped around them. When they finally drew apart, Clair looked down in embarrassment, her face flushed with color. Andy looked across the corral to keep from staring at the dress that had betrayed her. "I'm still hungry," he said.

"I kin cook real good," she said softly. "Now don't you look at me, Andy. Go an' talk to pa for a few minutes while I go inside an' put on another dress."

Andy stood and left the corral. He heard the sound of water dripping as Clair stepped out of the trough. Under the lean-to,

Andy found Bear carefully sizing a horseshoe with a sly, happy grin on his face. He looked up as Andy approached. "Chocolates and flowers, eh?" he said.

"Works every time, Bear," Andy answered.

•   •   •

When the train arrived at nine-thirty that morning, Gage, Stark, and Dutch were outside on the platform, waiting for it, a battered, surly little group, but they weren't wasting any time getting out of Willow Creek, not after what Andy had said to Dutch the night before. I'd opened the station at the usual time, seven-thirty, and already I'd heard the news of what had happened in town the night before.

Jackson, Reno, and Reb Cotton were still over at Doc Simes place. It didn't look as if they were going to be doing any traveling in the next few days. Jackson was still unconscious; had been from the time Andy hit him with the axe handle between the shoulder blades. Smelling salts had had no effect on him and Doc Simes was getting worried. Reno had a broken arm and a concussion. Reb Cotton had an ugly knot on his forehead and his wrist was shattered. Doc did all he could for it, setting the bones as best he could, but it was a terrible break and Doc figured that until the day the Lord took him, Reb would be doing well to use that hand just for hitching up his pants, once the bones had mended.

Like everyone else, I'd heard the shots in town the night before, but hadn't gone out to investigate. Like I said before, I ain't no hero. But the next morning the town was fairly jumping with the news of what Andy had done to Reb Cotton and his men, and all with the handle of an axe. I had breakfast over at the Miner's Cafe that morning so I could fill up on news as well as food and coffee. Cost me thirty-five cents, but it was worth every penny.

By ten that morning the locomotive had deposited several boxcars in the yard and had turned around, ready for the run back to Rock Springs. One by one, the men climbed aboard the coach. Dutch was unhurt but wary, and he looked behind him a lot. Gage walked like a man with a splitting headache, which I reckoned was true enough, considering he'd broke a nail keg with his skull. He wore a turban bandage so thick on his head there was no room left for his hat. Stark was stooped over with an arm held against his lower ribs. He had an ugly bruise on his cheek and was nursing the blackest eye I've ever seen in my life. I breathed a sigh of relief when the train pulled out and I was left alone at the station. Those men weren't very friendly, nor very happy.

· · ·

It wasn't until two-thirty that afternoon that O'Meara finally arrived for the meeting at the Overland Hotel. With Clevis Willis trailing behind him, he stalked in off the street and looked around the lobby.

"Over here, Will." Albert Fairbanks motioned toward the two men. O'Meara and Clevis crossed the lobby and passed through a door at the rear of the building. O'Meara stopped for a moment inside the doorway to Albert Fairbanks' office and glared at Andy, who was seated at a large square table alongside Bear. A nervous twitch tugged at O'Meara's left eye. Sheriff Heede was sitting toward the far end of the table looking as if he wished he were anywhere else but in that room.

"You busted up a lot of good men last night," O'Meara said furiously. He stomped into the room, jerked a chair from under the table, and sat down heavily across from Andy. Clevis leaned against a wall nearby.

"They could have avoided it by not attacking me in the Lucky Lady," Andy replied smoothly. "Six against one, and they had guns. Seemed like they needed settlin' down some. You oughta be more careful about who you hire, Will."

O'Meara glowered at Andy, but said nothing. He appeared restive, tapping on the arm of his chair in moody silence, scowling out a window at the mountains behind the hotel. Albert Fairbanks cleared his throat uncomfortably and looked down at the table. "This's your meeting, Andy. I reckon I'll leave it up to you now."

"Thank you, Albert," Andy said. He looked around the table then faced O'Meara. "I asked to meet with you, Will, because I want all this trouble between us to end. It serves no one. People have been hurt, and killed, and it's not going to stop unless we stop. Violence isn't a beast with a mind of its own. There's no one to blame but ourselves, and we've had enough of it, I should think. It's time we quit."

O'Meara sneered. "And just how do you propose t' do that?"

"The simplest way. Just end it. You keep what you have, I keep what I have, and we go on with our lives in peace." He held out a hand toward O'Meara.

O'Meara ignored the gesture. "You keepin' the Little Muddy?"

"Of course. It's mine."

"Then why in hell're you wastin' my time, boy?" O'Meara thundered. "That's a hell of a deal, all right! You win, I lose. I would have figured you for more damn sense than that."

Andy withdrew his hand slowly. "I'm not winning anything, Will. Let's get that straight at least. The Little Muddy belongs to the Bar-O. It did before you came to this valley and that's the way it's going to stay. I'm just appealing to you to end the violence once and for all. You keep what's yours. Let me keep what's mine.

"This is goin' t' be a mighty short meeting if you don't stop whistlin' that same old tune."

"You deny that the Little Muddy belongs to the Bar-O then?"

"You ain't got no cows, boy. I need that water."

"I sold my stock because they were being shot by vandals, Will. And there's no need for us to pretend we don't know who those vandals were and who hired them. There's not a man in this room who doesn't know it was Reb Cotton and his men, and that you hired them to do it."

"That's a damned lie!" O'Meara shouted.

O'Meara's outburst had no visible effect on Andy. "Because Reb Cotton and his men were killing my stock—on your orders—I had to sell my stock, and now that I have no cows you claim I don't need the water. That makes as much sense as cutting off a man's foot then telling him he doesn't need two boots because he doesn't have two feet." Andy leaned forward. "The Bar-O is going to restock as soon as this thing between us is settled, and I'll be needing that water.

"But it's going to be a dry summer. We can all see that. If it'll help, I'll hold off restocking the Bar-O until fall or even next spring and you can have the use of the Little Muddy until then, for fifty cents a head."

"Well," Albert Fairbanks said. "That certainly sounds fair enough—"

O'Meara's face turned the color of ripe beets and veins in his temples pulsed. He stood and put his hands on the table. "The Bar-O is finished," he said, eyes pinched and ugly. "And I need that damn water, this year an' the next an' the next after that."

"I'm just offering you a way to save the Circle-K, Will."

O'Meara blinked and stared at Andy. "You threatening my reservoirs again?"

Andy's voice was quiet, almost without emotion. "I'll do whatever it takes to save the Bar-O, Will."

"By God!" O'Meara roared. "By Thunder, if I catch you within five miles of those reservoirs I'll have you staked to an anthill with your eyelids cut off!"

"Now, Will—" broke in Albert Fairbanks. "There ain't no call to—"

"Save it, Albert!" O'Meara raged. "Keep your talk to yourself. No one threatens my reservoirs. *No one!*" He turned on Andy again. "I've got men guarding my reservoirs right now and I'll be posting more. They'll have orders to shoot at anything that moves, day or night. You keep away, boy."

Andy shook his head sadly. "That your final word, Will?"

O'Meara glared at Andy, then gave him a nasty smile. "You'll get my final word soon enough," he said. "When you get it, you'll know it." He looked around the table at the other men. "Good day, gentlemen," he said curtly, and he stalked out of the room.

Clevis nodded briefly to Andy before following O'Meara out.

17

Sheriff Heede yawned. "Well now. Wonder what he meant by that?" He stood and ambled toward the door. "Be seein' you gents. I got business t' attend to."

It was unlikely that Heede had anything better to do than to locate a cool spot in the shade on the west side of Main, but Andy said nothing; he had more important things to worry about than Sheriff Heede's studied indifference to the trouble that was building.

"O'Meara said you threatened to blow up his reservoirs," Bear said. "Is that true?"

Andy nodded. "The day I went out to his ranch."

Bear pursed his lips and drummed his fingers thoughtfully on the table in front of him. "I reckon that's why he sent Tripp and Aaron after you that day."

Albert Fairbank's eyes narrowed but he remained quiet.

Andy walked to the window that faced the rear of the hotel and stared out at the mountains for a while. When he spoke again his voice was tired, resigned. "I guess I knew O'Meara wouldn't listen to reason, but I had to try. I wanted everyone to hear it."

"You were fair enough, I'd say," Albert answered uneasily.

Andy caught his tone. "It's not your fight, Albert. I wanted you and Bear here today to make sure O'Meara didn't try anything foolish, but this is my fight now."

Albert Fairbanks cleared his throat uncomfortably. "You can't keep on with it, Andy," he said. "He's got too many men."

"I can't do much else."

"Appears to me you've been lucky so far," Albert insisted. "But you heard what Will said. He'll have those guards posted at his reservoirs, you can count on it."

Andy shrugged his shoulders. "Like I told O'Meara, I'll do what I have to do."

"Well," said Albert, "that's all I care to hear on the subject. I don't wish you ill, Andrew; don't know as I wish you luck either. It's a bad situation. I'm just sorry it's come to this. You take care now, and make sure you don't bite off more'n you can chew."

Andy gave Albert a half-hearted smile. "Thanks," he said. He looked at Bear. "Ready to get on back?"

Bear nodded glumly.

They said their good-byes to Albert and departed. On the boardwalk outside, Bear stared at Andy as if seeing him for the first time. "You ain't serious?" he asked. "About goin' after O'Meara's reservoirs, I mean?"

"I reckon I am, Bear," Andy replied. "But first I'll see about that reply O'Meara mentioned, although I can't imagine it'll be anything pleasant."

• • •

The afternoon sun scorched the earth. Waves of heat rose off the valley floor causing the Bar-O buildings to quiver in the distance. Andy perspired lightly as he placed the saddle on Pete's back. It was almost six in the afternoon and although the peak of the day's heat was over the temperature was still in the mid-nineties.

"You could wait till it was cooler," a voice said from behind him. He turned and found Clair watching him from the shade of a willow tree that drooped over the corral.

Pete took a deep breath and puffed out his chest as Andy pulled the cinch. Pete knew the routine. Andy waited until Pete exhaled again before retightening the cinch. He turned to Clair. She was wearing a pale blue dress that matched the color of her eyes, although her eyes were a deeper, more vibrant shade of blue. Her chestnut hair fell around her shoulders in a shower of loose curls. Andy went and stood in the shadows with her. "That's a mighty pretty dress you've got on," he said.

Color blossomed in her face and she looked down at her shoes. "You could have supper here," she said quietly.

"I've got to be getting back to the ranch, Clair. Bear already talked me out of going back once."

She nodded and looked off toward the west, started to say something, stopped, twisted her hands nervously, and finally in a low voice said, "What happened this morning—" Her voice trailed off. She turned from Andy and pulled at a tuft of horse hair caught in a crack in the wood of the corral fence. Andy came up behind her and touched her shoulder. She spun around. In a voice so quiet he could barely hear her, she said, "Did you mean it this morning? I mean . . . what happened—"

He put an arm around her waist and drew her near. Her eyes widened and she studied his face intently. "What do you think it meant?" he asked.

She dropped her eyes to the front of his shirt. "I don't know," she whispered. "I don't know what t'—"

He cupped a hand under her chin, lifted her face and kissed her gently, the way he had kissed her that morning. Behind them Pete snorted impatiently and stamped at the dust. The kiss ended and Clair looked into Andy's eyes. "What—?"

He put a finger on her lips. "When all this trouble is over we'll talk," he said firmly. "About the future."

She stared at him, her breath caught in her throat, then she looked quickly down at her hands. "I'd like that," she said. "Oh, Andy, I would sure like that."

He touched the side of her face then walked back to Pete. He got a book from the saddle bag and handed it to Clair. "Keep this for me, will you?"

She looked at it curiously. "What kind of a book is this, Andy?"

"Tables of integrals and mathematical functions."

She wrinkled her nose at him but folded the book protectively to her breast. "I'll take real good care of it."

"I know."

He stepped into the saddle and with a last smile to Clair rode out of the yard toward the west, into the hot, dusty-yellow grass of the valley.

The heat faded rapidly after the sun set. Andy sat on the porch with the Winchester leaning against the railing in front of him, listening to the silence that descended over the valley, watching the darkness deepen until the quarter-moon spread its cold, pale light over the land. The windmill loomed over the yard, a gaunt and bony specter silhouetted against the luminous black of the sky. The whiskering sound of a bat rose and faded rapidly into nothingness. A melancholy chorus of crickets chirruped far away in the fields to either side of the ranch house. And from far away the unmistakable muffled beat of horses' hooves came rolling across the bowl of the prairie.

Andy stood and leaned against the railing, peering into the night. He could see nothing, but he knew that riders were coming, six, maybe seven of them, still several miles away, riding swiftly in the moonlight. He went into the house and grabbed a bedroll that he had made up earlier, then he went outside, picked up the Winchester, and raced for the barn. Pete was in a stall, munching hay in the musty gloom. Andy found the bridle and stepped into Pete's stall. "Easy," he said. Pete nickered in protest as Andy slipped the bridle over his head. "I know this isn't quite what you had in mind, old boy, but it's time we were moving on." He spoke softly to the horse as he threw the saddle on Pete's back and edged him out of the stall. He jammed the rifle into the scabbard and led Pete out of the barn into the pale shafts of moonlight that were spearing through the aspens. Pete's ears lifted; he turned his head toward the east.

"You hear them too, boy," Andy said. "They're not on the way here for a social visit."

The sounds were closer now. Andy tied the bedroll on the back of the saddle and turned Pete toward the hills, riding for the line of cedar and pine that bordered the prairie. When he reached the trees he looped the reins around a branch and rubbed Pete's neck, speaking a few hurried words of reassurance in his ear. Then he grabbed the Winchester and ran back toward the ranch buildings.

Men were loping horses into the yard in front of the house as Andy sprinted into the field behind the corral and crept closer under the cover of tall grass. He kept low, raced to the edge of the barn, and slid into the dark, narrow space between the barn and an old equipment shed, peering into the yard. He counted four men in front of the main house. Inside the barn someone threw something heavy against a wall. Five. Distant voices came from the direction of Miles' and Nell's cabin. So that made seven, maybe more. There was little he could do against so many. Two of the men in the yard held torches. They'd come to burn the house and there was nothing he could do to stop them.

Another crash came from inside the barn accompanied by a savage curse. The familiar, pungent odor of kerosene filled the air. Andy stepped into the shadows at the end of the barn and risked a quick look inside. At first he saw nothing, but the sound of splashing liquid continued and suddenly a man came out of the darkness, backing toward him, pouring kerosene from a five gallon can. Before Andy could react the man was almost beside him.

The man looked up and saw Andy, a shapeless form in the shadows. "That you Eric? I got it all set t'—"

Andy swung the butt of the Winchester into the man's face. It caught him under the chin and he dropped the can, slammed against the side of the barn, and slid to the ground, unconscious. Andy looked toward the house. Two men were in the yard talking, but neither one looked toward the barn. Noise was evidently expected this evening. Andy dragged the man inside the barn and struck a match, painfully aware of the kerosene that soaked the straw-littered ground around him. In the flickering light he examined the man's face. It was one of the Circle-K cowhands, a man by the name of Matt Long. Blood trickled from the corner of his mouth and his left cheek was scraped and red.

A voice called out from the porch of the main house. "Anyone seen him? I want him, goddamnit! A hundred dollars t' the man who brings him to me." It was William O'Meara. Andy's eyes narrowed. So O'Meara was finally taking a personal hand in the dirty business he'd previously left to others. Andy strode to the mouth of the barn and looked toward the house. He raised the rifle to his shoulder, centered the sights on O'Meara's chest, eighty feet away, and put a gentle pressure on the trigger. He had the right. No one would fault him for killing the Circle-K owner, not here, now, at the very doorstep to his father's house with O'Meara's kerosene splashed everywhere waiting to be ignited. For several seconds the rifle stayed on O'Meara before Andy let his breath out and lowered the weapon. This, then, was O'Meara's final answer. There would be no peace until one or the other of them had forfeited everything, until the Little Muddy was once again controlled by just one man. And yet, even with his rifle's sights centered on O'Meara's heavy chest Andy had felt no hot surge of triumph, no sudden sense that victory was within his grasp. All he felt was a numb sensation in his fingertips and a cold-steel chill up his spine at the thought of killing a man from the shadows, even a man like O'Meara.

A dark shape crossed the yard and stopped at the wide, black entrance to the barn. Andy picked up the nearby can and backed out of the barn splashing kerosene as he went.

"You about done here?" It was the man Matt had mistaken Andy for—Eric Patterson.

Andy said nothing. He set the can down and hit Eric in the face with all his strength. Eric's jaw cracked and yielded and he landed heavily on his back in the loose dirt. Andy looked around quickly. Still no alarm was sounded, but moments later a man threw a flaming brand to the porch of the house. Andy dragged Eric into the barn, dumped him beside Matt, and peered out the door toward the house. Already the front of the house was an inferno. Orange light danced over the yard, softening the shadows.

O'Meara stood in front of the house watching the fire. A lump rose in Andy's throat as the hungry flames consumed the outside walls of the house. He should put a bullet in O'Meara's head or clear out, he thought; every minute he stayed in the barn only increased the danger of his being caught. He could do no good here. His time would come, later.

At that moment O'Meara turned from the blazing house and looked toward the barn. "What's holdin' you up in there? Matt? Eric?" He began walking in Andy's direction. "Get that damn fire goin'."

Once again Andy leveled his rifle at O'Meara and once again he thought better of it. He lowered the rifle and stepped to one side of the door. Matt and Eric were sprawled on the barn floor, out of O'Meara's line of sight. Andy peered through a wide, vertical crack in the door as O'Meara approached.

O'Meara stepped through the door, peering into the darkness. "Matt? Where in hell—" Andy rammed the stock of the rifle into the side of O'Meara's head, hard, and O'Meara reeled into a corner of the barn where he fell heavily against a leather harness and several wooden boxes, dazed but not out. Andy was instantly at his side. He grabbed O'Meara's coat and dragged him out of the harness into the flickering yellow light that came through the door of the barn. Across the yard, the house burned with a dull, angry roar. The heat prickled Andy's face.

Andy grabbed the front of O'Meara's shirt and lifted him part way off the ground. "I reckon this is proof enough that you're behind the trouble we've been having," he said.

O'Meara's eyes focused and he stared at Andy, inhaled sharply, about to cry out, and Andy slammed a fist into his stomach. O'Meara's eyes bulged in shock and pain. His face went chalky. He fell to the ground, struggling for breath.

Andy stood over him with the Winchester aimed at his chest. "Just so we understand each other, if you try to call out again, I'll kill you."

O'Meara groaned weakly and pushed himself to a sitting position. "Where in hell did you come from?" he gasped.

"I live here," Andy said caustically.

O'Meara stared at the bodies of Matt and Eric. "What'd you do t' them?"

"They'll be all right. Unless someone strikes a match and drops it, that is. That's kerosene you're sitting in."

O'Meara's eyes grew wide.

"This time you made a big mistake, Will," Andy said. "A very big mistake." Still watching O'Meara, he located a couple of lengths of rope in the debris that littered a corner of the barn.

"What're you doin'?" O'Meara asked.

"I'm going to tie you up and carry you out of here."

"The hell you are!"

"I don't have time to argue with you, Will. Now roll over on your stomach and shut up."

"You're crazy if you think—"

Andy punched him hard in the face, feeling something give beneath his fist. O'Meara collapsed, stunned. Andy rolled him over and tied his arms and legs. He found a remnant of cloth, someone's old shirt, and gagged O'Meara with it.

O'Meara struggled as Andy lifted him to his shoulders. "Stop fighting me, Will, or I'm going to hit you again," Andy said. O'Meara's squirming ceased but Andy felt the tension in O'Meara's body as he carried him through the black interior of the barn. When they reached the opposite end Andy unlatched a large door and pushed it open, just wide enough to squeeze through. Outside, he glanced around. The yard was much darker at this end of the barn, away from the burning house. As Andy watched, flames erupted from Miles' and Nell's cabin and he silently cursed O'Meara and his men. Through luck he had managed to capture O'Meara but the ranch buildings would be burned to the ground all the same.

He walked quickly to the edge of the barn, in the direction of the hills. As he passed the corner of the barn a dangerous metallic double-click sounded, almost in his ear.

"Hold it right there," Tripp said, shoving the muzzle of a gun into Andy's ribs. "Move suddenlike and you're a dead man."

•   •   •

"Pa!" Clair shouted. She ran into the house from the back yard where she'd been sitting in the still of the evening, looking across the prairie toward the Bar-O, drifting on the pleasant thoughts that had enveloped her from the instant Andy had ridden away. "Pa, Andy's house! It's burning!"

Bear Buchanan rushed to the back door and stepped out into the yard. Abigail appeared at his side and held his arm, watching in silence. Clair sobbed brokenly. Bright patches of light appeared where there should have been darkness, orange-red beacons that flickered and sparkled against the black base of the hills. Bear could just make out the separation between one point of light and another; the large one would be Andy's house, the smaller one to the left would be Miles' and Nell's place.

Clair clung to Bear for support. "He's all right, ain't he, pa?" she asked with tears in her eyes, searching his face desperately for a sign of hope. "He's got t' be all right, pa. He's *got* to!"

Bear rested a hand gently on her head. "Sure," he said with a lot more conviction than he felt. "Andy can take care of himself, hon. He'll be all right." But inside, a dark, poisonous fear slowly crept through him.

•   •   •

"Turn around," Tripp said. "Real slow."

Andy faced Tripp carefully with O'Meara's heavy body still draped over his shoulders.

"Drop the rifle."

Andy let it fall.

Tripp backed up a few paces, covering Andy. "Snake! Aaron!" he shouted. An answering call came from over by the bunkhouse. "Get over here," Tripp yelled. A grin crossed his face and he said to Andy, "Maybe you ought t' put Mr. O'Meara down, boy."

Andy lifted his arms, straightened his back, and dumped O'Meara heavily on the ground behind him. O'Meara made a furious, muffled sound, cursing into the gag. Tripp's eyes glinted. "Reckon Mr. O'Meara ain't goin' t' like that very much," he said.

Moments later Snake and Aaron arrived, dark demons in the firelight. Snake stared wide-eyed when he saw Andy. "Goddamn," he said softly. "Well I'll be good an' goddamned, Tripp, you got him."

Aaron stared at his father in surprise, the soiled white bandage on his head visible under his hat.

"Maybe you'd like to untie your pa there, young'n?" Tripp suggested sardonically.

"Oh, yeah, sure," Aaron said. He knelt by his father and untied the ropes.

Once his hands were free, O'Meara ripped the gag out of his mouth. He staggered to his feet, rubbing his wrists. "I'll kill you, you stupid sonofabitch," he raged. He swung a powerful fist that caught Andy on the side of the face. In that instant Andy saw Tripp's gun lift and center on his chest. O'Meara threw another fist into Andy's face and a cloud of tiny lights blazed in back of Andy's eyes. He fell against the side of the barn, still aware, somehow, of Tripp's gun. O'Meara punched him again with a thick, heavy fist and Andy fell to his hands and knees, his mind swimming darkly. A boot caught him in the stomach and another crunched into his ribs. Andy slumped to the ground and O'Meara kicked him in the side of the head. From some dark and distant place the blows continued to land, but there was surprisingly little pain. The rich odor of earth was close and a soothing pillow of fine, cool dust pressed against his cheek.

Something slammed into him again and then the silent, peaceful blackness came.

18

His throat was dry; he smelled the pungent odor of molding hay. Somewhere, far away, a bird sang.

He tried to open his eyes. The effort sent daggers of pain lancing through his head. His eyelids felt leaden. When he finally forced his eyes open he was met by a dim, fuzzy blue spot of color set against a patchwork background of dark, mottled shadows. His eyes focused slowly and he found himself staring down at his knees, lying on his side on dusty ground littered with hay.

His face throbbed. Dimly, he recalled O'Meara punching him and heavy boots pounding into his sides. When? How long ago?

He tried to move his arms and found they were tied behind his back. His legs were tied too. Groaning, he tried to sit up.

"Thought you was goin' t' be out all day," Tripp said.

Andy twisted his head, trying to locate Tripp. As he looked around he found he was inside a barn. Brilliant blue sky was visible beyond a set of open doors. Andy squinted uneasily at the light. So they were still out at his ranch. That was crazy. After they burned down the house he figured they would have burned down the barn then cleared out. His head spun unpleasantly. He looked around and finally spotted Tripp, sitting on a bale of hay ten or twelve feet away, smoking a cigarette, watching him. Nearby, Aaron was pacing restlessly across the opening to the barn. Andy tried again to sit up, without success. His ribs ached. He hoped none had been broken.

Tripp watched, amused.

"I could use some water," Andy said, his voice cracking.

"No doubt," Tripp answered. "You were busy last night."

Andy struggled, ignoring the pain in his ribs, and was able to work himself into a sitting position. From his new perspective he found he was in a barn, all right, but not at his ranch. A buckboard sat nearby, to his left.

"This the Circle-K?" he asked, looking around.

Tripp nodded.

"What time is it?"

"An hour before noon, thereabouts."

"Where's O'Meara?"

"Jest full of questions, ain't you?" Tripp said, pleased with himself. "You don't really want t' know where Will is, boy. That's like wantin' t' know where the bullet is that's goin' t' blow your brains out." He looked thoughtfully at Andy for a minute then said, "He's asleep."

Andy blinked. "Asleep?"

"He's a mite sore. Seems some simple-minded fool worked him over a bit last night."

Unable to contain himself any longer, Aaron interrupted his restless pacing and stared down at Andy. "You're goin' t' die," he hissed.

"You're a real brave man, Aaron," Andy said with weary sarcasm.

Aaron sucked in his breath and took a step toward Andy. Tripp's voice lashed out. "Simmer down, kid! Your pa don't want anythin' t' happen t' him just yet."

"Christ!" Aaron said angrily. He thrust his face closer to Andy's. "I'm goin' t' enjoy watchin' you die," he growled. His hand went to the soiled bandage that covered his head.

"You fall off your horse, Aaron?"

Aaron's hands clenched into fists and he turned to Tripp. "What's keepin' pa?" he demanded.

Tripp took a long, slow puff on his cigarette. "Sleep," he said. "You want t' go wake him?"

The wall behind Andy was nearly hidden by a tall stack of baled hay. To his right, not far from the door, was a mound of straw. The interior of the barn was cool, smelling of horses and leather. It would be almost pleasant, Andy thought, if his hands and legs weren't tied, his face didn't ache so much, and Tripp wasn't watching him with death in his eyes.

Andy leaned back against a half bale of hay. His fingers felt for the knots that bound his wrists. They felt like rocks but Andy's fingers dug in, searching for weaknesses, his wrists twisting slowly in an effort to loosen the bonds.

There was a formidable intensity in Tripp, Andy discovered that afternoon. Given another set of circumstances, Tripp's intelligence, ability to concentrate, and relentless sense of duty might have carried him far in life, perhaps as the owner of a large, successful ranch or as the mayor of a large city like Denver or even San Francisco. But Tripp, knowingly or unknowingly, had made a decision about who and what he wanted to be, and that was scum. During the interminable passing of time, as noon came and went, Tripp watched Andy with a dogged, unwavering attention while Aaron paced and complained and relieved his boredom in trivial ways. He was restless. He wanted action. And when he looked at Andy malice flared in his eyes; but it soon became apparent that Aaron was unable to remain focused on any one task for very long. Tripp rolled an occasional cigarette and smoked it down to a black stub, but he never once let his guard down, his eyes never left Andy's, and that's why it took Andy so long to untie his hands and why he never got the slightest opportunity to untie his legs.

With his hands hidden behind his back Andy worked at the knots, never once allowing his labors to show in his face or in the movement of his arms or shoulders. The knots were tough, but in time they yielded to his methodical twisting and pulling. After two hours the rope slipped off his wrists and he rested, trying to think of how he could untie the ropes from around his ankles. Left alone for even one minute he might have succeeded, but under Tripp's steady, inflexible gaze it was impossible. All Andy could do is sit in the cool gloom of the barn, mind spinning, hoping for a break.

"Riders comin'!" a man shouted. Andy looked up quickly at Tripp; Tripp's eyes gleamed. Snake Haskins stuck his head inside the barn. "There's riders comin'," he said breathlessly. "Three of 'em, 'bout a half-mile off. You best keep him quiet."

Snake left and Tripp eased his gun from its holster. "You will be quiet, won't you?" he asked softly.

Aaron drew his gun and squatted in front of Andy. "One peep outta you, you sonofa—" Andy pulled his hands from behind his back and swung a haymaker into Aaron's jaw in a single lightning movement. Aaron flew several feet across the barn and collapsed against a wheel of the buckboard, gun lying on the ground beside him. Andy struggled to his feet.

Tripp leveled his gun at Andy's chest. "Hold it right there," he said with iron in his voice. "Sit back down or I'll blow you wide open, boy. An' don't think for a second I wouldn't enjoy doin' it."

For a long moment Andy stood there, swaying on his feet, staring at Tripp, then he sank back to the ground. Tripp smiled with thin, bloodless lips. He glanced at Aaron lying unconscious on the ground then looked at Andy with a measure of respect in his eyes. "Heard tell you could throw a punch. Looks like the stories weren't exaggerated much."

The sound of horses loping into the yard in front of the main house reached the men in the barn. A man's voice called out. "O'Meara. Will O'Meara." It was Bear Buchanan.

Andy started.

"I know what you're thinkin'," Tripp said in a low voice. "If you call out, you've signed their death warrants."

Andy's shout died in his throat. "They'd be missed back in town," he said in disbelief. "There's more than one out there. You'd never get away with it."

Tripp's eyes gleamed. "You willin' t' take that chance, boy? You willin' t' gamble their lives against that thought?" The gun in his hand was as steady as an oak stump, his smile entirely untroubled.

Andy stared at Tripp, then closed his eyes and leaned back. "Thought not," Tripp said, stonily. He kept his gun on Andy as he dragged Aaron to the loose heap of straw near the entrance. Piling several armfuls of straw on Aaron, Tripp buried him. "Let's hope he stays out for a while," he said, grinning. "Wouldn't want folks wonderin' how he got knocked out or what he was doin' under there, would we?" He waved his gun at Andy. "You next, boy. I'm not goin' t' get close enough t' you t' give you the chance t' take a swing at me, if that's what you're thinkin', so you jest stand up an' hop on over here."

Andy stood awkwardly as Tripp backed away from the straw. Andy hopped across the floor, ribs throbbing at the jarring movement.

"You jest lie down right over there." Tripp pointed to one side of the straw heap where it butted against the end of the stacked bales. Andy lowered himself to the ground and Tripp approached, gun still pointed at Andy's chest. "I'm not goin' t' gag you," Tripp said, pleasantly. "Not with your hands free and handy. But if you call out you won't be savin' yourself, you'll just be killin' your friends. I don't give a damn either way, so I reckon I'll let you decide if you want company when you die. Keep quiet an' keep your hands away from that rope around your legs an' they'll leave here alive." When he finished speaking Tripp grabbed a few handfuls of straw and tossed them over Andy from a safe distance.

Soon Andy was buried. Dim brown light filtered through the straw; sound was muffled. The weight of the straw pressed into him gently and he held his hands in front of his face to keep the straw out of his eyes. From a distance he heard Tripp say, "I'll be right here the whole time, boy. Lie still now, hear?"

Bear called out again, "Will. Where are you, Will?" He was flanked on either side by Sheriff Heede and Albert Fairbanks, both of whom appeared ill at ease.

O'Meara came to the front porch of the house, tucking in his shirt. "What the hell you want, Bear?" He said curtly, nodding to the sheriff and to Albert.

"I'm lookin' for Andrew Stillman," Bear said. "His ranch was burned out last night."

"Sorry t' hear it."

"I'll just bet you are."

O'Meara chose to ignore the sarcasm. "So you're lookin' for him. You want some of my men t' lend a hand?"

"I reckon you know what I want, Will. Where is he?"

"Don't know what the hell you're talkin' about, Bear."

"I rode over to the Bar-O early this mornin'," Bear said. "Everything was burned to the ground. Andy's horse was tied to a tree in the hills above his house but Andy wasn't anywhere around. I figure you had a hand in what happened."

O'Meara's face grew rigid. "Talk like that could get you in a whole lot of trouble, Bear."

"I want him, Will."

"I ain't seen him."

"What happened t' your face? Looks t' me like you took a fist."

"Goddamned horse throwed me."

Bear snorted derisively. "I'll just bet it did." He twisted in his saddle and looked toward the bunkhouse. "I don't see many people around here," he observed.

"I've got six men protectin' my reservoirs from that damned maniac," O'Meara said. "The rest are out tendin' stock. I'm runnin' a ranch here, not a goddamn hotel."

Heede glanced around nervously. Albert appeared bemused, staring down at his saddle horn. Bear's eyes swept the house behind O'Meara. "Where's Jill?" he asked. "And Jason?"

"Rock Springs," O'Meara said, a faint grin working the corners of his mouth. "I sent Jason t' pick up some things I need. Jill went with him."

Bear stared at him. "Mind if we have a look around?"

Heede cleared his throat uncomfortably. "Maybe that's not actually necessary—"

"Not necessary!" Bear turned on the sheriff. "What the hell you draw your pay for, John?"

Heede glanced uncertainly at O'Meara.

O'Meara spread his hands wide. "Be my guest, Bear. Look around all you want."

Albert leaned toward Bear. In a low voice he said, "I reckon Andy isn't here."

Bear nodded, sadly. "We'll look around all the same," he said, but his heart was leaden. He figured O'Meara had taken Andy somewhere else already, either that or Andy was already dead, lying under a pile of loose stones somewhere in the hills. The thought numbed him. He couldn't face Clair again without Andy. It had been bad enough that morning, watching her face crumple when he returned from Andy's ranch alone, leading Andy's horse. It would be worse, far worse, this afternoon.

Tripp was repairing his saddle in the shade of the barn when Bear and the others walked in. He pushed a long needle through several layers of leather and looked up in surprise as the men entered the barn.

Bear glanced around the barn. "Saddle broke?" he asked Tripp.

"Needed work. You know what they say, 'A stitch in time . . .'" Tripp cast him a grin.

Bear studied the saddle for a moment, observing that it needed considerably less work than Tripp was giving it, and Tripp was an unlikely sort to do work that wasn't absolutely necessary. Bear looked around the barn carefully, followed at a little distance by Albert and the sheriff. He searched through a pile of boxes and riding gear at the far end of the barn. Walking back, he stared hopelessly at the bales of hay and the tools and equipment stacked against opposite sides of the barn. He lifted a canvas tarp and found several battered saddles underneath needing work. Looking up, he saw nothing but dusty, cobwebbed rafters.

"Let's go check the bunkhouse," he said in a hollow tone, and the three men left the barn.

In the shadows, Tripp continued to work methodically on his saddle.

Half an hour later Bear and the others mounted their horses in front of the house with William O'Meara watching from the porch. Bear glared at him. "Mark my words, Will. You leave that boy alone." The words were an empty threat in the hot afternoon air. It was likely that Andy was dead already, Bear thought. And if he wasn't, then he soon would be, and there was nothing he could do to help. As the three men wheeled their horses and rode out of the yard, Bear's helplessness felt like a razor-sharp knife twisting in his chest.

In the barn Tripp pulled his gun. "You can get up now, boy," he said loudly. Andy churned out of the hay and sat up. "You done real good," Tripp said. "You must be mighty fine friends with those fellers."

He grabbed Aaron by the heels and dragged him out of the hay; moments later O'Meara appeared in the door to the barn, his squat frame casting a dark shadow in the square of light that fell through the door. "I want him out of here," he said, clearly shaken by the unexpected visitors. He aimed a thick finger at Andy. "I want him—" His voice tailed off as he saw Aaron. His eyes narrowed to slits. "What happened in here?"

"Aaron don't take punches so well," Tripp drawled.

"What—who?"

"Seems our prisoner is mighty handy with his hands. He slipped his ropes and punched Aaron in the face. I hid them both under the hay while those men from town were nosin' around."

O'Meara mopped a sheen of perspiration from his forehead. "Good work," he said. He jerked a thumb at Andy and said, "Get him out of here. Take him out t' the line camp at

Antelope Ridge."

"I ain't never been there."

"Aaron'll show you the way." O'Meara kicked his son's foot. "Get up." He kicked him again. "Get up you worthless, no-account—"

Aaron groaned. He rolled over, a grimace of pain on his face.

"Bring me some water," O'Meara said to Tripp. "And go find Snake." Tripp shrugged and left the barn. O'Meara waited impatiently, glaring alternately at his son and then at Andy until Tripp returned. Snake Haskins dogged his heels, carrying a bucket of water. O'Meara took the bucket and dumped the water on Aaron's face. Aaron gasped and sputtered but William O'Meara paid him no attention. He turned to Tripp and said, "I want the three of you t' take the prisoner out t' the line camp an' hold him there overnight. I got things t' take care of here but I'll be along tomorrow morning." He looked down at Andy, sitting on the ground, and touched the welt on the side of his face where Andy had hit him with the butt of the rifle. "You're goin' t' die just as slow as I can kill you, boy."

Tripp said, "Aaron don't look ready t' ride much."

"Oh, he'll ride," O'Meara replied. "He'll ride even if it kills him, I reckon." He squatted down in front of Andy, just out of reach, and looked him over. When he rose he said to Tripp, "Give him water, and food if he kin chew it. I don't want him hurt much more than he is already before I arrive tomorrow. I want him healthy enough t' feel all the pain I have in store for him." His eyes pierced Tripp. "I'm countin' on you, Tripp. He slipped his ropes once already. Don't let it happen again."

Tripp grinned. "It won't."

•   •   •

The line camp was fifteen miles from the main ranch buildings of the Circle-K, located on the lower slopes of Antelope Ridge almost due south of the ranch. The cabin was shabby but stout, with walls made of pine logs cut from the nearby forest and a steep, sloped roof built on a framework of cut lumber. It had been built in the lee of a stand of pine trees and brush a quarter mile above the edge of the prairie, for years serving as a lonely outpost in the winter months for those cowhands assigned to watch over O'Meara's southern range.

When the little procession was half a mile from the cabin, Andy looked back over the valley. The Union Pacific spur coursed through the valley bottom, a faint line that disappeared around the tip of Crooked Neck Ridge which now blocked his view of Willow Creek. In town, Clair would be frantic, he knew, and his chest ached bitterly at the thought.

The horses continued climbing out of the heat of the prairie; the valley disappeared behind the thickening brush and timber. They wound through the pine trees for several minutes until Aaron called out, "There she is."

"Snake," Tripp said. "Climb on higher up an' watch our back trail for a while."

"Aw, Tripp," Snake complained. "It ain't gonna be light much longer anyway." The sun hung like a swollen orange over the western mountains.

"Are you goin' t' do what I ask, or ain't you?"

Snake glowered at Tripp briefly then lowered his eyes. "I'm goin'," he said. He went around the cabin and Andy heard his horse tearing through the brush as he climbed the hill. Aaron opened the cabin and Tripp, with a coil of rope looped over one shoulder and his gun drawn, motioned Andy inside.

Thick, stale air filled the room. The cabin was a simple rectangle, roughly twelve by fifteen feet, lit by a single, tiny window that faced east, caked with years of grime. In the gray-tinged light Andy saw that the cabin was furnished with two bunks set against the right-hand wall under the window and a table with two decrepit chairs that dominated the center of the room. The far wall was half-covered by a massive stone fireplace—the sole source of heat for the cabin's occupants in the winter months. A crude cupboard with double doors hung on one wall to the right of the door, canted at a slight angle.

Cobwebs brushed Andy's face and with bound hands he swept them away clumsily. For a moment Tripp surveyed the room, examining the walls and the meager furnishings. Finally he looked up. Square, open beams ran the length of the room and Tripp grunted in satisfaction. "Get over there against that wall," he said, and after Andy had walked to the other side of the room and had turned around Tripp ordered Aaron to pull his gun. Then he set his own guns on one of the bunks across the room from Andy. He placed the coil of rope on the table.

"I'm going t' make this simple," he said to Andy. "You just relax and Aaron here won't have t' put a bullet in your gut. How's that?" Aaron grinned at Andy. The paleness of his face along with the gray-white of his bandage gave his face the appearance of a grinning death's-head. Tripp pulled a knife and cut two twelve-foot lengths of rope from the coil he'd brought inside. Then he sliced through the rope that held Andy's wrists. "You just relax," he said. "Aaron might not be much with his fists but he's a fair hand with a gun."

Tripp tied the center of one of the lengths of rope around Andy's left wrist, letting the two ends trail out some five feet. The knot was solid, a tight, doubled square knot, and Tripp positioned the knot at the back of Andy's wrist where his fingers couldn't reach it. Once that was done, Tripp dragged a chair across the room and stood on it as he tied the two loose ends of the rope around one of the roof beams. He climbed down and tied Andy's other hand, in the same fashion, to a beam near the opposite side of the room. When he was finished Andy was standing spread-eagled against the wall with his hands about six inches above his head. He couldn't reach his head with either of his hands and his hands wouldn't reach closer than about four feet of each other.

"Reckon that ought t' hold you," Tripp chuckled.

Snake returned an hour later when the western sky had faded to the color of dark rust and black shadows lay under the trees. Already the thin mountain air had grown chilly. Aaron had found a bin of firewood at the rear of the cabin and was setting a couple of logs in the fireplace when Snake opened the door. A battered lantern filled the room with yellow light.

"Ain't no one followin' us," Snake said sullenly.

"Now we're sure of it," Tripp answered. "Maybe you'd like t' rustle up the grub now."

"Aw, Tripp. I'm bushed. Have Aaron do it."

"Aaron's busy. Besides, I know your cookin' wouldn't kill us."

Snake grumbled and began rooting through a canvas pack. He banged the pans and tossed a can of beans on the table. "Easy there," Tripp said. "Anything you spill, you eat."

Snake heated the beans over the fire and the men ate warm

beans and cold biscuits in silence. After they were through, Tripp untied Andy's ropes from the roof beams and motioned for him to take a seat at the table. Andy ate with the ropes dangling from his wrists and three guns trained on him. When he was through, Tripp stood him back against the wall and secured the ends of the ropes to the beams again.

Half an hour went by and Aaron and Snake grew restless. Tripp was content to do nothing but roll cigarettes and smoke them with his feet kicked up on the table while he watched Andy, but this was too much for Aaron who paced nervously, occasionally glaring at Andy and at the walls. After a while he noticed the cupboard hanging on the wall near the door, opened it, and searched through the shelves. He grunted in satisfaction, withdrew a soiled deck of cards and tossed it on the table. He opened the cupboard door on the other side. "Well, lookee here," he said, pleased at what he'd found. He pulled a nearly-full bottle of whiskey and several glasses from the cupboard and set them on the table beside the cards.

Snake's eyes came alive. "Well, now, I could sure use a little of that." He reached for the bottle and picked up one of the glasses.

"Put it away," Tripp commanded. "No one touches so much as a drop of it."

"Aw, Tripp," Snake complained. "What's a little taste gonna hurt? I'm mighty dry after the ride up here."

"Same here," Aaron added.

"Have some water," Tripp said.

"Ain't the same," Snake said sullenly.

"We're supposed t' watch the prisoner. This ain't no damn party."

"He ain't goin' nowhere," Aaron said.

"He ain't if we watch him every minute," Tripp answered. "An' that's exactly why somebody's goin' t' watch him every minute, every second, all night long, an' that's why you're goin' t' put that damn bottle right back where you found it. I ain't goin' t' chance havin' someone sleepin' when they're supposed t' be watchin'."

Snake was furious. His eyes followed the bottle as if mesmerized as Aaron put it away and shut the cupboard door with a bang. Snake picked up the cards and shuffled them several times, licking his lips. The glasses still sat on the table, tantalizing him. He stared at them with a saturnine expression on his face as his fingers manipulated the cards.

"Got anythin' against poker?" he asked Tripp.

Tripp shrugged and said nothing.

Snake looked up at Aaron. "You in?" he asked.

"What stakes?"

"How about dime ante?"

"We ain't got no chips, Snake."

"We kin use rocks."

"Sure," Aaron said. "How about you go get them?"

Snake was silent for a moment, then he grinned. "How about we don't gamble money?"

Aaron blinked. "Yeah, what then?"

Snake's grin widened, he jerked a thumb at Andy. "Him. We bet on him. Pieces of him. Toes, fingers, ears. The winner gets t' cut off what he wins." He pulled a long-bladed knife from a sheath at his belt and rammed its point into the top of the table.

"Christ," Tripp said. He grabbed a length of two-by-four with a blackened end that was leaning against the wall near the fireplace and stoked the fire. Then he sat on one of the bunks, pulled out a gun, and removed the bullets from it, one at a time. He held the gun against the light, looked down the barrel, and began wiping the mechanism with the tail of his shirt.

Aaron's eyes gleamed. "You in, Tripp?"

Tripp shook his head. "I'm watchin' the prisoner."

"Christ, Tripp. Where's he gonna go?"

"Nowhere," Tripp replied. "He ain't goin' nowhere. Not with me watchin' him he ain't."

Aaron muttered something unintelligible then picked up the cards. "How we gonna divide him up?" he asked, pointing at Andy.

Snake looked at Andy critically, like a man buying a horse he doesn't really need, avoiding Andy's eyes. He was quiet for about thirty seconds then he said, "Toes is worth toes. Fingers is worth five toes. Thumbs and ears is worth ten toes and eyelids is worth twenty toes. We each start out with half of him." He pulled the knife from the table and slipped it back into its sheath.

"That's a hell of a fine idea!" Aaron exclaimed with something like wonder in his voice.

"Christ," Tripp said in disgust.

Aaron shuffled the cards. "I'll deal first," he said. "Five card stud. Ante a toe."

"I'm in," Snake said, staring at the imaginary pot on the table. From force of habit he curled his fingers around a nearby glass.

Aaron dealt a card to each of them, face down. Then, face up, he dealt the nine of diamonds to Snake and the six of clubs to himself. "Nine bets," he said.

"One toe."

Aaron checked his hole card. "I'll raise a toe."

"Call." The gristly, imaginary pot grew. Tripp shook his head, but looked at Andy and smiled a little in spite of himself.

Aaron dealt Snake a card and said, "Queen of diamonds. Possible flush." He dealt himself the six of hearts and smiled. "Two sixes. The pair bets a finger."

Snake scowled at Aaron's sixes. He checked his hole card. "Call," he said.

Aaron dealt another card to Snake. "Three of clubs, busted the flush." He dealt a card to himself. "Six of spades. Three sixes bets an ear."

Snake cursed. "Fold," he said angrily. "Gimme them damn cards."

Aaron grinned, then stared at the table thoughtfully. "Let's see now," he said. His brow furrowed. "You lost a toe, then two toes, then a finger. That's . . ." He counted on his fingers. "How much was fingers worth?"

"Four toes," Snake said.

Andy laughed, startling the men. "There's no honor among thieves," he said.

"Shut up!" Snake yelled.

"I'm surprised at you, Tripp," Andy said. "Why would a man like you waste his time with these morons, anyway?"

An angry, strangled sound came from Snake. He whirled out of his chair and threw his glass at Andy's head. Andy jerked his head to one side and the glass shattered against the wall, inches above his left shoulder. "I tol' you t' shut your goddamned face," Snake snarled.

Andy stared at him and said, "I'm surprised you had the guts to shoot my father in the back, Snake."

A thin, cruel smile curled Snake's lips. "So you figured out who done it, eh?"

"I never had any doubt."

"Your pa wasn't much," Snake said, savoring the words. "He died easy, jest like you're goin' t' die—nice an' easy. Except that you're goin' t' die a whole lot slower."

"It's not hard to kill a man when you shoot him in the back," Andy said. "That's how a coward kills, Snake, and that's how I knew it was you. And I'll bet the whole time you were back-shooting my father your guts were knotted and quivering with fear."

The blood drained from Snake's face. "You shut up, boy! I'm warning you." He took a step toward Andy.

Tripp's voice cut through the tension in the air. "Easy there, Snake. Leave him alone. He ain't supposed t' be hurt before tomorrow."

"O'Meara said he ain't supposed t' be hurt *much*," Snake said savagely. "He didn't say we couldn't have a little fun." He slipped his knife from its sheath and held the gleaming tip of the blade an inch from Andy's left eye, twirling it with practiced fingers. "I'm goin' t' cut your eyelids off myself," he hissed.

"How are you going to manage that with my back to you, you back-shooting, yellow-bellied bag of snail slime?" Andy said.

Snake let out a howl of rage, jumped back, and swung a fist into Andy's stomach. Andy tensed his stomach muscles against the blow, grinning at Snake. Snake trembled with fury and threw a punch at Andy's face, a punch that missed by half an inch as Andy jerked his head quickly to the right. He swung a leg up and kicked Snake in the chest. Snake crashed backwards into a chair, breaking its back and several of its legs.

Tripp watched, amused.

Snake got to his feet unsteadily. "You . . . you sonofabitch!" he wheezed. He looked wildly around the room and his eyes fell on the two-by-four near the hearth. He picked it up and advanced toward Andy.

"No," Tripp said sharply.

But Snake had gone too far to stop. With all his strength he rammed the end of the two-by-four into Andy's solar plexus. A bright burst of light exploded behind Andy's eyes and pain shot through his body. Snake stepped back, drawing the two-by-four back, ready to ram it again into Andy's stomach. Andy's eyes gaped. He saw Tripp leap off the bunk, his gun aimed at Snake.

"Drop it!" Tripp barked. "Now!"

Through a dark, hazy curtain the room rippled in front of Andy's eyes. He saw Snake waver then drop the length of wood, and he felt a brief surge of gratitude toward Tripp. He tried to draw air into his lungs, but the blow had paralyzed him. He stared at Tripp with his mouth open, his eyes wide, unable to make a sound, unable to inhale the slightest bit of air, as if an invisible band of steel were constricting his chest. The room swam darkly. His legs buckled and sudden tension yanked his arms up as the ropes kept him from falling to the floor. The room dimmed.

This was what it was like to drown. This was what it was like to die.

19

A faint sound like the distant chatter of insects buzzed in his head for a moment, then went away. It came again, then faded. Andy reached out, mentally, trying to identify the curious, rhythmic sound, slowly becoming aware that his body was experiencing great pain. The sound was gone. His eyes fluttered open and he found himself staring at the floor.

His arms felt as if red-hot pokers had been pushed through his flesh from his wrists to his shoulders. He gasped and his stomach throbbed with agony. The pain helped him throw off the lethargy that gripped him and suddenly he realized he was hanging by his arms, held by the ropes that Tripp had tied over the beams. His knees were bent, buckled from the time he'd lost consciousness. He stood, unsteadily, and leaned against the wall, eyes closed, arms still outstretched and on fire. The whirring sound started again and he looked up; Snake was sitting at the table shuffling the cards, occupying the one useable chair remaining in the room. The other was in a corner, twisted and broken. The lantern had been turned low, bathing the room in somber, orange light.

He wondered how long he had been unconscious. Outside the sky was dark, the tiny window stared back at him like a square, charcoal eye. Tripp was asleep on one of the bunks; Aaron was asleep on the other.

Suddenly Andy thought about Clair. She was back in town, almost certainly worried about him, perhaps wondering where he was and what had happened to him. He groaned, silently. At that moment the pain in his arms was nothing like the anguish he felt knowing he would never see her again. They could have had so much together. Now it was over before it had even began.

What time was it? he wondered. How long did he have? An hour? Two? Maybe three? No, not that long. The sky was completely black, which meant the moon had already set; dawn could not be too far off. And after Tripp and Aaron awoke and O'Meara finally arrived, except for enduring whatever inhuman pain they'd planned for him, his life would be over. Tripp had shown the unimaginative tenacity of a bulldog during the times he had watched Andy; when Tripp was awake again there would be no possibility of escape.

Andy looked around, forcing himself to think clearly. The bottom of the cup Snake had thrown at him lay in a corner of the room nearly six feet away, its edges sharp and jagged, but there was no way he could reach it even if Snake wasn't watching. He looked up at the ropes that held him. They were tied around parallel roof beams about nine feet apart, each rope forming a large loop that circled the shaft of a beam. He saw that it would be possible to slide the ropes four or five feet along the length of the beams before the ropes were stopped by a cross-beam, and he mentally projected himself that additional distance into the room. From there he would be able to touch the table with an outstretched foot. If he could draw the table closer he could stand on it and the ropes would be greatly loosened; given time, he could then untie the ropes with the aid of his teeth. The thought was tantalizing, but with Snake watching him it was impossible.

Andy looked at Snake, who was playing solitaire with a bored expression on his face. The outlaw yawned. Not once had he looked up since Andy had regained consciousness so he was startled when Andy said, "I reckon Tripp appreciates having you around, Snake." He kept his voice low, praying that Tripp wouldn't wake up.

Snake jumped. He looked up at Andy with ugly, red-rimmed eyes. "Well, you're awake. Too bad. Just don't start nothin' you can't finish, boy."

"Must be mighty convenient for Tripp," Andy repeated.

"What?"

"Having someone he can give orders to. Someone he can snap his fingers at who'll lick his boots and crawl around at his feet like a dog."

Snake was out of his chair and across the room in an instant. He jerked his knife from its sheath and stood to one side of Andy, keeping well away from Andy's feet. He pressed the tip of the blade against the side of Andy's neck. "I tol' you not t' start nothin' you couldn't finish," he said, his voice a sibilant, deadly whisper.

Andy looked at him contemptuously. "Go play with your cards, Snake. You heard what Tripp told you. You can't touch me."

Snake increased the pressure of the blade fractionally and Andy felt the point dig into his throat. "You keep talkin' an' I might just cut out that tongue of yours, boy."

"I wouldn't bet on it," Andy said, his voice low and mocking. "You aren't man enough to go against anything Tripp says."

"Keep talking, you sonofabitch, an' I'll cut out your damned eyes."

"Talk is cheap, Snake. But that comes easy to a coward. Tripp tells you to go up the ridge and up you go. Tripp tells you to cook supper and you cook it. Tripp tells you not to touch me and you wouldn't lay a finger on me for all the gold in California or all the horse manure you could eat in a week."

Snake's eyes gleamed in fury.

"You're one of life's complete cowards," Andy pressed.

"Over there in that cabinet is a bottle of whiskey and you and I both know you'd like a drink, and that you can hold your liquor as well as the next man." Andy stared right into Snake's eyes. "But you can't touch that whiskey any more than you can touch me, Snake, because Tripp told you not to, and you're such a miserable goddamned coward you wouldn't draw a breath of air if Tripp didn't give you permission first."

Snake's face was livid. He picked up the two-by-four with trembling hands.

Andy grinned at him. "What do you suppose Tripp would do to you if I yelled out and he caught you about to hit me with that again? Turns your legs to jelly just thinking about it, doesn't it?"

"I'll kill you," Snake said savagely, helplessly, setting the two-by-four on the floor in haste. "I'll cut out your goddamn heart and feed it t' the coyotes."

"No you won't. And you won't touch that whiskey either, you sorry egg-sucking coward. Go back and play with your cards."

Snake paled. He backed away from Andy like a man backing out of a cave infested with rattlesnakes. A nerve twitched over one eye and his forehead glistened with perspiration. "I'll show you," he said. His voice was a mixture of poisonous rage and slinking fear. He walked to the cupboard and stood before it hesitantly. Andy laughed, a quiet sound of derision, and Snake reached up suddenly and opened the cupboard door. He pulled out the bottle and glared at Andy triumphantly. He opened the bottle, glanced nervously at Tripp, and put the bottle to his lips. He took a tiny swallow and Andy laughed quietly again. Snake's face colored. He poured several ounces of the brown liquid into one of the glasses on the table and drank it in one long draught. Then he crossed the room and pressed the point of his knife under Andy's armpit. "As easily as I drank that red-eye I could push this knife right into your heart," he said.

"One tiny sip doesn't prove a damn thing, Snake," Andy sneered. "I reckon you have about as much courage as a little schoolgirl's pet rabbit."

Snake's fingers trembled, then a slow, cunning smile played across his face. "I see what you're up to," he said. "You want me t' kill you now, nice an' quick, so's you won't die slow an' painful come morning." He stepped back and returned the knife to its sheath. "Well, it ain't goin' t' work, boy. It'll take you all day t' die tomorrow, an' you won't be callin' anyone a coward at the time, neither. You'll be too busy screamin' and beggin' t' die t' be callin' anyone a coward."

"Better hope Tripp doesn't catch you with that whiskey, Snake."

Snake grinned, a trifle uncertainly, and sat down again at the table. He poured an inch and a half of whiskey into the glass, took a swallow, shuffled the cards again, and dealt himself a hand of solitaire which he played listlessly, glancing up occasionally at Andy.

"You've got more guts than I figured you for," Andy said.

Snake grinned, with effort, and took another swallow.

Andy looked at the window again. Outside, the sky was still dark. The fire Aaron had built was now only a bed of orange-red coals. Snake continued to empty the bottle. As the alcohol overcame his inhibitions he drank more freely. Finally he pushed the cards aside, yawned hugely, and leaned back in his chair with his heels on the edge of the table. Pulling his gun, he aimed it unsteadily at Andy's head. "Bang," he said, then he snickered, grinning foolishly. He set the gun on the table before him and folded his arms across his chest. He peered through dull, heavy-lidded eyes at Andy. "Think about mornin', you son'vabitch. Come mornin', you're gonna die."

Five minutes later Snake was dead asleep, breathing deeply, his legs still propped up on the table. Sweat formed on Andy's forehead. He hadn't counted on Snake's falling asleep in contact with the table. Now, if he drew it closer, Snake's legs would come crashing to the floor, and even if Snake were too drunk to wake up, the noise would almost certainly wake Tripp. Or Aaron.

Still, there was nothing else to try. Certainly there was no way to get free where he was, even if no one was guarding him. He took a small step into the room and the ropes trailed behind him. He shook them, rattling them gently, trying to slide them along the beams. His progress was painfully slow. The ropes inched forward, caught on snags, inched forward again. Andy's arms ached. He glanced out the window and for a moment his heart caught in his chest. Against the black of the mountainside he could see the ethereal, almost invisible scarlet glow of the coming dawn.

Redoubling his efforts he tugged and shook and bumped the ropes along the beams. Five minutes later he had moved the contrary ropes the distance to the cross-beam where they would go no farther. Andy stuck out his right leg and found he could indeed touch the edge of the table. His toe found a lip under the table's edge; without too much effort he would be able to draw the table toward him.

And if he did, Snake's feet would fall.

Andy glanced out the window again. The sky had lightened to a heavy rose color trimmed with flakes of dull orange. Beads of perspiration gathered at Andy's hairline like translucent pearls.

To make a mistake now was to die.

In the lantern's pale light he checked the room around him. The two-by-four Snake had rammed into his stomach was lying on the floor eight inches beyond the reach of his left foot and a rounded dowel from the broken back of the chair, was nearby, inches from Andy's straining, outstretched foot. He thought swiftly. What could he do with the dowel if he could get it?

He might be able to pull the two-by-four within reach.

Then . . . what?

He looked around the room for a use for the two-by-four. A gleam of light in the corner behind him caught his eye—the jagged bottom of the glass Snake had thrown at him. With the two-by-four he could scrape the piece of glass out of the corner . . . or could he? Would the length of wood reach? It was about four feet long. And even if the board reached, could he use it to pull the glass within reach of his feet? How much noise would that make?

And then what? What could he possibly do with the glass at his feet and his hands spread-eagled above his head?

He pondered the problems and alternatives desperately, aware of the spreading light in the sky outside. It would take time, perhaps too much time, to slide the ropes back along the beams to the wall if he chose to go after the glass, if he could use the dowel to get the two-by-four. Or he could be up on the table in less than a minute if Snake, Tripp, and Aaron didn't wake up when Snake's feet hit the floor. Such a terrible if. If any of the outlaws awoke, Andy's life would end in a slow and terrible death.

His head spun with the agony of the decision, while, outside, the slow turn of the earth lightened the sky.

The dowel. How could he reach the dowel? He stretched his left foot out as far as it would reach, his right arm straining against the rope. His toe fell three inches short.

His moccasins. With his right foot he worked the moccasin part way off his left foot and with his toes wedged in the heel portion of the moccasin the limp leather extended several inches beyond the reach of his toes. He held his foot out, lowered the tip of the moccasin just beyond the dowel, and pulled. The dowel made a dry, scratching sound and shifted an inch closer. Again he reached out with the moccasin and this time the dowel moved within reach of his toes.

He had the dowel! He took another long look at Snake's legs still resting on the table and decided to try to get the two-by-four.

He maneuvered the dowel clumsily until it was trapped between his feet and all his weight was supported by his arms. With his teeth clenched against the fiery pain that raked his arms and shoulders, he reached out with the dowel and forced his mind to concentrate on the task of drawing the two-by-four closer. On his first attempt the dowel scraped across the top of the two-by-four without moving it and Andy stifled a groan. His arms felt as if they were being ripped from their sockets. He reached out again and this time the tip of the dowel went beyond one end of the board and swung it around several inches on a gritty pivot. Again he held out the dowel and pulled and this time the two-by-four rasped loudly against the floor, spun, and bumped against his feet.

Now he had to decide—spend several precious minutes working his way back to the wall, perhaps longer now that he had the two-by-four, and try to retrieve the piece of glass—or pull the table out from under Snake's legs. If he chose the latter and no one woke up he could be on the table and free within minutes.

Outside, a cheery yellow glow lit the eastern sky.

Andy looked at Snake's scarred, heavy boots and made his

decision. His toes sought the two-by-four and he drew it closer, grimacing at the noise it made against the grit that covered the cabin floor.

Mercifully, the grain of the beams allowed the ropes to slide more easily on the return trip to the wall; still, the short journey was a nightmare of pain and noise that seemed to last forever. For three or four long minutes there was no sound in the cabin save that of Aaron's dry snoring, the occasional pop of an ember, and the hideous rasp of the two-by-four. It wasn't until Andy had managed to return once again to his place against the wall that Tripp rolled over on his bunk, opened his eyes, and stared at him!

Andy felt the marrow in his bones freeze, the breath catch in his throat. He didn't want to die. He watched as a sleepy grin creased the corners of Tripp's mouth, and for a long and breathless moment Tripp looked at Andy, his face frozen in a malevolent mask. Then Tripp closed his eyes and turned his face again to the wall.

For nearly a full minute Andy stood there, his heart hammering, his head reeling in bewilderment, expecting Tripp to jump up at any moment with an awful laugh and sweep the two-by-four away. He would slap Snake awake, curse him for falling asleep, wake Aaron, and they would all watch him until O'Meara arrived from the ranch. Then they would watch him die.

Another minute passed. A fragment of frozen, aching time.

Then, abruptly, Andy realized what had happened. Tripp had seen, in that brief glance, exactly what he'd expected to see. Andy was still standing against the wall where he had been before, still tied, and Snake, with his back to Tripp, appeared to be watching Andy with his feet propped up on the table. There was still a chance.

Carefully Andy slid the two-by-four toward the broken piece of glass, just inches from the corner of the room, hanging again by his arms as he used both feet to inch the far end of the board around the glass. His arms felt as if acid, not blood, were running in his veins. He tilted his head forward, saw the far end of the two-by-four go beyond the glass, and thrust his end of the board out, twisting it, trying to lever the glass closer. The wood growled horribly against the floor and the glass moved several inches closer.

He glanced up at Tripp but the outlaw remained still. Outside, Andy could just discern the green of the closer trees, even through the crusted dirt of the window.

He repositioned the two-by-four, trapping the glass once again against the wall, sweeping it toward him—gritting his teeth at the awful noise. A half-dozen times the long, stealthy, rasping sound tore at his heart until the glass had finally moved to where he could touch it with the tip of his left foot. He pulled it toward him then slid the sharp, gleaming piece of glass over to the other side of his body, to his right foot. After another quick glance at Tripp, he worked both the moccasin and the sock off his right foot and carefully, gingerly, gripped the broken piece of glass between his toes and lifted it off the floor, again fighting the deadly, crippling pain that tore at his joints and muscles as he hung by his arms. He levered his legs over his head, his back pressed firmly against the wall, until the fingers of his right hand just brushed the glass. He needed another inch, and he strained his stomach muscles further, forcing his legs higher, until his hand finally closed around the serrated edges of the glass.

His swung his legs back to the floor and stood up. He had done it. He had the glass! His fingers couldn't reach the tough knots that had been tied behind his wrists but with the glass, in time, he could cut the ropes. Hope surged through him and his thoughts turned briefly to Clair again, thoughts that he pushed aside with effort. Now was not the time.

Across the room, Tripp stirred.

Andy closed his hand around the glass and watched Tripp. Tripp rolled onto his back, eyes closed, breathing lightly. He wouldn't sleep much longer. Andy held an edge of the glass against the rope and pressed, rubbing it across the fibers as he put weight on the rope to give it tension to cut against. The fibers made a dry hissing sound as they parted and a small slit appeared in the rope. The light in the cabin came equally from the lantern and from the light of the new day.

He found an edge of the glass that was blessedly sharp and within a minute one entire strand of the three-stranded rope parted. Andy worked feverishly on the remaining strands, listening to Tripp's uneven breathing.

Another strand parted. Andy's pulse quickened and he pulled harder on the last remaining strand, working steadily with the knifelike piece of glass. The fibers protested, rustling like dry grass in a summer's breeze, yarns popping until one final yarn remained and suddenly the rope snapped, the loose end slithered upwards over the beam, and Andy caught it as it fell off the other side.

Without bothering to look at Tripp, Andy set both the glass and the end of the rope on the floor. He stepped to his left and began working furiously with his teeth and fingers on the knots that held his left wrist.

With desperate strength and the bitter taste of hemp in his mouth, Andy tore at the knots. It took nearly a minute and his jaws ached with the strain, but finally he pulled his hand free and turned toward the room.

Tripp had thrown an arm across his eyes. "Snake," he called out suddenly in a gruff voice heavily laden with sleep. "Drag your butt outta that goddamn chair an' put on some coffee, willya?"

Andy took two quick steps toward Snake.

Tripp sat up. "Snake—" He saw Andy and his eyes widened. He let out a startled warning—half yell, half squawk—and reached for his gun, spinning wildly toward Andy. Snake's eyes flew open. He jerked his feet off the table. He scrabbled at his empty holster, staring in shock at Andy, jumping to his feet just as Andy leaped aside and the sound of Tripp's gun boomed in the confines of the cabin.

Snake grunted. He took a stumbling half-step forward and collapsed as Andy swept the bottle from the table and hurled it at Tripp with all his strength. It bounced off the side of Tripp's head with a hard bony sound and shattered against the wall. Tripp's arms flew wide. He fell back against the wall, gun clattering to the floor. Aaron had swung his feet to the floor and was fumbling for his gun with terror in his eyes. Andy leaped toward him and kicked him in the pit of the stomach with the side of his foot. Aaron slammed against the wall and fell to the floor, curled into a tight ball, making agonized animal sounds.

Andy grabbed Snake's gun from the table. Tripp was unconscious and Aaron was on the floor, holding his stomach with both hands. Andy swung the gun to cover Snake. A bright red stain was spreading across the back of Snake's shirt. He lay unmoving with his face pressed against the floor.

Andy rolled Snake onto his back. His eyes were covered with a milky film and blood bubbled thickly in his mouth, coloring his tobacco-stained teeth. He blinked, once. His eyes appeared to focus on Andy for several seconds, then he exhaled, blood spattering his lips, and he died.

For a long moment Andy stood in the middle of the room with the gun in his hand, staring down at Snake. The realization that he had beaten the three of them dawned slowly. Tripp was still out. Aaron was on the floor breathing in long, wrenching gasps, and Snake was dead, shot in the chest by Tripp. Andy's legs suddenly felt weak and he sat down heavily on the chair. It had been so close. So terribly close.

A minute later he began untying the rope that still trailed from his right wrist. His thoughts turned to Clair again, and to Kit and Amy, and as he worked at the knot his vision began to blur.

20

Tripp was still unconscious. A good-sized knot was already forming on his forehead as Andy tied his hands securely behind his back and bound his legs at the ankles. He did the same to Aaron who made a series of weak sounds, offering no resistance.

Minutes later, Tripp came to with a weak groan, eyelids fluttering open to reveal a glazed and vacant look. His face was pinched in pain, and as the seconds passed an expression of malice began to shimmer darkly in his eyes. He craned his head around and stared malevolently at Andy. "How'd you git outta them ropes?" he asked thickly. "The way I had them fixed, ain't nobody coulda got out of 'em. Not with a man watchin' him every minute."

"Then you should have had a man watching, Tripp," Andy replied. "Last night I asked you what you were doing in the company of morons. Seems Snake had a little too much to drink and he dozed off."

Tripp's eyes shone with fury. "I'll kill that stupid sonofabitch," he said with murderous intensity. "I'll blow off his goddamn—"

"Again?" Andy arched an eyebrow.

"Huh?"

"You already killed him once, Tripp. You want to do it again?"

Tripp lifted his head and stared for a moment at Snake who was still lying on the floor in a dark, glistening pool of blood. Tripp lowered his head. "Serves him right," he said evenly. "Serves the sonofabitch just exactly right."

"I thought he was your friend."

"He didn't have no friends. Stupid, dumb sonofabitch."

Clearly, Tripp felt not the slightest remorse over Snake's death. In the past Snake had been occasionally useful to Tripp, and now, with Snake dead, Tripp displayed no more concern over him than he would in finding that his cigarette had somehow gone out.

Andy gathered together all the weapons in the room, cramming them into the canvas pack along with the remaining food. He took the pack with him and went out back and saddled one of the horses, leading it to the front of the cabin, tying its reins to a tree outside. Inside the cabin, Tripp had worked himself to a sitting position on the floor. Aaron hadn't moved; his face was a pasty white, the color of clotted cream.

"Now what, boy?" Tripp said harshly.

While saddling the horse Andy had considered what to do with the two men. His thoughts, he discovered with a sense of annoyance, had been uncomfortably scattered and confused. Under the circumstances, putting a bullet in both Tripp's and Aaron's heads seemed like only common sense, and yet he found the thought impossible to contemplate seriously. Snake's unfortunate association with Tripp had ended, finally, with a sort of dull, prescient inevitability, a man who was, perhaps, as much victim as killer. Still, he was gone and Andy felt nothing but relief at his passing. Tripp and Aaron were another matter. It bothered Andy that he felt unable to mete out the swift justice they so richly deserved. For a dozen reasons it was unthinkable, he thought with a certain bitterness, to allow Tripp and Aaron to go free, not the least of which was the probability that the two men together, or at least Tripp alone, would lie in wait in some dark corner and come after him again when he least expected it; and yet, the thought of placing the muzzle of a gun against their heads and pulling the trigger was equally unthinkable. And too, was it a sign of strength to kill a man, even when the killing was warranted? Andy felt as if he had been cheated in some sly, unfathomable fashion, that his hands were somehow still tied. If only Tripp and Aaron had also been killed during the brief struggle that morning. If only they had died during that one brief, immeasurable moment when the killing would have been justified. But the opportunity had slipped away. Now it came down to coldly putting bullets in their heads or just climbing on the horse outside and riding away, leaving them unharmed to free each other or await O'Meara's arrival from the ranch.

He found he couldn't do that either, and yet he had to do something with them, and quickly.

His brow furrowed as he covered Snake's body with a dirty blanket. Finally he answered Tripp's question. "Now you take a little walk," he said. "You and Aaron."

"Yeah? Where to?"

Andy ignored the question. He untied the legs of the two men. "Get up," he commanded.

The two men stood clumsily. "I can't pull my boots on with my hands tied," Tripp complained.

"You won't be needing boots."

"Huh?"

Andy crossed the room, picked up both Tripp's and Aaron's boots, and tossed them on the coals in the fireplace.

"Hey, goddamnit!" Tripp yelled. "Them's good boots!"

"Like I said," Andy said, his eyes piercing Tripp, "you won't be needing them." He set several pieces of kindling on the coals around the boots and within seconds small yellow flames rose from the embers. Thick black smoke began to pour off the worn, grimy leather.

Tripp groaned. "Them was sixty dollar boots."

"Sit down," Andy ordered.

"What for?"

"Take off your socks."

"Like hell!" Tripp said incredulously.

Andy shoved Tripp across a bunk. Tripp's head cracked on the wall. He rolled over and tried to raise himself to his elbows as Andy reached down and yanked the socks off his feet. "You too," he said to Aaron. Aaron sat on the edge of the bunk, brooding but compliant, and held his feet out for Andy, one at a time, as Andy stripped off his socks and threw them, along with Tripp's, into the fire that was building.

"Get on your feet."

Aaron stood but Tripp glared at Andy defiantly. Andy grabbed the front of Tripp's shirt with one hand and wrenched Tripp off the bunk in a single, powerful motion, ignoring the pain that flared in his arms. "Get outside," he said.

"I'll see you dead," Tripp said, voice low and vicious. "One of these days I'll carve out your goddamned heart."

Andy's eyes were icy. "I'm a fool, Tripp. I should kill you right now. After today, if I ever see you again, I won't think twice about it—I'll kill you quicker than I'd kill a scorpion in my bedroll. Now are you going to get outside or will I have the pleasure of throwing you out?"

Tripp's eyes blazed with hatred for a long moment then he turned and followed Aaron out the door. Andy left too, pulling the door shut on the sight of Snake's body, half-hidden under the soiled blanket. He climbed into the saddle as Tripp and Aaron watched uneasily, standing barefoot in the clearing at the front of the cabin, hands still tied behind their backs. "All right," Andy said. "Get moving."

"Which way?" Aaron asked.

"Down the hill; same way we came up yesterday."

"Without boots?"

"Without boots."

"I ain't goin' nowhere," Tripp said, "an' that's a stone fact."

"You're going," Andy said softly. "You can walk or I can drag you, Tripp, but one way or the other, you're going."

"I'll rot in hell before I take a single goddamn step, you sorry sonofabitch."

"Your choice," Andy said quietly. He dismounted, untied a

length of rope from the rear jockey of the saddle, and walked over to Tripp. "Lie down," he said.

"What d'you think you're—"

It was time, Andy decided, to end Tripp's resistance once and for all. He grabbed the front of Tripp's shirt and kicked his legs out from under him; Tripp landed heavily on his back, the wind knocked out of him, and Andy threw a quick loop around his legs. He tied Tripp's legs together tightly and climbed back in the saddle, wrapping the other end of the rope around the saddle horn.

"Goddamnit!" Tripp shouted, futilely. "Untie my legs, boy!"

"You walk on up ahead," Andy said to Aaron, ignoring Tripp. Aaron stared at Tripp and licked his lips nervously then did as he was told. Andy nudged his horse into a walk and Tripp followed feet first, body carving a rounded furrow in the pine needles and small granite stones that covered the forest floor.

"Stop," Tripp screamed furiously. "Goddamnit, boy, you turn me loose or I'll—"

"That's right, Tripp," Andy returned sardonically. "Tell me what you'll do."

Tripp began to scream an unbroken string of savage curses. He howled in rage as his shirt was pulled out of his Levis and his back scraped roughly over the rocky trail. His hands dug into the rough ground, pressed in by the weight of his body; he twisted to one side to save his hands and was dragged with all his weight on one shoulder. Quickly the shirt tore away and Tripp's shoulder scraped along the ground, rocks cutting into his flesh.

He held out for longer than Andy thought he would. For over two hundred yards Tripp was dragged, yelling obscenities, threats, and foul curses, until he finally gave in. "Christ, okay!" he bellowed in pain and fury. "Stop! I'll walk, goddamnit!"

With a sharp word to Aaron, Andy reined the horse and stepped to the ground. Tripp was breathing heavily, gasping in pain as Andy untied his legs. "Now walk," Andy said. "If I have to drag you again I won't stop until you're a bloody corpse and that's a solemn promise."

Tripp gritted his teeth in agony. "When I find you again, I'll hang you upside down from a tree and skin you alive, boy, an' that's a promise, too. An' when I'm done, I'll stake your screaming carcass to an anthill."

A shiver of disgust passed through Andy. "There's a sickness in you that only death will cure," he said, gathering up the rope.

Tripp staggered to his feet awkwardly and walked past the horse, past Aaron, and continued down the trail. Andy mounted the horse again and there was no further trouble as they left the hills and marched out into the prairie.

The sky was a flawless, pale blue that morning, hinting subtly at the heat to come as they hiked toward the golden sunlit peaks that marked the western edge of the valley. The valley floor was still in shadow but that would soon change. They passed quickly through the valley floor—Andy ignoring the groans and cries of pain of the two men as their tender feet found hidden rocks and stickers amid the tough blades of dry grass. Andy kept a lookout for O'Meara, but he saw nothing moving on the prairie, no tell-tale sign of dust, no black speck moving just below the timberline on the trail they had taken the day before, and soon the sun rose from behind the hills, sweeping with it the early morning chill from the land, warming Andy's back and soothing the biting ache that still remained in his arms and shoulders.

For over three hours he marched them through the prairie with the furnace heat building around them, sun glaring off endless miles of pale ochre grass. They crossed the tracks of the Union Pacific and after an hour or so Andy steered them northwest, angling toward the very center of the valley floor. In time, at odd intervals, Andy caught sight of a gleaming smear of fresh blood on a rock or on a crushed blade of grass. Tripp's and Aaron's feet were taking the punishment badly.

They had made seven or eight miles when Aaron stumbled and fell, landing heavily on one shoulder. "I—I can't go on," he gasped, eyes glazed in fear. "Please don't drag me, Andy. I—I never meant you no harm."

Tripp's face wrinkled in disgust.

Andy looked around. They were four or five miles beyond the Union Pacific tracks, at least fifteen miles from O'Meara's ranch. The ground was cracked with heat, the hills remote; it was as good a place to leave them as any. He rested his hands on the saddle horn, facing the two men. "I never want to see either of you in this valley again," he said simply. "I reckon you can understand that, Tripp. If I see you again, I'll figure you're here to kill me, so I *will* kill you."

"Enjoy your last few days alive, boy," Tripp snarled. "Next time I see you, you're a dead man."

Andy ignored him. "You too, Aaron. You're no longer welcome in these parts. If you want to live, get out." He wheeled his horse and nudged it into an easy lope. Within minutes the two men were out of sight.

· · ·

As Andy rode back toward town he considered his situation carefully. In truth, it wasn't much worse than it had been two days ago; other than a number of new lumps and bruises and a weariness burrowing deep into his bones, he was none the worse for his ordeal at O'Meara's hands and at the line camp. The only thing that had changed was the fact—clear enough now—that O'Meara was adamantly and inflexibly determined to have the Little Muddy no matter what the cost, including murder, and that single, unequivocal fact was the one thing Andy needed upon which to act. There was only one way left to attack the Circle-K and break O'Meara's power once and for all, and that was to dynamite Upper Badger reservoir. Without that water the Circle-K would be finished.

Of course O'Meara would continue to keep guards posted at the dams and their number would undoubtedly be increased as soon as he learned that Andy had escaped. Andy was faced, now, with the problem of finding a way to destroy the reservoir, even though the dam was swarming, day and night, with O'Meara's men.

He kept to the hollows of the valley as he rode toward town, watching for signs of trouble, thinking carefully about O'Meara's dams.

· · ·

For two interminable days Clair had been frantic, unable to sleep, unable to concentrate on anything—she lived, minute to minute, watching for Andy, sweeping the horizon with a look that had become, as the hours passed without further news, a nightmarish, agonizing vigil. Numbing terror gripped her as she became increasingly certain of his death,.

The day before, when Bear returned alone from Andy's ranch leading Andy's horse, she had wept, miserably, inconsolably, in Abigail's arms, yet with some faint measure of hope still intact. Now, twenty-four hours later, despair had settled like a block of ice in her chest, her hands were weak, her fingertips chilled and numb.

A few minutes before noon, three hours after Andy had left Tripp and Aaron in the prairie, her watchfulness paid off as she saw a rider coming from the southwest, three hundred yards away. Her heart leaped. She shaded her eyes, squinting into the brightness of the day.

"Oh my God!" she screamed. "It's Andy!" "Ma! Pa! It's Andy!" She bolted out of the yard and ran to him, lifting the hem of her dress as she went. She met him almost a hundred yards from the house. Andy looped the reins around the saddle horn and stepped to the ground as she drew near. She ran, calling out his name, through a shifting, blinding curtain of tears and almost collapsed in his arms. He caught her and held her close, his eyes closed for a moment, feeling her pressed against him, trembling, her arms tight about his neck, then he opened his eyes again and searched the prairie reflexively for signs of trouble. She sobbed in his arms, face pressed tightly into his neck.

"Oh, A-Andy," she cried. "W-Where on earth h-have you been? I was s-so worried . . . we were all so worried . . . I waited so . . . so long . . . Pa found your horse . . . in the hills—" Her voice dissolved into painful, wracking sobs. They held each other for what seemed to Andy like an impossibly long time, her crying abating slowly as her tortured, pent-up emotions worked their way to the surface. Andy saw Bear and Abby under a willow tree, watching, but keeping their distance. This, they understood, was Clair and Andy's moment, a bond that would never be broken.

It was minutes before Clair finally backed out of his arms and looked at him. "Oh God, Andy!" she said as she brushed away her tears and noticed, for the first time, the cuts and bruises that still covered his face from the beating O'Meara had given him. "What happened to you?"

"It's nothing," he said.

"Nothing?" she cried. "But, Andy . . . your poor face!"

"I had some trouble. It's over now."

"I—we— thought—" She couldn't finish the sentence. Fresh tears formed in her eyes. "When you didn't come back— Oh, Andy, it's been so awful, so terrible, wondering, not knowing—"

He pulled her toward him and kissed her lightly. "I need a bath," he said. "And a few hours sleep. I'm bushed."

She looked at him, noticing for the first time the haggard appearance of his face behind the bruises. He hadn't slept properly in several days although he'd slept, after a fashion, in the cabin while hanging by his arms.

"Of course," she said. A smile appeared on her pale, drawn face, the first smile she'd managed in over thirty-six hours, and she pinched her nose at him.

"I know," he said, picking up the reins. "After the water's ready I reckon you'd better make yourself scarce for half an hour."

"Pooh! You're no fun," she said, her old humor starting to come back although her eyes were still pink with recent tears.

Together they walked back toward the house. Bear was waiting for them at the corral. When they reached the gate Clair let go of Andy's arm. "I'll go get that bath ready," she said, hurrying off toward the house.

Bear stared after her. "Bath? Did she say bath?"

"That she did, Bear."

Bear grinned and shook his head. "You ain't been back five minutes an' already you got the situation under control." His smile faded and his eyes narrowed. "Where've you been, Andy? Whose horse is this? We been worried plumb sick around here, wonderin' what happened t' you. I went out t' O'Meara's ranch yesterday, with Albert an' the sheriff, lookin' for you."

"I know, I heard you."

"Heard us—" Bear said, startled. "Heard what? Where?"

"I was in the barn buried under a pile of straw when you and the others came in. Tripp was there, guarding me."

Bear sighed. "I reckon you got a story t' tell."

"I do," Andy said. "But it'll have to keep. Right now I need that bath. And some food. And a favor."

"Just name it."

"Take this horse over to the livery and get him a stall under O'Meara's name. I don't want anyone calling me a horse thief."

"O'Meara's horse, eh?"

"One of them, yes."

Bear wagged his head in exasperation. "Willow Creek's been a sight more interestin' since you got back, Andy, an' that's a fact."

. . .

Andy awoke at five that afternoon. His arms still ached and he couldn't find his clothes. "Clair," he called.

She appeared in the doorway. "Hello, sleepyhead," she said sweetly.

"Where are my clothes?"

"I washed 'em."

Andy grunted. "I reckon they needed it."

"Somethin' fierce."

"They still wet?"

"Damp."

"I'll wear them damp."

"Only if I get 'em for you." She took a tiny step into the room.

"Out!" He pointed at the door.

"This is *my* room," she said coquettishly. "You've been sleeping in my bed."

"It isn't your bed until I'm out of it, young lady. Now go get me my clothes."

She turned toward the door, her eyes dancing. "Are you always so grumpy when you wake up, mister?"

"Only when I can't find my pants," Andy grumbled.

She returned a minute later, tossed his clothes on the bed, and gave him another coy smile. "Grump," she said and she left the room, closing the door gently behind her.

21

"What's this?" Bear picked up a book Andy had open on the desk. It floated on a sea of papers containing calculations and hand-sketched diagrams. It was the book Andy had asked Clair to keep for him. "There ain't nothin' in here but a mess of numbers," Bear said, perplexed and somewhat wary.

"A table of integrals and mathematical functions. That part's a table of logarithms, Bear."

Clair was sitting almost at Andy's elbow, resting her chin on her palms as she watched Andy work. Outside, through the multipaned window, the setting sun was spreading ribbons of color across the sky. Clair looked up at her father. "Andy learned all about them in college," she said proudly. She beamed at him.

"Loggy-rhythms," Bear mused. "Seems I heard somethin' about them once, long time ago." With apparent effort he sorted through a dusty, layered memory. "There was some feller from New York," he said at last, "all decked out in fancy clothes in Merrick's Hardware Store in Beaver Falls when we used t' live in Pennsylvania. He was talkin' about these here loggy-rhythms. Talkin' up a storm, he was. The man was a durn fool. First he was speakin' English and the next thing you knew he was speakin' some kinda foreign language an' didn't seem t' know he'd done it, neither."

"Oh, pa," Clair said. "Let Andy work."

Bear ignored her and leafed through the book. "How do these loggy-rhythms work, anyhow?"

Andy grinned and winked at Clair. "Well, Bear, you use logarithms to multiply and divide numbers easily. You can even raise numbers to powers and take square roots or cube roots."

Bear frowned. "Square roots? Cube roots?" he said suspiciously.

"Sure," Andy replied. "See, you start with some number, then you move the decimal point over until you have a number between one and ten. The number of places you moved the point over is the characteristic and in this table you look up the mantissa—"

"Just like that other feller!" Bear interrupted, his brow furrowed and clouded. "Dad-burn it all, Andy—sounds like English, but it ain't. That what they taught you at that college?" Without pausing, he waved a ham-sized hand at a diagram Andy had drawn. "An' what's this here thing, anyway? Looks like a well casing or a tank of some sort."

"It's more like a tank than a well casing, Bear. Anyway, when I get through figuring out exactly what I need, I'd like you to build it for me."

Bear's face cleared remarkably and he set the book back on the table, staring at the diagram with sudden interest. "I won't need loggy-rhythms, will I?"

"No. I'll do that part."

"Okay, then. This here's business," he said to Clair. "Why don't you go help your ma?"

"I want t' listen," Clair said.

"You ain't too old for me t' tan your bottom for you, little lady. Now run along."

"I am so too old, pa!" Clair said, indignantly. "Years too old an' you know it." In spite of her words she stood up and edged toward the door as Bear took her chair. "You stayin' the night, Andy?" Clair asked.

"He is," Bear answered for Andy. "Maybe you'd like t' fix up a bed on the couch for him."

"I will," Clair said, her eyes shimmering. "With extra pillows, too."

She left the room and Bear rolled his eyes at the ceiling. "With extra pillows, too," he mimicked in a squeaky baritone.

Andy grinned at him and Bear settled down, studying the diagram thoughtfully. After a few minutes he said, "I don't know what it is, Andy, but I'd be willin' t' bet it ain't nothin' but trouble." He stared at Andy. "You still ain't said how you got your face all banged up an' where you've been the last two days."

"I haven't had time, Bear."

"Well, you got time now. Why don't you tell me that story you promised me?"

Andy sighed and pushed himself back from the desk. He stretched out his feet, folded his hands across his stomach, and told Bear all that had happened to him since he'd left Bear's house two days earlier.

When he was through Bear's face was ashen. "Gawd, Andy," he said quietly. "Don't never breathe a word of this t' Clair. You're lucky t' be alive! Hell, you'll be lucky t' be alive next week with Tripp and Aaron still runnin' round loose. You shoulda put bullets in that pair when you had the chance."

"I wanted to, Bear. I thought about it, but I just couldn't do it."

"Too bad. They'll be gunnin' for you now, you kin count on it. Tripp ain't the sort t' quit, not after what you done t' him. Aaron might fold up, but not Tripp." He picked up the diagram and stared at it. "What is this thing, anyway? You fixin' t' give them murderin' bastards another chance at you?"

"It's a bomb," Andy said evenly.

"A bomb?" Bear said in surprise. He turned the diagram sideways, then upside-down. "Ain't like nothin' I ever seen before."

"It's one of a kind, Bear."

Bear set the diagram back down on the desk. "You want t' tell me how it works?"

Andy explained the idea behind the bomb then told Bear how he intended to use it, omitting the more esoteric details. When he was finished Bear shook his head. "What I ought t' do," he said slowly, "is hold a shotgun weddin', right here an' now—get you an' Clair hitched up good an' proper—an' then run you two the hell out of the territory." He jabbed a calloused, accusatory finger at the paper. "If O'Meara's men don't get you, this thing will."

"I need you to build it for me."

"Be a damn fool if I did."

"I can make this work," Andy said earnestly. "And with the reservoirs gone O'Meara would be finished."

Bear cupped a hand under his chin, his mouth set in a grim, straight line, his eyes morose. "You ain't quittin', are you, Andy? O'Meara and his men cut you up, chase you all over town, burn down your ranch, and come within a star's twinkle of killin' you, an' you still ain't got the sense t' quit."

"I can't give up now."

Bear was silent for nearly a full minute. "Well, I reckon there ain't nothin' I kin do or say t' make you quit," he said finally. "You got a streak of pure mule in you from somewhere. So I'll build your bomb for you, but it might be best if you didn't mention anything about this t' Clair. She's already done enough worryin' over your damn fool hide."

"I won't, and thanks, Bear."

"Thanks for nothin'," Bear said, staring at the diagram gloomily. "I'm jest makin' it easier for you t' go an' get yourself killed. You let that happen, son, an' I'll never speak to you again."

•   •   •

The next morning Andy waited across the street from Peliter & Owens Hardware Store for ten minutes until Jack Peliter finally ambled down the boardwalk and opened the front door. Andy was nervous, standing out in the open, wondering what had become of Tripp and Aaron. He waited until Jack Peliter disappeared inside, then he crossed Main Street and, when the street was clear, he slipped quickly into the store after him. Jack was standing behind the counter when Andy came through the door. "Good morning," Andy said.

Jack Peliter looked up and smiled nervously. "Why, howdy there, Andy," he replied, his voice uneasy, yet filled with genuine warmth.

"Got a minute?"

Jack hesitated, but not for long. "Reckon so," he said and walked to the door, locked it, and pulled the shades over the front windows. He faced Andy and smiled apologetically. "You understand how it is, Andy."

Andy nodded. "Of course. I don't want to cause you any trouble, Jack."

"You needing another axe handle?" Jack's eyes glimmered with dark, subterranean humor.

Andy's eyes swept the shelves in the store which were laden with boxes and barrels and tools and objects of every description. A keg of nails stood near the counter and a shiny new well pump was lying on the floor at the rear of the store. Andy faced Jack Peliter and grinned wryly, "No, no axe handle this time, Jack. What I need is two gallons of axle grease, about twenty burlap sacks, two hundred yards of rope, and . . . and one other thing."

"Well, I can help you with the first three items, at least. That last one seems a mite vague, though."

"It's got to be kept confidential, Jack."

Jack Peliter's face grew serious. "Your being here today has got to be kept confidential, Andy—at least as far as that's possible. I don't know how many people saw you come in—"

"I didn't see anyone on the street, Jack."

"—but," the older man continued, "when you leave, might be best if you go out the back."

"That's what I had in mind," Andy said. He paused, then asked, "You got any dynamite?"

Jack Peliter was visibly startled. His face paled and he said, "Then it's true, is it? Those stories about you thinking about blowing up O'Meara's reservoirs?"

"They're true," Andy answered solemnly. "I hate like hell to do it, but we can't afford to have O'Meara in this valley any longer. He's trying to run me out. It's my right to do the same to him."

"If O'Meara was to find out . . ." Jack's voice trailed off. "The dirty sonofabitch," he said vehemently.

"I need dynamite, Jack."

"I'd give it to you for nothing just to see those damned reservoirs washed down the mountain along with every last bit of O'Meara's influence in this valley, but I don't have any right now, Andy. Tincup Smith picked up the last shipment, a month, maybe a month and a half ago —all hundred pounds of it. I don't reckon he'll be back for more for another five months."

"So Tincup has dynamite?"

Jack Peliter nodded. "He ain't likely to part with any of it though. He doesn't find much color in that mine of his. Just enough to keep him in dynamite, bacon, flour, and shotgun shells. Story has it he uses dynamite just for show, just for the excitement of having it around and to listen to the noise it makes. He doesn't cotton to folks much. All he seems to care about is dynamite, fair to middling whiskey, and his mule,

Jeb—probably in that order, too."

"Has Tincup ever had any trouble with O'Meara?"

"Couldn't say, Andy. Seems like O'Meara alienates about everyone he comes in contact with, but Tincup only comes to town two or three times a year. He might never have met O'Meara for all I know."

"Do you know where Tincup's mine is?"

Jack shook his head. "Not exactly. I'm not sure anyone's ever seen it. All I know is it's up north about thirty miles, in the canyon where Grizzly Creek empties into the Green River. If you follow Grizzly Creek into the hills for five or six miles, keeping your eyes peeled, you might spot his shack somewhere. That's about the best I can do."

"Thanks, Jack."

"I wouldn't drop in on him if I was you, Andy. He's about as unpredictable as a rattlesnake in a tree. Heard he guards that canyon as if he owned every last inch of it. If you want dynamite, I could order you some—take two or three weeks to get it in, though."

"Thanks anyway," Andy said. "But I reckon I'll take my chances with Tincup. How much do I owe you for the other things?"

"I'll put 'em on your bill, Andy. If you blow O'Meara's reservoirs, they're on the house; if you don't, well, just try to return what you don't use."

"I can pay for them, Jack."

Jack shook his head. "It's worth it to me, Andy. Makes me feel good, like I'm helping you fight O'Meara. Besides, supplying you with what you need is the easy part. I don't see how you're going to get anywhere near those dams of his. I hear tell he's got guards all over hell up there."

Andy grinned, glancing toward the rear of the store. "Thanks, Jack," he said. "You can deliver everything to Bear's place. He'll be expecting them."

Jack Peliter walked to the back and unlocked the door. He turned to Andy again. "I wish you luck," he said. "Just thought you oughta know—O'Meara went and bought out my entire stock of storm lanterns several days ago. Word has it he's got both dams lit up like a couple of Christmas trees."

Andy thanked him again and slipped out the door.

.   .   .

Pete, Andy's bay horse, picked his way over the narrow rocky trail that wound up the twisted canyon, his shod hooves ringing dully as they struck rocks, the sound dampened by the thick brush that grew in the canyon bottom. The air was cool in the gorge, with its steep, majestic sides and overarching canopy of trees. A pleasant breeze rustled through the needles of the pines, its gentle soughing pierced by the occasional bright cry of a jay.

It was no wonder Tincup chose to live in these mountains, Andy thought. The natural beauty of the land seemed to cascade around him like water: pale, opalescent beams of sunshine lancing through the trees; the light-dark symmetry of shadow cast by the canyon's walls; the unending, rippling melody of Grizzly Creek; geologic layers of ragged rock carved by wind and water into mystic statues; moist, loamy dirt overlaid with soft, copper-colored pine needles. And, too, it was perhaps no wonder that Tincup felt the need at times to shatter the relentless, almost ponderous silence of this sanctuary with the heavy booming roll of an occasional dynamite blast, a transitory disturbance that echoed again and again off the canyon walls and proclaimed, if both briefly and falsely, the mastery of man over the wild and impervious nature around him.

Andy felt small in that vast canyon, pleasantly small. Small enough that all the acts of desperate violence he had engaged in during the past several days seemed somehow less significant, less real, overshadowed by the glorious indifference of the canyon. He suddenly envisioned himself living out the rest of his days in a place such as this, with Clair at his side, the two of them as quiet and as filled with inner harmony as the raw beauty around them.

A bluejay with bright, black eyes swooped across the trail and landed in the lime-green shadows of a huge lodgepole pine, scolding him for trespassing. In one of the oversized saddle bags that Bear had given him, one bottle clanked against another with a hard, glassy sound and Andy dragged himself out of his reverie. Amy was somewhere in Cheyenne, trusting him to bring them all back to the Bar-O someday. In town, Clair was waiting. He had obligations.

His thoughts intruded on the wild beauty of the canyon and

once again he scanned the hills for some sign of Tincup's shack.

"That's 'bout far enough, sonny."

The voice seemed to float out of the rocks and the trees around him in the mid-afternoon shadow of the canyon. Andy reined Pete to a halt. He looked around but saw no one.

"You kin git on back same way you come in." The voice was cracked with age, energetic, dry, inhospitable.

"I'm looking for Tincup Smith," Andy called to the shadows.

"And who might you be?"

The voice came from behind a clump of brush at the base of a tree thirty feet off the trail, ten feet above Andy's head. He saw, then, the twin black circles of a double-barreled shotgun held with the steadiness of wooden pilings driven into the ground, aimed directly at his chest.

"You mind putting that scatter-gun down?" Andy asked.

"Not fer all the gold in these hills, sonny."

"Heard that isn't much."

Andy heard a quiet, private cackle, then Tincup said, "You heard right. But I still ain't heard your name yet an' my finger's gettin' plumb weary on this here trigger."

"Andrew Stillman, Tincup. I've come to talk with you."

"Stillman," the voice said. There was a pause. The creek gurgled. "Henry's boy?"

"His oldest."

"How's Henry doin' these days?"

"My father is dead," Andy said. "Shot in the back."

There was another moment of silence then the muzzle of the shotgun withdrew into the brush. Tincup stood up and came into the open, staring down at Andy from the steep slope of the hill. His shoulders were thin and bony under his shirt and his black suspenders held up a baggy pair of worn Levis that could have stayed up in no other way. His thick, grey beard was nearly a foot long and it was puffed out along his cheeks making it impossible to see his neck. A thick grey moustache blended so completely with his beard that it was hard to determine where his mouth might be. His eyes were bright and dark, like those of the bird Andy had seen earlier, and Andy realized that Tincup was, in some ways, as wild as the rest of the canyon, hiding behind his beard, now, in much the same way as he had hidden behind the brush only moments earlier.

"Sorry t' hear that," Tincup said, his voice gruff but filled with an unassuming, almost childlike sincerity. "Truly am. They's more ways t' die in th' city than out here, purely unnecess'ry too, t' my way of thinkin'." He deposited his meager bulk on a nearby rock and squinted at Andy. "I don't need no conversation, sonny." He gestured around him. "Got all I kin handle, right here."

Andy swiveled in his saddle, withdrew a bottle from the saddle bag, and held it up.

Tincup's eyes glowed appreciatively. "Well now, that'll buy you a few minutes I reckon, though I'll tell ya right now I ain't got all that much t' say." He stood up and ambled down the rocky slope with the grace of an antelope. "If'n you're willin' t' part with that there bottle you must have a powerful thirst for conversation. Might's well come on up t' th' cabin."

Tincup Smith turned and walked up the trail for a hundred yards, went past a heavy outcropping of granite that bulged from the side of the canyon, then turned and climbed a narrow, almost invisible trail that scaled the steep wall of the canyon in a series of tight switchbacks. Andy got off Pete's back and led him up the trail. After a hike of about three hundred yards they entered a clearing at the base of an enormous granite cliff. A crude little shack, a tilted almost dwarflike structure that blended happily into the surroundings, was nestled into a pocket formed by a half-dozen trees and wild brush, all overshadowed by the ominous, looming white rock, and Andy realized that he would never have found Tincup if Tincup hadn't allowed himself to be found.

Andy removed the saddle bags and turned Pete loose to graze on a small patch of meadow grass with Tincup's mule, Jeb. Tincup waved a bony hand at the shack and said, simply, "This here's home."

"A man surely couldn't ask for a better one."

Tincup looked down at the ground, embarrassed. "Other than you, now, your pa is th' only other man to've seen it."

"My father?" Andy said in surprise.

Tincup nodded uncomfortably. "Ol' Henry was somethin' kinda special," he said. "The only man I ever called a friend in these parts." He stared at Andy for several seconds. "You got his eyes, an' most of th' rest of his face, Andrew. I'm plumb sorry t' hear they got him." He looked up at the hills contemplatively. "Up here you got bear, an' cougar, an' sometimes they're hungry an' a nuisance, but they ain't mean and they ain't greedy, an' they never say one thing when they mean another. They got no poison in'em, not like city folk." He paused then added: "Hard t' die nat'rally in th' city." He fell quiet after this lengthy speech, lost in thought for several seconds, then he rubbed his hands together in anticipation. "Now then, I believe you got somethin' fer me?"

Andy reached into the saddlebag and pulled out two bottles of Tincup's favorite brand of whiskey. Tincup's eyes shone like dark moons. "I reckon you want more'n jest talk," he said, eyeing the bottles eagerly.

Andy nodded, handing him the whiskey. "Dynamite," he said. "But the whiskey is yours to keep in any case."

Tincup took the bottles and nodded toward the shack. "Reckon we kin talk jest as well settin' as standin'." He led the way toward the shack and set two chairs out in the cool shade of the bluff in front of the little cabin. He held one bottle in his hands, caressing the cool, smooth glass lovingly. "What'd'ya want t' know about dynamite?" he asked.

"I need some. About fifty pounds."

Tincup held the bottle, staring at the label sadly. "Fifty pounds," he mused. "That's a whole case, Andrew. I ain't so sure I kin help you."

"You don't have that much?"

"Oh, I got a full case, all right," Tincup said in a low voice. "But my dynamite, Andrew . . . "

"High density, high velocity?"

Tincup gave Andy a sharp glance. "You know somethin' about dynamite? How?"

"I went to college back east. Civil engineering. I had a class on explosives." He shrugged depreciatingly. "We blew up rocks in a quarry on weekends."

Tincup's eyes kindled with a curious brightness. He looked at Andy like a man seeing his single greatest love repeated in another man's eyes, and he bent forward eagerly. "It's high density, high velocity sticks," he said. "Gotta be," he jerked a thumb at the bluff behind them. "Granite don't take nothin' else." He chuckled softly. "You shoulda been here for th' fourth of Ju-ly. While ever'one in town was celebratin' with their puny firecrackers and what all, I took five sticks up to ol' General Custer up there near th' top o' th' ridge,"—he pointed at a spot high on the opposite canyon wall—"an' stuck thirty yards of fuse in the primer stick an' set it right under th' base of th' General." He faced Andy. "Sometimes I give names t' things around here," he explained. "Kinda keeps me from bein' lonesome sometimes. General Custer is th' name I give t' a big rock 'cross the way. Anyway th' General was granite, prob'ly twenty feet across, balanced kinda delicate, musta weighed three, four hundred tons.

"I lit that fuse—thirty yards give me 'bout an hour—an' high-tailed it down the side of th' hill with th' General perched right over my head. I got back here with two minutes t' spare an' I was settin' jest where I am now with a jug o' red-eye t' my lips when that charge went off. General Custer sorta jumped an inch or two, kinda like th' blast scared it off its nest, and then it slid off th' mountain and started rollin'. I hope t' tell you, that was a sight! The General was a mean sonofabitch, all right. I named that rock jest right. Never seen nothin' like it. Damn rock fell nine hundred feet soundin' like th' devil himself poundin' down th' mountain."

He peered up at the ridge. "Some days I kinda miss th' General though," he said with a trace of sadness in his voice. "Canyon wall looks kinda bare without 'im. Might be I shouldn'ta done 'er."

Andy was silent for several minutes, visualizing General Custer crashing down the side of the canyon, giving Tincup time to come off the telling of his story. Finally he asked, "How well do you know William O'Meara?"

Tincup frowned. "Circle-K?"

"Yes."

"Irishman with a red face, eyes like a copperhead, voice like a man grindin' an axe?"

Andy smiled, "Sounds like you two've met."

Tincup spat expertly on a rock that sat innocuously in the yard, apparently for the express purpose of providing a target. "O'Meara's one dog-mean sonofabitch," he said. "I ain't got no use fer th' man."

"It was one of Will O'Meara's men who shot my father in the back."

Tincup was silent for a minute. He appeared to be resting peacefully, his eyes nearly closed. When he spoke his voice was surprisingly soft. "What d'you need dynamite for, Andrew?"

"I want to blow up O'Meara's reservoirs."

Tincup's face registered nothing. He stared up at the spot that General Custer had vacated, several weeks before. "You'll need a whole case," he said slowly. "I reckon I kin spare that much for a good cause."

"I'll order you another case in town," Andy said. "When it comes in I'll pack it up here to you myself."

Tincup Smith appeared not to have heard him. "It's gonna be quiet in these hills," he said slowly as if he were trying to fathom exactly what that meant. He shook off the thought and turned to Andy. "What'd they teach you at that college, Andrew? You know how t' rig a primer charge? You know how t' split safety fuse so's th' powder don't come out?"

Andy smiled. "Couldn't be any better teacher than you in the whole doggone world, Tincup. I reckon I could do with a refresher course."

22

Jack Peliter's information had been correct, Andy thought with a wry grin: viewed from a distance the dam did have the appearance of a Christmas tree, if a sparsely-lit one at that. Lanterns had been strategically placed, two at the base of the dam, two more at the top, and a single lantern, carried by an unseen hand, slowly criss-crossed the face of the dam in irregular patterns.

Not that the dam required the additional light of the lanterns, Andy noted critically. In just a few days the moon would be full; it hung high now over the western mountains, bathing the valley in cool, silver light. Even without the lanterns no one could hope to get close enough to the dam to plant a charge. From his vantage point just below the crest of the ridge, Andy could see water shimmering behind the dam. The face of the dam was speckled with numerous small, dark bushes that had taken root since the earthen dam had been built. A hundred yards behind the face of the dam, the Rock of Gibraltar was a low, dark mound, covered by scraggly brush, rising less than two feet out of the water.

The reservoir was as full as Andy had ever seen it. Even more so, perhaps, than it had been five days earlier when he had first scouted the dam and the surrounding hills, the night after he'd returned from his visit with Tincup. Badger Creek was still flowing with the last of the water the shrinking snow pack would give up for the summer. In another two weeks the creek would be dry.

For the past five days Andy had spent part of his time in the hills and part of his time at Bear's house. He tried to keep his presence at the blacksmith's home hidden, arriving before dawn, leaving after dusk, sleeping, for the most part, in the daytime, packing the needed supplies by night over a little-used trail that traversed the northern end of Crooked Neck Ridge. From there he crossed another, higher ridge to the east that looked out over O'Meara's reservoir. At the end of the reservoir, far from the dam and fifty yards away from the water, he carefully concealed his equipment in a dense stand of brush.

The bomb had been the most difficult thing to pack across the mountains. Bear had done a fine job on it, building it with the knowledge that Andy's life might very well depend on its working properly. It was a hollow cylinder made of sheet metal, six feet long, two and a quarter feet in diameter, with a watertight steel cap fitted into one end, three inches from the rim. Fitting that cap and sealing it with lead had occupied the major portion of Bear's time. A reinforced steel shelf had been built inside the cylinder, fifteen inches below the end cap, and half a dozen iron straps girded the cylinder. When completed, it weighed just over two hundred pounds. Filled with fifty pounds of dynamite, it would still take more than eight hundred pounds of ballast to sink the bomb into the reservoir, and for that purpose Andy had fashioned a strong wire cage out of twisted strands of baling wire that would later be fastened to three holes near the rim of the open end of the bomb. When the time came to sink the bomb, the cage would be filled with granite rocks. The bomb would then be submerged in the reservoir with its open end downward, retaining air the same way a cup retains air when inserted upside down in water.

As the days passed, Andy packed the remaining supplies over the hills to the northern end of the reservoir: the case of dynamite (containing eighty-five sticks), two hundred yards of rope, two pulleys, a length of safety fuse, matches, burlap sacks, three woolen blankets, the wire cage, soap, and extra clothing. In the hills half a mile from the reservoir, he cut a number of logs and dragged them to the reservoir. There he built a crude raft which he hid in some overhanging bushes at the water's edge, fifty yards from the place where he intended to launch the bomb.

Andy determined that there was only one good place at the reservoir from which to launch the bomb properly: at a small cove, out of sight of the dam which was fully five hundred yards distant, where a granite cliff had been partially submerged when the reservoir was filled. The water was deep, fifteen feet or so, within a few feet of the rocky bank, and the limbs of a giant cottonwood tree overhung the pool. It would have made a perfect swimming hole had O'Meara allowed swimming in the reservoir. Some days earlier, Andy had rigged a pulley in a thick branch of the cottonwood, twenty feet above the water, fitted it with a rope that ran the length of the limb to the pulley and back, and tied both the pulley and the ropes out of sight.

The preparations had been, of necessity, elaborate, and through all of Andy's comings and goings Clair maintained a quiet, restrained watchfulness, aware of the recent conspiratorial air that had blossomed quite unexpectedly between Andy and her father. Something was afoot, that much was clear, something they didn't want her to know about.

During the final evening in which Andy stayed at Bear's house, one night before he planned to dynamite the reservoir, Clair caught Andy and her father exchanging significant glances across the dinner table. She said nothing at the time, but later, when dawn was near and Andy stole through the house like a wraith and went outside to saddle Pete, she slipped on a dress, wrapped a shawl around her shoulders, and followed him.

Outside, the eastern sky was tinged a deep purple-blue. Several stars still hung in the sky. She stayed in the shadows of the small stable, watching silently as Andy wrapped containers of axle grease in burlap and stowed them in his saddle bags.

When he was nearly done, she asked quietly, "What's the grease for, Andy?"

Her voice startled him. He looked around and she stepped out of the darkness toward him. "Nothing, Clair," he said without conviction. "Nothing important."

"I want to know." She stood two feet from him, arms folded across her body against the morning chill, shivering. "I'm so scared, Andy."

"Of what?"

She looked down, avoiding his eyes. "Of . . . of whatever it is you're doin'."

"And what's that?" his voice was gentle.

"I don't know. Everything. You comin' an' goin' at all hours of the day an' night. You an' pa, sneaking' around like a couple of thieves." She gestured at the bulging saddle bags. "What's the grease for, Andy," she asked again.

Andy grinned crookedly. "I'm going to wear it to keep warm."

Her head jerked up and her eyes flashed with anger. "I'm serious, Andy!"

"So am I." He held out his arms to her.

She backed away, retreating into the darkness of the stable, her eyes blazing, until her shoulders found the wall. "I ain't . . . I'm not—a little girl, Andrew Stillman!" Her eyes reflected the dim light of the coming dawn. "You an' pa have been sneaking around for days now an' I want t' know what you're up to. I don't want you t' treat me like a little girl. I'm a woman now, Andy. *I want to know!*" Her voice broke and filled with the sounds of tears. "I—I love you, Andy. I thought I lost you once. I don't want t' lose you again. I want to know what you're doing."

Andy went to her, held out his arms again. "Clair—"

"*No!*" She whirled out of his reach. "No," she whispered. "I don't want you t' hold me—I want you t' *talk* to me." She stepped out of the blackness of the stable into the yard and the sunrise painted reddish streaks in her hair.

"If I tell you, Clair—you'll try to stop me. Right now I don't need that."

"*I'm not a child*!" she cried. Tears glistened on her cheeks. She held one hand to her face and one arm across her body, sobbing quietly. "Maybe . . . maybe I w-won't like what you're doin' . . . but I won't try t' stop you, Andy. I won't get in your way. I just want to know!"

"I'm going to dynamite Upper Badger Reservoir," Andy said, more abruptly than he'd intended. "That'll wash out Lower Badger too. Is that what you wanted to hear?"

She stared at him with wide, unblinking eyes.

Andy's voice fell to little more than a whisper. "Maybe you're right," he said. "If you're going to marry me I reckon you've got the right to know what I'm doing." He reached out and pulled her into the shadows.

She stood like a statue in his arms. "Marry . . . married?" she said faintly. "Oh, Andy. I'd hoped . . . that is, you never actually said . . ."

Her body warmed his hands where his fingers gripped her slender waist. "I didn't mean to ask you like that," he said awkwardly. "I wanted to wait until this was over—" He held her at arm's length and peered into her face. "Will you . . . marry me, I mean?"

Her face was a pale shadow in the ruddy light in the yard. "Oh God, yes, Andy," she said breathlessly. "Of course. I never wanted anything more in my whole life." She pulled into his arms, pressing her face into his shoulder. They clung together for a moment then he felt her face tilt up to his. Her breath warmed his cheek. "You mean it?" she asked. "You're goin' t' destroy O'Meara's reservoirs?"

Andy nodded uncomfortably.

He felt her body begin to tremble against his. "I heard rumors," she whispered. "Folks . . . folks talkin'." She stifled a sob. "Oh, dear God—" She pressed her face into his neck. "But it's better knowin' than wonderin', Andy. It's better knowin'."

Her hair was soft against his face. He touched it gently. "You're right," he said. "You're not a little girl any longer."

• • •

Eighteen hours later, as he observed the dam in the moonlight, he felt the lingering pressure of her lips on his, the ghost of her body trembling in his arms. Reluctantly, he shook the ghosts away.

There was too much to do. It was time to go.

He ran quickly, silently, along the backbone of the ridge for half a mile then angled down the slope toward the water. The giant cottonwood loomed darkly against the moonlit sky. Andy went to where the bomb was hanging from a limb of the tree over a small bed of mesquite coals that lay in a low, sunken pit in the ground. Earlier that evening, just after sundown, he had strapped the dynamite into the head of the bomb on the shelf near the sealed end. The dynamite had been heating in the sun all day, and before placing it in the bomb he had wrapped it, all eighty-five sticks, in a thick nest of burlap to hold the heat. After the dynamite was safely in place he hung the open end of the bomb over the coals to keep the dynamite warm while the sun set and a chill settled over the night hills. The moon rose slowly over the reservoir. It was imperative that the dynamite not be allowed to freeze—and the nitroglycerin in the dynamite would freeze at just fifty-two degrees Fahrenheit. The bomb, when submerged, would be surrounded by water with a temperature of less than thirty-five degrees for as long as two or three hours. The burlap was needed to prevent freezing of the nitro.

The fuse had been inserted into a blasting cap imbedded in the primer stick just as Tincup had shown him. The fuse was three yards long—six minutes worth—tied carefully to wooden spacers that were fastened to pieces of metal Bear had fixed to the inside of the bomb. Andy had split the end of the fuse carefully, as Tincup had shown him, and it trailed down the inside of the bomb to within three feet of the bottom skirt. Eighteen inches from the end of the fuse, to one side, Andy had pressed a wad of putty onto a line of metal tabs fixed to the inside of the bomb. Into the putty he had inserted the ends of a dozen wooden matches, their tips pointed upward, toward the head of the bomb.

A dozen chances to light the fuse.

He would have to light the match in total darkness in the air space inside the bomb while holding his breath, fourteen feet under water. A tab outside the lower skirt of the cylinder, just under the row of matches, would help him locate the matches in the darkness. Several inches to the right of the matches, a patch of sheet metal had been roughened—a place on which to strike the matches—and to the right of this patch was the end of the fuse, but he would be able to see that when the match lit.

Two nights earlier Andy had hung the bomb from a tree limb with its bottom skirt a few feet off the ground and had gone through the motions—without the dynamite installed—of holding his breath, finding a match in the darkness of the cylinder, striking it, and lighting the fuse. He had even tried it with wet hands coated with grease. In the end he succeeded ten times in a row.

It would be much harder, he knew, swimming in the frigid blackness of the water.

It was time to sink the bomb in the reservoir.

Andy tied the rope that passed through the pulley over the water to the thick wire hanger that held the bomb suspended over the coals. He dragged a heavy pine log out of the bushes nearby and rolled it carefully into the water. Leafy branches cut from a bush had been tied to the log. Two free-ended ropes, that had been tied around the middle of the log, trailed slackly in the water; one rope was two feet long, the other, seven. Later, both ropes would be tied to the bomb. From further up the bank he retrieved the raft, eight logs bound tightly together with ropes. Near the water's edge he had piled dozens of granite rocks, each weighing from ten to twenty pounds. A fresh set of clothing awaited him up Badger Creek, three hundred yards from the end of the reservoir. Two cakes of soap were wrapped inside the bundle of clothing.

Everything was poised and waiting now. To keep the dynamite as warm as possible he had waited until the last minute to remove the bomb from the coals. He took one last look around. Once he had begun, everything had to go smoothly. The bomb had to be sunk, the dynamite floated to the dam, the fuse lit, and he had to get the hell away from the bomb—all before the dynamite froze.

Moonlight, cold and pale, slanted through the leaves of the tree from the western sky.

Andy kicked dirt over the coals, and with that gesture there was no turning back.

Quickly, he attached the wire cage to the bottom of the bomb. Two ropes had thus far been tied to the bomb; one passing through a pulley high in the tree overhead and the other passing through the pulley out over the water. For five minutes Andy pulled on one rope and let off slack on the other, slowly maneuvering the bomb out over the water until it was suspended over the cove by just one rope. His hands ached. He held the rope, walking it around the trunk of the tree, then backed it off, hand over hand, lowering the bomb with care until the cage was submerged and the lower rim of the cylinder had slid six inches into the gently rippling water of the reservoir. That done, he tied the rope to the base of a small, sturdy pine that grew near the water's edge. Taking one last look around, he stripped off his clothing and began coating himself with a thick layer of grease, grinning as he worked. Clair hadn't believed him.

The water in the reservoir was icy cold. A man immersed without protection in that water would die in less than fifteen or twenty minutes and Andy estimated he would be in the water for at least half an hour as he set the bomb in place, lit the fuse, and retreated to the Rock of Gibraltar. The grease would prevent excessive loss of body heat during that time. He spread the grease liberally, feeling more than a little foolish in the bright moonlight, then he rubbed grease completely through the fabric of his clothing and donned his pants and shirt again. He felt sticky and absurd but already the thick coat of grease was warming him.

He placed a dozen granite rocks on the raft, climbed aboard the unsteady, swaying craft, and pushed off toward the bomb, ten feet from shore. He slid off the raft into the water beside the bomb and instantly the water began drawing heat from his body—slowly but inexorably, through the thick coating of grease.

The sooner he got out of that water, the better.

Quickly he lifted rocks off the raft and lowered them through the water into the cage, painfully aware of the matches and the fuse inside the bomb. He had lowered the bottom edge of the bomb into the water to avoid splashing water inside the cylinder where the critical components might have gotten wet.

Creaking slightly, the wires that held the cage straightened under the weight of the rocks. Once all the rocks were in the cage Andy pulled the raft to shore by means of a tether rope. He regained the shore, not cold, but not warm, either. He untied the rope that held the bomb and lowered the bomb deeper into the water, watching the water inch up the side of the cylinder until the bomb was almost floating on the cushion of air that had been trapped inside. Once this had been accomplished, Andy tied the rope to the pine again.

Twice he repeated the entire process—rafting stones out to the bomb, placing them in the cage, returning to shore, lowering the bomb deeper still into the black water until at last the top of the bomb floated less than four inches out of the water. Another five or six rocks would submerge it.

As the bomb had sunk deeper into the water, water pressure had compressed the air inside the cylinder into a smaller and smaller volume. Andy had allowed for that. The lost volume was lost buoyancy. Once the bomb had been fully submerged it would sink of its own accord, which would compress the air within even more, which, in turn, would further increase the bomb's tendency to sink. Therefore, by itself, the bomb would sink rapidly to the bottom, rendering it useless. The interaction of these several forces and pressures was rather subtle and Andy was thankful for his engineering education, although he found it ironic that the first practical application of the principles he had struggled to learn would be used to destroy rather than to build.

Andy untied both ropes that had held the bomb over the tree and the bomb bobbed freely in the water, a few inches above the surface. To keep it from sinking to the bottom once he put the few remaining rocks into the cage, Andy floated the pine log out to the bomb and tied the two ropes that had been previously tied to the log to the wire hanger at the top of the bomb. Once the remaining ballast was placed into the cage, the log would act as a float, a float that would not attract the attention of the men at the dam, and it would prevent the bomb from sinking to the bottom.

Andy loaded several rocks into the cage and the bomb slipped gently beneath the water. The float log rolled over, sank an inch, and took the weight of the bomb. The bomb was now ready to be floated out to the dam. An hour had passed since the bomb had been removed from the coals. The water would now be removing heat from the dynamite at the maximum rate. Andy hoped the burlap was doing its job, keeping the dynamite warm enough beneath the icy water.

He stowed a hundred yards of rope on the raft, the remainder of one of the cans of grease, and a board which would serve as a crude paddle. A knife was at his belt. He cut a short length of spare rope and tied it, as a means of towing the bomb, from the raft to the float log that now held the bomb hidden under eighteen inches of water. In the daytime the bomb would have been visible beneath the reservoir's clear water, but at night it was nothing but black on black.

There was nothing left to do now but transport the bomb as quickly as possible to the dam. He glanced up at the sky. From the position of the moon he judged the hour to be about one o'clock; in three and a half hours the sun would begin to light the sky in the east and the men guarding the dam would see him if he were still out on the water. But he didn't have that long anyway.

Before then, the dynamite would have frozen.

23

Andy kneeled on the raft and paddled slowly out of the cove with the bomb, an awkward, hidden cargo, in tow behind him.

Up until that time the moon had seemed a friend, its light making the business of getting the bomb safely into the water easier. But now that he was on the open surface of the man-made lake, it seemed as if the moon was leering at him—a grinning specter with a tilted, shining face, spotlighting him for the men traversing the top of the dam. Yet even in that light, the outlines of distant objects were indistinct, and the contours of the raft were broken by leafy branches Andy had fixed to it. After his initial fears had lessened, Andy realized he was probably no more visible to the men on the dam than they were to him, and they weren't expecting trouble to come from over the water.

The bottom of the rock-filled cage was thirteen or fourteen feet below the water's surface, so Andy followed a broad arc across the reservoir designed to pass over its deeper portions. The lake was a shimmering, shifting plain of glass surrounded by dark spires of trees that thrust into the pale gray-black of the sky. Water lapped at the sides of the raft. In the distance, Andy could see the lanterns that had been placed at either side of the top of the dam. Ahead and to his right, the Rock of Gibraltar bulged out of the water, dark and low, like the back of some gigantic, reposing beast.

It took some forty minutes of hard paddling to reach a point a hundred yards from the dam, twenty yards to one side of the island. Once there, Andy untied the tow rope from the float log and, abandoning the bomb for the moment, he paddled the raft slowly to the island. When he was several feet from the dank mound of earth he stepped off the raft into water halfway to his knees. The bottom was soft, yet not muddy, held together by grasses that had been caught by the rising water. Crouching low to keep his silhouette from showing, Andy tethered the raft to a shrub then transferred the blankets to the island. He then tied one end of the large coil of rope to the stoutest shrub he could find and tied the other end around his waist. From the container of grease he removed the last of the gooey substance and smeared a fresh, thick coating over his hands, into his hair, and over his face.

Ahead of him, the rim of the dam rose blackly out of the water; to his left, the dark shape of the float log floated quietly. He waded out into the water until it was chest deep then swam toward the log, making as little noise as possible. From that point on, he knew, it would be a race against time, against the unyielding cold of the water.

Andy reached the log and propelled it toward the dam with powerful, silent, underwater kicks. He kept his hands out of the water, trying to preserve their warmth as long as possible. As the lights drew nearer, he saw the dark form of a man walking across the top of the dam, his feet less than three feet above the surface of the water. Andy couldn't determine whether or not the cowhand on the dam was looking in the direction of the approaching log. He hoped the log wasn't moving too fast and he made sure he did not splash.

Cold seeped into his body through the grease. Behind him, the rope uncoiled slowly as he drew closer to the dam.

Ten minutes after leaving the island he reached a point twenty feet from the dam, approximately midway between the two lanterns at the point where he had determined the dam to be the most vulnerable. Below him, the bomb was suspended under the water by the shorter of the two ropes tied to the float log. He was cold. Only with effort could he keep his teeth from chattering.

He looked around. Piled against the face of the dam and extending outwards for a distance of several feet was a gently bobbing carpet of driftwood floating in a layer of yellow-white scum. To one side of the dam, a dark shape moved near one of the lanterns.

Andy pulled the knife from its sheath, cut the shorter of the two ropes, and lowered the bomb further into the depths. The float log bounced rhythmically when the slack in the second, longer, rope ran out. The bomb had almost reached its final position, the dynamite now eight feet under water. Andy carefully pushed the log closer to the dam. Twelve feet from the rim he felt a gentle resistance as the cage touched the bottom of the reservoir as the earth sloped up to the dam.

Boots scraped on hard earth and Andy looked up. A guard had begun his slow walk between the lanterns, his gait slow and unsteady with the repetition of the drill. Andy's heart pounded hollowly; his legs felt weak. The bomb was ready; all that remained was to light the fuse and get back to the island. The rope at his waist tugged at him, beckoning to him, he thought a bit whimsically, perhaps dangerously—a slender umbilical cord calling him back to the safety of the island. The grease on his hands was sticky. And cold.

The slow-moving form drew nearer.

Andy took several deep, quiet breaths, watching the guard approach, and when he felt the tingle of excess oxygen flooding his body, he gripped the rope that passed between the bomb and the float log and pulled himself under the water, beyond the illuminating glare of the moon, beyond the range of one danger and into the frigid, murky depths of another.

Below him, the cylindrical body of the bomb hovered: another dark moon, floating in yet a darker sea. He couldn't see the ballast cage below the bomb. He inched downward, passing along the length of the cylinder, feeling water pressure building in his ears. Ten feet. Twelve. His fingers reached the lower rim of the bomb and he pulled himself downward yet another two feet until his feet touched the rocks in the cage, four feet below the bottom of the cylinder. The mass of the bomb shifted at his touch, rotating as he gripped the rim and felt for the tab that marked the spot under the matches. He found it, finally, and put his head and shoulders into the open mouth of the bomb.

His head broke the surface of the water nearly two feet beyond the lower edge of the cylinder just as he'd expected, the air having been compressed by the pressure of the water at that depth to two-thirds of its former volume. Inside, the cylinder was utterly black. With his eyes open Andy could see nothing at all. The drip of water from his hair echoed with a faint, unearthly hollow sound inside the bomb as he groped for the putty that held the matches. He found it, and touched the slender stick of a match, shocked at the degree of numbness that had already crept with the silence of death into his fingers. He pulled a match free and struck it on the side of the cylinder, just to the right of the putty.

The tip broke off with a dry snap and the bomb rang with a deep, low sound, like the striking of a distant gong. Blood rushed in Andy's ears, a rhythmic surge and hiss. Water lapped softly at the insides of the bomb.

He exhaled slowly and drew in a breath of fresh air. He found another match and struck it twice, willing his hand to be steady. The match didn't light; on the third attempt it twisted out of his fingers and fell into the water.

For a moment he was gripped by a cold feeling of a different kind. What was wrong? Had the matches somehow gotten wet? Or was he just clumsy with cold? He shivered, let out his breath in a soft sigh and took another deep breath. His hands trembled as he felt once again for the putty in the darkness, aware, in some separate chamber of his mind, of the guard above who was walking the crest of the dam, perhaps fewer than twenty feet away. He found a match, pulled it out of the putty, and dropped it. A wave of despair swept through him. His teeth chattered. His fingers closed slowly around the end of yet another match, pulled it free, and again his body started its insistent cry for oxygen. He touched the match against the side of the cylinder carefully and scraped. The match flared, blindingly, in the confines of the bomb, startling him. He dropped it into the water. With an angry hiss the match went out. Spots of light danced in Andy's vision in the sudden darkness.

He took another deep breath and his mind cleared. In the abysmal blackness he pulled another match from the putty, forcing himself to concentrate on the motions he had practiced two nights earlier. The roughened side of the cylinder was just to the right of the putty. He located it in his mind then scratched the head of the match carefully on the side of the bomb, willing steadiness into his fingers. Nothing happened. He tried again and this time the match crackled and sputtered into dazzling flame. He held his breath and gripped the match tightly, turning his head slightly to the right. The split end of the fuse dangled, waiting.

Carefully, Andy touched the fragile flame to the end of the thick cord. At first nothing happened, then the fuse ignited, throwing off a tiny stream of yellow sparks. Gray smoke curled upwards. Andy blinked, dropped the match, then slipped slowly and carefully beneath the surface of the water. The last thing he remembered hearing before leaving the bomb was the surprisingly loud hissing of the fuse.

And now, he had six minutes to get back to the island.

He kicked gently upward, finally breaking the surface of the water. The cool night air felt warm against his face after the biting cold of the water. The moon was blinding. He had surfaced with great care, not knowing whether the guard was still close by or not. He groped, with the least possible movement, for the float log that held the bomb. He squinted and finally saw the guard, thirty feet to his left, unmoving, staring abstractedly over the still waters of the reservoir. Andy pulled himself slowly under the cover of a leafy branch tied to the log, breathing slowly and deeply. His toes felt numb and his arms and legs ached. The cold tunneled into him relentlessly. He kept his fingers out of the water as he clung to the log, watching the guard, aware of the dynamite barely a yard below his feet.

The guard, having completed his private ruminations, began walking back in Andy's direction and Andy slid still further under the sheltering brush, hoping the grease on his face wasn't reflecting too much light. The dry scrape of the man's boots drew near and Andy, against his will and better judgment, half-expected to hear a cry of alarm and the sudden explosion of a gun in his face.

Dirt crunched. Stopped. Crunched again. And the guard stopped almost opposite the log, staring out over the water, his face dark under the shadow of his hat. For a long moment Andy held his breath.

A man's voice called from the distance. "Hey, Ned. You want some coffee?"

The man on the dam turned his head. "You damn right," he said, and walked away.

Andy breathed a quiet sigh of relief and began taking up the slack of the rope quickly, pulling it, not hand over hand, but sliding his right hand along the rope, gripping it, then sliding the left hand up to meet the right. He kept up a steady rhythm, hauling the rope without having to open and close his fingers more than a fraction of an inch.

He reeled in nearly ten yards of rope before it tightened and he began to move slowly toward the island; twenty seconds lost, in addition to the minute the guard's attention had been on the water, during which time Andy treaded water only a few feet from where the bomb floated and the fuse hissed in quiet solitude, approaching the dynamite at the rate of eighteen inches to the minute, eight feet under the water. Once the rope was taut he slid the knife out of its sheath and cut the rope from around his waist to reduce the drag during the return trip. He lay partially on his side in the water, pulling his way toward the island, looking up at the sky. The moon had continued its slow westward trek until it now peered at him through the trees that grew on the crown of the ridge. Black fingers of shadow trailed out over the reservoir at the water's edge.

His fingers ached. That was good. It meant he could still use them.

He slid out the right hand and pulled. Slide and pull. Water gurgled quietly around him.

How long had it been since he'd lit the fuse? he wondered. Three minutes? Four? The frigid water numbed his brain, slowing his thoughts until time became a meaningless, flexible abstraction. He concentrated on the rhythm of his work, pushing his right hand along the rope and pulling it toward him, gripping the rope with his left hand, pushing out again with the right. Below his knees, his legs had numbed beyond all feeling. His fingers opened and closed automatically, reluctantly, and he felt the strength draining from them. Behind him the dam seemed farther away. Ahead of him the island seemed little closer.

Mechanically he pulled himself through the water. Another minute. Or was it? Perhaps it was two. It might have been ten. The fuse might have gone out. The moon seemed to have been suspended in the trees forever.

Slide out the right hand. Close the fingers. Sluggish.

Pull.

Open the fingers of the left hand—slowly, so slowly.

Slide.

Dull pain. But where?

Cold bored into him, yet less unpleasant now, with almost soothing gentleness.

Close the fingers.

The moon was lodged in the trees, a bright eye, mocking him. Behind him the dam was a dark and distant line. It required too much effort to turn his head so he didn't try to see how much farther it was to the island.

Slide.

Grip.

He felt nothing. Five seconds passed.

Had his hand closed? He couldn't tell.

The moon laughed silently down at him, also frozen.

Clair . . . Oh God, Clair . . .

An invisible fist closed around him, squeezing air from his lungs, driving him a few inches closer to the island. The world filled with the sound of thunder, quite a remarkable sound, he thought sluggishly, rich and deep and close, fading quickly and returning, expanded now, from the distant hills.

He rolled over in the water, gazing at a star.

A column of water rose a hundred feet into the air, a thick, white pillar glowing in the moonlight—lit, momentarily, at its base by an eerie blue-white flash of light. A piece of the dam fifteen feet wide and four feet high disappeared in an instant from its rim. A solid, dark gout of water poured through the breach with a growing roar while thick drops that had been blown into the air by the initial explosion rained down heavily, followed by a fine spreading mist. Water thundered down the face of the dam, eroding the earth deeply and quickly as it went. After half a minute a cracked portion of the dam near the center gave way with a deep rumbling sound and several hundred tons of earth and mud cascaded down the remaining face of the dam, pushed by the awesome force of the water behind it.

Downstream, Badger Creek swelled, overflowed its banks, and a rumbling wall of black, churning water raced toward Lower Badger Reservoir, two miles away.

With some distant part of his brain, Andy was aware of what had happened; yet he felt no particular elation at his success, wondering, still, whether or not his fingers had closed around the rope. Again he tried to close his fingers but felt nothing, no movement of his fingers, no pressure of the rope on his fingertips. Then, soon, he felt the slow, insistent suck of water around him.

The reservoir was draining. Without the rope to hold him, the water would sweep him away.

He couldn't tell whether or not he was holding the rope until it was pulled from his feeble grasp and began to slide across his shoulder. In a last, desperate attempt at survival Andy wrapped the rope around his arm in a clumsy corkscrewing motion and folded his arm across his chest, clamping it with his other arm.

Water streamed over his face.

He tried to kick his legs but they felt somehow disconnected; and yet, he found to his faint surprise that it mattered little to him and he felt at peace, not quite as cold as he had been only minutes ago. His shoulder struck something, but what it was he could not say.

"Easy there, Andrew," a voice said, or seemed to say.

• • •

The deep, rolling sound that came out of the hills wasn't like that of thunder—it was somehow more focused, more purposeful. And too, the night was clear, without clouds.

William O'Meara woke up, went to the window, and stuck his head out, listening.

In the waning moonlight he saw Clevis Willis walk out of the bunkhouse, an ear cocked toward the north. O'Meara called down to him, "You hear that?"

"Weren't thunder," came the laconic reply.

"By God," O'Meara's voice filled with rage. "He's at the reservoirs. That sonofabitch is at the reservoirs!" His voice raised to a furious shout. "Get everybody up! I want every man saddled and ready t' ride in two minutes. Two minutes, goddamnit!"

He pulled on pants and boots and was buttoning a shirt as he stormed out the door to his room. Jill stood with wide eyes and an alarmed, pale face at the entrance to her room. "Pa!" she cried. "What is it?"

"The reservoirs," he muttered hoarsely. "That sonofabitch is at the reservoirs."

Jason came out of his room, buckling his belt. He cast a quick, tense look at Jill then followed his father out of the house.

• • •

The two men guarding Lower Badger Reservoir stood poised with their rifles, listening. There was no mistaking the sound that had echoed throughout the canyon from somewhere above them only minutes earlier, and after the sound had finally expended itself against the hills the night was filled with a heavy, expectant silence.

And then, a minute or so later, another sound reached their ears.

They watched, eyes straining as they peered through the gloom toward the opposite end of the reservoir where the creek entered from above. The noise grew, swelled to an evil roar all its own, and suddenly a wall of foaming, muddy water broke from the darkness under the trees, cascading high over the banks of the creek. The men stood at the top of the dam, transfixed and gaping. "Jesus," one man whispered.

"Don't jest look at it, Bill," cried the other, springing into sudden life. "Run for it!"

Together the two men raced across the top of the dam with the water rising slowly just below their feet. They reached the safety of the hillside above the reservoir and the man named Bill looked back in time to see black water pour over the face of the dam in a broad, flat wave, slowly at first, then with increasing volume. In less than a minute the earthen dam eroded, the angry water ripping out the weaker sections, and finally the entire dam seemed to give way all at once.

The two men watched in awe as the thick, muddy water pushed aside everything in its path and hurled down the gorge on its way toward the open prairie.

• • •

Clair stood in the corral with a blanket wrapped around her shoulders, unable to sleep, eyes burning, gently stroking the neck of a pale buckskin. The horse stood with its neck hung low. Its eyes were nearly closed as it savored her unexpected attentions, its shadow black on the broken, hoof-pocked dirt of the corral.

Clair gazed into the western sky, into the low-hanging face of the moon, studying it intently as if it could somehow give her news of Andy. It gazed back, unblinking, old placid poker-face, and at that instant a deep, low sound, like the distant boom of a huge gun, came from afar.

"Oh God, Andy," she whispered.

Her hands trembled.

• • •

With Badger Creek to their left, they rode toward the opening in the nearby hills—Will O'Meara, Clevis Willis, Jason, seven tired cowhands. Behind them, the dust swirled in the moonlight like pale mist. Other than the rhythmic breathing of their horses and the dull beat of hooves in the soft earth of the prairie, they rode in silence, with O'Meara in the lead, until he held up his hand and reined his horse to a sudden halt.

Clevis pulled up alongside and stared into the darkness. O'Meara leaned forward in his saddle. "You hear that?"

Clevis was silent a moment. They were little more than a mile from the ranch; ahead, the mountains loomed dark against the sky. Nearby, Badger Creek, a peaceful, gossamer thread of silver in the moonlight, cut through the rising swell of the prairie. "Water," Clevis said, flatly.

"Sweet Jesus," O'Meara breathed.

The raging water appeared, a sleek and oily foaming mass in the moonlight, thundering down on them, following the gentle course of Badger Creek like some crazed beast, three hundred yards away. The men spurred their horses and climbed a gentle slope that rose at right angles to Badger Creek. The torrent swept toward them, thick and savage in the bowl of the creek, spreading a dark stain across the land to either side with its spent waters.

The men turned and held their ground where the water posed them no danger. They watched in horrified fascination as the water in the creek roared by, carrying limbs and brush. It crept up the slope toward them and beyond, swirling gently at the feet of their nervous horses.

O'Meara was beside himself with helpless rage and he hurled curse after furious curse at the dark, roiling water. "*I'll kill him!*" he screamed, his face a hideous, contorted mask. "That miserable, rotten sonofabitch! Bastard. *Bastard!*" And with that final epithet he uttered a weird strangled cry and twisted partway around in his saddle, staring at Clevis with wide, surprised eyes, mouth open in pain. He reached a hand out to his foreman. His eyes bulged then rolled back in his head and he fell from the saddle into the rippling, inky water.

"Pa!" Jason shouted. Both he and Clevis were off their horses in an instant. The water was six inches deep. William O'Meara had landed on his back, his horse shying away. Together Jason and Clevis dragged the Circle-K owner toward higher ground.

Clevis ripped O'Meara's shirt open and put an ear to his chest but he could hear nothing over the roaring of the passing water. He looked up at the men still on horseback. "You, there, Whitey, Sonny, get on back t' the ranch and bring the buckboard out, fast!" Clevis looked across O'Meara's body at Jason, his face a grim, impenetrable mask.

• • •

Overhead, a star twinkled. His head throbbed, his fingers were on fire with pain, yet he ignored the agony that blazed throughout his body as he gazed at that star, trying to fathom its solitary meaning.

A bird cried out, a thin, reedy sound. A tiny sound compared to—

The dam. The explosion.

He was lying on his back. He lifted his head and tried to reach out but something warm and soft held his arms. He smelled the pungent, weedy odor of ancient mire, earth that had been long submerged. Somewhere, a frog croaked with a forlorn, lonely sound.

"You okay?" a voice asked. Andy twisted his head weakly toward the sound and found himself staring into a dark, gnomelike face. He tried to answer but his voice wouldn't work. Darkness swept over him again and the face disappeared into the mist.

· · ·

He felt cold; not just chilled, but soaked to the soul with deadly ice. His heart hammered yet felt weak, as if it might burst at any moment. He felt sick. He tried to draw a deeper breath and pain ripped at his lungs. His eyes opened on a dull blue sky.

"Jest about gave up on ya fer a while there," someone said in a low voice. "Reckon you'll make it though. Good const'tution."

Andy turned his head and stared into the face of Tincup Smith. "What—?" he said in a cracked voice.

Tincup hushed him with a quick gesture. "I seen a couple of fellers over by th' dam a couple a minutes ago," he said. "Or what's left of 'er, anyway. Best if we don't make any noise right now."

Andy discovered he had been wrapped in the blankets he'd left on the island. His body ached and his mouth felt strangely immobile when he tried to speak. "W-Where are we?" he asked.

"On th' only dry spot in th' middle of th' biggest damn mudhole west of the Mississip," Tincup replied with evident satisfaction.

Andy took another breath and winced. He rested for

several minutes then pushed himself to a partial sitting position, surprising himself when he succeeded. The day had just begun, the sky still considerably lighter toward the east than the west. He found himself on the Rock of Gibraltar, lying behind a hedge of scraggly brush. Nearby, the raft had partially sunk into a slick, tilted plain of mud, still held by a rope to the island. Andy lifted his gaze and his mind reeled at the alien sight of over forty acres of dark, smooth, gleaming mud spread across the bottom of the valley.

Tincup grinned at him, displaying a set of tobacco-stained teeth. He sat on the ground with his shotgun cradled across his bony knees. "Blew 'er t' Kingdom Come," he observed with gleaming eyes. "Never seen nothin' like it, I ain't. Not in this lifetime, nor any other."

But for a trickle of water that wound its way serenely through what had been the deepest part of the reservoir, the reservoir was entirely empty, nothing more, now, than a muddy bowl swept clean of all but a few ancient, decaying trees.

"What are you doing here, Tincup?" Andy asked, his voice ragged but usable.

Tincup cackled. "Didn't figger this was somethin' I could rightly miss, Andrew. B'sides, I didn't have anythin' else t' do. Been here five days now, me an' Jeb, hidin' out, watchin', waitin' fer th' show. Damnedest thing I ever seen, that contraption you blew th' dam with." He raised his eyes and stared intently toward the remains of the dam. "Don't see no one about jest now," he said. "Figger you kin stand? Someone's goin' t' see that raft sooner or later, an' I'd be jest as happy if we wasn't here when they did."

With a struggle that lasted several minutes Andy disentangled himself from the blankets and got unsteadily to his feet as Tincup kept a lookout on the wreckage of the dam and scanned the surrounding hills. Then, with Tincup supporting Andy most of the way, they hiked across the low ridge, slimy with mud ten inches deep that sucked at their feet, to the safety of the trees. His joints ached and his entire body felt brittle and old, yet Andy found himself starting to feel good again. He had done it! The reservoir was gone. O'Meara was finished. Clair was waiting. He picked up his stride and he and the old miner disappeared into the trees.

Across the glistening, empty valley the frog croaked again. Above them, a bird peeped plaintively in the hills.

24

It was past ten that morning when Andy finally drew within a half mile of the town of Willow Creek. He rode at an easy lope, scanning the prairie alertly for signs of trouble. That morning, as he and Tincup had hiked through the trees around the reservoir, he had thought, being slightly overwhelmed with his first sense of victory, that he had beaten O'Meara. Now, although the reservoir had been destroyed and O'Meara could not help but lose much of his stock, he realized O'Meara would be more determined than ever to kill him. And, somewhere out there, Tripp and Aaron would be waiting.

The open prairie seemed full of hidden danger.

His joints were still stiff and his muscles ached. His fingers felt like someone had beaten them with hammers. As he rode he realized, fully now, just how close he'd come to dying in the frigid water. Another minute or two, possibly less, and he would have, and it was only the fortuitous appearance of Tincup that had saved him.

Yet Tincup seemed oblivious of the part he had played, recounting over and over with undiminished glee the glorious explosion he'd witnessed when the dynamite went off: the flash of light, the thick column of water and spray, the booming sound that stayed in the hills long after, the roar of the water draining from the reservoir. This, to him, was the great event of the night, not his wading chest-deep in water out to the Rock of Gibraltar after seeing that Andy was in trouble, or his grabbing Andy under the arms and bracing himself against the dark waters that threatened to carry them both away, or his staying by Andy's side after wrapping him in blankets, with his shotgun at the ready. All these things were, in Tincup's estimation, without significance when compared to the glory of the detonation that had reduced O'Meara's reservoir to a bowl of drying mud.

In the hills, at the far end of the reservoir, Andy had worked with the bar of soap trying to clean off the grease in the tiny stream of water still flowing in Badger Creek, and, throughout his ablutions which required the better part of an hour and stung like fire as the cold water flayed his raw nerves, Tincup told the story of the explosion repeatedly, with untiring effervescent enthusiasm.

How did you get out to the island? Andy would ask, and Tincup would answer something like: "Jest walked out, didn't need no bath neither. 'Leastwise not *this* week!" and continued his description of the events just prior to those he seemed so inclined to forget.

Andy donned the clothing he had stashed, having been only partially successful with the soap, and as he and Tincup followed the stream out of the hills for some distance then pursued a deer trail that came out into a meadow where the old miner had left Jeb, not far from where Andy had picketed Pete, Andy said, "Why don't you come back to town with me, Tincup? It's on your way and I reckon you could use a good meal."

Tincup shook his head. "Not fer all the gold in these hills, sonny."

Andy grinned and said, "Heard tell that ain't much."

"You heard right," Tincup replied with a gruff cackle, and when Andy tried again to get Tincup to accompany him to Willow Creek, Tincup shook his head and said, sadly, "Too many ways t' die in th' city, Andrew. Ain't my kinda folk, anyways, but yer always welcome out my way, 'specially if'n you bring a bottle."

Andy approached the town from due east, coming through a dry wash behind Booth's Mercantile. Clair didn't see him until he'd almost reached Main Street even though she'd been watching for him since before dawn. Bear was in the Blacksmith Shop, working, his mind elsewhere.

"It's Andy, Pa!" Clair cried and she hurried across the street toward him. Andy dismounted when he saw her and she ran to his arms. "Andy," she said with relief. "Thank God you're all right!"

Andy held her, breathing in the delicious fragrance of her hair as she whispered in his ear, "I heard it, Andy. Last night—late—I heard it, the dam . . . Everybody's been talkin' about it this mornin' but no one knew what happened to you." She leaned back in his arms and stared at him with wide, blue eyes. "What's wrong with your hair?" she asked.

Andy's face broke into a tired grin. "Grease," he said. "I told you I was going to wear it."

She laughed, a bit unsteadily, and said, "You look awful." Then her smile faded and she began pulling him toward the blacksmith shop. "You can't stay out here," she said in a frightened voice. "Mr. O'Meara's been brought to town. Some of his men might be around."

"O'Meara? I would have thought he'd be up at the reservoir or maybe looking over his range."

"He's hurt, Andy. Folks say he might be dyin'. He's over at Doc Simes' place now."

"Dying?" Andy said in amazement. "What happened?"

"I heard tell he had a stroke. He was brought to town in a buckboard just after dawn. I saw it go by."

Together they walked past the mercantile toward the street. Andy asked, "Have you seen Tripp or Aaron?"

Clair shook her head. "Clevis and Jason and Sonny brought Mr. O'Meara in. I didn't see anyone else."

Andy nodded and together they started to cross the street, but before they'd reached the other side Jason O'Meara approached on horseback and came to a halt ten feet from them. Clair's fingers tightened on Andy's arm.

"I'm glad t' see you're all right," Jason said. Andy studied Jason's face warily. Jason's shoulders sagged; he held up a hand then let it drop limply back to the pommel of his saddle. "I ain't got no fight with you, Andy."

"Glad to hear it."

Jason's eyes were rimmed with red; weary lines creased his face. When he spoke his voice was heavy with exhaustion. "Don't like t' say it, but my pa was . . . is . . . a, a fool, Andy." He looked down at his hands. "Guess I've been somethin' of a fool too, for longer than I care t' think on it."

Andy said nothing. Clair's hand trembled.

"I reckon I own the Circle-K now," Jason said quietly. "Even if pa lives he ain't never goin' t' be the same again, least that's what Doc Simes says. You an' me, Andy—we ain't got no quarrel an' I say, right here an' now, that the trouble between the Circle-K an' the Bar-O is finished. I've already told my cowhands that you ain't t' be bothered an' I'll kill the man that does. This war is over, far as I'm concerned. If you want t' end it too, I'd be mighty pleased t' shake on it." Jason leaned down and extended his hand toward Andy.

Andy took Jason's hand and the two men held the grip for a long, solemn moment. Bear came over and stood next to Clair.

Jason straightened in the saddle and smiled thinly. "The Circle-K still needs them reservoirs, Andy. This might sound strange, but I'd like you t' oversee the rebuilding. I don't know how much engineers get paid, but it's worth three hundred dollars a month t' me. If you'll do it, that is."

Andy was silent for a moment. "I'll have to think on that a while, Jason."

Jason nodded. "One more thing," he said. "I'll pay four thousand dollars for the use of the Little Muddy until the end of October. I gotta save as much of the herd as I can, Andy."

"I don't have to think that over, Jason. You can use the Little Muddy until the beginning of March if you need it, and any Bar-O range more than two miles south of the . . . the house." Andy ended with the abrupt realization that the house was gone.

Jason's eyes were somber. "As soon as things settle down a bit, me an' some of the boy'll be out t' start work rebuildin' everythin' my pa burned down. You just say where you want it. You got my word on that."

"I couldn't ask for anything more fair than that," Andy said. He paused, then added, "I'm glad you're not going to let the Circle-K fold up, Jason."

"I didn't agree with much of anythin' my pa's done in the last four months—maybe the last four years. I don't know what come over him." Jason jerked his head in the direction of Doc Simes' office. "Maybe—" His voice choked suddenly. "Maybe it's better—this way." He looked down at his saddle horn for a long moment. When he looked up again his voice was tightly controlled. "I ain't seen Tripp or Aaron since last night, Andy. You better keep a lookout for those two. Tripp ain't talked of nothin' but killing you for days now. He's plumb crazy, dangerous as a rabid dog."

Again Clair's fingers tightened on Andy's arm. "I'll be careful," Andy said.

Jason nodded. "Be seein' ya, Andy. You too, Clair, Bear." He kicked his horse into a lope to the end of Main Street and disappeared down the dusty path that led south, toward the Circle-K.

Bear looked after him. "That's a mighty good man there," he said to no one in particular. "You best be doin' like he says," he cautioned Andy. "You oughta hole up somewhere for a day or two 'til Tripp an' Aaron are found."

"Like here?" Andy indicated Bear's house.

"Of *course* here." Bear grinned. "Anyway, I'd hog-tie you if'n you tried t' leave, so, if'n you think on it, you ain't really got no choice."

Andy smiled wearily. "I won't put you to the trouble. I'll just put up Pete, and then I could use a bath and a place to sleep. But before any of that I reckon I'd better ask you for permission to marry Clair." He put his arm around Clair's waist and Clair smiled up at him, her face alive with happiness.

Bear looked from Andy to Clair and back to Andy again. A grin widened on his face. "Well I'll be doggoned, Andy! Of course you got my permission. I been waitin' most of a month for you t' ask. Didn't want t' have t' beat it out of you, though." His eyes twinkled with merriment. "You know, for a college feller, you seem a mite slow t' me."

Andy led Pete through the cool shadows of the yard between the house and the shop, his arm still curled around Clair's waist. Bear went into the house to break the news to Abigail. In the stable Andy stripped off Pete's saddle and bridle and turned the horse loose in the corral. When he turned from the saddle rack, Clair was waiting for him.

He pulled her into his arms and held her close.

Several minutes later they came out of the stable and walked into the sunlit yard behind the house, Clair again holding Andy's arm. She talked excitedly. "Oh, Andy, when— when do you think we can do it—get married?"

"Pretty eager, ain't you?" Andy drawled.

She gripped his arm tighter. "Don't fun with me, mister." Her voice fell to a whisper. "Feels like I've been waitin' for—"

The gunshot, although it came from the street, seemed to explode almost in their faces. Andy reeled backwards and fell to one side. Blood spread darkly over his left shoulder. The gunshot lingered for a moment in the late morning air, echoing up and down the street. Clair screamed and dropped to his side. "Andy! Oh no, *Andy!*"

Another shot whined over their heads, and as Andy scrabbled in the dust, pulling Clair behind a storage shed set under the filtered shade of a willow tree, he heard Tripp's angry voice—"Goddamn it! Wait 'til you got a better shot, you dumb sonofabitch!"

Andy grimaced in pain as he got to his feet and pulled Clair to the far side of the shed. Her face was white with shock. "Run," he said. "Get to the house!"

"I can't leave you!" she cried hysterically. Tears filled her eyes and she stared in horror at the blood spreading over his shoulder.

"If you don't go in the next two seconds, you'll kill me, Clair." His eyes pleaded. "Now *go!*"

Her eyes widened and she turned and fled for the back of the house. Andy heard her footsteps. Moments later he heard the sounds of men running toward him from the street. Tripp and Aaron were coming. He ran through the yard, dropped to the ground, and rolled under a pine log fence. On the other side he got to his feet and looked around. Beyond, the prairie stretched out for miles. Out there, they would run him down and kill him.

A slug whined past his face and he felt the shock of its passing. He ducked, turned to his right, and sprinted toward the back of Beringer's General Store a hundred feet away. As he ran, another shot rang out behind him.

• • •

Abigail and Bear were talking in the kitchen when they heard the first shot. They stood, staring at each other in confusion for several seconds, then Clair screamed and another shot rang out. Abigail's face drained of color. Bear ran to the back door just in time to catch Clair as she stumbled into his arms.

"Pa!" she screamed in terror. "Andy's shot! He's hurt bad!"

Bear glanced up and saw Andy roll under the fence out back. Tripp and Aaron appeared at the side of the house; Aaron fired his gun. Andy ducked and ran toward town. Tripp saw Bear with Clair in his arms, framed in the doorway to the house, and he swiveled his gun and fired a quick shot at them. The slug burrowed into the wood an inch from Bear's head; he pulled Clair inside and together they fell to the floor. Abigail cried out in terror.

"Bastards!" Bear shouted. He ran into the living room and grabbed a shotgun from a wall rack, then ran toward the back door of the house.

Abigail grabbed Bear's arm but he pulled her fingers away. "No," she pleaded. "No, please." Behind them, Clair got to her feet, sobbing.

A gunshot boomed in the distance.

"I got to," Bear said. He held the shotgun across his chest, looked at his wife for a moment, then bolted out the door, crossed the fence at the rear of the yard, and ran in the direction Andy had taken.

Clair ran from the kitchen to the living room followed closely by Abigail. From a drawer Clair pulled out Bear's old Army Colt. The gun looked enormous in her hands. "What are you doing?" Abigail cried.

"I've got t' help him, ma!"

"No," Abigail said in a husky voice. "No, Clair. You *can't*—" She grabbed Clair's arm.

"Let *go*, ma!" Clair screamed. She whirled, pulled loose, and raced to the front door. Sobbing, half-blinded by tears, she jerked the door open and ran out into the street.

The streets were strangely deserted. Vaguely, Clair realized the sound of gunfire must have driven everyone indoors. She ran down the middle of Main Street, tears drying on her face. Her tears had come as a first reaction to the crisis—uncontrollable when she first saw the red stain spreading over Andy's shirt. She had felt utterly overwhelmed and helpless, seeing him hurt like that, not knowing what to do—but as she ran toward Beringer's General Store with the heavy Colt in her hands there was no time for tears. Andy needed her. She would die, if necessary, trying to help him. The heavy gun felt ponderous and alien in her hands and she felt terribly weak and inadequate, but at least there was no time for tears.

Another shot rumbled through the town, coming from somewhere behind the bakery, just up the street. In the distance a man cursed. Clair's throat constricted painfully with the horror of her thoughts. Oh God, Andy—

No one was on the streets, no one to help. Another shot rang out, this time behind the hardware store. Something heavy and metallic crashed against wood. Then another gunshot. Clair felt her tears threaten again. *No!*

Her dress flew around her ankles as she ran. She turned into the alley between the bank and the hardware store, where cool shadows were filled with old crates and boxes, and rough-cut lumber leaned against the walls. Suddenly she froze. Ahead, just beyond the far end of the alley, she heard the sound of men running, then Tripp's angry voice: "That way! No, *that* way, goddamnit! Circle around, you dumb sonofabitch—cut him off!"

Clair's chest tightened. A wave of despair filled her.

A shot sounded nearby, horribly loud. Clair leaped—almost fell—behind a wooden crate halfway down the alley. Her heart pounded sickly in her chest. She cocked the gun and held it out in front of her, barely able to keep the heavy gun level. Her hands trembled uncontrollably.

Where was pa?

Dear God, where was *Andy?*

A man ran into the far end of the alley. She heard footsteps before she saw who it was, and she pressed herself against the wall of the hardware store, the gun straining her wrists, her finger wrapped around the trigger. A man appeared, running full out in the dim alley.

It was Aaron.

Fifteen feet away, he saw her. His eyes widened in surprise. His stride broke. His gun lifted.

Her finger jerked spasmodically on the trigger and the Colt roared in her hands. It ripped from her grasp and flew over her head, clattering into the shadows somewhere behind her. The bullet caught Aaron in the right eye and blew a hole the size of his fist out the back of his head. He lifted several inches off the ground then fell sideways into an empty nail keg, dead before he hit the ground. He rolled onto his back, left eye staring with chilling, vacant surprise at the pale blue of the sky.

•   •   •

Andy raced across Water Street, running from between Kinsey's Boarding House and the bank toward the back of Goldman's General Store, holding his shoulder, trying to stem the flow of blood. From behind the hardware store Tripp shouted something to Aaron. Seconds later a loud shot rang out, a shot that was strangely muffled. He kept his head down and ran past the rear of the store. His shoulder was on fire and his legs felt strangely weak. He was losing too much blood.

Somewhere in the distance he heard Tripp curse.

Fifty yards of open ground separated Goldman's store from the livery stable. As he ran, Andy looked around for a place in which to hide; but there was no place to go except to the livery which lay ahead. And beyond that, the prairie stretched out with deadly, undulating flatness. If he went out there, they would run him down and kill him. The weather-worn, two-story stable was his only hope; a chance to stay alive for another minute before help arrived or Tripp and Aaron killed him.

Five yards from the rear doors to the stable a bullet burned a shallow furrow across his ribs. He ran on, with jerky strides, passed through the open doors, and fell to his knees just inside the stable. Except for a number of horses that stared at him with sleepy eyes, the livery was deserted. Andy got to his feet and looked around the cool, dark shadows inside the peak-roofed, cob-webbed livery. The loft caught his eye. A place to hide.

A wooden ladder, consisting of boards nailed between two heavy support columns, led upward into the loft. Andy climbed the ladder clumsily, shoulder blazing in agony. In the loft he stumbled past a row of neatly stacked bales of hay, slipped into a narrow space between two stacks of bales, and backed against the wall. The darkness comforted him. From his vantage point in the loft he could see out over a low railing into the livery where the horses flicked their eyes around questioningly. To his left, from the direction in which he had come, the bales of hay rose six inches higher than his head. Several bales to his right had been removed, forming a rough, flat surface, waist-high. Overhead, hanging from a rafter, was a scythe with a long, wicked blade that reflected hidden points of light. Andy grabbed the wooden handle of the scythe and lifted it from its place over the rafter just as Tripp stepped into the livery. The tip of the scythe caught on the beam, held, and sprang back, ringing musically.

Tripp glanced up, his face a black, soulless silhouette against the light that spilled through the open doors. Andy held his breath.

"That was your last mistake, boy," Tripp said softly. He crossed the floor swiftly and began to climb the ladder to the loft, the butt of the gun in his hand striking the ladder's rungs with every step.

Andy swung the scythe down and rested the blade on the bales of hay to his right, gripping the handle tightly in both hands. "This is murder, Tripp," he called out. "There's no way you can get away with it, not after chasing me all the way through town."

Tripp laughed, an ugly, hollow sound in the darkness. He stood in the loft. "Nobody does what you done t' me, boy," he said with murderous, icy calm. "Nobody. Not ever. If they catch me they kin string me up, but you're a dead man." His boots hissed in the straw that littered the floor.

Andy leaned forward several inches and in the gloom he saw Tripp's gun, held in front of him close to his body, barely six feet away.

Five feet.

Andy tightened his grip on the scythe. Blood roared in his ears.

Four.

Bear raced through the rear doors of the livery, shotgun sweeping the shadows in front of him. "Andy!" he called out.

Tripp twisted, leveled his gun at Bear and fired just as Andy took a single step forward and swung the scythe with all his waning strength. Tripp's gun boomed in the confines of the loft. He whirled quickly back to face Andy, his eyes wide and bulging with horror a hundredth of a second before the razor-sharp blade ripped through his throat and out the back of his neck. His body fell backward to the floor, blood spurting from the severed arteries in his neck. His head fell to the floor with a heavy thud and came to rest almost at Andy's feet, tongue protruding, coated with bits of straw, dead eyes glaring malevolently at Andy. Andy slumped to the floor and sat with a bale of hay at his back.

"Andy!" Bear shouted. He sat up with the shotgun lying across his legs, holding his right arm with his left hand, blood oozing between his fingers.

"Tripp's dead." Andy's voice floated weakly from the loft, strained and distant.

Clair ran into the livery through the front doors, blinking in the gloom. "*Pa!*" she cried, running to him. "*You're hurt!*" She looked around wildly. "Where's Andy?"

Bear pointed toward the loft. "Up there. I ain't hurt bad. You go see about Andy."

Clair scrambled up the ladder and hurried between the dark, looming bales of hay, gasping when she saw Tripp's decapitated body. Then she saw Andy and she stepped over Tripp, lifting her skirts automatically. Her face filled with horror when she saw Tripp's head, lying at Andy's feet. She kicked it away with a tiny squeal of disgust and fright, then sank down beside Andy to the cool, straw-littered floor of the loft.

Tears flooded her face as she touched him. "Oh God, Andy—"

He reached up, held her hands. "I'll . . . be all right . . ." He struggled weakly, trying to get to his feet. "Aaron—"

"He's dead," she said. She put her arms around him and buried her face against his chest, crying weakly. "I-I shot him, Andy. I killed him."

Andy relaxed and leaned back. He tilted his head back and breathed shallowly, comforting her, touching her hair, feeling its silky texture with his fingertips, savoring its fresh, clean scent. The light in the loft was decidedly gray, he thought sluggishly.

Dark really.

Almost like a moonless night.

EPILOGUE

It wasn't until next spring that I visited the grave, and even then it wasn't like I felt obligated; I was just curious—that, or maybe I just wanted to be sure he was really dead. Hell, maybe I just wanted to get away from the telegraph office and any excuse would have served. I sure picked a mighty fine day, though. It was the middle of May and the winter chill that had hung around all through a wet and leaden April had finally burned off. The sky was blue and the mountains were crowned with a new winter's season of crystal-white snow. Flowers poked out of the ground everywhere.

With the warm weather, the spring run-off had started in earnest; Jason's reservoirs were filling and Andy was watching over them like an old mother hen.

The wedding last September was one of the finest ever seen in these parts. Clair was so beautiful in her long white dress that it just about broke my heart all over again to look at her. Her face was glowing with happiness, her eyes fairly danced with blue, and her beautiful chestnut hair swirled around her shoulders in light brown curls. To have looked at her that day you'd never have guessed that only a month earlier she'd blown Aaron's brains entirely out the back of his head. But then, women always seemed a little more resilient out west.

Bear looked uncomfortable in his suit, but pleased as punch as he gave the bride away. I saw more than a little moisture in his eyes but you'd never get him to admit it now. Amy made the cutest bride's maid you ever saw, all decked out in a lovely, pale-blue silk dress. She hung around Andy like a shadow, stealing secret glances at her sister-in-law all evening long. There was some concern about who was going to be the best man; Andy first asked Miles but Miles claimed he was "too blamed old" which Andy said was a lot of nonsense. In the end it was Jason O'Meara who passed the ring to Andy which sure pleased a lot of folks who'd seen enough shooting and burning and fighting in the valley to last them a lifetime. Jill, looking cold and lovely, but with a pinched look about her eyes, accompanied Jason to the festivities. Afterwards, folks said the green of her dress had perfectly matched the look in her eyes.

Tincup Smith was there too, nervous as a bird, staring at the townsfolk with dark suspicion, yet looking at Andy just as proudly as if he were his own son. He steered clear of the crowds as much as possible and didn't talk much to anyone except Andy and Clair, and, of course, to little Amy.

Two-Bit had come back from Montana and Slim was back from Rock Springs. Miles had lost track of Stringer. Seems he'd left Salt Lake City headed west, and never kept in touch after that. Of course Paul Armstrong was there, having never left. He and Grace Beringer had announced their engagement a week before Andy and Clair's wedding, and during the ceremony Grace held tightly to Paul's arm looking at him in pretty much the same way Clair looked at Andy. More than once that evening I thought I caught Grace winking at Clair, the two of them smiling secretly, but I might have been mistaken.

There must have been a hundred people at the ceremony and, when Andy finally kissed the bride, I thought folks all the way down in Rock Springs could hear the whooping and hollering.

. . .

The graveyard was on a little knoll just north of town, not a hundred yards from where Willow Creek flowed through the valley. A dusty little path wound to the top of the hill, if you could call it a hill, and when you got to the top you weren't twenty feet above the town of Willow Creek a quarter mile away.

I turned and looked back. The town and the hills looked quiet, now. The Circle-K was still behind Crooked Neck Ridge, and William O'Meara was still there, too. The stroke hadn't killed him after all, though most folks figured he'd have been better off if it had. The entire left side of his body was paralyzed, from the muscles of his face to the toes of his foot. He couldn't talk, couldn't walk, couldn't even feed himself properly, but whenever Andy's name was mentioned, his eye— his right eye—grew abnormally bright and he tried to say something, but it was just a murky croak and nobody ever figured out what it was.

In the first couple of days after Andy had dynamited the reservoir, Jason negotiated a quick deal with a ranch up north on the Green River. He drove twenty-two hundred head of cattle fifty miles in three days to some open range owned by a small rancher who was pleased to let Jason keep his cattle there until the middle of October for six thousand dollars. In all, Jason saved fifty-two hundred head. Thirty-eight hundred of the herd died.

And while Andy was rebuilding Jason's dams I managed to get in six games of chess with him. He wasn't bad. I reckon he could've handled Doc okay, but I wore him out, all six games. I wouldn't have cared to challenge him to a range war, though. He was pretty doggone good at that.

I turned back and stared at the graveyard. It wasn't much to look at—dusty, barren, a dry, tired-looking place. But you don't expect much of cemeteries, anyway. I reckoned the hill, small though it was, took a lot of wind in the winter. A picket fence that had weathered some twenty years framed the yard, separating one expanse of prairie from the other.

The grave had been dug to one side of the yard, almost by the fence in the northwest corner, as if the townspeople had been reluctant to put him down with decent folk. It wasn't much of a headstone—but I reckon he was lucky at that: just a hunk of two-by-eight with a few words, already fading, scratched into the wood. Next year you might not be able to read it at all. Even so, it warmed me some to read the epitaph:

Here Lies
DEAN TRIPP
Killed August 2, 1885
Thank God

I thought that last line was sort of irreverent, but then, I reckon folks weren't feeling very reverent last year at the time.

Couldn't say as I blamed them any.

65739078R00149

Made in the USA
Middletown, DE
03 March 2018